Jill Mansell worked for many years at the Burden Neurological Hospital, Bristol, and now writes full time. Her novels PERFECT TIMING, MIXED DOUBLES, HEAD OVER HEELS, MIRANDA'S BIG MISTAKE, KISS, GOOD AT GAMES, SHEER MISCHIEF, FAST FRIENDS, MILLIE'S FLING and STAYING AT DAISY'S are also available from Headline.

Also by Jill Mansell

Staying at Daisy's
Millie's Fling
Good At Games
Miranda's Big Mistake
Head Over Heels
Mixed Doubles
Perfect Timing
Fast Friends
Kiss
Sheer Mischief
Open House
Two's Company

Solo

Jill Mansell

headline

First published in 1991
by Bantam Press, a division of Transworld Publishers Ltd

This paperback edition published in 2002
by HEADLINE BOOK PUBLISHING

10

ISBN 0 7472 6745 6

Typeset in Times by Avon Dataset Ltd, Bidford-on-Avon, Warks

Printed and bound in Great Britain by
Mackays of Chatham plc, Chatham, Kent

HEADLINE BOOK PUBLISHING
A division of Hodder Headline
338 Euston Road
London NW1 3BH

www.headline.co.uk
www.hodderheadline.com

For my brother, Paul,
because I'm proud of him.
And because now
he'll have to read this book . . .

Chapter 1

Parties full of strangers bored the knickers off Tessa.

'Well, you're damn well coming to this one,' declared Holly impatiently. 'You haven't been out for weeks and it's going to be brilliant. *Everyone's* going. And just think, play your cards right . . . show a bit of leg . . . a bit of cleavage . . . and you, too, could find a husband like mine!'

Tessa wiped her hands on her already paint-streaked sweat-shirt and picked up the bottle of ridiculously expensive Chardonnay which Holly always insisted on buying because she liked the label, and which neither of them properly appreciated. Pouring herself half a mugful and wincing at its icy dryness she said, 'I don't have a cleavage.'

'What God didn't give you, Sellotape will,' pronounced Holly. 'They showed us how on *Blue Peter*.'

'And I haven't been out for weeks' – Tessa mimicked Holly's despairing tones – 'because I have been working. Working pays the rent. It even occasionally allows me to eat. I simply can't afford to mix in your kind of social circles.'

'You can't afford not to,' countered Holly. 'These are the people who commission poverty-stricken artists to paint absurdly flattering portraits of their revolting children.'

'Besides,' Tessa went on, surveying the almost-finished canvas before her and beginning to realize that Holly wasn't going to let her wriggle out of this one, 'you aren't married.'

1

Holly grinned, refilling her own mug with a flourish. 'Ah! I didn't say I *had* a husband, I said I'd *found* him. All that remains now is to exert a little gentle pressure.'

'And I suppose he'll be there tonight.'

'There is that small chance,' conceded Holly smugly. 'After all, it is his party.'

From the living-room window of Tessa's tiny cottage, perched on the side of one of the rolling, north-facing hills overlooking the spectacular elegance of the city of Bath, she could see in the far distance the equally spectacular and elegant Charrington Grange Hotel.

Even if Holly hadn't been working there for the past two months and regaling her with endless details about it, Tessa would have heard of it. Everyone knew of the Charrington Grange Hotel, owned and run by the Monahan brothers and built up from nothing – well, scarcely anything – over the last fifteen years into one of the foremost country hotels in England. Originally a gracious Georgian residence commanding breath-taking views across the city from its position at the very top of the south-facing hills above Bath, it had fallen into hideous disrepair during its forty-year occupation by an elderly and eccentric Monahan maiden aunt. By the time of her eventual death the roof was barely intact, the walls of the gracefully proportioned rooms were streaked with damp and the entire place was overrun by the dotty old woman's grand passion – several hundred decidedly un-housetrained cats.

Pulling every conceivable string between them, the notorious Monahan brothers, Ross and Max, had somehow managed to raise the vast amount of capital necessary to transform the crumbling old house into an opulent hotel catering to the very wealthiest clientele.

The Press had had a field day at the time. The very idea that Max Monahan, moody and unpredictable, and Ross, with his mile-long reputation for carousing, heart-breaking and generally misbehaving, could pull off such a stunt was so ridiculous it was laughable. Max, the elder brother by two years, having been sent down from Oxford following a particularly outrageous prank involving a prostitute dressed as a nun and a visiting trade union leader, had rapidly established himself as a star broker on the Stock Exchange. Six months later, the day after his twenty-first birthday, he had abandoned this glittering new career, disappearing to the Caribbean and returning eighteen months later with the completed manuscripts of not one but two fat novels. These thrillers, with their winning combination of sex, violence, tension and wit were wildly successful, yet at the time Max had doubted whether he would want to do it again. It had been fun finding out that he could, but it was scarcely what he termed a proper job.

In the end, however, the vast sums of money offered, the luxury of being virtually his own boss, the flexible hours and the ease with which he conjured up fresh plots, won the day. To Max Monahan, writing was a doddle and the rewards were too great to pass up. He rapidly became established as one of those few lucky writers whose books were read by everyone. Over the years he had grown more level headed and now, with his astute business brain and almost ruthless determination to pile success upon success, he was recognized as the more down to earth of the two brothers. The Charrington Grange Hotel was owned jointly between them and although Max didn't work there full-time he was involved in all the major decision-making and both he and Ross still lived there. Blockbuster novels remained his major – and considerable – source of income, but the hotel acted as an antidote to the solitude which writing entailed, and because he didn't need to sweat over a word processor for eight hours a day like some writers he'd heard of, there was still plenty of time left over in which to enjoy himself.

Ross Monahan, on the other hand, devoted his entire life to enjoyment. Tessa had never made a particular point of reading the gossip columns but even she was aware of his wicked reputation. Expelled from more schools than anyone cared to remember, his notorious passion for fun was equalled only by his stunning good looks and lethal charm. Incapable of remaining in one place for more than a few weeks, in his early twenties he was the archetypal playboy, his outrageous exploits hitting the papers almost weekly. Men despised and envied him; women – apart from those whose hearts he had broken – adored him.

If everyone had been amazed when he had appointed himself manager of The Charrington Grange, they had been well and truly astounded when they finally realized what an out-and-out success he was actually making of the job.

And fifteen years on, Ross Monahan was still doing it, running the hotel with such panache and enjoyment that he had made it seem scarcely like work at all. Having always moved in the most glittering and outrageous circles, he had turned The Grange into a kind of open house for those who played as hard as he did. It was quite simply *the* place to stay if you wanted to have a really good time – and could afford to pay for it.

And according to Holly, Ross Monahan was absolutely lethal with women.

'Gorgeous, gorgeous!' she had informed Tessa, shortly after

going to work for him. 'But definitely dangerous to know. When I first met him I made a solemn vow with myself not to get involved.'

'But you have,' guessed Tessa, observing the sheepish look in her friend's eyes. Holly had shrugged and smiled. 'Given half a chance I would have done,' she'd admitted. 'But the bastard isn't interested. For God's sake, Tess, he treats me like a friend!'

And now Holly was planning on treating him like a brother-in-law. She was passionately in love with Max, only Max didn't know it yet. Tessa, who adored Holly but sometimes despaired of her, suspected that it would all end in tears and that most of them would land on her own inadequately small shoulders.

Meanwhile, Holly was returning in less than two hours to pick her up and take her along to this horrible party. And she really didn't have a single suitable thing to wear.

Two hours later, gloomily surveying the other women at the party, Tessa realized that she'd been even more right than she'd feared.

'I *told* you,' hissed Holly, grabbing her arm and trying to drag her backwards through the French windows leading on to the terrace. 'Look, hardly anyone's noticed yet. Why don't we whizz back to my place and find you something decent to put on? You can't stay here dressed like that.'

'Stop panicking.' Tessa dug her heels in like a dog and prised Holly's fingers off her elbow. 'I'm being understated. If anyone says anything I'll tell them that designer labels are *passé*.'

'Mine isn't,' retaliated Holly, shocked. In order to reassure herself, she glanced in a nearby mirror, admiring the strapless, emerald-green Fendi creation which enhanced her generous breasts – no need for Sellotape there – and expertly played down her slightly too-generous hips. Then she turned back to face Tessa, whose black, cotton-jersey dress was looking plainer by the second. In Holly's eyes the severity of the cut did Tessa no favours at all, encasing her as it did from neck to knees and almost completely obscuring the enviably slim figure beneath. Worse still, she was wearing no jewellery whatsoever and her fingernails, although at least scrubbed clean of oil paint, were unvarnished. Sometimes she didn't understand her friend at all.

'Oh well,' said Tessa with more hope than conviction, 'maybe I'd better just go home.'

'Shut up!' shrieked Holly, so vigorously that her breasts jiggled in their casings. 'I've got you here and you're not running away now. Oxfam dress or no Oxfam dress, you're staying.'

Tessa grinned. 'How did you know it was from Oxfam?'

Holly raised her eyebrows. 'It's the only place you ever shop, stupid.'

Ross Monahan was doing what he did best: circulating, having fun and idly wondering whom he might take to bed with him at the end of the evening. It was a game which amused him, particularly when so many of the women were so blatantly obvious. Jennifer Johnson, with her rich-but-thick fiancé standing less than six feet away, had pressed herself against him and all but stuck her tongue in his ear. Sally Paige-Latimer had made a particular point of telling him that she didn't have to get back to London until tomorrow evening and that daft bitch Clarissa Fox had actually taken his hand and shoved it down the front of her dress so that he might experience – first-hand, so to speak –

the wonder of her expensive new silicone implants.

Liberating a fresh glass of champagne from the tray of a passing waiter, Ross loosened his bow tie and moved across to the fireplace at the far end of the room, from which strategic position he could see exactly what was going on in both the ballroom and the hall beyond. The party was going well; the two hundred or so guests were clearly enjoying themselves judging by the amount of noise and laughter, and Max, in particular, appeared to be having a good time. At present he was being cornered by Holly King, who was looking like an over-decorated Christmas tree, but whose incredible boobs undoubtedly owed nothing to silicone. Watching her now as she tossed back her equally bouncy red-gold hair for the third time in less than a minute and placed her hand on Max's arm as she spoke, Ross was amused to find his suspicions confirmed. Holly was besotted with his brother. And a big, curvy, talkative red-head like Holly was just about the last type of woman that Max would ever go for.

For a moment Ross almost felt sorry for Holly, of whom he was extremely fond. He had had his doubts about her when she'd applied for the job on reception, noting her appallingly patchy c.v. and recognizing that her family's wealth meant that if she didn't feel like working she didn't have to. But sensing his concern, she had assured him that she would work 'like stink', and for a moment she had so reminded Ross of himself that he had given in. He had taken the risk and Holly hadn't let him down. In the two months since she had been working at The Grange she had committed some appalling *faux pas*, but her sense of humour, punctuality and willingness to learn had more than made up for it. And the customers adored her, despite her appalling dress sense.

Then he stiffened. Clarissa-better-than-natural-Fox was bee-lining towards him once more and right now he simply couldn't face her. Them. Whatever, he had to escape.

Taking a sharp left turn and assuming his purposeful I'm-the-Manager expression, Ross stepped through the open French windows out on to the terrace. Couples, couples everywhere. If he didn't move fast, Clarissa would catch up with him and do something even more outrageous in the open air. All of a sudden the memory of her overpowering perfume and ungentle fingers was almost nauseating.

Tessa, sitting alone on a grassy slope beyond the terrace, was hugging her knees and wondering whether this was really the most boring night of her life or whether there had been another she'd forgotten about. Maybe there was something lacking in her character, she decided, unconcerned. Apart from the spectacular view before her, she couldn't think of one single, even halfway decent, reason for being here. Holly had disappeared with Max, she didn't know anyone else and no-one had shown the slightest inclination to strike up a conversation with her. According to Holly, of course, she should gatecrash their cliquey little groups and announce with suitable drama: 'I'm an artist! And talented too! Wanna portrait of your wife . . . husband . . . brats . . . pets?'

But she couldn't. And leaving now was the best idea she'd had in years.

The next moment a hand touched her shoulder and she leapt a mile.

'Sshh,' said Ross, easing himself into a sitting position beside her and sliding his arm around her waist. Behind them, he could hear the fast, neurotic tap of Clarissa's too-high heels as she searched the terrace. Tilting his dark head towards Tessa's, he murmured, 'I need saving.'

'So I've heard.' Recognizing him at once, she couldn't help smiling. 'Although I rather had the impression that you were beyond redemption.'

Ross pinched the inside of her elbow in retaliation. 'All lies. I've been a virgin since I was twelve. Speaking of which' – with his free hand he grasped Tessa's slender fingers and raised them to his lips – 'I don't believe I've had the pleasure. You are?'

'I am a guest at your brother's party,' said Tessa, unable to prevent herself admiring the chiselled perfection of his mouth. 'And you are a bullshitter, Mr Monahan. I warn you, I'm quite immune to bullshit.'

Ross laughed. In the background Clarissa's footsteps faded in despondent retreat, but all of a sudden Clarissa no longer mattered. This girl, this guest-at-his-brother's party, was quite beautiful. She was also a natural blonde with slanting green eyes and silky dark eyelashes who was wearing no make-up whatsoever, no overpowering perfume and none of that disgusting lacquer with which so many women solidified their hair. In her highnecked, plain black dress, bare brown legs and flat black leather shoes, she was more alluring than any of the other exposed and over-made-up women he had seen tonight.

He noticed the empty wine glass on the grass beside her. 'Look, can I get you anything?'

'A taxi would be nice.' Tessa, who had also heard the retreating female footsteps, began to rise to her feet. Alarmed, Ross yanked her back down beside him.

'You can't be serious! Apart from the fact that it's not even nine o'clock, we've only just met.'

'Maybe the excitement is simply too much for me,' she replied, her voice betraying her amusement. 'Maybe I can't wait to rush home and record every thrilling detail in my diary. Maybe I just don't like parties.'

'Maybe you don't like me,' countered Ross, feeling absurdly put out. He wasn't used to being laughed at, however gently. And he certainly wasn't accustomed to being rejected. This girl wasn't playing games, he realized, she meant it.

Tessa shrugged. 'I don't know you.'

'Then at least give me a chance.' Now it was his turn to stand up, pulling her with him and keeping a firm grip on her hand. She wore no rings, and her unpainted nails were cut short. 'You could begin by telling me your name.'

'Where are we going?' countered Tessa. He was walking so fast she almost had to run to keep up. 'If you're thinking of showing me your etchings, forget it.'

'What do you think I am?' Pretending to be affronted, then realizing that it wasn't such a pretence after all, he pulled her in the direction of the conservatory. 'We're going to get to know each other. In the non-biblical sense, of course.'

Three hours later Ross silently conceded defeat. He knew nothing more about her now than he had when he'd first spotted her sitting alone on the grassy slope beyond the terrace. Every question was parried, every overture firmly rebuffed. However hard he tried, she remained totally unimpressed. He had practically told her his life story and he still didn't even know her name.

He had never wanted a woman more badly in his life.

'You really shouldn't be here with me,' said Tessa, allowing him to refill her glass from the bottle he had retrieved from its hiding place behind a huge tropical fern. The conservatory, with its domed glass roof, stained-glass side-panels and strategically positioned amber-tinted spotlighting, was like a small jungle. And since Ross had taken the precaution of locking the door behind him, they were both unobserved and uninterrupted, surrounded only by lush foliage and the scent of exotic blooms. In the distance could be heard the muted sounds of revelry, as the party continued without them.

Ross leaned back in his seat, white wrought-iron and strewn with silk cushions, and stuck his feet up on the table. 'Why on earth not?'

'People will wonder where you are.'

He winked. 'It's my party and I'll hide if I want to. What's the matter – am I boring you?'

In order to avoid answering, Tessa sipped her drink. Despite her cool front she actually wasn't having as easy a time of it as Ross supposed. Initially, being only too aware of his horrendous reputation, she had taken everything he said with a bucket of salt. And although maybe she still did, he was managing to get to her anyway. This side of Ross Monahan, the side that was charming and funny and so effortlessly capable of winning people over, was bloody hard to resist. Particularly, thought Tessa ruefully, when he had managed to fill her glass with Bollinger at least twice as often as he had his own.

'Stop ignoring me,' said Ross, snapping a feathery fern off at the stem and trailing its slender tip across the back of Tessa's knuckles. 'I asked you a question. *Am* I boring you?'

'To death,' she smiled, moving her hand out of reach. 'But don't stop. Yet.'

Chapter 2

I must be drunk, thought Tessa, kicking off her shoes and sinking into a sitting position on the edge of the vast, canopied bed. When a man like Ross Monahan urged you to spend the night at his place and assured you that you were quite welcome to the bed – he would be *happy* to sleep on the settee – you knew you were playing with fire.

Either drunk or crazy, she told herself as she pulled her dress over her head, threw it in the direction of a large, red-velvet chair and wrapped herself in the dark blue towelling robe he had left for her.

But she knew she wasn't that drunk. She was enjoying the game which had begun so many hours earlier. The challenge had been thrown down and she couldn't resist it. She was going to seriously enjoy being the only woman in the history of the world to have slept in Ross's bed . . . alone.

His suite of rooms on the top floor of the hotel was as sumptuous as she had imagined, particularly since seeing the rest of The Grange earlier. Like stowaways, they had remained closeted in the conservatory until the early hours of the morning when the last guests had departed, either roaring off into the night in their smart cars or retiring to their rooms in the hotel.

Then, taking her hand, Ross had given her the full guided tour, showing her the elegant sitting rooms, the restaurant, the squash courts, the superb gym and the spectacular indoor swimming-pool built inside a second, even larger, conservatory, illuminated by underwater lighting and surrounded on three sides by more tropical vegetation. Ross was as proud of the hotel as a new father. Tessa had been touched by his enthusiasm. But if he was under the impression that she would be so overwhelmed by this display of his success that she would leap into bed with him, he was going to be disappointed.

Saying no was much, much more fun.

Firmly securing the belt of the far-too-big robe around her waist, she threw back the bedcovers and slid between cool white sheets, just as a cautious knock sounded at the door.

'It's OK, I'm decent.'

'Pity,' said Ross lightly. He was still dressed, and carrying a folded blanket over one arm.

Tessa gestured at the bed. 'This is awfully kind of you. You'll probably have a terrible time trying to sleep on that settee.'

'Probably.' He gave her a mournful look, then grinned. 'But I'll survive.'

She watched him fling the blanket over the narrow leather Chesterfield. 'And it's four-thirty now. Nearly time to get up again anyway.'

'Don't remind me.'

'I'm very grateful.'

'Absolutely no problem.'

Tessa pulled the covers up to her chin and smiled at him. 'You're a true gentleman.'

'I believe you,' said Ross. 'Thousands wouldn't.'

She watched him hover for a few seconds beside the sofa, wondering no doubt if she might change her mind. Then, giving him one last big smile, she plumped up her pillows and turned over. 'Mmm, well, thanks again. Good night.'

Tessa didn't know what time it was when she shifted in her sleep and first realized that she was no longer alone in the bed. Her bare leg was resting against another bare leg, definitely not her own. Sleepily, almost subconsciously, she stretched out her hand and encountered a smooth, warm back. She became aware of the very faint scent of aftershave and toothpaste, and the quiet, regular breathing of someone deeply and peacefully asleep.

To her great surprise, Tessa was neither shocked nor annoyed by this invasion of her privacy. It was, after all, his bed and a narrow, slippery leather Chesterfield was about as conducive to a good night's sleep as a tin bath.

In fact, she realized drowsily, she had forgotten quite how nice it felt to lie next to another body, accidentally brushing against an arm or a hip, sharing each other's warmth and enjoying the primal instincts of simply being together.

With a guilty start she came properly awake. For the way her fingertips were trailing down Ross's spine wasn't in the least bit accidental. And, without even realizing it, her own left leg had managed to fit against the curve of his right one with all the snugness of a missing piece in a jigsaw.

This was taking the enjoyment of sharing each other's warmth a little too far.

Regretfully easing her leg back to her own side of the bed and removing her hand from his back, she closed her eyes and attempted to distract her mind from its traitorous wanderings. She had always believed that physical intimacy – not just sex – was something like a video recorder or a Magimix: what you didn't have, you didn't miss, it just faded from your mind and became unimportant.

It had been almost a year since her last relationship had ended. At first, of course, she *had* missed the hugs and the kisses – and the sex – but certainly not enough to go rampaging round Bath in search of males, any males, with whom to satisfy the need for physical contact.

And pretty soon she had become used to being and sleeping alone once more. The withdrawal symptoms had been mild. Because hugging and kissing and sex weren't physical addictions like heroin. They were something that was nice but also quite possible to live without.

On the other hand, a year was a long time.

Faintly appalled by her own weakness, Tessa realized that what she was experiencing now was a surge of sexual longing. Her fingers had found their way back to Ross's shoulder and the need to touch him had grown, become a compulsion.

My God, I'm a nymphomaniac, she thought, smiling to herself in the darkness, but at the same time almost frightened by the strength of her feelings. Her stomach was taut with anticipation, her breathing shallow. Adrenalin was pumping through her body, galvanized both by her desires and her daring as she rolled fractionally closer towards the warm, perfect, wonderful-smelling and oh-so-forbidden body lying just inches from her own. And of course it was the very worst body in the world to have engendered such feelings for, because Ross Monahan had the most awful reputation in the world as a womanizer.

She had so enjoyed herself earlier, proving to him that she was immune to his legendary charms. And now look at me, thought Tessa, helpless and inwardly squirming with lust. A pathetic wreck, at the mercy of her hormones. Sometimes, just sometimes, nature was a real bitch.

'I hope you realize and appreciate,' murmured Ross almost inaudibly, 'what incredible self-control I've been exercising for the last twenty minutes.'

Tessa let out a shriek and sprang away from him as if she'd been electrocuted. Shocked to the core and hideously embarrassed to realize that he'd been awake the entire time, she buried her face in the pillow and shuddered with mortification. How he must be laughing at her now.

Slowly, very slowly, he turned over. 'I didn't say stop,' he pointed out gently.

Tessa, still buried in the pillows, couldn't speak. When his hand touched her hair she remained utterly rigid. The humiliation was unendurable.

'In case you're interested,' continued Ross, his tone almost conversational, 'I would rate that very same twenty minutes as possibly the most erotic of my entire life.'

'Shut up,' squeaked Tessa, wishing she were dead. But to add further to her dreadful shame the seeds of longing were still there. His fingers were now lightly exploring the sensitive skin at the back of her neck and she wasn't pushing him away. She couldn't push him away. The sensations he was evoking were absolutely exquisite.

'You know,' he murmured minutes later, 'this is what sex counsellors prescribe couples as therapy for impotence.'

With a tiny resurgence of her old spirit, Tessa retorted, 'How on earth would you know?' and gasped softly as his magical fingers slid along the line of her collarbone.

'I read it in a book.' There was a smile in his voice.

'The couple are finally so turned on by all the touching that in the end they can't help themselves and bingo! Problem cured.'

'Really,' whispered Tessa, because she couldn't think of anything else to say.

'Oh yes, really.' Reaching for her, Ross turned her over to face him finally. In the darkness she could see his eyes glittering like coal as he peeled open her towelling robe and slowly pushed it away from her shoulders. 'I'm beginning to think,' he said, tracing the outline of her mouth with the tip of his index finger, 'that these sex counsellors might really have a point.'

It was like being told to execute an intricate dance with a world champion, thought Tessa hazily, and suddenly discovering that you knew all the steps. Every response, every rhythm, was sheer perfection. They moved together, so finely tuned to each other's needs that there was no awkwardness, no hesitation . . . and no *doubt*. After all the anticipation they were both so ready that no further foreplay was necessary but still they continued, wordlessly prolonging the ecstasy, not wanting it to end a minute sooner than it might. When Ross kissed her mouth she felt faint with longing, her hands caressing him in return, her body pressing against his.

And when, finally, the waiting became unendurable they moved together at precisely the same moment and she caught her breath as he entered her. Closing her eyes so that he wouldn't see the tears of sheer happiness seeping beneath her lashes, all she could think of was: perfect. And just as she thought it, Ross murmured that very same word aloud.

* * *

17

'Well, that was rather pleasant,' said Ross afterwards, propping himself up on one elbow and grinning down at her. God, she was beautiful. With careful precision he smoothed a damp strand of blonde hair away from her cheek. He was a man of wide, possibly panoramic, experience with women, but he was truly shaken by the depth of emotion he was feeling now for this girl. Somehow it hadn't been just a great lay. And whatever else it was quite unnerved him. It was new, uncharted territory.

Because he didn't know what else to do, he resorted to banter. 'Think I should write to the sex counsellor and tell him I'm cured?'

'You must be relieved, after all those terrible years of celibacy,' said Tessa, misinterpreting the expression in his eyes. The fun was over, he'd got what he wanted and now he didn't know what to do with this girl so inconveniently still here in his bed.

Be fair, it was what we both wanted, she told herself. And it had been fantastic, after all.

But it was still just a tacky little one-night stand, nothing more, and now they had to pay for it, enduring all this terrible awkwardness, being polite to each other and pretending that they weren't complete strangers who had both simply happened to fancy a quickie . . .

In the cold light of dawn, which it was by this time, she realized that what had seemed miraculous and wonderful just minutes earlier, now appeared instead to be something sad and somewhat sleazy.

And Ross didn't help matters at all by choosing this particular moment to say, 'Look, I still don't know your name. You *have* to tell me who you are now.'

Tessa glanced out through the window at the pale grey sky

and the misty hills in the distance. Then she closed her eyes. 'I thought you knew. I'm your tart for the night.'

'I want to know,' he insisted, and she shook her head, sickened by the game he felt he had to play.

'What on earth for?'

'So that I can phone you.' His tone was half-joking, half-serious. He couldn't understand why she had so suddenly drawn away from him. This was a situation he had never encountered before.

'Oh, *please*!' sighed Tessa in deep despair. There was nothing else for it. To climb out of bed, hunt for her clothes and walk three miles home at six-fifteen in the morning was too humiliating, *too* sleazy and much, much more than she could handle right now.

So she took the only other alternative currently available, turned over on her side – away from Ross – and went back to sleep.

After dozing fitfully for a while Ross rose at seven-thirty. Gazing down at the girl in his bed with her long, glossy blonde hair strewn across the pillows and her left arm only half-covering her small but perfect breasts, he didn't dare awaken her. He couldn't stand it if she was going to carry on with that I'm-a-tart routine.

What the hell was he to do?

In the end, because there was no way he could miss his nine o'clock meeting with an extremely influential American businessman in Bath and because she had mentioned last night that the friend who had driven her to the party had left and she wasn't sure she had enough money on her to pay for a cab home, Ross stuck a rolled-up fifty-pound note into the top of the almost empty champagne bottle he had brought up to the room with him last night. Placing it on the bedside table, he scribbled a note and rested it against the bottle.

Then, still wishing that he had the nerve to kiss her awake, make love to her all over again and tell her what last night had really meant to him, he took what clothes he needed from the wardrobe and soundlessly left the room.

> Sorry, urgent business meeting – had to go.
> Please feel free to call room service for
> breakfast. And please *do* leave your phone
> number – I *will* call you. R.
> PS Money for cab home.

The wages of sin, thought Tessa, poking the rolled-up fifty-pound note into the bottle and watching it slowly unfurl as it soaked up the dregs of the champagne. That he had felt obliged to leave money for her just about said it all.

Holly's dark green sports car screamed to a halt outside Tessa's cottage at midday, as Tessa had known it would.

'So what happened to you?' Holly, incapable of wearing anything so mundane as jeans and a sweatshirt, looked like an explosion in a flowerbed. The scarlet, violet and pink jacket and dress were new and had obviously cost a bomb. Tessa suspected that she'd been misery-buying, which meant all had not gone according to plan with Max.

'I had a headache,' she said, clearing a pile of unprimed canvases off the sofa and gesturing to Holly to sit down. 'I couldn't find you to tell you I was leaving.'

'What time was that?'

Tessa pretended to think. 'Tennish? I caught a cab.'

'Lies!' exclaimed Holly triumphantly. '*I* drove back here at eleven-thirty and you weren't home then.'

'Must've been asleep.' Tessa turned away, gathering up a pile of old newspapers and carrying them through to the kitchen.

'Sweetie, I threw stones at your bedroom window.'

'I wondered why it was broken.'

'Tell me, tell me,' begged Holly, following her into the tiny kitchen and cornering her against the fridge. 'You've met someone gorgeous. Who *is* he?'

'What happened with Max?' countered Tessa, stalling for time. Holly grimaced and plucked meaningfully at her new clothes. 'The bastard cost me three hundred pounds. He was charming for almost ten minutes and then he introduced me to this French girl, Dominique something-or-other. She's a doctor, for heaven's sake. The next thing I knew they were dancing together and I was left holding up the wall. And she had a tattoo on her thigh,' she concluded with disgust. 'No doubt Max spent the rest of the night investigating it at extremely close quarters.'

'It's a very nice dress, anyway.'

'And it's very nice of you to say so, my dear.' Holly shook her head, smiling. 'But as a way of changing the conversation, it sucks. Now tell me this instant who you spent the night with, Tessa Duvall, or there'll be very big trouble indeed.'

Chapter 3

The day Tessa sat down and ate four banana sandwiches was the day she realized she was pregnant. For twenty-seven years she had hated bananas with a vengeance.

It was a shock, but not a huge shock. Incredibly, the subject of contraception simply hadn't crossed her mind at any stage during that fateful night in September. Not until the following day – when Holly, to whom she had steadfastly refused to name names, had made some flip remark about condoms – had she realized what a risk she had taken. After that the possibility that she might be pregnant had remained just that: a niggling but distant possibility. It couldn't happen to her, she kept telling herself; they'd only done it once. And for some bizarre reason she was also convinced that the year of celibacy preceding that night would somehow count in her favour.

But the weeks had passed, nothing had happened and the realization that what she had feared might happen had actually happened had been a gradual one – like slowly being poisoned with arsenic.

Tessa cursed herself for her stupidity. Knowing that she should put that night out of her memory hadn't helped at all. Despite everything she had ever heard about Ross Monahan, and knowing exactly what a terrible reputation he had, she had been unable to get him out of her mind. Despite all her efforts to the contrary she kept remembering his laughter, his dark flashing eyes, his absurd sense of humour and the way he had managed to persuade her that he really wasn't as bad as she'd been led to believe . . .

Which was all so much bullshit, of course. When she was being logical she recognized that much at least. And above all else Tessa was logical. When it came to the crunch she could rationalize the situation with bone-chilling practicality.

She and Ross were poles apart. Queen Victoria and Mick Jagger would have been a more likely proposition than Ross and herself.

There was no way on earth that they could ever be a couple.

It was just going to be so *hard*; forgetting someone not exactly forgettable was difficult enough, and now she was going to have a permanent reminder . . .

Remembering now how close she had come to revealing the identity of her one-night stand to Holly, Tessa shivered with relief. At least she had that to be grateful for. Holly was congenitally incapable of keeping a secret for more than thirty seconds. Going to bed with Ross had been an incredibly stupid thing to do, and having been caught out like this was humiliating beyond belief. The identity of the father of her child was something Tessa was quite definitely going to keep entirely to herself.

The two Christmas trees flanking the reception desk shimmered like belly dancers every time anyone walked past them, hundreds of silvery strands reflecting rainbows of light from the spectacular chandelier suspended above them.

Holly adored Christmas and all its decorations, but today she was too excited even to open the latest window in her Advent calendar.

She had been shocked to the core yesterday when Tessa had said over lunch, 'Oh, by the way, I've got a bit of news for you.' So shocked, horrified and amazed in fact that she'd needed a large brandy to steady herself.

Tessa, on the other hand, had been completely in control. Amused by Holly's extravagant reactions, she had smiled and explained quite simply that she had had two weeks in which to get used to the idea, and now that she had she was looking forward to it. It wasn't necessarily going to be easy, but she would cope.

It was typical of Tessa, of course, to put on this brave front and to dismiss with an airy gesture any suggestion that things might not be that easy. She was a survivor, the most fiercely independent girl Holly had ever known, and the last thing she would do was panic.

Over fettucine alla vongole and a glass of red wine Holly had tried and failed to discover the identity of the father. To her eternal frustration, Tessa just shook her head and dismissed him as easily as she had dismissed her other problems. He was a complete one-off, she insisted; there was absolutely no question of him being contacted and informed of the situation.

Tessa wasn't the least interested in slapping a paternity suit on a virtual stranger and dragging him through the courts in pursuit of money. This was *her* baby and *her* responsibility and she would manage perfectly well on her own.

Privately, Holly had thought her friend crazy. Aloud, she had declared expansively that she would do anything she could to help.

And in the middle of the night a wonderful idea had come to her. Hugging it to herself, amazed by her own brilliance, she had hardly been able to wait to get to work this morning. Any minute now Ross would appear and she would pounce on him before he had a chance to get into his office. Holly unthinkingly scrawled an extravagant doodle down the left-hand margin of the signing-in register and smiled a secret, congratulatory smile. She'd always adored the sound of the word entrepreneur and now here she was practically being one!

'So, you have a friend,' said Ross, struggling to make sense of Holly's excited babble and wishing he'd managed to catch more than three hours' sleep last night. 'A friend in need. Is usually a bloody nuisance,' he added, collapsing into the chair behind his desk and indicating that Holly should also sit down. Neither her alarmingly yellow dress nor her rather overpowering perfume were doing his hangover much good.

'Well, Tess isn't,' she informed him proudly. 'She's lovely. And that's the whole point – you'll be helping her and she'll be doing you a favour at the same time. She really is an extremely talented artist.'

'And you want us to display her work in the hotel,' said Ross, trying to slow Holly down. 'If she's so great, why doesn't she sell through an art gallery?'

Holly could see that her boss wasn't yet functioning on all cylinders. With exaggerated patience she said, 'She does, of course she does, but the only people who go into galleries are those who want to buy paintings.'

'Ye . . . es.' This was where he began to lose track. 'Holly, you couldn't run and get me a cup of coffee . . .?'

'In a minute.' If Holly knew anything it was how to press home an advantage. She was going to make the most of his fragile state while it lasted. 'The point is, if Tessa has her pictures hanging on your walls, they'll be seen by people who *hadn't* planned on buying anything! So when they see them and fall in love with them and then realize that they *can* buy them, they'll be even more pleased than if they'd wanted a painting in the first place. Don't you see . . .?' She shook her head, urging him to understand. 'Everyone likes to say they saw something and simply *had* to have it. It's a wild, romantic gesture . . . it makes them feel dashing and spontaneous . . .!'

'OK, OK.' Ross put up his hand to stop her. 'And what exactly do we get in return, apart from wild guests making romantic gestures all over the place and probably getting themselves arrested into the bargain?'

'Ten per cent,' replied Holly promptly.

Ross had never needed a cup of coffee more badly in his life. 'We're not having bloody price tags on them,' he grumbled, weakening.

'Heavens, no! Just a discreet notice on the reception desk,' Holly soothingly assured him. She was already planning to tell the guests about Tessa's paintings whenever they strayed within a twelve-foot radius of her desk.

'And I'd have to see her work first before I agreed to anything.' He was privately both surprised and faintly intrigued that Holly, with her wealthy background and razzle-dazzle social life, should be such great friends with a pregnant, poverty-stricken artist. He had met one or two of her friends before and if he'd offered them a stick of charcoal they'd have been more likely to try and smoke it. 'So, who is she? Would I have heard of her?'

'God no,' declared Holly. 'She's not the least bit interested in the kind of socializing I do. We've been best friends since we were eight when her mother came to work for my mother, but to look at us you'd never think it. She's the exact opposite of me.'

'In that case I like her already,' said Ross with a half-hearted attempt at humour. 'At least she might have the decency to bring me a cup of coffee.'

'She'd be more likely to call you a lazy bum and tell you to make your own,' Holly replied. 'You couldn't charm your way around Tessa like you do with everyone else. She won't tolerate bullshit.'

Somewhere in the depths of Ross's memory a distant chord was struck. But it was too distant to pursue; Holly was rattling on again, moving in to close the deal. 'In fact I did manage to drag her along here to Max's party a couple of months ago,' she continued, jiggling her knee up and down in her anxiety to hear him say 'yes', 'but she didn't stay long. You probably wouldn't have noticed her . . .'

Ross stopped thinking about coffee. For a few seconds he actually stopped breathing. No distant chord this time; instead he heard a bloody great gong.

Staring at a point on the wall beyond her, he ran through in his mind Holly's earlier words: 'She's the exact opposite of me . . . She won't tolerate bullshit.' And: 'I managed to drag her along to Max's party.'

Christ, it *had* to be her. It had to be.

'So?' Holly clicked her fingers to regain his attention. 'Can I tell her it's on?' Ross, she thought, was really in a bad way this morning. He was looking positively shell-shocked.

'No, you bloody well can't. Was this her idea?' His hangover forgotten, he was trying to make sense of it all. Or even some of it.

'Of course not!' Holly glared at him, indignant and proud. 'She doesn't have a clue about any of this. I *told* you, it's my own plan. She only told me yesterday that she was pregnant and I came up with this brilliant idea last night.'

'This baby,' said Ross, wondering at his ability to sound merely curious when the question he was about to ask could have such earth-shattering repercussions. 'Who's the boyfriend?'

'Oh,' Holly flicked her wrist, a gesture of disdain, 'no boyfriend. He was simply a one-night stand who disappeared off the scene. In fact it's a bit of a coincidence because apparently it all happened on the night of Max's party . . .'

Chapter 4

The Grosvenor House Hotel, supremely elegant and swarming with the celebrities who had descended upon it for the occasion, was coping admirably with the invasion.

Max, who had co-written the screenplay for a film nominated for several awards today – including best screenplay – wasn't coping well at all.

It was the kind of glitzy, self-congratulatory show-bizzy affair that made him wonder why on earth he hadn't stuck to his guns and said no. He didn't want to be here. He was too busy to be here. And who gave a damn anyway, whether he was here or not? In a room containing six hundred guests, did one more or less make any difference?

He was later to come to the conclusion that it did.

Francine Lalonde, voluptuous star of dozens of films, both French and English, chose that precise moment to make her customary late entrance. Up on the stage a grey-haired young man was receiving his award for best costume design from an older, balder man, but no one was paying any attention.

'Oh hell,' drawled Francine Lalonde in the husky, laid-back tones which had helped to make her famous. 'They bloody well started without me.'

Max, despite having written on numerous occasions about love at first sight, had never seriously entertained the idea of such a dubious philosophy. It simply wasn't feasible. How, after all, could you fall in love with someone you didn't know?

But quite suddenly, blindingly, he understood. He just knew that whatever the other person said, thought, felt or did would be absolutely *right*.

And when Francine Lalonde, catching his eye, first winked at him, then insinuated her way towards his table, he knew, too, that everything she did would indeed be right.

'I'm afraid I'm making a disturbance,' she whispered, sliding into the vacant seat on Max's left and winking at him again. 'I'd better be quiet before I am told off.'

Seldom if ever stuck for words, Max simply nodded. It was all he could manage to do. He had seen several of her films over the years and had admired her beauty in a detached way, but nothing could have prepared him for this real-life encounter. She looked like a perfect, just-ripe fruit and smelled of honey. Her glossy chestnut hair, elongated sherry-brown eyes and pouting coral lips made a gentle mockery of the stick-thin blondes who tried and failed to acquire the kind of sexual allure which was only ever born, not made. Not for Francine Lalonde the artificial aids employed by so many in their pursuit of glamour; her hair swung at her shoulders, lacquer-free, she wore no flashy jewellery and her plain apricot silk dress moulded to the feminine curves of her body rather than vice versa. She was a real woman. She didn't have to try.

Max, by devastating contrast, felt like a fifteen-year-old all over again.

His state of tongue-tied bliss, however, couldn't last. Francine Lalonde was one of the guests of honour at this ceremony and her place was at one of the far more prestigious tables at the front, close to the stage. But as the organizer arrived to bear her off, she turned to Max and briefly covered his hand with her own.

'Such a shame, they are taking me away,' she murmured. 'And you look so clever, so interesting. I do enjoy a man who is clever. *Bonne chance, m'sieur . . .*'

The rest of the ceremony passed by Max in a blur with only brief flashes of exquisite clarity. From his position at the back of the room he was no longer able to see her but when she stepped on to the stage amid thunderous applause, first to present the award to the most promising young actor and then to receive her own for best actress he felt himself holding his breath, concentrating on her every word and smile and willing the moment to prolong itself indefinitely. His mind raced as he sought for some way to see her again. He *had* to see her again. And he needed, too, to ensure that the second meeting would captivate her to such an extent that it would automatically be followed by a third . . . and a fourth . . .

'Where are you going?' hissed the man on his right, the director of the film Max had co-written. 'They're just about to announce Best Film – you can't leave now!'

'Sorry,' said Max, sounding anything but. 'Emergency. I have to go. Good luck . . .'

The ceremony, dragging on and over-running as such ceremonies invariably did, finally ended just before five-thirty. By the time Francine had exchanged greetings and air-kisses with a hundred or so old colleagues and distant friends she was more than ready to fall into her waiting limousine and contemplate with pleasure a quiet evening back at her hotel. A hot bath, a relaxing drink, an expertly administered massage maybe, or . . .

'I've been asked to give you this, madam,' said Tomkiss her pompous driver, and Francine regarded the large, gift-wrapped parcel with mild curiosity. The prospect of that hot bath, however, was more inviting.

'How charming. But do you think it is a bomb, Tomkiss?'

'It doesn't tick, madam,' he replied stiffly, still holding the parcel towards her.

She suppressed a faint smile. Tomkiss had no sense of humour whatsoever. 'Well, that is a good sign. Throw it into the car then, and I'll look at it later.'

'The gentleman asked me to make sure you opened it right away, madam.'

Francine, now openly amused and enjoying the brief diversion, said, 'You mean he gave you money to ensure your co-operation? How much, I wonder. Twenty pounds?'

'Er . . . fifty, madam.'

'Tomkiss, you must be careful! You know how easily I fall in love with wealthy men. Look, I shall sit in the car and open my parcel. Is that allowed or must I shiver on the pavement in order to fulfil this present-giver's wishes?'

'Inside the car will be adequate I'm sure, madam,' said Tomkiss, who was beginning to harbour the suspicion that she was making fun of him.

'That's most kind of you,' replied Francine gravely. 'What a truly good man you are.'

Most of her admirers gave her flowers, jewellery, perfume. Having untied the scarlet silk ribbons and pulled away the chic midnight-blue wrapping paper, she smiled. Some men gave her chocolates, some paintings. One had even presented her with a Rolls-Royce Silver Shadow.

But none before had ever given her a wicker basket containing six fat bundles of fresh asparagus, a dozen perfect artichokes and two lobsters.

Opening the envelope which nestled cosily between the lobsters she pulled out a folded piece of newspaper. *The Times* crossword, completed. In the margin beneath it were written only two words: 'Clever enough?'

The door beside her opened. 'Well?' said Max, his dark eyes glittering, his expression carefully controlled. 'Am I?'

'You certainly are,' purred Francine, patting the seat beside her. 'I'm impressed. Come with me back to my hotel, clever man. I have a suite at the Ritz. Maybe, when we get there, you'll be able to impress me some more.'

Max felt as if he'd died and gone straight to heaven. As the evening progressed he found himself falling more and more under Francine Lalonde's spell. She was everything he had ever wanted in a woman. Even when she did things he actively disliked in other women – like smoking endless cigarettes – he didn't care. It was as much a part of her as her expressive hands, deliciously dry sense of humour and faintly accented English. He simply couldn't imagine her *not* smoking. It would have been all wrong . . .

He loved her healthy appetite, the sheer pleasure with which she bit into a tender green asparagus tip, rolling her eyes in appreciation and laughing when the melted butter ran down her fingers. She extracted every morsel of succulent flesh from the cracked lobster claws with an air of triumph that was almost childish, yet a moment later her pink tongue would be darting lasciviously between parted lips, reminding him that she was a forty-year-old sex-symbol desired by men the world over and supremely aware of her own sexuality.

'The most delicious meal I have ever eaten,' declared Francine finally, holding up her hands. 'But maybe,' she added with a lazy smile, 'also the messiest. Look, melted butter everywhere. I think I better take my bath. Max, could you unzip me?'

Better and better, thought Max, wiping his own hands on a linen napkin and rising to his feet as Francine turned her back to him.

The zip slid slowly, noiselessly from neck to waist revealing an oyster satin camisole beneath. For a second his fingers hesitated, hovering over her spine as he battled with his emotions, but he was too late. Francine, smiling at him over her shoulder, was already making her way towards the bathroom.

'I'm afraid I take very long baths. Will you be OK out here?'

'I'll be OK,' Max assured her with a slight smile as he admired her swaying walk. 'If you have a newspaper around I'll do the crossword.'

'So clever,' said Francine, stepping out of her high-heeled shoes and leaving them in her wake. As she disappeared through the doorway she added dreamily, 'And such a magnificent body, too . . .'

When she emerged from the bathroom over an hour later, wrapped in a pale yellow silk robe and with her wet hair combed away from her face, she looked surprised to find Max still there.

'My God, I forgot all about you,' she murmured distractedly, softening the insult with a smile and reaching for her half-empty wine glass. 'Did you see a hairdryer, *chéri*? I'm sure I left it around here somewhere.'

She hadn't only changed, she seemed almost to have forgotten who he was. Their earlier rapport might never have existed. Max felt as if he'd been punched very hard in the stomach. Silently he handed her the hairdryer, which had been lying on the floor beneath the coffee table.

'Look,' said Francine with a hint of apology. 'It's been wonderful. Maybe some other time it will be wonderful all over again, but I'm really very tired right now. All I want to do is go to bed.'

It was all Max wanted to do as well, but he was damned if he was going to say it aloud and give her the satisfaction of further humiliating him. That kind of masochism wasn't his style at all.

'You do look tired,' he replied evenly, matching her veiled insult with one of his own, but inwardly longing to pull her into his arms. 'And I really do have to get back to Bath.'

'Of course you do. I have to be in Scotland by nine o'clock tomorrow morning. Hey, it's a hard life we have, don't you think?' She laughed, pulling a comb out of her pocket and shaking her head so that droplets of water sprayed from her hair. Then she moved towards Max, put her arm around his neck and kissed his cheek.

'I really am sorry, Max. I'm not always easy to be with. My manager says I am a cold and hot person. Sometimes he says I am loopy, you know?'

He nodded, unsmiling. It hurt too much to smile.

'But be in touch, yes? I will like to see you again when I am not so tired.'

'Maybe.'

Francine pouted, parodying his clipped tones. 'Maybe. *Mon Dieu!* Is that a maybe yes or a maybe no? Come on, Max. Don't sulk with me. It's so bloody British!'

He gathered his dinner-jacket and discarded bow tie from the back of the settee and headed towards the door. Opening it, he turned to gaze at her once more, assessing her as if she were a somewhat bizarre abstract painting in an art gallery.

'It's just maybe,' he said, as casually as he knew how. 'And don't pout like that, Francine. It's *so* bloody Gallic.'

Chapter 5

When she pulled open her front door Ross experienced afresh that jolt of longing. In a baggy, white cotton sweater and primrose-yellow cut-offs, her long, curling blonde hair fastened in a disorganized topknot and her face once again devoid of make-up, she looked as stunning as he had remembered.

At the same time he longed to pick her up and shake her. What the hell did she think she was playing at, anyway?

'Hello, Tessa,' he said slowly. And waited.

Tessa couldn't believe this was happening. Why was he here? How had he found her? How much did he know and how on earth did he know anything anyway?

Logically, she realized that all this was in some way connected with Holly. But she still couldn't figure out how, since Holly didn't know anything either. And Ross, she sensed with mounting unease, wasn't going to give her any time at all in which to gather her thoughts.

'Hi.' Wiping her paint-stained hands with a tissue she stood aside to allow him in, since that was obviously why he had come here. She glanced at her watch. 'Can I get you a drink?'

'No.' Ross had had several hours in which to gather his own thoughts and he had assumed that it would give him the advantage, but now that he was here he found himself most uncharacteristically at a loss for words. He could scarcely even remember what he had planned to say.

'I paint,' said Tessa unnecessarily, nodding towards the easel set up beside the window. Ross glanced in turn at the jar of brushes on the window-sill, the blank canvases propped against a chair, the paint palette balanced across its arms and the half-dozen or so framed paintings hanging on the whitewashed living-room walls. With barely a hint of sarcasm, he said, 'Really?'

'I'm afraid the place is in a bit of a mess . . .'

'Oh, do shut up.' He pushed his hands into his pockets and turned to face her, his dark eyes flashing, his determination renewed. 'Tessa, why the bloody hell did you do it?'

'Do what?' Unnerved by his attack she moved across to the window, looking out as if she was expecting another visitor. But there was only Ross's car, a sleek white Mercedes, glittering in the cold December sunlight and serving as a cruel reminder of the difference in their lives.

'Everything.' He gestured with his hands, almost knocking her latest painting from its easel. 'Why did you slope off that morning without leaving me your phone number? Why did you push the money into the bottle? Why wouldn't you even tell me your name?'

Tessa shrugged. 'None of those things seemed relevant at the time, I suppose.'

'Why the hell not?' he demanded. 'What could be more relevant than leaving me with some means of contacting you? I told you I wanted to see you again, dammit.'

'But there would have been no point in us seeing each other again,' she tried to explain. It was clear in her own mind, but from the look on Ross's face he obviously didn't understand at all. Although that, she realized, was because he simply wasn't used to being run out on. His pride had been hurt. She had resisted an irresistible man and now he was challenging her to admit that she'd been wrong. He needed reassurance.

And since he appeared not to know about the baby, she felt she could afford to humour him.

'What *would* have been the point?' she said, her tone reasonable. 'Look at how different we are, the two of us. I'm poor and you're wealthy. You're wildly successful and I'm not the least bit successful – yet. We're different in every way possible . . .'

'I don't know anything about you,' he interjected. 'You wouldn't tell me a single bloody thing about yourself in all those hours we spent together.'

'Take it from me,' she said solemnly, 'we're different. Look, nothing would ever have happened – I mean *properly* happened – if we'd carried on seeing each other. You can have any woman you want, for heaven's sake. I knew that I couldn't compete. So I saved us both a bit of embarrassment and slipped away quietly. Don't you see it was the best thing to do?'

'No, I do not,' declared Ross, his knuckles white. 'And if all these so-called differences were so important to you, why the fuck did you sleep with me in the first place?'

For the first time since his arrival, Tessa smiled. Her green eyes narrowed and she tilted her head slightly to one side as she considered her answer. And despite himself, despite the fact that this beautiful, self-willed girl confused and irritated him beyond belief, Ross smiled too.

'OK, I know.' He pushed his fingers through his dark hair. 'That was the dumbest question I've ever asked in my life.'

'It was nice.'

'A nice question?' He grinned, deliberately misunderstanding her. Quite suddenly the challenge and tension between them had dissipated.

'The question was dumb. The sleeping with you was nice.'

'You really thought so?' Now he was openly teasing her. 'You aren't just saying that to be kind?'

'Actually I am. You know how it is with you men and your fragile egos. We wouldn't want you getting impotent again, after all.'

Ross took a step towards her. What he desperately wanted to do was pull her into his arms, slide that baggy sweater off her shoulders and tumble her into bed. But all he did was take a single step forwards. He was beginning – maybe – to learn how to deal with Tessa Duvall.

'Wouldn't we?' he challenged softly.

Tessa realized at once what he was doing and she was shaken by how badly she wanted him to do it. It was all happening again, the tidal wave of adrenalin, that surge of sexual desire so powerful that her knees were actually trembling, the longing to touch and explore, to give and receive pleasure . . .

But this time she *wasn't* going to give in. The reasons she had given Ross for not seeing him again hadn't been part of some elaborate game; she had been speaking the truth. And it had been hard enough trying to get him out of her mind after just one night. If she gave in now it would only make matters worse. She was going to kick the habit before it got completely out of hand.

This time she was going to say no.

Or she would have done if Ross hadn't chosen precisely that moment to pull her gently but firmly into his arms.

* * *

Unaccustomed as he was to being turned down, Ross couldn't believe that Tessa was doing so *again*. Even worse, she didn't even have the decency to take him seriously.

'What's so funny?' he demanded, falling back against the pillows and watching her laugh at him.

'You are.' Tessa leaned across and kissed the tip of his nose. 'I bet you say that to all the girls. You really should be more careful, one of these days someone's going to take you up on it.'

'I have never asked anyone to marry me before,' declared Ross, outraged. 'And I didn't plan that when the occasion arose I would be laughed at. Now will you bloody well marry me or not?'

'Not!' giggled Tessa, wishing that he would see the funny side. 'Look, this is absurd. You don't propose marriage to people just because it's fun going to bed with them. There's no need to worry,' she went on, whispering in his ear, 'I won't tell anyone. Your reputation shall remain intact.'

'Ah,' said Ross, equally softly, 'but what about your reputation? You're the one who's pregnant, after all.'

He watched her freeze. Then, jerking away from him, she covered her face with her hands. When she didn't say anything, Ross went on, 'Holly told me about it. She explained that you'd had a one-night stand with some guy you met at Max's party and that you weren't going to see him again because he was off the scene. But I'm not off the scene, am I? I'm here and you're pregnant and I've asked you to marry me. How the hell can you be so *stubborn*?'

'I've told you.' Tessa's tone was flat, uncompromising. 'It wouldn't work and it's stupid to even pretend that it might.'

'But you're having my child.' Again he was torn between wanting to hug her and shake some sense into her. Then a thought struck him. 'You are going to have it, aren't you?'

'Of course I am.'

'Then why didn't you want me to know about it?'

'Oh, please!' exclaimed Tessa, her green eyes flashing. 'What was I supposed to do, trail into the hotel and ask you for money?'

'In your situation it's what most girls would do.'

'Well, I'm not most girls,' she retaliated harshly. 'And I don't beg from anyone. I'll manage perfectly well by myself.'

'A child needs a father.' Ross was aware that he sounded unbelievably pompous but he couldn't help himself. 'It isn't fair to deprive it of a parent simply because you're too bloody obstinate to want to share it. And how's it going to feel when it grows up enough to understand that it's illegitimate? What about the stigma?'

He was quite unprepared for Tessa's reaction. Swinging round, she hit him as hard as she could on the side of the head, so fiercely that for a second Ross saw real stars.

'Jesus,' he muttered, touching his temple and somehow expecting to see blood.

'Exactly.' Tessa was shaking with fury, her tone icy with disdain. 'He was illegitimate too. So was I. And I don't think it did either of us such terrible harm.'

Now that he understood he was appalled by his own insensitivity. Risking life and limb, he pulled her into his arms. Burying his face in her long hair, he said urgently, 'I'm sorry, I'm really sorry. I only said it because you'd shot down every other argument I could think of. I didn't mean a word of it anyway.'

For endless seconds Tessa said nothing, staring instead at the Prussian-blue ceiling of her bedroom. Finally, she patted his arm in a gesture that was curiously maternal.

'I'm sorry as well. I shouldn't have hit you like that.' She paused, then broke into a grin. 'But just think how annoyed I would have been if I really was illegitimate.'

Holly was up to her ears on reception when Tessa strolled past, arm in arm with Ross. She did a classic double-take but Tessa, the bitch, simply winked and carried on walking, leaving Holly to deal with a party of excitable Mafia-types who seemed to think that if they spoke slowly and loudly enough in their incomprehensible Sicilian dialect she would somehow miraculously understand them.

Boiling with curiosity, she had to endure another hour of chaos and frustration before Tessa finally emerged from the restaurant alone. By some miracle there was no one requiring attention and the phone was silent. Holly darted out from behind the desk and frogmarched Tessa into the ladies' cloakroom.

'Tell me everything,' she demanded, glancing at her watch. 'And in less than thirty seconds. Ross will kill me if he finds out I'm missing – he has some very strange ideas about women's bladders.'

'OK,' said Tessa, mimicking Holly's rapid-fire line of speech. Holding up the fingers of one hand she began ticking them off. 'We met. We had a quickie. He asked me to marry him. I turned him down. I slapped his face. Shit, I've run out of fingers. Never mind. And he agreed to let me sell my paintings in the hotel.'

Tessa relished the ensuing silence. She had never in her entire life seen Holly so completely stuck for words.

'You met, you . . . *what*!' shrieked Holly, visibly paling beneath her heavy make-up. 'Come on, stop kidding around. Tell me what's going on.'

'Would I lie to you?' asked Tessa with an innocent shrug. Examining her reflection in one of the gilded mirrors lining the walls, she licked her index finger and smoothed her eyebrows. 'Let me just say,' she added casually, 'that your boss has a definite talent for persuasion.'

Holly was aware of the expression 'gob-smacked'. Now, for the first time in her life, she understood exactly what it meant.

'Jesus Christ,' she exploded. 'You really did go to bed with him. Tessa, you can tell me. Are you drunk?'

'Me?' With wounded eyes Tessa gazed at her friend's reflection in the mirror. 'Of course I'm not drunk.'

'But you're pregnant! You know you're pregnant and Ross knows you're pregnant. I knew he was a bastard but I can't believe that even Ross would do something so unbelievably shitty.'

Seizing Holly's wrist and enjoying herself more than she had in years, Tessa peered at the slim gold watch and shook her head. 'Your thirty seconds are up, Holl. And because I wouldn't want you to think bad things about your boss I'll let you into a secret. It wasn't shitty . . . it was great.'

Frustrated beyond belief, Holly did what Ross had so longed to do earlier. Grabbing Tessa's shoulders she shook her. Hard.

'Stop it!' she shrieked. 'What are you *doing*? Tell me what's going on before I go out of my mind!'

Tessa grinned. She couldn't help it. And Holly was right; if she didn't let her in on the secret her friend was in danger of going seriously barmy.

'Relax. If it makes you any happier, Ross was only going where no man other than him had gone before. For the last year, anyway.'

The shock was too much for Holly. Plonking herself down on a rose-pink velvet upholstered chair, she breathed, 'You mean . . .?'

'He's the father,' supplied Tessa with an audible sigh of relief. After all, if you couldn't tell your best friend, who could you tell? 'But it really isn't common knowledge, so hold the phone calls if you can.'

'Ross? You and Ross? Oh Tessa, what have I done?'

Much as she had patted Ross's arm earlier, Tessa now did the same to Holly. 'I know, I know. It's all your fault. It's practically your baby. But don't worry, I promise I won't sting you for maintenance.'

When she returned to the restaurant she found Max sitting at the table. Ross had disappeared.

'He had to go and sort out some problem about double-booking,' said Max, lighting a cigarette and casting Tessa a look which wasn't exactly favourable. 'Our receptionist has disappeared. My name is Max, by the way.'

'I know.' Tessa sat down. 'And I'm Tessa Duvall.'

'So I've heard.' Watching her as she relaxed in her chair, seemingly unconcerned by his taciturn expression, he knew that he had been right. During a highly uncharacteristic brother-to-brother discussion earlier that evening he had listened with mounting disbelief to Ross's story. Finally he had told his brother that he was off his head. Ross wasn't in love; he had fallen prey to a smart, manipulative girl who recognized a five-star meal ticket when she saw one. And this girl was playing a particularly clever game. Ross might have been crazy enough to offer to marry her but if she'd accepted him right away he would have begun to doubt her soon enough to bring him to his senses. As it was, Tessa was playing it cool, appearing to reject him in order to pique his interest and only make him that much more determined to succeed.

This was what Ross refused to accept, but in this case Max was in the advantageous position of not being besotted by an innocent smile, a mane of tumbling golden hair, a pair of beguiling emerald-green eyes and presumably a startling talent for seduction.

Tessa, in turn, studying the volatile man sitting across the table from her, decided that although only two years separated Ross and Max, no one would even think to question it if they were told it was a decade. Max's hair, black and straight, was streaked with silver; the dark Monahan eyes – so very like his brother's in shape and colour – were fanned with more than their share of creases and lines and at this moment entirely lacking in humour, and the wide, nicely defined mouth was turned down at the corners.

Altogether, she decided, he bore more than a passing resemblance to a large and dangerously incensed tiger. For some reason – and she suspected she knew what that might be – Max Monahan, tonight, was not in a party mood.

'What are you thinking?' she asked, regarding him over the rim of her water glass. 'Or can I guess?'

The famous dark brown eyes narrowed. 'I'm sure you can.'

'Don't worry, I'm really not going to marry him.'

'Bloody right,' said Max icily. 'Particularly if I have anything to do with it. But just for the record, let me tell you that I understand exactly what you're up to. Ross might be infatuated with you, carried away by the whole romantic idea of a whirlwind marriage and fatherhood, but I'm not. And I'm going to make damn sure that he realizes what you are before he makes a complete fool of himself.'

It was ironic, thought Tessa, that she and Max should be on the same side but that he refused to accept it. It could even almost be amusing, but amusing or not she still had her pride. And to be accused like this of deliberately laying a trap for Ross in order to inveigle him into marriage wasn't nice.

'And what exactly am I?' she countered, challenging him. If Holly ever got her bizarre wish and married this cold, cynical inquisitor, she was damned if she'd be a bridesmaid.

'A gold-digger,' he declared flatly.

'OK,' said Tessa, placing her elbows on the table and preparing for battle. 'It doesn't really matter to me what you think, since this hypothetical marriage isn't going to take place anyway and that means we're never going to become in-laws. But it does piss me off to think that you automatically assume the very worst about me when you don't even *know* me.'

'I know enough.' Max shot her a dismissive glance and stubbed out his cigarette.

'Then you should know that I never had the slightest intention of contacting your brother. It was only by the merest coincidence that he found out who I was.'

'Oh, of course!' he exclaimed, feigning wonder. 'The very merest coincidence! Your oldest friend just happened to tell Ross all about you. Come *on*, Miss Duvall. Neither of us were born yesterday. And if you want my honest opinion I doubt very much indeed whether this baby, *if* it exists, was ever anything to do with my brother in the first place.'

This was too much. Trembling with rage, Tessa sprang to her feet. She could take so much, but Max Monahan's humiliating insults were way below the belt.

'Don't judge everyone by your own revolting standards,' she said in a low voice, picking up the half-full bottle of claret which stood on the table between them. Their table was a corner one and she moved around it, blocking the view of the other diners in the busy, noisy restaurant and tipping the contents of the bottle into Max's lap. 'And don't wet your pants worrying about your brother,' she added with a deliberately sweet smile. 'You're both grown men, after all.'

Chapter 6

It was easy enough to ignore whatever Max had to say on the subject of Tessa, but Ross was finding it a little more difficult maintaining a relationship with someone who flatly refused to see him. Furious with Max, she was quite unfairly venting her anger on Ross instead. When he phoned she would repeat the unflattering, almost slanderous, comments which Max had showered upon her. When he drove to her cottage demanding to see her, she stated quite plainly that nothing would give her less pleasure – which was a damn lie – and refused to let him in.

It was a ridiculous situation. He had done everything he could to bring both Tessa and Max to their senses but, for as long as they clung to their obstinate beliefs, he was stuck.

When Antonia rang him on Christmas Eve he was at such a loose end that he accepted her invitation at once. Since he obviously wasn't getting anywhere with Tessa he might as well have a little fun where he could.

'Darling, will you stop worrying about me!' Antonia, sitting naked before the dressing-table mirror, fiddled with the awkward catch on the back of one of her earrings.

Richard Seymour-Smith regarded his wife from the doorway, jangling his car keys in the nervous manner she found so irritating. 'I do worry. I don't like to think of you being here on your own, particularly on Christmas Eve. Why don't you change your mind and come with me? Father will be delighted to see you.'

'Really, I'll be fine,' she insisted. Richard's father was a pompous old bore whose disapproval of her was silent but obvious. She reached out to her husband and tilted her head, proffering her powdered cheek for a kiss. 'You two can spend a nice comfortable evening together talking about business and politics, all those things I don't understand. I'm going to enjoy a lazy night in front of the television, stuffing myself with brandy and chocolates and watching myself get fat.'

'You have a perfect body,' Richard told her, as she had known he would. 'OK, I'm going. I'll be back by midnight at the latest. And be careful, sweetheart. Don't let any strangers into the house.' There had been a spate of burglaries in the area recently and their isolated home would be a prime target.

'I won't,' said Antonia with perfect truth. ''Bye, darling. And give my love to your father.'

Ross, as usual, was late. By the time his white Mercedes careered to a halt at the top of the snowy drive, Antonia was already halfway down a bottle of white wine. Since it was already dark outside, the porch lights were switched on and as she went to greet him she smiled at the thought of his response when he saw her silhouetted against the open doorway wearing only a white satin camisole and high heels.

'Holy cow,' breathed Ross. This was what he most liked about Antonia, you always knew where you were with her. And it was usually in bed. 'Get inside, quick. What if someone sees you?'

She stared mockingly past him at the tree-lined drive, the acres of unremitting darkness. 'Oh, there can't be more than a couple of hundred people hiding out there. Don't be so boring, Ross. Ever made love in the snow?'

She trailed her hand down the front of his shirt, feeling the warmth of his body and the hard, sculpted muscles of his torso.

'Ever made love to a man with a dick the size of an acorn?' he countered. 'It's freezing out here.' And he pulled her with him into the hall, kicking the door shut behind them. Any half-hearted ideas he may have harboured about remaining faithful to Tessa were melting as fast as the snowflakes in his hair. Tessa appeared to want nothing further to do with him and he was only human, after all. When someone like Antonia was wrapping themselves around you, saying no wasn't the response which sprang most naturally to mind.

They made love in the sitting room, in front of the fire, with the ease and expertise of two people who have known each other intimately for over a year and who understand how to give and receive maximum pleasure.

Afterwards, as Antonia lay in his arms with one smooth, brown leg tucked between his and her head against his shoulder, Ross experienced a surge of disappointment so acute that it hit him like a punch in the stomach.

It wasn't the sex; that had been fine. Technically perfect. But somehow sex alone was no longer enough.

Antonia, he realized, wasn't the person he had most wanted to make love to. She wasn't Tessa. And that part of him which had become emotionally involved with Tessa was now crying out in protest at having been abandoned.

Great, thought Ross with almost comic despair. Not content with dumping me, she has to wreck my sex life, too.

*   *   *

51

Holly, not for the first time, despaired of Tessa. It was Christmas Day and for the past week Ross had been sloping around the hotel like a funeral on legs, terrifying the younger waitresses and generally dispensing gloom and despondency. Today, it seemed, was no exception.

How Tessa could refuse to see him, Holly didn't understand. She had every right, of course, to be furious with Max but, when all was said and done, it wasn't his opinion of her that counted.

If Holly had been in Tessa's position, she would have leapt at the opportunity and clung on to Ross with both hands.

And as it was, she had made no progress at all with Max. Convinced that she and Tessa had hatched Tessa's grand plan between them, he was no longer even speaking to her.

The huge bunch of mistletoe she had bought and hung hopefully above her desk had been a complete waste of money.

Reminding herself what a bastard he'd been – and his general mood had been particularly surly ever since he'd returned from that smart ceremony in London without an award – Holly couldn't understand why she was still so crazy about him. But then, she thought ruefully, it never did work like that anyway. In her experience the bigger the bastard the more irresistible she found them.

By mid-afternoon Ross began to show signs of cheering up. Two extremely pretty daughters of an Irish racehorse trainer dragged him without too much of a struggle into the ballroom where a rumbustious game of charades was in progress and cheating was rife. The eighty-five guests, having enjoyed a six-course lunch and vast amounts of champagne, were showing no signs at all of wanting to sleep it off. Holly was due to finish her shift at three-thirty and she was looking forward to getting home. Her parents, who invariably spent the winter months in the Caribbean, had sent her an intriguingly large Christmas parcel which by some miracle she had managed not to open too soon and Tessa would be busy preparing a late lunch for the two of them. Since the death of Tessa's mother five years earlier, they had always spent Christmas Day together.

She was less than amused therefore, when Sylvie Nash – the receptionist scheduled to take over from her and work the late shift – phoned in sick. She didn't even have the decency to do the deed herself. Holly gritted her teeth as she listened to Sylvie's boyfriend's drunken excuses. Sylvie had a migraine attack; she was in agony, laid up in bed and so ill that she couldn't even crawl to the phone. That Sylvie was in bed Holly didn't doubt, but a headache was the last thing she was likely to be suffering from.

'I'm really sorry, darling.' Ross attempted to placate her when she relayed the message to him. Holly slapped his hand away.

'I *can't* stay here,' she wailed. 'I have other plans, dammit.'

'Please, you can't let us down. And this isn't such a terrible place to spend Christmas. Tonight's party's going to be wild . . .'

'Oh, shut up, Ross. Tessa's waiting for me at my flat. Apart from the fact that she's spent hours preparing lunch for the two of us, I'm not bloody well going to let her spend Christmas on her own.'

Holly was unaware that Max, who had overheard her noisy protests, was standing behind her.

'Look,' said Ross suddenly, sounding more interested. 'Couldn't we get Tessa here? Would she come if you talked to her and explained the situation?'

'Of course she wouldn't!' exploded Holly with derision. 'Thanks to your pig of a brother she wouldn't set foot in this place and I don't bloody well blame her.'

'I'm not that much of a pig,' remonstrated Max with a slight smile. Holly jumped at the sound of his voice but realized at once that it was too late to back down. Whirling round to face him, her grey eyes sparking with anger, she snapped, 'Yes, you are. You behaved appallingly towards her and she'd done nothing to deserve it.'

Luckily, Max was in a good mood. He also recognized the fact that unless Tessa came to the hotel, Holly would walk out on them. And an hotel can't function on all cylinders without a receptionist, even on Christmas Day.

'Give me your address,' he said. Holly had longed for months to hear him say those words, but for entirely different reasons. 'And for Christ's sake, cheer up. I'll go and pick her up myself.'

Tessa was sitting cross-legged in the window-seat of Holly's sitting room, idly sketching the view of The Circus, that famous uninterrupted circle of slender Georgian houses whose perspective it was so difficult to get exactly right. Through the uncurtained illuminated windows of other houses she could see parties in progress, Christmas trees glittering and people having fun. Living alone, Tessa was used to solitude but Christmas was somehow different. Holly's elegant, high-ceilinged flat smelled deliciously of roasting turkey, pine needles and beeswax candles and the latest Tom Cruise movie was being premièred on television, but Tessa felt unaccountably edgy. She wanted Holly to return and her friend was already fifteen minutes late.

Because of her elevated position she didn't spot Max letting himself in through the front door three floors below. When she heard Holly's key turning in the door to the flat, she slid off the window-seat and ran through to the hallway to greet her.

Coming face to face with Max Monahan wasn't quite the Christmas surprise she'd been waiting for.

'Ho, ho, ho,' he said quietly, handing her an icy bottle of Veuve Cliquot. 'I didn't bring red wine, you notice. This seemed safer.'

'I can't imagine what on earth you're doing here,' said Tessa, realizing how rude she sounded, but too stunned to do anything about it. 'And where's Holly?'

Max popped the cork on the champagne and, ignoring Tessa's protests that she had given up alcohol, half-filled her glass. As he did so he explained Holly's dilemma.

'She called me a pig,' he concluded. 'I told her that if I could forgive you for wrecking my suit last week, you could forgive me for speaking my mind.'

'Ah,' said Tessa warily, 'but have you changed your mind at all, or am I still a lying, cheating, money-grabbing tart?'

Max drained his own glass, strode into the kitchen and switched off the oven. 'You could well be, but I'm prepared to admit that since I don't know you I shouldn't have made those kind of remarks. So, for now I'll hold fire. How's that?'

'You're still a pig,' Tessa told him, a hint of a smile playing on her lips. 'But I can cope with that. OK, let's go.'

'Merry Christmas,' said Ross, wondering whether he dared give Tessa a kiss. He wasn't accustomed to feeling like a nervous teenager on a first date – indeed, he had rampaged through his teens with careless abandon – but seeing Tessa enter the hotel with Max had done strange things to him. And now here she was, in a simple scarlet wool sweater and a matching short skirt, and her dark stockinged legs were just as spectacular as he remembered.

He hesitated, then gestured towards the scarlet bow with which her shining hair was fastened into a topknot. 'Very festive. You look . . . wonderful.'

'I look hungry,' said Tessa, who wasn't comfortable receiving compliments. 'My lunch is in the oven back at the flat. Any chance of a leftover drumstick?'

Ross had already organized that. As he led her through to the deserted restaurant she saw that only one table, in the very centre of the room, was set. Crimson and white roses were artfully arranged in silver vases. Half a dozen fat candles cast their amber glow over the dazzlingly white linen tablecloth, enhancing the glitter of silver cutlery and elegant crystal glasses. A frosted ice-bucket held yet another unopened bottle of champagne.

The table was set for two. After helping Tessa into her seat Ross sat down in the chair facing her.

'You weren't expecting me to turn up then,' she said with a trace of irony.

'I hoped you would. I would have come and fetched you myself but you might have refused. It was up to Max to make the first move and apologize.' He glimpsed the expression in her green eyes and added sharply, 'He *did* apologize, of course?'

'In his own way.' Tessa, inhaling the scent of the roses, reminded herself that Ross's irresistible charm was the exact reason she wasn't going to allow herself to become involved with him. Falling prey to that charm, those stunning good looks and that breathtaking body, would only lead to tears, maybe not before bedtime but, undoubtedly in the only-too-foreseeable near future.

Complications like that, she had decided, were just what she didn't need.

Ross didn't help matters by leaning back in his chair, fixing her with a seductive smile and saying, 'So, here we are. Our very first Christmas together. Now aren't you glad you came?'

His glittering dark brown eyes were mesmerizing. He was doing it again, thought Tessa; deliberately trying to seduce her. She smiled back at him.

'I don't know yet,' she replied slowly, picking up her fork and tracing figures of eight on the linen tablecloth. 'It rather depends on the food.'

Chapter 7

By mid-evening the ballroom was packed with Christmas revellers in various stages of abandon.

Antonia, her black-stockinged legs carefully crossed so that her split-to-the-thigh black and bronze dress fell open to reveal as much leg as possible, smoked a rare cigarette and watched the proceedings at the top table with an expression of detached amusement.

Inwardly she was far from amused. Curiosity mingled with a distinct sensation of unease. So accustomed to getting her own way that she could scarcely remember what failure felt like, she realized via some inexplicable sixth sense that she was now facing a real threat. The perfect, effortless order of her life was in danger of falling apart.

And no matter how carefully she scrutinized the girl with whom Ross was sitting, she couldn't for the life of her understand why.

OK, she thought, trying again. She's pretty. But then so are a thousand other girls and they at least made the best of themselves. This one wasn't even wearing any make-up. Her tousled blonde hair, Antonia judged with an expert's eye, hadn't been within screaming distance of a hairdresser for months. The scarlet angora outfit was simple but bearable, although scarcely appropriate to an evening such as this. And the flat black leather pumps, Antonia decided, were frankly *passé*. Along with every other *Vogue* devotee Antonia had got rid of all her own similarly styled shoes a year ago, chucking them into a box and giving them to her daily woman to cart down to Oxfam. This girl obviously didn't have a clue as far as current styles were concerned.

And yet . . . and yet here was Ross, looking as if he were constantly having to force himself not to touch this underdressed, unfashionable girl. It wasn't the Ross Antonia knew, so laid back that he was practically horizontal and barely bothering to conceal his amusement when women made fools of themselves in their efforts to gain his attention.

This time, however, he was the one who was interested. Antonia would almost have called it besotted. And with a gut-wrenching spasm of jealousy, she realized that the threat to her own happiness was even deeper than she had first imagined.

Sipping her vodka and tonic and listening to the rattle of the ice-cubes as her hand shook with a mixture of fear and fury, Antonia decided that something would most definitely have to be done. She and Ross had the perfect arrangement; he didn't mind the fact that she had a husband and she didn't concern herself with the endless river of women with which he amused himself . . . as long as that was all it was. Amusement.

The trouble was, she had always felt she knew Ross well enough to be confident that his way of life wouldn't change. She simply hadn't allowed for the possibility that one day he might fall in love.

That was the great threat. And when Antonia was threatened, she retaliated.

* * *

Thankfully Ross's mood had undergone a dramatic improvement since Tessa's arrival and as a result he had put away his whip. Holly, allowed to join in the fun as long as she kept an ear out for the phone in reception, was having a whale of a time flirting outrageously with a French film producer whose soulful brown eyes could have melted her ice any time if only she wasn't so madly in love with Max. She was only encouraging him in the hope that Max might notice and be suddenly overcome by a wave of Heathcliffian jealousy and sweep her into his arms. So far all he had managed was a wink and a grin as he danced past her table with Mrs Ellis, the slender, enigmatic divorcée from Room 12, in his arms, but at least it was a start. Only this afternoon she'd called him a pig. A man had his pride, after all.

Holly smiled at the waiflike new waitress whose name was Grace and helped herself to a canapé from the tray Grace was carrying somewhat inexpertly in both hands as she steered her way between the tables. At that moment she noticed for the first time the sinuous figure of Antonia Seymour-Smith rising from her seat at the far end of the room. Shit, thought Holly, glancing anxiously across at Tessa and Ross. She hadn't expected Antonia to be here tonight. Uncomfortably she recognized the irony of the fact that, although she was incapable of keeping secrets, she hadn't yet found the right moment to tell Tessa about Antonia's only semi-secret involvement with Ross. By some miracle her husband appeared to be unaware of the situation but it was otherwise common knowledge that the two of them had been conducting a long-running, not terribly discreet, affair.

The French producer was murmuring something Gallic and

seductive in the direction of her cleavage but Holly was no longer listening. The waitress, Grace, was standing motionless beside her and they were both gazing in the same direction. As Antonia made her way across the crowded room, her own eyes fixed unwaveringly upon Ross and Tessa, Holly's heart sank. She didn't know what Antonia was planning but she knew she wasn't going to like it one little bit.

Having earlier made the mistake of doodling a caricature of the Irish racehorse trainer on the back of a piece of Christmas wrapping paper, Tessa now found herself besieged by requests for lightning sketches of other guests.

'Sign your name clearly,' Ross instructed her as she concentrated upon capturing the roly-poly – but not too roly-poly – likeness of T. J. Henderson, a second-generation Texan oil baron visiting the UK with his dim, but incredibly over-endowed, nineteen-year-old daughter. 'And charge them a fortune, otherwise they won't appreciate it.'

Tessa smiled and shook her head. These two-minute sketches were for fun, not for profit. T. J. Henderson roared with laughter and slapped his fat knee.

'Make me look real pretty, hon, and all you have to do is name your price. I'll pay it!'

'Good heavens,' protested Antonia, appearing quite suddenly at Tessa's side. 'You make her sound like some kind of prostitute.'

Ross's eyes narrowed. He and Antonia had an unspoken understanding and so far she had never let him down. Normally she observed from a distance and teased him afterwards. Trust her to choose tonight of all nights – and Tessa of all the women she had ever seen him with – to stick her oar in. He watched with mounting annoyance as she placed her bronze-tipped fingers upon Tessa's shoulder.

'Antonia,' he said, partly as a means of introduction, partly warning her not to misbehave. 'This is Tessa Duvall. She's going to be selling her paintings through the hotel.'

'She must be very talented,' remarked Antonia, smiling at T. J. Henderson in such a way that only Ross caught the *double entendre*.

'Where's Richard?' he demanded, wishing fervently that he could tell Antonia to take a hike.

She switched her smile in his direction and he saw the icy determination in her dark blue eyes. 'Oh he's here, in the other bar. Christmas Day or no Christmas Day, he's managed to find someone to talk business with. Why, at this very moment I imagine he's discussing something riveting like personal allowances or the fluctuation of the Deutschmark. Which is why,' she continued smoothly, meeting the annoyance in his eyes with a careless shrug, 'I preferred to join your party. And who could blame me?'

In the time it had taken Antonia to demonstrate her boredom with her husband, Tessa had both sized up the situation and finished the sketch. This sleek blonde with the expensive haircut and a body honed by exercise was one of Ross's famous line of exes. With detached amusement and admirable presence of mind she signed her name to the caricature with a clear, bold hand and said, 'This one's on me. Thank goodness I'm not a prostitute – I'd be bankrupt within a week.'

'Don't say that.' Antonia slid into the chair next to her. 'You're obviously very gifted. Just make sure old Ross here doesn't take advantage.'

Ross wasn't used to feeling helpless. Glancing around he

glimpsed Holly, looking equally apprehensive at the far end of the ballroom.

'He won't,' said Tessa, smiling at Antonia.

'He might,' replied Antonia, knowing that she shouldn't say it but out of sheer desperation going ahead anyway. 'Ross thrives on taking advantage. Why, he did it to me only last night. I wouldn't have mentioned it, of course, only it scarcely seems fair on you not to know how he behaves when one's back is turned . . .'

'She's history,' declared Holly, the light of battle in her eyes. 'She's a complete tart and you mustn't let her get to you. If you do, you're crazy.'

'I'm not crazy,' Tessa informed her from the depths of the back seat of Max's car. 'But I do have a few remaining scruples. If anyone's a tart, it's Ross Monahan. And it just goes to show,' she went on, her voice even, 'that my decision not to have any more to do with him was the right one all along.'

Max, pulling up outside Tessa's cottage, was experiencing an uncomfortable conflict of emotions. He hadn't yet made up his mind about Tessa, but he had to admit that she had handled tonight's awkwardness with admirable dignity. Until now he had regarded Antonia with good-natured disdain, understanding the situation and disapproving of it but at the same time deriving some satisfaction from knowing that at least their affair was in the long run meaningless.

'I'm sorry about tonight,' he said, wrenching on the handbrake. Tessa was out of the car in less than two seconds.

'Don't be,' she retaliated shortly. 'I'm just pleased that someone had the decency to put me in the picture. Even if it did have to be Antonia Seymour-Smith.'

'It's what he's like.' Max gestured despair with upturned palms. 'I thought you realized that.'

'I did,' replied Tessa through the open window. 'But he exceeded even my sordid expectations. Thanks for the lift home.'

'Would you like to come in for coffee?' asked Holly, when they finally reached her flat. 'We have turkey if you feel like it,' she added out of sheer desperation. This was the very first time she and Max had been together away from the hotel and she wanted to make the most of the opportunity.

'Maybe some other time.' Max was scarcely listening, functioning on automatic pilot. Holly was an efficient receptionist but in other respects she interested him about as much as botulism.

Uppermost in his mind at the moment was a slowly forming plan to see Francine Lalonde again. Since he couldn't get her out of his mind he had decided to take positive action instead. The trick, of course, was to disguise the fact that it was a plan. If she thought for one second that he was chasing after her like some stage-struck fan, it wouldn't work at all.

'Oh, but you must,' Holly blurted out now. 'You have time for a quick drink, surely!'

'I'm driving. Look, I really should—'

'Of course you are! I have fresh orange juice, though. You could have that, with some cold turkey and walnut stuffing . . .'

'Holly, no.' The time had come to be firm. 'I have to get back. We're very grateful to you for working so hard today.' He leaned towards her and for a heart-stopping moment Holly thought he was going to kiss her. But it didn't happen and Max opened the passenger door instead.

'No problem. It was my pleasure,' she told him with a brave smile. To herself she added, 'Well it could have been.'

It was almost midnight by the time Grace arrived home. The living-room light was still on which meant that her mother was waiting up for her, no doubt engrossed in some late-night film and steadily demolishing the box of Thornton's continental selection which Grace had given her that morning.

Reversing her mother's ancient Fiat – rusty but reliable – into the only available parking space, Grace realized how much she was looking forward to telling her about her day. Mattie's insatiable curiosity always used to drive her wild; by nature a quiet girl who kept her thoughts to herself it had seemed like an unpleasant intrusion of privacy, but in the past month, since taking the waitressing job at The Grange, Grace was now only too happy to talk about it. Indeed, it was practically a compulsion. During the last couple of years at school she had been irritated beyond belief by the girls who constantly rabbited on about their boyfriends, their every sentence prefaced by, 'Darren says . . . ' and, 'Colin thinks . . . ' Now, however, she understood their one-track minds and their need to talk about the most important person in their lives. Now that she, too, had fallen in love she understood completely. Writing pages of details in her diary was fine in its own way, but the need to speak that magical name aloud was irresistible . . .

Mattie Jameson was indeed watching television, an old black-and-white Bing Crosby film that she must have seen a dozen times before but enjoyed all the more for knowing that it had a happy ending. Life was too short, she always declared, to waste watching miserable films. She had no patience at all with Ingmar Bergman.

Comfortably ensconced before the fire, wrapped up in her favourite pink-and-white dressing gown and with her light brown hair waving around her face, she looked younger than her forty years. Her face softened and she broke into a welcoming smile as Grace moved towards her. Putting down her cup of milky coffee, she held out her arms for their customary hug. She smelled deliciously of the magnolia soap and bubble bath which had been another of Grace's presents to her.

'You're late. How was work?'

'Oh, fine.' Grace kissed her mother's soft cheek. 'Busy, of course.'

'Hotels always are at this time of year. Can't understand for the life of me why some people should want to spend their Christmases in an hotel instead of their own homes, but there you are . . .'

'Probably so that they don't have to do all the hard work themselves.' Grace slipped out of her coat, helped herself to a satsuma from the fruit bowl and sat down at her mother's feet, propping her back against the armchair so that she could see the television and talk without having to engage in actual eye contact.

Mattie's shrewd grey eyes missed nothing and Grace found conversation easier when she wasn't being subjected to their silent interrogation. She didn't want to give herself away completely.

'Have a chocolate.' Mattie handed her the box of Thornton's, two-thirds empty. After years of half-heartedly attempting to diet, she had finally come to terms with the fact that size ten dresses and self-denial weren't for her. Now, her figure comfortably rounded, she ate what she liked and enjoyed every moment of it. 'So. Who was there today, anyone exciting?'

'That Texan oil baron gave me a five-pound tip. The French film director I told you about tried to pinch my bottom,' recounted Grace, gazing dreamily into space. 'I was pouring brandy sauce at the time and half of it ended up in his wine glass. When I told Ross he said I shouldn't worry about it, that all Frenchmen suffered from MTF and that next time I should pour the sauce over his head.'

'MTF?'

'Must Touch Flesh.' Grace smiled, remembering the incident. 'Then Ross said that it was probably my own fault anyway for having such a pinchable bum.'

Over the rim of her coffee cup Mattie gravely regarded the back of her daughter's head. 'I hope *he* managed to keep his hands off you, at least.'

'Mum!' said Grace, scandalized. 'He's the manager! Anyway, he had enough problems of his own this evening. He brought a new girl-friend along to the hotel and that mistress of his, Antonia Seymour-Smith, was there with her husband Richard. Well, Antonia must have been really jealous because she went right up to the new girl-friend and told her – in front of Ross and some of the guests – all about their affair.'

Some people never changed, thought Mattie. Aloud she said: 'And what happened then?'

'I couldn't hear all of it, I wasn't close enough. The new girl-friend didn't say much, but Ross dragged Antonia through to the bar and dumped her on Richard, telling him that his wife was drunk and that it was time she went home. Of course Antonia couldn't argue because Richard doesn't know about the affair so she had to shut up. They left, and five minutes later, Ross's girl-friend disappeared with Max. Holly, one of the receptionists, went with them.'

'Just like a soap opera,' remarked Mattie idly. 'Was Ross furious?'

'Mad as hell.' Grace was sounding positively delighted. 'He tried to stop the girl leaving but she wouldn't even speak to him. And he was so cross with Antonia that he's not going to want her any more . . .'

'Well, well. Don't some people lead complicated lives.' Mattie felt she'd heard enough about Ross Monahan for one evening. 'Look, that nice film's ended. Are you ready for something to eat before bed, darling? How about some nice baked ham and pickles?'

Chapter 8

The snow looked so gorgeous, thought Tessa, why on earth did it have to go and spoil itself by being so damn cold?

Rubbing her gloved hands together and blowing on her wrists, she surveyed the narrow lane ahead, banked high on either side with drifts of snow like frozen waves and more suited to a bobsleigh than to the bicycle which was her only available form of transport.

Still, all she had to do was wheel the bike down this lane. As soon as she met the main road, she reminded herself, she'd be fine. And cycling into the centre of Bath was going to be a hell of a lot easier than either walking it or waiting for a country bus which might never arrive.

Tessa was pleased to discover that she had been right. Pushing the bike downhill was no problem and when she reached the junction she saw that the main road had indeed been lavishly gritted. What had been snow was now charcoal-grey slush, less picturesque but immeasurably easier to negotiate. Her toes numb with cold and her breath materializing as opalescent clouds before her, she swung her leg over the crossbar and pushed cautiously out into the traffic.

Less than two minutes later the bicycle, mangled and crushed almost beyond recognition, catapulted into the ditch. The articulated lorry, undamaged, skidded to a halt twenty yards further down the road.

The lorry driver, realizing that he was sliding out of control, had managed to sound his horn just in time. Tessa, glancing over her shoulder, had seen the monster behind her, felt the first brush of its chrome bumper against her rear wheel and taken a flying leap in the direction of the snow-packed left-hand verge.

When she later recovered her sense of humour she recognized the irony of narrowly avoiding a lorry carrying several thousand tins of dog food. At the time, it was a toss-up which of them was the more shaken by the accident, herself or the driver of the lorry.

'Bleedin' 'ell,' he croaked, white-faced and trembling. 'I thought you'd gone under the wheels. You OK, love? I just lost control. Bleedin' 'ell.'

Tessa had actually had a pretty soft, if cold, landing. Accepting the lorry driver's clammy outstretched hand and pulling herself to her feet, she nodded and managed a ghost of a smile. 'I think I'm fine. Nothing broken, anyway. And don't worry, it wasn't your fault.' She wondered whether she should go and see her local doctor. When accidents like this happened in television serials the pregnant mother invariably collapsed, clutching her stomach and screaming: 'Oh God, the baby.'

In reality, however, she felt perfectly OK. 'The bike's looking a bit wrinkled,' she observed, stuffing her hands into the pockets of her faded denims and starting to shiver. 'I don't think I'll be getting far on that. Look, if you could give me a lift to my friend's house I'd be awfully grateful.' The lorry would never have managed to squeeze along the narrow, snow-choked lane to her cottage but Holly would hopefully be able to give her a lift home later.

' 'Course I will, love. Come on, give us yer arm. Bleedin' 'ell, I really thought you'd copped it. Gave me an 'elluva turn.'

All Tessa appeared to want was to carry on with her own life in her own way, and Holly, though convinced that her friend was quite mad, had until now been prepared to humour her.

But the very calmness with which Tessa had relayed the story of the accident which could so easily have had tragic — if not fatal — consequences infuriated Holly beyond belief.

And when she arrived at The Grange later that same afternoon to find Ross in reception, engrossed in a far-from-businesslike tête-à-tête with the pouting Swedish girl-friend of a rock star currently staying at the hotel, her anger knew no bounds. Looking at Ross, in a charcoal-grey suit which must have cost hundreds of pounds, a green-and-grey pin-striped shirt and highly polished Italian leather shoes, with his out-of-season tan and expensively casual haircut, and at the Swedish girl's floor-length leather coat the colour of beech leaves, she was overwhelmed by the absolute unfairness of it all. Holly would be the last person in the world to describe herself as a Socialist, but at this precise moment she experienced a surge of longing to strip Ross of his carefree, overprivileged lifestyle and spectacular wealth and shower it instead upon all those who needed and deserved it so much more than he did.

As she stood there watching them Ross glanced up and saw her. Normally he would have greeted Holly with a grin and a brief exchange of banter, teasing her about whatever new outfit she might be wearing or remarking upon her hairstyle. But at that moment the girl in the leather coat leaned forward and reached up on tiptoe to whisper something in his ear, huge diamonds flashing as she rested her left hand against his chest. Ross returned his attention to her, ignoring Holly, and that was the final kick in the teeth, the ultimate insult. Quivering with rage on Tessa's behalf, because Tessa would never dream of causing a scene on her own behalf and that was why she was trapped in her world, so very different from Ross's, Holly ripped off her raspberry-pink cashmere jacket, slammed it down on the reception desk and marched over to Ross and the girl.

'Holly! Heavens, you look cross. More problems with those Italians in the Berkeley Suite?'

She took a deep breath. 'I just want you to know, Mr Monahan, that while you've been here, canoodling in comfort and having *fun*,' – she hissed the word 'fun' through gritted teeth – 'I have been with Tessa. She was almost killed today when her bicycle was crushed by a lorry. She's extremely lucky to be alive . . .' Faltering, Holly realized that she hadn't planned her diatribe in advance. Spontaneity was all very well but now she was stuck. The horrified expression on Ross's face, though, was most gratifying.

'. . . I just thought you should know, that's all,' she concluded in triumph as a distinct pallor invaded his deep tan. Then, turning to the Swedish girl, she added in a voice loaded with meaning, 'After all, they were close. Once.'

Ross, pulling up outside the cottage, thought at first that Tessa was out. Then he realized that although no lights were on, a faint amber glow was discernible through the downstairs windows. She must be watching television in the dark.

'Oh God, not again,' said Tessa, when she saw who it was.

'Lovely to see you, too,' he retaliated, wounded by her lack of enthusiasm. Then he held up his hands in apology. 'I'm sorry. I came to see how you were. May I come in?'

'Good old Holly.' Tessa, aware of how ungracious she was sounding but forced to do something to conceal her traitorous true feelings – a perverse form of pleasure – stood aside to allow him in. 'I wouldn't take off your jacket if I were you; I've had trouble with the fire. The logs are wet.'

Ross believed her. The fire, spluttering in the fireplace, was indeed in a sorry state. He was at first intrigued to see that the subdued amber lighting came not from the television but from clusters of candles, then appalled when he realized that the candles weren't there to create a romantic atmosphere, but to compensate for the lack of electrical power in the cottage.

'For Christ's sake!' he exploded, 'I don't believe this. Today you were almost killed. Tonight you're all alone in a freezing cold house. What the hell's happened to the power?'

Tessa, with some amusement, said, 'Last night's snow must have brought the lines down. Don't you ever have power cuts at The Grange?'

'We have an emergency generator.'

She shrugged. 'Well, I don't, so maybe I'm more used to coping with it than you are. Look, why don't you sit down? Are you hungry?'

'No ... yes,' he amended rapidly, realizing that she was inviting him to stay and eat. This small advance in their so-far volatile relationship gave him ridiculous pleasure.

'Then sit,' instructed Tessa, disappearing into the minute candle-lit kitchen. 'I'll be with you in a couple of minutes. Lucky I've got a gas oven,' she added with a grin.

Ross didn't sit. Instead he prowled, admiring the skill with which she had transformed a small L-shaped sitting-room into a place of charm and comfort. The ceiling, painted a deep shade of crimson, offset the whitewashed walls which, in turn, provided the perfect backdrop for her paintings. Huge bowls of artlessly arranged dried flowers jostled for space in the deep window-seats with hand-painted silk cushions and a cleverly glazed marmalade clay cat. The crimson carpet was old and faded in some places and the heavy white lace curtains slightly frayed at the edges, but the idiosyncratic mixture of brass candelabra, silver-framed photographs, stained-glass terraria and assorted bowls of marbles, handpainted eggs, silk flowers and trailing ferns was so welcoming that Ross felt immediately at home. Junk-shop mixtures weren't his style at all, but Tessa had created an environment in which it was impossible to be uncomfortable.

After stoking up the fire and at last teasing it into flames, he turned his attention to her paintings, which on his previous visit he had not had time to properly examine.

Here were further examples of Tessa's refusal to be pigeon-holed. Intrigued and impressed, Ross first examined the largest of the oil paintings, hung above the fireplace. Executed in deep, dark colours, it depicted a mountain storm in all its uncom-promising glory.

To the right of this bold, clever piece of work hung a mistily impressionistic watercolour, and further still to the right a medium-sized oil in a plain silver frame depicted a party in an art gallery, capturing expressions on faces, moments of indiscre-tion, anxiety and joy, laughter and sidelong glances with humour and wicked accuracy.

He had always admired artists for their ability to do what he could never do himself, but he was particularly impressed by these examples of Tessa's talent. And the variety of styles which she was able to adopt – and master – further convinced him that she had a real and unusual gift. Moving around the room he smiled at a small, as yet unframed portrait of Holly which captured exactly her talents for outrageous dressing and having fun. Tessa hadn't indulged in any unnecessary flattery but her obvious affection for her subject shone through; in her electric-blue, extravagantly frilled – and filled – dress, with a pink carnation tucked behind one ear and a wide smile, Holly was shown as the original good-time saloon girl, breaking the hearts of every cowboy in town and enjoying every minute while it lasted.

Tessa, pushing open the door with her knee and coming in with a tray, saw Ross examining the portrait.

'You're lucky you didn't get a Christmas card from Holly with that picture on the front,' she observed with a wry smile. 'She wanted to have three hundred printed so that she could send them out to all her friends with a postscript telling them that for just two hundred pounds they, too, could be captured on canvas by Tessa Duvall.'

He took the tray from her and placed it on the low, black coffee table in front of the fire. Two plates of creamy lasagne wafted their aromatic scent of garlic and herbs, and she had opened a bottle of Chianti to accompany the meal. Knowing that Tessa had stopped drinking, Ross was touched by her hospitality.

'It's a good idea. You shouldn't knock it,' he told her. 'Something like that could work very well indeed.'

Tessa shrugged. 'I know. But as someone remarked the other week' – she didn't bother to remind him who that had been and

Ross decided to ignore the oblique reference to Antonia, to pretend that she didn't exist – 'it's too much like touting for custom. I'd feel like a prostitute, selling myself . . . I'm afraid I find it all rather embarrassing.'

At her insistence he occupied the armchair while Tessa sat cross-legged on the floor. The logs had dried out now and the fire was burning brightly. The piping hot lasagne was delicious, the wine at just the right temperature and the candlelight seductive. Tessa, simply dressed as always in white denims and a dark blue V-necked lambswool sweater, with her long hair worn loose and her cheeks flushed from the heat of the fire, looked infinitely desirable.

'So, tell me what happened this morning,' said Ross, banishing such wayward thoughts firmly from his mind. 'You seem to have recovered remarkably well. Did the hospital give you the all-clear?'

Tessa, swallowing a mouthful of lasagne, shook her head. 'I wasn't hurt. There was no need to see a doctor. All I did was take a flying leap into a ditch full of snow.'

'You were riding a *bicycle*, for Christ's sake!' exploded Ross, his dark eyebrows raised in despair. 'In weather like this you were asking for trouble. What is it you have, some kind of death wish?'

She grinned. 'A Raleigh Sport, as a matter of fact. Or it was until earlier today.'

'And what will you do now?' he demanded, waving his fork in the direction of the window, indicating the thick snow outside.

Tessa tilted her head on one side, appearing to give the matter some consideration.

'I thought I'd give it a title,' she said finally. 'Maybe call it, "Splat" or, "Crunch" and exhibit it at the Tate Modern.'

'Look,' said Ross, fixing her with dark, slanting eyes and willing her to be serious, 'you can make all the jokes you want but whether you like it or not I am concerned about your safety. You're carrying my child and I cannot just stand by and watch you take stupid risks with your life. With both your lives.'

Touched by his concern, but at the same time filled with indignation that he should think so badly of her, Tessa glared back at him. 'I know, I know, I should have driven into town in my new Lamborghini,' she snapped. 'Ross, you don't seem to understand. When I can afford a car I'll buy one, but until that day comes I have to rely on something less expensive. For heaven's sake, from the expression on your face anyone would think I'd parachuted blindfold out of a plane. And it wasn't my bike that caused the accident anyway, it was the lorry.'

'Is the baby really OK?' he said, changing the subject abruptly.

Recognizing that he had taken in what she had to say, Tessa nodded. 'Perfectly, as far as I can tell.'

'You're nearly four months now; are you starting to show?'

She couldn't help smiling at this. He sounded like a midwife. Any minute now he'd be whisking out a stethoscope and listening for the foetal heartbeat. 'Yes, I've put on a few pounds and my jeans won't do up,' she assured him solemnly. 'Hence the baggy sweater, which covers a multitude of sins.'

'And your boobs are bigger,' remarked Ross, studying her chest with undisguised curiosity.

This time Tessa burst out laughing. 'Yes, my boobs are bigger. Before long I'll have a cleavage to rival Holly's. Pregnancy has its advantages after all!'

Later, when they had finished eating, Ross said, 'Tell me about your mysterious past. Where did you do your art training?'

'No mysteries.' Tessa, still sitting on the floor, was peeling an orange and dividing it neatly into segments. 'And no formal training. My mother encouraged me to paint when I was young and gave me constructive criticism as soon as I was old enough to cope with it. She was a great art lover, completely self-educated but with a real eye. And she was a wonderful teacher . . . she taught me to appreciate the magic of Van Dyck and Michelangelo, Brueghel and Canaletto when all I was interested in was Toulouse-Lautrec. When I was very young we spent whole days at a time in the National Gallery.'

'You lived in London?' Ross sensed that tonight she was in the mood to talk. And now, more than ever, he wanted to know about Tessa's past, to learn more, much more, about the fiercely independent girl sitting before him.

'My father died when I was a year old. He had a brain tumour and my mother spent that year nursing both of us. Then there was only me to look after.' Gazing into the leaping flames she paused for a few seconds, lost in thought, then shrugged and offered him a peeled orange segment. 'When I was seven Mum met a man, an artist. He was big and handsome, with long blond hair and a dark moustache and his name was Tom Charteris. We both adored him, but like a lot of artists he was selfish. Arrogant. He allowed Mum to support him for a few months, then he left her for a woman who could afford to keep him in more style. Mum was devastated because she'd believed in him, done everything she could for him. She couldn't believe that he'd dumped her. That was when we moved to Bath. She got a job as a live-in housekeeper at Holly's parents' home and that was when I first met Holly. We were poles apart, of course. Suzannah and Michael King were seriously wealthy. They still are, for that matter, but even then they lived a life that was way out of our league. Holly was jet-setting all over the world with them while my mother kept their house clean, polishing their silver and dusting their Chippendale chairs. But every time they came back from Gstaad, Barbados or New York, Holly and I would pick up our friendship where it had left off and it was to her parents' credit really that they didn't attempt to separate us. I was only the housekeeper's daughter, after all.'

'That's a ludicrous idea,' intercepted Ross, enraged at Tessa's Victorian attitude.

'Not so ludicrous. Holly went to a smart school, filled with suitably high-born potential friends. They wanted the best for her. Happily, Holly refused to have her friends chosen for her and her parents knew better than to try and change her mind. They were my first-ever customers and the paintings they bought when I was twenty still hang in their sitting room today. When Mum died two years later they offered me a home.'

'Which you refused, naturally.'

'I was an adult. I was quite capable of looking after myself,' replied Tessa in matter-of-fact tones.

Ross shrugged. 'I'm surprised you didn't share a flat with Holly.'

'Oh, she suggested that, of course, but I couldn't have afforded to pay half the rent on the kind of place Holly could bear to live in and I wouldn't allow her to subsidize me. So, I found this cottage – I rent it from a farmer who lives further down the valley – and made it my home. I've been here five years now.'

'And you manage to support yourself by selling your work? Why haven't you sold these?' Ross gestured towards the paintings on the walls. 'I'd like to buy the party picture. May I?'

'I manage to support myself now,' she told him with a self-deprecating shrug. 'Just about. But until last year I was doing odd jobs here and there, to pay the rent. I worked as a charlady for a while, then as a croupier in the Royale Casino in Bath. I did a bit of waitressing, a lot of baby-sitting and a terrible, six-week stint as a tour guide for visiting Japanese and American tourists. I thought I'd go blind. All those flash-bulbs . . .'

'I'm impressed,' said Ross, smiling at the expression on her face. 'But I'd still like to buy that painting. Very much.'

'Not for sale, I'm afraid. I gave them to my mother. When she died I found I couldn't bear to part with them, so they stay here. Sorry.'

He shook his head, dismissing her apology, then brightened.

'But I can commission you to paint something for me. You'd agree to that, wouldn't you?'

'Of course.' Tessa allowed him a glimmer of a smile. 'What was it you wanted, a portrait of Antonia Seymour-Smith?'

Here it came, thought Ross. He might have known that she would get around to the subject of Antonia sooner or later. How to wreck a perfectly good evening in three seconds flat, he thought bitterly. She must have been taking lessons from Max.

'Look,' he said in his most reasonable voice, 'I'm sorry about what happened at the hotel, but as I tried to tell you at the time it was only a casual affair. She meant . . . she *means* nothing to me. If you hadn't constantly refused to see me I would never have gone to her house on Christmas Eve.'

Tessa, having listened patiently to his reasoning, now shook her head.

'I wasn't accusing you of treachery – of being unfaithful to me, if you like – and that certainly wasn't why I left. I'd made it quite plain to you that we had no relationship. As a free agent you could do whatever you liked, with whomever you liked . . .'

'Then why the bloody hell did you leave?' demanded Ross, by now thoroughly perplexed.

'Watch my lips.' Leaning towards him, speaking slowly and carefully, Tessa repeated: 'You can have an affair with whomever you like. But you don't even *like* Antonia – by your own admission she means nothing to you. And that's what I find so bizarre, the fact that you can carry on an affair with someone for whom you have no feelings. Particularly,' she added a moment later, just as Ross opened his mouth to protest, 'when she's so obviously besotted with you.'

'But she isn't besotted with me,' he retaliated. 'We both know it isn't that kind of relationship. She has her husband, I have my . . . friends, and now and again we arrange to meet. No complications, no awkwardness and no harm done.'

'But it *was* awkward on Christmas night,' Tessa reminded him, 'because Antonia may have set out believing that she wouldn't allow herself to fall in love with you, but it didn't work out that way. Sooner or later emotions were bound to come into it, because for some reason women are like that. And now they have, for her. She's involved and you're not. It's all going to be messy and difficult and very, very sad.'

Something in her tone of voice aroused Ross's interest.

Forgetting for the moment that he was supposed to be defending himself, he said, 'This is something you've had experience of. You've been through it yourself.'

Tessa silently marvelled at his stupidity. He really, *really* didn't have a clue.

'No,' she said, touching the rim of the crimson candle which flickered between them and experiencing that momentary flash of pain as melted wax ran over the tip of her finger, then rapidly cooled and hardened. The pain subsided as quickly as it had come. 'No, I haven't been through it myself. I'm far too smart to get involved with that kind of man.'

When he rose to leave shortly afterwards Ross gave her a decorous kiss on the cheek – the kind of kiss one offered a shrivelled maiden aunt – and thanked her formally for dinner. Tessa, stiff with restraint, fought down the humiliating urge to slide her arms around him and stood instead by the door with a fixed smile and fists clenched tightly behind her back.

Not until Ross had left and she had returned to the sitting room did she see his keys still lying on the coffee table, next to the burned-down crimson candle. Snatching them up, she raced back to the front door. Barefoot, she ran down the snowy path. The dark outline of Ross's figure was only just discernible fifty yards further along the lane.

'Your keys!' shouted Tessa, gasping as an icy blast of air hit her lungs. 'Your car! What are you *doing*?'

The dark silhouette stopped, turning to face her. 'Your keys,' replied Ross. 'Your car. And I suppose that what I'm doing is trying to prove to you that I can occasionally be a gentleman.'

'But it's your car,' repeated Tessa, dazed and dismayed. 'It's a Mercedes.'

In the darkness, Ross was smiling. 'And you'd set your heart on a Lamborghini,' he said consolingly. 'I'm sorry.'

'But this is ridiculous . . .' she protested through chattering teeth. Her feet burned with cold and it even hurt to breathe.

'It's a damn sight less ridiculous than the idea of you skidding around in the snow on a bicycle.'

'But—'

'Oh, do shut up, Tess.' Ross was also frozen. Being a gentleman was bloody hard work and he only possessed so much self-control. The sight of Tessa, with her blonde hair gleaming in the moonlight and her feet ridiculously bare in the snow, was almost too much for him. Raising one hand in a farewell salute, he turned to leave. 'And if it makes you any happier,' he added, sensing that she was still standing there behind him mouthing 'buts', 'I'm not doing it for your sake. We do have a child to consider, after all.'

Chapter 9

Holly, arranging a vast bowl of pink tulips in reception, was so deeply involved in planning her campaign – codenamed Get Max – that she didn't notice Grace, wearing a slightly shorter-than-usual uniform and rather too much coral lipstick, slip into the manager's office with a tray. She was so engrossed that she also failed to observe Dr Timothy Stratton-Staines from Room Seven as he made his way briskly out to his car with a small leather suitcase in his hand.

Having come to the reasonable conclusion that Max simply wasn't susceptible to love at first sight and that after this length of time he had come to regard her merely as a receptionist rather than as potential love interest, Holly had decided that a properly planned campaign was what was required. Max needed a bit of helping along and she had all sorts of tricks up her sleeve. It wasn't cheating, she'd explained to Tessa when she'd outlined her plans, it was simply a matter of making Max realize that there was more to her than met the eye and that basically he just didn't know what he was missing.

Which was why, having done a bit of serious research, she was at this moment wearing a blindingly efficient navy-blue suit from Jaeger and a plain white silk shirt buttoned all the way up to the neck. Her legs were encased in opaque, dark blue stockings and matching low-heeled court shoes, and her hair was pulled back in a bun so tight that her temples ached. Incapable of showing a bare face to so much as the milkman, she had been forced to compromise with the make-up, limiting herself to smoky grey eye-shadow, subtle lipstick and scarcely any blusher at all.

In Holly's own opinion she looked an absolute fright but she had paid a great deal of attention yesterday to Caroline Mortimer, Max's high-flying and ruthlessly elegant literary agent, when she had arrived to have lunch with him. In her late thirties, Caroline Mortimer had real cheekbones and a ballerina's svelte figure. She had probably invented power-dressing single-handed. Holly had taken in every detail, noting the severity of the beige suit, the matching beige fingernails and lipgloss. The immaculate dark chignon was a work of art and apart from a matt-black watch her hands were bare of jewellery.

As far as Holly was concerned, Caroline Mortimer looked positively alarming. Max, on the other hand, had appeared to find her irresistible. It surely wasn't necessary for him to put on an act with Ms Mortimer, after all; he was successful enough not to have to feign adoration in order to win favour. This led her to the inescapable conclusion that Max actually liked women who dressed in that dynamic manner. Certainly he would never have lingered over a three-and-a-half-hour lunch and disappeared up to his apartment with her for a further two hours – supposedly to discuss his work-in-progress – if he didn't find her attractive.

Holly had been shocked rather than upset at the time, somehow imagining the relationship between author and agent to be sacrosanct, comparable to that of doctor and patient, with actual sex forbidden.

But the perfect chignon had shown slight but definite signs of wear and tear when Ms Mortimer had finally left the hotel and now all Holly had to hope was that her own transformation might – please God! – have a similar effect upon Max. She certainly hoped so; this bloody awful outfit had cost an absolute bomb.

Ross was sitting at his desk and was busy on the phone when Grace tapped on the door and entered the office without waiting for his reply. Then, apparently overcome by her own daring, she hovered halfway between the door and the desk, paralysed by indecision and clutching her loaded tray as if it were a dead animal.

'Any car, Mike,' said Ross into the phone, raising a questioning eyebrow in Grace's direction but receiving no response. 'Well, you know what I mean. Anything decent, maybe another Merc. Maybe a Lamborghini? No, no, not part exchange . . . it's gone to a friend. Yeah, I just felt like a change.'

Grace had already observed that Ross's car was missing from its customary position at the head of the gravelled driveway. Dazzled by her own daring – her stars had said that this was a day for taking chances – she waited for him to conclude his conversation with Mike Donnelly, who was a great friend of Ross's and who owned the smartest car showrooms in Bath, and finally managed to place the heavy tray on the edge of his impressive, overcrowded leather-topped desk.

'What's this?' said Ross, leaning back in his chair and frowning. 'Do I have a meeting with someone?'

'No . . . w . . . well, I don't think so,' stammered Grace, her cheeks reddening. 'I don't know. I just thought you'd like some coffee and something to eat.'

Ross was struggling to remember her name, a facility which normally came easily to him. But this young girl, so quiet and normally so colourless – although at the moment she was positively scarlet – was someone whose identity currently eluded him.

To compensate for this lack, he gave her a dazzling smile.

'Of course. What a marvellous idea. I usually have to beg Holly on bended knees for coffee and she thinks the whole world takes it black, without sugar.'

'I thought . . . ' said Grace, quite overwhelmed by his smile, 'I thought that maybe I could bring you a tray every morning. Just coffee and toast, maybe . . . or if you'd prefer a proper breakfast, I could always—'

'Just coffee would be fine,' interjected Ross, who never ate breakfast. 'But yes, that sounds great.' The phrase 'grace and favour' sprang into his mind and quite suddenly it came back to him. When he had interviewed her a couple of months ago the thought of that same phrase had made him smile.

Leaning across the desk, he poured himself some coffee, adding plenty of cream and sugar. 'Thank you, Grace. Excellent idea.' Then he sat back, pulled a folder from the pile on his desk and flipped it open.

Realizing that this was a gesture of dismissal and at the same time breathing in the faint but intoxicating scent of his aftershave, Grace went for it.

'I've got a car,' she blurted out, further emboldened by the fact that he'd actually remembered her name. 'If you needed a lift I could drive you anywhere you wanted to go.'

Ross glanced up, amused. He may have struggled to recall her name but he was well acquainted with her car, having noticed it in the hotel car park a few weeks ago. It had been necessary to have a quiet word with Hugh Stone, the deputy manager, about shifting rust heaps like Grace's unprepossessing little Fiat to a less conspicuous parking area behind the kitchens. A week ago he might have passed a scathing comment in response to such an offer – he needed to get to Manchester and Grace's car didn't look as if it were capable of crawling further than the end of the drive – but quite suddenly he recalled Tessa's own biting remarks as she had reminded him that not everyone was able to afford the sporty, prestigious models he took so easily for granted.

'That's very kind of you,' he said, smiling at the young waitress and noticing for the first time the abbreviated hemline of her skirt. 'But Max has a spare. I'll use one of his for a couple of days until Mike comes up with something for me. Just one suggestion,' he added, as she turned to leave. Grace swung back, her face pink and eager, her heart pounding.

'Yes, Mr Monahan?'

'The uniform.' He nodded at her thin legs. 'We don't want to raise the blood pressure of our male guests too drastically, after all. Maybe it could be returned to its usual length . . .?'

Max wasn't having a good day.

Yesterday, by contrast, had been extremely satisfactory. Caroline had brought him up to date with the sales figures of his latest novel and was forging ahead with her negotiations for a lucrative contract with the Americans for the film rights to last year's bestseller. She was as slick with money as she was in bed and Max had spent a thoroughly enjoyable day witnessing both attributes to the full.

Which only served to accentuate the difference between then and now. Sitting down as usual at eight-thirty to confront his word processor, he had been irritated beyond belief to discover that nothing was going according to plan. A glitch in the computer had wiped two entire chapters from disc. He had discovered a fatal flaw in the plot. His normally effortless fluency had deserted him. And, to add final insult to injury, the coffee percolator had blown a fuse.

Since working without a constant supply of decent black coffee was a physical impossibility for Max, he stormed downstairs in a less-than-sunny mood in search of a replacement percolator and – hopefully – inspiration.

What he found, on the phone in reception and deeply involved in a conversation obviously *not* connected with business, was Holly. Max frowned, unable to decide whether she looked more like a spinster librarian or a stripogram dressed up to look like a spinster librarian.

Holly, who had been rabbiting on about bikinis and the price of flights to Barbados, skidded to a halt in mid-syllable the moment she spotted Max, started gabbling instead about the availability of The Grange's honeymoon suite and slammed down the phone ten seconds later. As she opened her mouth to speak to Max it rang again. Propping himself against the desk he listened, his frown deepening, as she informed the caller in brisk tones that no, every room in the hotel was currently full and that maybe he should try The Royal instead.

'Max!' Having replaced the receiver for the second time she gave him the benefit of her dazzling smile. Then, remembering her newly adopted image of sleek sophistication, hastily modified it to a mysterious semi-smirk. 'Max, how may I help you? If you don't mind me saying so you're looking a trifle harassed.'

'A trifle harassed?' he echoed, disbelief temporarily over-coming his irritation. What in heaven's name was Holly up to now?

She blushed. It was the first time he'd seen her blush, probably because it was also the first time he'd seen her without a face caked in make-up.

'Sorry, Max. What's up?'

'You tell me. When I looked out of my window a few minutes ago I saw that chap with the terrible toupee leave the hotel, complete with suitcase. Isn't his room free?'

'Dr Stratton-Staines? He hasn't checked out.' Holly tried not to sound as sickened as she felt. The good doctor might wear an ill-fitting wig but he had devoted his life to helping young children stricken with cancer, otherwise she would never have agreed to let him pay his bill at the end of the week when his new cheque-book arrived, instead of in advance as hotel procedure demanded.

'Better send someone up to check his room,' said Max, looking grimmer by the minute. 'Looks like he's done a runner.'

He had, reported Grace five minutes later, by which time Max had ruthlessly extracted the story of the missing cheque-book from Holly.

'Christ, you're gullible,' he snapped. 'And what on earth were you doing when he and his suitcase slipped past you in reception? Daydreaming, I suppose.'

'Yes,' agreed Holly unhappily. At least Max didn't know – would never know – that the subject of her daydreams had been himself. And he was such a bad-tempered old bastard that she sometimes wondered why she even bothered.

'You're hopeless,' he went on, with a disparaging glance at

her tailored, dark blue suit and crisp white shirt. He couldn't help comparing her with Francine Lalonde, who exuded so much femininity without even having to think about it. She would certainly never be seen dead in an outfit like this, he thought with renewed longing for the beautiful woman whom he now hadn't seen for two long months. 'Efficiency is in the mind, Holly. Not the wardrobe. And my coffee percolator's broken. If it's not too much to ask I'd be grateful if you could organize a replacement, right away. Some of us,' he added cruelly, 'have work to do, after all.'

Chapter 10

The painting was coming along well. Tessa, stepping back from the canvas, allowed herself a smile of satisfaction. After seven hours of intense application the picture was three-quarters completed. The scene, recognizably set in the ballroom at The Grange, was – as Ross had requested – that of a party in full swing, bright, colourful and buzzing with laughter and high spirits.

She was definitely pleased with it. The composition, which could have been tricky, had worked well and, although she had included no recognizable faces, the eye was drawn naturally to a single figure, glass in hand, lounging against the huge fireplace. A back view of a tall, dark-haired man in a dinner jacket, the casual stance was unmistakable, the slight tilt of the head as recognizable as any face. Ross would be amused, Tessa thought, to see himself depicted as the dark stranger, alone in a crowd. If he even recognized himself, of course. It was hardly a view he would be familiar with, after all.

It was midday before the post arrived, the postman's progress impeded by the weather. No snow had fallen for three days but sunny days and freezing night temperatures had resulted in lethally icy roads. Tessa felt particularly sorry for him when he was forced to make his hazardous way to her isolated cottage with nothing more riveting than banking circulars.

When she went to retrieve her mail, however, she was glad

he'd made the effort. Ripping open the grey envelope addressed in flamboyant magenta ink, the first words she saw were: '. . . so I'll see you at 1.30 on Thursday.'

It was absolutely typical of Dominic, she thought with a mixture of exasperation and delight, to invite himself to stay for an unspecified period without giving her a chance to object. Not that she *would* object, but it wouldn't even occur to him that there might be reasons why he couldn't stay with her. That wasn't the way Dominic's mind worked.

Skimming through the rest of the letter she caught up with a year's worth of news in just under a minute. He was thinking of getting married again but his current wife was behaving in a most unfeeling manner and refused point-blank to divorce him. His life-size sculptures were much in demand and selling well through a small, but prestigious, gallery in Truro, Cornwall. He had fallen from a step ladder and sustained a broken leg, which was very boring indeed. He had therefore decided to get away from it all for a while and recuperate in the company of the most gorgeous piece of skirt in the south-west . . . apart from the woman he was going to marry, naturally. He would travel up by train, arrive in Bath at 1.30 on Thursday and hitch a lift or something out to her place. And if she could rustle up some food, great. If not, he'd take her out somewhere cheap, fun and noisy and they could get drunk together. Maybe he'd break his other leg . . .

Dominic Taylor hadn't changed a bit. Apart from the off-white plaster cast encasing his left leg from ankle to thigh he looked exactly the same. With his bright blue, permanently laughing eyes, very short white-blond hair and thin, brown face, he echoed every girl's dream of a Scandinavian god. Tessa was always amazed that although he was of only medium height he gave the appearance of being tall. His scuffed leather flying jacket, when she hugged him, bore the faint scent of the sea.

'Tessa, you're fat!'

Bone-thin himself, and as acutely perceptive as ever, Dominic registered the addition of those few extra pounds at once.

'And you're a temporary cripple,' retaliated Tessa, tapping his plaster cast with her knuckles. 'So watch what you say. A girl can take offence, you know, to those kind of remarks.'

'You look gorgeous.' He kissed her. 'And I certainly didn't expect you to come and meet me. I hope you aren't planning to take me home on a bicycle built for two.'

'Don't mock. I've gone up in the world.'

'A car?'

Tessa smiled. 'Yes, a real car. And there's no need to look so surprised, you aren't the only great and successful artist in England. Since my last one-woman exhibition I've been rich beyond my wildest dreams.'

'Bloody hell!' declared Dominic, when she unlocked the passenger door of the white Mercedes and gestured for him to climb in. 'You were being serious.'

Tessa, taking his crutches from him and throwing them on to the back seat, was enjoying herself enormously. 'Why? Didn't you think I was talented enough to be a success?'

Having levered himself into the passenger seat at last, he blew her a kiss. 'Of course you're talented enough,' he said, turning up the quadrophonic stereo and getting blasted by Rachmaninov at full tilt. 'I just can't get over the fact that you've been more successful than me!'

* * *

Max, who had spent a pleasant lunchtime in Beaumont's wine bar in Bath with a couple of friends, wasn't too surprised at first when he stepped out on to the pavement and spotted the familiar white Mercedes parked on the other side of the road on double yellow lines.

When he drew closer, however, and saw an unknown, fair-haired male lounging in the passenger seat smoking a cigarette, his suspicions were aroused. Ross had a habit of abandoning his car in the city for two or three days at a time when he didn't need it; now it appeared that a couple of joyriders had taken advantage of his generosity.

'Who's driving this car?' he demanded, addressing the blond passenger through the half-opened window.

Dominic, quite unperturbed, returned his steely dark gaze with faint amusement.

'A stylish, stunningly attractive, outrageously talented girl, since you ask. Why? Did you want to hitch a lift?'

'Now look,' began Max, fully prepared to act first and ask unnecessary questions later. 'This car belongs to—'

'Hello, Max,' said Tessa, coming up behind him and sizing up the situation at once. Max clearly had no idea that Ross had passed the car over to her.

'Tessa.' He acknowledged her with a curt nod, his thick black brows drawn into a ferocious line. So the car hadn't been stolen, he surmised rapidly. But he'd still like to know why Tessa was driving it, and who the bloody hell her companion was, jumped-up little smart-arse.

Her arms full of groceries from the Italian delicatessen across the street, Tessa stood her ground, casting around in her mind for the most tactful way of explaining Ross's ludicrously extravagant gesture, then wondering why on earth she should bother. What Ross chose to do with his own car was, after all, none of Max's business.

'He wanted me to have it,' she said, in reply to the unspoken question hanging between them. Out of the corner of her eye she saw Dominic's triumphant smile and knew that it was also one of relief. No artist liked to know that a fellow artist was making *that* much more money than themselves.

'He *gave* you this car?' Max looked neither triumphant nor relieved, but downright disgusted. 'I don't believe I'm hearing this.'

Tessa had never had any intention of keeping the car. As soon as the snow and ice melted she was going to return it to Ross. But Max's nasty, suspicious nature and complete lack of humour infuriated her beyond belief.

'At least I refused to marry him,' she said, opening the rear door and dumping the bag of groceries on the back seat. 'Think about it, Max. What's more important, your car or your freedom? Ross got off lightly, and you of all people should be pleased. Giving me the Merc. was a small price to pay, don't you think?'

'You shouldn't have put your hand on my knee just as I was driving away,' she reprimanded Dominic much later, as they sat in front of the fire finishing off their meal.

'Why not?' countered Dominic, his eyes glittering with mischief. 'He was a pompous bastard.'

'I know.' Tessa smiled. 'He still is. But you still shouldn't have done it – he's going to get the wrong impression and go around bad-mouthing me to anyone who'll listen.'

'And who's going to listen? Someone called Ross, presumably. Is he as shitty as his brother?'

Tessa gazed into the flickering flames of the fire. 'Not quite as shitty. He has his moments. Max is convinced that I'm an evil, scheming bitch; at least Ross doesn't think that.'

'You'll notice,' said Dominic, with an ostentatious glance at his watch, 'that six hours have elapsed since we met. I've been very good, very patient. But I think it's time you finally told me what's going on. Pass me my wine glass – no, refill it first – and start from the very beginning . . .'

It was almost midnight before Max bumped into Ross in the hotel bar. Waiting until Ross had disentangled himself from a group of over-bright theatrical types, he then moved across to join him.

'I saw your car today.'

'And?' Ross out-stared him, a belligerent expression on his face.

'And, coincidentally, Tessa was driving it. If you ask me, you're making a bloody fool of yourself.'

'Look.' Ross put down his drink. 'Don't jump to conclusions. Tessa needed a car. What you don't realize is that she was knocked off her bicycle the other day. She's lucky to be alive. And as long as she's carrying my child I'm going to make sure she has a safe mode of transport. I just don't want her to get killed, OK?'

'Fine,' countered Max. 'Very commendable. So long as you realize that she's using your life-saving car to jaunt around town with her smart-alec boyfriend.'

* * *

Mattie couldn't believe that she was doing this, sneaking into her daughter's room to read the secret diary which she knew existed but which she'd never yet set eyes on.

But Grace worried her. Severely. And when her daughter had casually let drop the information that Ross had – in no uncertain terms – admired her figure, Mattie's anxieties had reached such a pitch that she realized she had to intervene.

According to Grace, Ross was demanding that she – and only she – brought him coffee every day. That he talked to her far more than he did to any of the other waitresses. And that he was definitely displaying a more-than-casual interest in her.

It didn't take Mattie long to unearth the crimson, leather-bound book she was looking for. Hopelessly untidy herself, her daughter's passion for neatness and order never failed to amaze her. It also made it ridiculously easy to find anything she wanted. The diary was on the bottom shelf of the bedside table, beneath three copies of *The Caterer* and a box of peach-shaded tissues.

When Mattie had finished reading, she shuddered and closed the diary on her lap. Looking up, she was confronted by her reflection in the wardrobe mirror, pale and resigned and suddenly looking older than her forty years.

It was no good; she would have to act. Teenage crushes might be a normal phenomenon, but now that she knew the extent of her daughter's infatuation with Ross she couldn't afford to take any chances.

Grace had to be told that Ross Monahan was her father.

Chapter 11

'Max!' cried Francine, pushing back her wide-brimmed straw hat and flinging her arms around him with such enthusiasm that he could feel the warm swell of her famous breasts pressing against his chest. 'My God, you came to rescue me from hell! You are a true knight in shining armour.'

He couldn't help it. When she had stopped hugging him he slowly removed her sunglasses. Her sherry-brown eyes danced, while members of the film crew and assorted extras looked on with interest.

'Yes, it's really me,' she assured him, still clutching his arm. 'And I promise not to behave badly this time. I'm *much* too glad to see you to behave badly . . .'

It was all very gratifying. Being called in at twenty-four-hours' notice to replace a temperamental scriptwriter was certainly lucrative but it wasn't Max's favourite pastime. He didn't care for office politics, nor for the personality clashes which notoriously abounded on film sets – particularly when the filming wasn't going well. The new writer inevitably became enmeshed in the jealousies, arguments and power struggles. It was far simpler to say that you were committed elsewhere and to refuse the offer with polite regret.

But when Jack Weston had called him yesterday from Amalfi and told him that the star of his troubled film had personally recommended Max Monahan for the job, he hadn't put up too much of a struggle. Astounded that she had even remembered his name and with his self-confidence boosted no end by her evident trust in him, he realized how badly he needed to see her again.

And the thought that she wanted to see him again was, of course, an intoxicating one. Whether she wanted him as a scriptwriter or a lover was another matter. Hoping that it would be both, Max had agreed to fly out right away.

And now he was here on the Neapolitan Riviera, in a small, sunlit piazza with Francine in his arms and a harassed but evidently relieved director in a pink baseball cap bearing down upon him.

'You must be Max.' He stuck out a damp, hairy hand. 'Thanks for coming. If nothing else,' he added wryly, 'you look as if you might be able to cheer Francine up. She hasn't exactly been a ray of sunshine around here recently. She didn't hit it off with the scriptwriter, I'm afraid.'

'Hit it off?' echoed Francine, her dark brows lifting. 'If I had a gun I would have shot it off, no problem! Jumped-up little pansy,' she declared, outraged. 'He was jealous because his boyfriend preferred me. I didn't want his ugly boyfriend but he went crackers every time he saw him looking at me. And he kept changing the script, giving me more and more stupid lines. My character would never even *think* such lines . . . oh, Max! This morning he flew back to London and now you are here to make me better again. I'm so glad to *see* you . . .!'

'You'll have to see him later, Francine,' said Jack Weston firmly. 'The script comes first. Max and I can start work on it over lunch.'

They sat at a long, bleached-wood table outside the Ristorante il Saraceno, untidy piles of much-corrected script spread out before them amid bowls of steaming garlic-drenched pasta, carafes of red local wine and a profusion of glasses. Far below them, beneath the spectacular rocky cliffs and pastel pink-and-yellow houses, lay the Bay of Salerno. Aquamarine water glittered in the February sunlight. Small fishing boats chugged lazily into port and out again. In bars and restaurants all over the picturesque town, Italians were eating, drinking, meeting friends and making the most of their lunch break.

Max barely had time to notice, let alone appreciate, the stunning beauty of his surroundings. There was no time at all to linger over the exquisite food laid out before him. The wine remained untouched in his glass as he scrutinized the messy script and listened to Jack Weston's verbal synopsis of what the storyline was meant to convey and the myriad reasons why it had managed to veer so wildly off course.

Francine had undoubtedly worsened the situation by clashing horns with the talented but volatile young writer, but she had been right about the changes he had been making along the way. By subtly altering her character the impetus of the plot had been lost and as a result the credibility of the storyline was floundering badly. At a conservative estimate, reckoned Jack Weston as he pushed his plate to one side and re-lit a plump, well-chewed Monte Cristo cigar, they were running three weeks behind schedule and maybe half a million over budget.

'A hiccup's a hiccup,' he told Max, his tanned face creasing with pain as he kneaded his chest, 'but figures like that give me indigestion. The trouble with Francine is that she's so damned stubborn. Once she makes up her mind about something, that's it. And she wants her character to go the other way, grabbing all the sympathy ... it just wouldn't work. She's hell-bent on protecting her image but I'm the one who has to protect the film. Can you make her see sense, Max? Can you re-write her part so that we're all happy?'

'I don't know,' replied Max honestly. Francine was an enigma, to whom he was hopelessly attracted but unable as yet to figure out. Taking a sip of bitingly strong espresso, he grinned reassuringly at the director. 'But give me the rest of the afternoon to start work on the script. This evening I'll speak to Francine. One way or another we'll give it a bloody good try.'

'OK, I understand,' she said finally, tilting her head to one side and biting her lower lip like a small child. 'I really do, Max. You're telling me that my character has to be sometimes a bitch otherwise she will be too sickly, like a rum baba, and make the audience want to vomit.'

'Well, something like that.' Max, relieved and at the same time trying not to smile, slipped his jacket around her shoulders. The temperature had dropped now and Francine was shivering beside him. 'Your audience don't want to see you playing a weak female, taking everything that's thrown at her. They know you too well. They know you're a real woman who gets what she wants.'

'And you are an even cleverer man than I first thought,' replied Francine, bending down at the water's edge and removing her flat, ivory leather shoes. Casually, almost without appearing to think about it, she tossed them into the sea.

'You'll hurt your feet,' said Max. They were thirty yards of rocky beach away from the grassy slopes of the hotel's exotic, floodlit gardens.

She pushed back her shining hair with one hand in order to smile up at him. 'I'm a real woman who gets what she wants,' she reminded him softly. 'And I want you to carry me, all the way back to my bed.'

The next week passed more quickly than any other Max could remember. He had seldom had such a good time on so little sleep. By day he worked, throwing himself into the task of transforming the film script from something flawed into something truly great. The weather was perfect with temperatures in the high sixties, a nice change from the recent icy conditions back home but not too hot to divert him from his work.

By night, it was a different story. Francine, miraculous Francine, diverted him in the most enticing manner possible. Sometimes they ate dinner with the rest of the film crew; more often they melted into the back streets of Amalfi, finding small, family run trattorias where they could be alone together, talking incessantly and lingering for hours over delectable food and endless cups of *cappuccino*.

Francine had captivated him totally. During the course of their evenings she could make him laugh, impress him with her mixture of intelligence, wit and perspicacity, and infuriate him with her own personal brand of peculiar female logic. Her husky voice, with that charismatic French accent which grew more pronounced with excitement or emotion, mesmerized him. The clothes she wore, silky outfits in ice-cream colours, were as bare of ornamentation as the rest of her. She wore barely any make-up and it suited her – she exuded glamour anyway, simply because she *was* Francine Lalonde.

And every evening, when they finally left to return to their hotel at around midnight, the magic continued. Francine was a skilful seducer and an insatiable mistress. Their lovemaking was exhilarating. How Francine managed to crawl out of bed and into make-up at five-thirty every morning, Max couldn't imagine.

'All finished!' sighed Francine, taking a sip of celebratory champagne and sliding her bare leg between his. 'And the script is a masterpiece. Max, you have been a true genius. This time we shall *all* win awards, I know.'

'I'm not sure they hand out awards for this kind of thing.' He dropped a kiss on her shoulder and glanced at his watch. 'We really should be getting dressed. Jack's booked Dino's restaurant and we're expected at nine.'

'But darling,' protested Francine, squirming with pleasure as his warm mouth travelled to the nape of her neck. 'It's such a waste of your last night. I thought we would stay here instead and make love.'

A faint smile touched the corners of Max's mouth as he kissed the satiny hollow of her throat. 'And *I* thought,' he murmured slowly, 'that I may as well stay on. You have another two or three weeks of filming ahead of you yet. I've finished rewriting the script but there's no reason why I have to rush back to England now. I can just as easily work on my novel out here. And we can be together . . .'

'But that isn't possible!' exclaimed Francine, drawing away slightly. 'Max, you told me that you planned to leave when the film script was all sorted out.'

Mimicking her accent, he said lightly, 'I changed my plans.

Very un-English of me, I know, but I've decided to stay on. So you see, it wasn't impossible after all.'

Francine, shifting on to her side, smiled. 'Well no,' she said slowly, 'of course it isn't impossible that you stay here, but you have to understand, darling, that I have made some other small plans.'

'What are you talking about?' His eyes darkened. 'What kind of other plans?'

'Oh, sweetheart, don't be naïve.' Francine pouted. 'Surely you understand how these things are. I thought you would be leaving tomorrow so I telephoned Jacques in Paris. He's coming down to stay with me. I can't be on my own, *chéri*. I so hate it when I am left alone.'

Max felt as though a part of him had died. The happiness he had experienced over the last ten days was eradicated at a single sweep. He hadn't been building a meaningful relationship at all; he'd merely been babysitting.

'Oh Max, now you're angry with me,' said Francine with a sorrowful shake of her head. 'But I can't apologize. It's simply how I am. And it doesn't mean that I haven't had a wonderful time with you, either. It's been great, but now you have to go back to your home and I will carry on working, first here . . . then in Normandy . . . then New York . . . you see, darling, that is what my life is like. Not too settled. And it is why I am like this, as well. I like you a lot but I'm not the settling-down kind.' She shrugged, struggling to explain. 'We shall see each other again, Max. And it will be so much more romantic than just being together all the time, getting bored and trying to pretend that everything is OK because that's how proper couples are supposed to be. Max, please stop looking at me that way. Can't you see that what I'm saying is right?'

He looked away, sickened by her cold logic, her bluntness and cynicism. Until recently he had shared those same harsh views, which only served to increase the irony of the situation. It had never occurred to him that they might one day be thrown back in his face.

'If that's how you really feel,' he said evenly, 'then you *are* right. And don't worry, I won't embarrass you by staying. I'll leave tonight.'

'But Max,' shrieked Francine, 'you mustn't do that! You can't possibly leave tonight. We were going to stay here and make love . . .' She clung to him, her brown eyes alight with promise, sensual fingers trailing across his flat, tautly muscled stomach.

Max managed a faint smile. To refuse such an offer would be downright masochistic. Rolling on to his back and breathing in the faint, honeyed scent of her voluptuous nakedness, he prepared to give himself up to sheer, unadulterated pleasure. 'Oh well,' he murmured in bored tones, 'if you really insist . . .'

Chapter 12

When Lady Roberta McPherson, the organizer of the Clifton Midsummer Ball, realized that the ticket holders comprised an embarrassing surfeit of males she had flown into a panic. In a desperate attempt to at least partially redeem the situation – and save both the ball and herself from eternal shame – she had immediately instructed her daughter to invite forty of her most respectable female friends to the ball, free of charge. No hippies, no fatties and no ugly girls were to be asked, she had urgently stressed; only attractive girls with pleasant personalities, lovely smiles and a decent sense of decorum.

Happily, Mattie Jameson was curvaceous but not fat. At twenty-two years of age she had a sweet, slightly rounded face, shoulder-length hair that was very nearly blonde, a shy but charming smile and a perfectly adequate personality.

She had almost fainted with pleasure when the glamorous but absent-minded Corinne McPherson, who worked at the same advertising agency as Mattie as a personal assistant to the director, and for whom Mattie – a lowly typist – was endlessly covering up, had invited her to the Midsummer Ball. It was the most thrilling thing ever to have happened to her and she had promptly blown an entire week's wages on a long, romantically flounced, sunflower-yellow Laura Ashley dress, sprigged with tiny blue forget-me-nots, which she felt were a wonderful omen.

Whatever happened, Mattie knew she would never forget this, her very first ball.

Halfway through the evening, however, her spirits began to droop. Idiotically she had assumed that since Corinne had invited her, they would spend at least some time together. It hadn't occurred to her that Corinne and her equally smart friends would be whooping it up at one of the top tables while Mattie would be stuck on table thirty-seven in the farthest corner of the vast marquee with a party of middle-aged bankers and their done-up wives. She had tried her very hardest to smile and join in with their conversation but even prising their names out of them had been an uphill struggle. And although her experience of homosexuals was limited, the spare man to whom she had been allocated was so obviously gay that there seemed little point in attempting to bowl him over with her charm.

Gazing longingly at Corinne and the rest of her party who had now spilled on to the dance floor and who were so obviously – and noisily – enjoying themselves, Mattie realized that in order to reach the ladies' loo she would have to walk right past them. It wasn't much but it was better than staying put and missing out completely on all the action. And there was always the faint chance that someone might see her, be captivated by her smile and ask her to dance. Mattie had devoured enough Mills & Boons in her time to know that such things *could* happen . . .

The trouble was, of course, that nothing happened. Absolutely nothing at all, despite the fact that she meandered past the dance floor so slowly that one of the waitresses asked her if she was feeling unwell.

Feeling badly let down by Mills & Boon, Mattie returned five minutes later to her lonely seat – the bankers were now dancing – and consoled herself with a glass of red wine. When the fieldmouse ran over her foot a few seconds later she let out a scream loud enough to attract plenty of attention from guests sitting at nearby tables. But Mattie didn't even notice them. Her knee, having jack-knifed in a reflex of shock and revulsion, crashed against the underside of the table and toppled her wine glass into her lap. She gazed aghast at the hideous crimson stain as it spread like fungus over her precious new dress.

When she finally looked up and saw the expressions of curiosity on the faces of all those watching her, she realized that she was on her own. Her plight was a source of mild amusement, nothing more. No one here was going to help her.

She headed for the ladies' cloakroom at the speed of light this time. Head down, cheeks burning with mortification and with her full skirts bunched together at the front in an attempt to hide the terrible stain, Mattie elbowed her way through the crowds dancing to the band's own rousing version of an old Rolling Stones hit. And by supreme irony someone did on this occasion attempt to draw her on to the dance floor.

'C'mon, sweetheart, wanna boogie?' urged an extremely drunk and overweight man in his fifties, his face even redder than her own as a result of his frantic exertions, an aura of sweat emanating unpleasantly from his overheated body.

'No, thank you,' said Mattie, unshed tears misting her vision, and his leer changed abruptly to a sneer.

'You girls, you're all a washte of time.' He released his damp hold on her arm. 'I only wanted a bit of fun. You're not so pretty anyway . . .'

* * *

When Ross pushed open the door to the ladies' cloakroom and saw Mattie fully occupied at one of the basins he stood and admired the view for a few seconds before making his presence known. He didn't recognize her from the back but with her yellow dress pulled up to her thighs to reveal a pair of shapely legs in flesh-coloured stockings and narrow white suspenders, she presented an alluring sight. If he didn't know her already maybe it would be worth making the effort to do so.

When he coughed gently she spun round in shock, the front of her skirt – which had been soaking in the basin – clinging to her legs and dripping water on to the floor at her feet.

'This is the ladies' cloakroom,' squeaked Mattie, unnerved by the unexpected presence of such a gorgeous-looking boy.

Ross grinned. Although he was more than a little drunk he disguised it well. 'I know, I'm sorry. I was actually looking for Susie Rossiter. You haven't seen her anywhere, have you?'

Mattie shook her head. Ross, amused by her predicament and by her dumbfounded expression, made his way over to her.

'Red wine?' He nodded at the front of her dress.

Standing there dripping, she gazed back idiotically. She had never in her life seen such eyes, dark and thickly lashed and glittering with sensuality. He was quite simply the most beautiful boy she'd ever encountered.

Finally she nodded, glancing down at the puddle at her feet. It looked for all the world as if she'd wet herself. 'A mouse ran over my foot.'

'Of course,' agreed Ross, nodding slowly.

'Oh! I meant that I jumped a mile and knocked over my drink,' explained Mattie hurriedly, sensing his doubt. Then her face fell. 'I don't know what I'm going to do now. I can't very well go back in there with a sopping wet frock.'

Ross smiled. Susie Rossiter had vanished, presumably back to her ape-like but hugely wealthy boy-friend. He had completely lost interest in his own partner for the evening, a ravishing brunette called Cassandra with an irritating giggle and the bizarre belief that sex was something one only did with one's husband.

And although he sensed that socially this girl was way out of her depth here, she seemed pleasant enough to make it worth his while becoming further acquainted. He had nothing else to do for the next hour or so, after all.

'We'll go for a walk,' he said, taking her hand. 'Outside. Your dress will be dry in no time. I'm Ross Monahan, by the way.'

'My name's Mattie.'

It didn't occur to either of them for even a single second that she would refuse his offer. At eighteen, Ross had never been turned down by a female in his life.

And much later, when he laid her down on a secluded grassy bank beneath a midnight-blue sky glistening with stars it didn't occur to Mattie for one second to object when Ross, the expert seducer, gently relieved her of her virginity. It was her gift to him, her only means of thanking him for making this Midsummer Ball the happiest, most blissful and most gloriously memorable night of her entire life.

Mattie didn't know how she managed to live through the following week. As minute after minute crawled by in excruciating slow motion she existed in a state of exquisite torture, reliving every moment of her time with Ross in fabulous Technicolor. She could recall the scent of new-mown grass and the sweet taste of his mouth against her own, she could feel the silky texture of his dark hair and warm, tanned skin, and remember the husky tone of his voice as he had whispered in her ear that she was beautiful.

Most clearly of all she recollected how he had kissed her goodbye before helping her into the taxi, asking her for her phone number so that he could call her in the week. Trembling with sheer happiness she had pencilled both her home and work numbers on the back of his cigarette packet.

And all she'd lived for since then was the sound of the telephone ringing, which wasn't so easy in the office because the phones shrilled every couple of minutes and each time she felt that her heart might actually stop beating for good. At home, where she and her parents lived quietly, the phone seldom rang at all but Mattie, who didn't dare go out even for a few minutes, still spent every evening imagining that at any moment it might.

And the secret was hers alone. No one else knew what she was going through. Corinne McPherson, breezing into work at twenty to ten on Monday morning, had flashed a smile in Mattie's direction, asked her if she'd enjoyed herself at 'the bash', and disappeared without even waiting for a reply. Mattie, the muscles at the tops of her thighs still aching from their unaccustomed exertions, her eyes smarting from the make-up she wasn't used to wearing but which she felt she needed just in case Ross appeared miraculously in the doorway of the office and whisked her away to somewhere glamorous for lunch, didn't even mind. It *hadn't* been a dream, it had really happened. And any day now – any *minute* now – Ross would phone her, as he had promised he would. Her life was about to change beyond all recognition and she could scarcely contain herself, waiting for it to begin.

* * *

Her life, of course, did change beyond all recognition. The phone continued to ring but the caller was never Ross. Somehow seven days became fourteen. Inexplicably, fourteen days became twenty-eight. Finally, in a frenzy of confusion and wounded pride Mattie managed to corner Corinne one lunchtime and ask her very casually if she happened to know someone by the name of Ross Monahan.

'Ross!' exclaimed Corinne, shaking her head and laughing. 'He's a demon, darling. Absolutely lethal with the ladies. Ross is wonderful, just so long as you refuse to believe a single word he says. If I told you who he's rumoured to be having an affair with at this very moment in time, you simply *would* not believe me . . .'

With a chill of recognition Mattie realized that once again no one else was going to help her. Having clung stubbornly to the belief that he had in a careless moment thrown away the cigarette packet with her phone number on it, she now forced herself to face up to the unpalatable truth. During the course of that evening, as they had walked arm in arm across the sweeping emerald lawns she had definitely told him the name of the company she worked for. She had let him know that she was a friend of Corinne McPherson. She had also told him her surname and he had taken enough notice at the time to remark that one of his favourite restaurants was Jameson's, in Clifton.

When it came right down to the bottom line, if he'd lost her phone number but had really wanted to contact her he could easily have done so.

But he hadn't. And by the time Mattie faced up to that fact she had also realized that she was pregnant.

* * *

It wasn't easy being a single parent, but Mattie made the best of it. Reconciled to the fact that her staid parents had no intention of supporting the daughter who had brought such unforgivable shame upon the family name, she made the move from Bristol to Bath, existing in a tiny bedsit and not realizing until several years later that Ross – and his elder brother Max – lived in the same city.

It had come as an incredible shock to her when she had first read in the newspapers of the Monahan brothers' plans to transform the crumbling Charrington Grange into a luxury hotel. On countless occasions during those lonely, freezing nights with only her daughter for company, Mattie envisaged a confrontation between herself and the man – no longer a boy – who had caught her in that timeless and most clichéd trap of all.

But, by sheer force of will, she managed to persuade herself that she was better off – spiritually if not financially – on her own. Ross was the archetypal playboy, spreading himself around pretty indiscriminately and somehow managing to get away with it, and he was hardly likely to welcome her with open arms if she were to reveal herself – and their daughter – to him at this stage of his life. Gradually, almost without realizing it and simply because she had no alternative, Mattie came to terms with the fact that all she had been to Ross was a convenience, a temporary diversion. She began to take a perverse pride in her newfound independence, learning to pity Ross rather than resent him. He might have an outwardly glamorous, jet-setting lifestyle but could he possibly be more blessed and more contented than she was with her precious daughter?

And no one could have wished for a better child. As a baby, Grace slept through the night, seldom crying and often smiling. At the age of three she was cheerful, affectionate and obedient. Later, a quiet but diligent schoolgirl, she always did her homework without having to be asked and spent her spare time either reading or helping her mother around the house.

Grace only ever mentioned her father once, at the age of ten. Mattie, who had been bracing herself for that question for years, sat down with her daughter and told her everything. It was actually the plot of a romantic novel that she had read several months earlier but it had struck her at the time as the kindest and most sensible solution. As a result, she had explained to Grace that her father was an American soldier whom she had met while he was on holiday in England and with whom she had fallen deeply in love. He – Carl Shaunnessy – had been tall, dark and wonderfully handsome with a terrific sense of humour and a winning smile. And he had, of course, adored Mattie as much as she loved him. After six blissfully happy weeks together he had returned to the States to begin the preparations for their wedding. Mattie would join him a month later. Two days before she had been due to set sail she had received a telephone call from his only living relative, his adored grandmother. Carl had been killed in a tragic accident, burned to death in a blazing house as he – a mere passer-by – attempted to rescue two young children from their bedroom on the second floor. The children had been saved by Carl Shaunnessy's quick thinking and unselfish disregard for his own safety. He had died a hero. And Mattie had never loved another man since.

The story was so poignant that Mattie ended up in tears, while Grace considered the facts and nodded with grave, ten-year-old understanding.

And although Mattie was prepared to elaborate further, it had never been necessary. Grace had never mentioned the subject again. The past had been neatly tied up, like a parcel, and she appeared to be quite satisfied with the information she had received.

Mattie had been unable to hide her feelings when Grace announced that she had applied for a job at the Charrington Grange Hotel, but at least she had been able to disguise them. Gripped by genuine shock and an obscure premonition of doom, she had managed to pass off her disquiet as purely maternal concern. Grace had done well at school; she was a clever girl with a handful of GCSEs and could do so much better than this. While waitressing was a perfectly respectable occupation it was hardly going to lead to a glittering career. Notoriously badly paid and with long, unsocial hours, the opportunities for promotion were negligible. She wouldn't be using her qualifications. Her feet would ache dreadfully. And the man for whom she would be working was a careless, thoughtless, smooth-tongued unprincipled bastard.

But Mattie couldn't tell her that and Grace was nothing if not determined. Secretarial work had bored her and she had enjoyed her stints as a Saturday waitress in a city centre café when she'd still been at school. Working at the famous Charrington Grange Hotel was what she wanted to do and her mother's flustered objections didn't concern her in the least.

Chapter 13

Dominic had paid a great deal of attention to what Tessa had told him about her current situation. He had listened to the calm reasoning behind her decision not to become involved with Ross Monahan and – to his own great surprise – had agreed with it. Dominic himself thrived on uncertainty and the wild romance of see-sawing emotions. He was never truly happy unless there was some trauma about to erupt. But Tessa was different. Pride and independence were only part of it; she had to be in control and that included her emotions. She would never allow herself to be made a fool of, could not bear to tolerate either the humiliation or the knowledge of her own weakness. Luckily she had the necessary strength of will to carry it off. In all the years Dominic had known her, Tessa had retained her self-respect and he admired her for it.

But suppressing a natural attraction towards an eminently eligible man simply because 'it would only go wrong sooner or later' was something else. This time Dominic had a feeling that even Tessa Duvall might need a little help.

When Ross turned up at the cottage the following morning the last thing he was expecting was to be greeted at the door by a blond male wearing a scarlet satin dressing gown which was much too small for him. He also wore a plaster cast on one leg and an expression of amused curiosity.

'I was looking for Tessa,' said Ross, his eyes narrowing as

he realized that the dressing gown was one of hers.

'She's gone into Bath to buy some food.' Dominic, leaning against the doorpost, knew at once who the visitor was. Despite being thoroughly heterosexual, he could nevertheless recognize and appreciate that Ross Monahan was as physically perfect as Tessa had said he was. It must, he considered with some sympathy, make it very difficult for her. 'She should be back soon. Why don't you come in and wait?'

Since the purpose of his visit had been to prove his brother wrong, Ross was less than amused by the situation he now encountered, but he had to know exactly what was going on. With a brief nod he stepped inside and made his way into Tessa's small sitting room.

She had been working on the painting he had commissioned and he studied the almost-finished canvas, more to give himself time to gather his thoughts than to judge it. But despite his preoccupation his attention was caught at once. This painting was very good indeed, glowing with life, its vivid colours and brisk style enhancing the sense of fun, of wanting to be there. Surprised and amused, Ross recognized the figure by the fireplace, undoubtedly himself. A moment later he almost laughed aloud, for there on the extreme right-hand side of the painting was an equally unmistakable likeness of Max, engrossed in conversation and clearly besotted with the girl to whom he was speaking. The girl, no one he knew, was ugly with a capital U, grotesquely fat and with the features of one of those deep-sea fish nobody would ever want to eat. But Tessa had portrayed Max as a man in love, mesmerized by this hideous female and quite clearly longing to take her to bed.

'She's a clever girl,' he observed, as Dominic – his rival – hobbled precariously into the room with a six-pack of lager under his arm.

'You don't have to tell me,' replied Dominic with a deliberately disarming smile. 'I love her to death but it drives me crazy that she won't sell herself. An artist can't afford to be shy, for God's sake, they have to get out there and *push* . . .'

'My brother' – Ross pointed at the figure in the painting – 'won't be amused by this. It's great, but I can't believe she did this to him.'

'Believe it.' Dominic collapsed on to the settee and noisily opened a can of lager. He was a talented artist and although his first and most abiding love was sculpture he had the ability to turn his hand to any form of painting. Tessa's style hadn't been difficult to copy, but when she came home and saw what he had added to the canvas he sensed that she wouldn't be too amused either. It was, after all, almost blasphemous.

But necessary. And Dominic was just pleased that after only a brief exchange with Max Monahan he had remembered him accurately enough to fashion a recognizable likeness.

'Have a lager,' he said, tossing a can in Ross's direction. 'I'm sorry, I haven't introduced myself. Dominic Taylor.'

'Ross Monahan,' said Ross, reluctantly shaking his outstretched hand and realizing that he was telling Dominic nothing he didn't already know. 'And you're staying here with Tessa?'

'For a few weeks, maybe longer,' replied Dominic blithely. 'As I say, Tessa and I are very close. She's told me all about you, of course.'

Ross could feel his jaw tightening. 'And what exactly has she told you?'

'Oh, just the sordid details. One-night stand, unexpected pregnancy, all that.' Assuming with confidence that Ross wouldn't dare to take a swing at a cripple, he carried on. 'She knows that you screw around, that you aren't exactly ideal husband material, so she's going it alone. Well, fairly alone. When she phoned me I came at once, even though it was hardly the greatest timing as far as I was concerned.' He tapped his plaster cast with his knuckles for emphasis. 'But Tessa and I have always had a special relationship . . .' His voice trailed away and Ross, almost bursting with jealousy, wondered whether he could live with his conscience if he hit someone whose leg was in plaster.

'I don't screw around,' he replied coldly. 'And Tessa has some weird ideas about independence. I offered to marry her and that's more than I've ever done to any woman before. Her ideas are her own. I happen to think that her views on my suitability as a husband are wrong.'

Dominic was by this time enjoying himself hugely. He only hoped that Tessa wouldn't return now and land a bloody great spanner in the works. 'Look,' he said, assuming an eminently responsible tone of voice, 'she's made up her mind. Don't take offence, but who did she contact when she was in trouble? What Tessa and I share goes beyond money and privilege. We understand each other. And I'm not the kind of man who worries about a little matter like illegitimacy. If I love a child it doesn't concern me whether or not the mother is married. Similarly,' he added, as slowly and meaningfully as he could manage, 'if I love a woman, the fact that she might already have a child by somebody else is simply not a problem.'

* * *

'You didn't even wait for her to come back?' demanded Holly, aghast. She had heard Tessa talk about Dominic in the past but she was sure there had never been anything *intimate* between them. Privately, she could hardly wait to meet the man who had so thoroughly dented her boss's morale.

'He's staying at the cottage – which has only *one* bedroom – for an indefinite period,' snapped Ross, glowering at her. 'He was wearing one of her dressing gowns. And he informed me in no uncertain terms that he and Tessa had something "special" going on between them. What the hell did you expect me to do, under the circumstances?'

'But you said he'd got a broken leg,' argued Holly, realizing to her astonishment that she was almost feeling sorry for him. 'My father broke his leg during a skiing holiday a couple of years ago and his doctor told him he couldn't . . . you know . . . while he was still in plaster. Mummy was absolutely thrilled. So this Dominic can't be doing anything too special.'

'Bullshit,' snapped Ross irritably. 'I broke *my* leg when I was nineteen and it didn't stop me.'

'Now, now, calm down.' Holly patted his hand with a soothing gesture but Ross, unaccustomed to being soothed, glowered at her and snatched his hand away.

'She's a two-timing bitch. I can't believe she's behaving like this.'

'I'll speak to her. Don't worry.' Holly smiled reassuringly at him, forgiving him for his rudeness since it gave her the opportunity to drive over to Tessa's cottage and meet the 'cocky bastard' in person. 'I'll find out what's really going on.'

* * *

'He's in the bath,' said Tessa, before Holly had even had a chance to open her mouth. 'Oh, don't look so stunned, I guessed what would happen. The Grange grapevine lives on.'

'Well?' demanded Holly, giving her friend the benefit of one of her most searching looks. 'Is it true? Are you and Long John Silver as madly in love as Ross thinks you are? He's spitting teeth, by the way.'

'Probably do him good.' Tessa resumed her position before the easel set up in the centre of the room. 'And no,' she added over her shoulder, 'of course we aren't. Dominic's been up to his usual tricks, telling all sorts of ridiculous stories for his own amusement, and I haven't decided yet whether to scream at him or laugh. Which is why he's beaten a strategic retreat to the bathroom.'

'Interesting,' purred Holly. 'Do you think he'd like someone to wash his back for him?'

'Knowing Dominic, he'd far rather you washed his front for him. Holly, don't even think of it. For heaven's sake, you've got that look in your eyes and *you're* supposed to be in love with Mad Max.'

'I am,' Holly protested. 'But he was very rude about my new outfit the other day so I decided to go for a change of plan. A spot of jealousy never goes amiss. At least,' she added with a wink, 'it doesn't seem to have done you too much harm.'

'Games,' said Tessa, with a dismissive gesture. 'All this play acting . . . I can't stand it. It's so pointless. Why can't people just be honest with each other?'

'Less fun.'

'Less complicated. Will you look at what Dominic did to this picture? He told Ross that I'd done it. Dominic couldn't be truthful if his important little places depended on it.'

'He really did that?' Examining the wicked portrayal of Max, Holly's spirits lifted still further. 'That's incredible.' Inwardly, she quivered in expectation. Daring, dashing Dominic was getting better by the minute.

Chemistry was a funny thing, thought Dominic, ten minutes later. That infallible, unstoppable ring-through-the-nose had captivated and catapulted him into more trouble with the opposite sex than he had ever thought possible – although at the time, of course, it had all been wonderfully exhilarating.

What was happening now, he supposed, must be the flip-side. Anti-chemistry. Or maybe since it *was* chemistry, it was that of the lion facing the hyena.

Quite simply, he couldn't stand *anything* about Holly King. Every aspect of her looks, her voice and her personality irritated him beyond belief. Never, never before in his life had he disliked anyone more strongly. If he and this monster were the only two people on the planet, he thought with a shudder of revulsion, he would certainly die a virgin.

Saying as little as possible and wishing he could go for a long walk, Dominic sprawled in the only armchair with his plastered leg propped up on the coffee table and sullenly contemplated the fraying holes in the only remaining leg of his ancient Levis.

But it simply wasn't possible to forget that Holly was there. The comfortingly familiar scent of Tessa's oil paints had been overpowered by her cloying perfume. Her undoubtedly expensive clothes were a living nightmare – he'd never been a fan of Kandinsky and his work didn't look any better translated on to a silk jersey tent. Her make-up was equally unsubtle – it probably glowed in the dark – and her voice, well-bred and confident, was far too loud for the room.

She was the kind of woman to whom he sold his sculptures for ludicrously over-inflated prices, but that was purely business. He had never been forced to socialize with one of them before. And now he knew just how wise he'd been not to do so.

'We'd love to.' Tessa, speaking with a paint brush clenched between her teeth, sounded like a bad ventriloquist. She turned to look at Dominic, who had been paying no attention, and added, 'Wouldn't we?'

'What would we love to do?'

'Holly's invited us to dinner at her flat tonight. You'll adore it – she's a brilliant cook.'

'No,' said Dominic flatly. 'Sorry, but I can't.'

'Why on earth not?' wailed Holly, deeply offended. Here she was, pulling out all the stops, offering to make the kind of Chinese meal that took *hours* to prepare, and this gorgeous, insufferably rude man didn't even have the courtesy to think up a reasonable excuse for refusing her.

'Because I don't want to.' Congenitally self-centred, Dominic suffered no such qualms. 'I'd rather stay here. Is that allowed?' he added with undisguised sarcasm.

'Not only is it allowed,' interjected Tessa swiftly, wiping her brushes on a rag and tossing the lot into his lap, 'it's compulsory. You, selfish pig, can bloody well stay here, clean my brushes and keep your hands off my paintings. I'm going to Holly's for the evening. And I hope you have a rotten miserable time on your own.'

Chapter 14

The amber spotlighting amid the tropical foliage bathed the swimming-pool in seductive light, flattering Antonia's tanned body and creating a subtly decadent atmosphere which matched her mood.

Sleeking her wet hair away from her face she pulled herself out of the water in a single swift movement and rested at the pool's edge, glancing at her watch and realizing that it was almost ten o'clock. If Ross planned to swim this evening – as he fairly often did – he would be here any minute now and she would see him again for the first time in several weeks.

And they had been a decidedly unpleasant few weeks at that. Shocked by how much she had missed him, Antonia had initially decided that what she needed to do was diversify in order to put him out of her mind.

She had flirted like mad with a visiting Swiss banker whom she had met at a dull dinner party given by one of Richard's even duller business associates. The handsome banker had responded at first with pleasing alacrity and her confidence had been boosted no end, but the next day had been a nightmare. Having arranged to meet him for lunch at an intimate restaurant in Castle Combe, she had spent hours getting ready and told Richard a whole string of risky lies in order to get there, only to be stood up by the lily-livered bastard who hadn't even had the nerve to tell her in person, but had asked the *maitre d'* instead to make sure she received his note.

He was sorry, he wrote, but he'd had second thoughts. She was a very attractive woman, but he realized now that he loved his wife too much to risk spoiling their future for the sake of a moment's pleasure.

If that was as long as he was capable of lasting, she thought derisively, she hadn't missed much.

But the rejection had wounded her pride and with nothing else to occupy her mind Antonia often found herself thinking about Ross. Finally, after long, empty weeks away from The Grange, she had decided that she simply *had* to see him again. She would apologize for her behaviour on Christmas night. She would remind Ross – as if he could have forgotten! – what he had been missing. And then they would resume their easy, long-standing relationship of mutual enjoyment and understanding.

Boredom struck Dominic like a mallet. Slightly ashamed of his behaviour earlier – though more because he had annoyed Tessa than because he had hurt the ghastly Holly's feelings – he had cleaned the brushes she had hurled at him and even washed up the row of coffee mugs he'd used during the day.

Then, sitting down and preparing to enjoy a lazy evening in front of the fire with a sketch pad and charcoals, the dreaded boredom had enveloped him for no reason at all. Tessa, he thought darkly, had wished it upon him. He had to get out, go somewhere . . . *do* something . . . and because his soon to be ex-wife had taken his mobile in a fit of pique, he was trapped.

Less than half an hour later Dominic eased himself on to a stool, propped his crutches against the bar and ordered himself a celebratory cognac. More proficient with his crutches than even his own wife suspected, the journey to the end of the lane had nevertheless been chilly and somewhat hazardous. But he had correctly assumed that almost anyone would stop and offer a lift to such an obviously incapacitated young man, and almost anyone, in the shape of an ancient retired sheep farmer, had done just that – all the way to the elegantly illuminated front entrance of the Charrington Grange Hotel.

Being disabled, he had discovered, had its advantages after all.

It was also a great conversation-opener. Wherever he went, people asked him how he'd managed to break his leg and in order to brighten their day he'd invented a variety of wildly original stories.

'How did it happen, then?' asked the man occupying the next bar stool, exactly on cue. In his forties, with tired eyes behind steel-framed glasses and a world-weary air, he seemed in particular need of entertainment. Obligingly, Dominic launched into the version involving a light aircraft, a pilot with heart trouble, a crash-landing into the Mediterranean and thirty-six hours of bobbing about in the sea with nothing to eat or drink and only a circling shark's fin for company.

'I've been making up for it ever since,' he concluded, raising his empty glass and hoping that his neighbour, enthralled, would take the hint and buy him another.

'You've been making up a lot of things,' remarked the man with a wry smile. 'But I'll get you a drink anyway.'

Unperturbed but mildly curious, Dominic shook his hand. 'Dominic Taylor. How did you know I was lying?'

'Richard Seymour-Smith,' replied his neighbour, indicating

to the barman that refills were required. 'And I'm an accountant, so it was easy.' Glancing at the unoccupied bar stool to his left, he added: 'I also have a wife who's a consummate liar. The art of lie detecting, therefore, is a particular interest of mine.'

It didn't take long after that for Dominic to piece together the whole story. This clever, unassuming man was helplessly in love with his wife and was dealing with her infidelity in the only way he knew how; by closing his eyes and pretending that it didn't exist. It was easier than forcing a confrontation. He couldn't risk losing her. He couldn't imagine a life without Antonia. As far as he was concerned, an unfaithful wife was better than no wife at all.

At the mention of Antonia's name it all clicked into place. Dominic couldn't help admiring the irony of the situation. It took more self-control than he'd known he possessed to keep quiet about his own involvement in the complicated triangle.

When Richard excused himself in order to make a phone call, Dominic decided to explore a little of the hotel. Swinging expertly along on his crutches he passed through the reception area, winking and grinning at Sylvie Nash who was working the late shift and who, with her Barbie-doll face and figure, was far more his idea of what a receptionist should look like than Hurricane Holly.

Poking his head around the door leading into the crowded restaurant, he smartly withdrew when he spotted Max Monahan at a nearby table. He didn't need to be kicked out into the snow at this hour of the evening. He was enjoying himself. And he was also intensely interested in discovering the whereabouts of the feckless, shameless Antonia.

* * *

When Ross dived into the pool he thought he was alone. It wasn't until he surfaced for air that he saw her, sitting in the shadows, silently watching him.

'Antonia.' He spoke guardedly, acknowledging her presence, assuming that this meeting had been engineered.

'Hello Ross.' It was almost a whisper. 'I've missed you.'

When he didn't reply she raised her gaze, realizing that he was waiting for something more. 'I came to apologize,' she continued, her voice stronger, her eyes appraising his tanned, miraculously constructed body and her fingers flexing with longing at her side. 'I broke the rules and I'm sorry. But now I'm back.'

'So I see.' Ross couldn't help admiring her skills. Antonia certainly knew how to make the best of herself. In that topaz-yellow, barely-there bikini, with her hair slicked back and one toe now idly stirring the surface of the water she was looking good, innocent and provocative at the same time.

He knew exactly what she wanted and it wasn't swimming lessons.

He thought of Tessa, whom *he* wanted.

Then he thought of Dominic, living in Tessa's cottage and confronting Ross with a mixture of defiance and disdain and presumably, since there was only one bedroom, sharing her bed.

When Antonia, sensing that the moment was right, slid noiselessly into the water and swam in hypnotic slow motion towards him, Ross didn't move away.

Dominic, leaning against the heavy green-glass door so that it swung open just far enough for him to be able to view the proceedings unobserved, allowed himself a small, triumphant smile. It had crossed his mind in the past day or two that he and Ross were, in many ways, really rather alike. But being so close to Tessa brought out the Mary Whitehouse in him. Here, now, and under these particular circumstances they were on directly opposing sides. It was with enormous relish that he flung open the glass door and waved one of his crutches in abandoned greeting.

'Good evening, Mr Monahan!' He shielded his eyes in order to see more clearly, then with a somewhat over-exaggerated double-take, hobbled to the side of the pool, fixing Antonia with his most disarming smile.

'My word, what a surprise. Mrs Seymour-Smith, as I live and breathe, taking *full* advantage of the hotel's facilities.'

'Who the hell are you?' demanded Antonia, hastily tugging her bikini top back into place and thanking her lucky stars that the interruption hadn't come five minutes later.

'Private detective, Mrs Seymour-Smith, hired by your husband. And I must say, I'm shocked. Why, only this morning Mr Monahan assured me that he didn't screw around and now here you both are in—'

'You're a *what*?' shrieked Antonia, but Ross cut in.

'Don't panic,' he said rapidly, glaring at Dominic's departing figure and wishing now more than ever that he could flatten him. 'It's all bullshit. He isn't a private detective. Look, calm down. He's gone.'

'So am I,' snapped Antonia, wading in undignified haste towards the edge of the pool and hauling herself out. 'Your friend has a bizarre sense of humour and I'm afraid I don't find any of it amusing.'

'Neither do I,' replied Ross grimly, shooting a dark glance in the direction of the green-glass door through which Dominic had disappeared. 'And, for God's sake, don't call him my friend. He's certainly no friend of mine.'

'Darling, come and sit down. We must have a talk.'

Grace regarded her mother warily, wondering what this was going to be about. Surely she wasn't going to start on about contraception again? They'd been through all that a year ago.

Mattie, inwardly shaking, patted the settee beside her. However she worded it, Grace was going to receive the greatest shock of her life.

'Sweetheart, there's something I have to tell you,' she said hurriedly, taking the plunge and gripping Grace's fingers so tightly that her daughter flinched. 'I didn't imagine that it would ever be necessary, but I realize now that it is, and it's all my fault. You aren't going to be very pleased with me, Grace, when I tell you how I found out.'

'Found out what?' Grace was genuinely puzzled now. This was no lecture about sex education. And Mattie was looking positively grey with anxiety.

When her mother put her hand under one of the cushions and pulled out her diary Grace let out a shriek and made a wild grab for it.

'That's mine! You have no right to even touch it!'

'Darling, I've read it.' Mattie sank back, longing to put her arms around her daughter, but knowing that it was impossible. 'I've read all of it, which is why I have to talk to you now.'

'It's private!' snarled Grace, shuddering with fury. 'It's none of your business. You can't read my private things—'

'But I had to,' intercepted Mattie miserably, 'for very special reasons which I shall explain. Sweetheart, I didn't want to have to do this, but I do have to tell you something about Ross which will come as a huge shock to you.'

'Go on then.' Grace's expression was sullen. Presumably her mother was about to launch into a lecture on the dangers of older men. Chance, she thought to herself with a trace of bitterness, would be a fine thing.

'All right.' Mattie, her heart thundering against her ribs and her palms sticky with perspiration, closed her eyes. 'Darling, Ross Monahan was . . . is . . . your father.'

Chapter 15

The sun was shining and the snow had finally melted. Tessa parked the gleaming white Mercedes neatly at the top of the drive and gave the crimson leather upholstery an appreciative pat before jumping out. Opening the boot, she carefully lifted up the painting, wrapped in brown paper and secured with string.

'For God's sake, Tessa, are you crazy? Put that down.'

Ross, whose office overlooked the front drive, came towards her. Tessa's unexpected arrival had cheered him up enormously, quite making up for the fact that the little waitress who normally brought him his coffee was off sick yet again, forcing him to put up with the fiercely black, sugarless poison that Holly always served up.

Taking the large, surprisingly heavy, painting from her, he paused for a second to survey her figure, semi-disguised beneath the pink-and-grey sweatshirt and paler pink leggings but still recognizably changed since their last encounter.

'Thanks for the car.' Tessa dropped the keys into his jacket pocket. 'It was great.'

'It still is,' protested Ross. 'I hope.'

She laughed and to his great relief fell into step beside him. 'I didn't park it in any ditches, if that's what you mean. I even washed it yesterday.'

'By hand?' Ross was incredulous. There were machines for that kind of job, after all.

'By actual hand,' agreed Tessa, making gentle mockery of his surprise. 'And now I'm returning it. The snow's gone and yesterday I bought a new bicycle.'

He stopped short at the top of the steps, turning to look at her. 'It's your car,' he said, frowning. 'I gave it to you. I told you, I don't want you riding around on a bicycle. It isn't safe.'

'It's perfectly safe,' replied Tessa patiently, 'and it's very good exercise for me. I don't need your car, Ross. And when I do need one I'll buy my own.'

'Of all the stubborn females . . .' With both hands full he had to wait for her to hold the door open for him. 'And where's your friend today, anyway? At least he appeared to appreciate the damn car.'

This time Tessa kept her smile to herself. 'Dominic? Oh, his wife turned up on my doorstep this morning. She travelled up from Truro in order to have a serious conversation with him.'

'He's married?' Placing the painting on his desk he began to undo the string. 'Holly didn't tell me that.'

Tessa grinned, collapsing into his executive chair and running her fingers through her just-washed and still slightly damp hair. 'Well, she wouldn't, would she? And since when did a little obstacle like marriage stop anyone from playing around?'

'*Touché*. But if they were married to the right partners they wouldn't need to. If I were happily married,' he added casually, 'I wouldn't dream of sleeping with anyone else.'

'Enough,' protested Tessa, who was enjoying herself. 'The thought of you with a halo is more than anyone could cope with. Now shut up and look at your painting.'

Ross, the archetypal man-who-had-everything, gazed at the completed picture in silence for almost a full minute. In order not to detract from the intricate scene, Tessa had finished it with a dove-grey mount and a narrow, completely plain, silver frame. It was exactly what he had wanted, and more. The composition was masterly, the colours perfect, the details wickedly accurate and the touches of humour sublime.

'If you really hate it,' she said finally, 'I could always cut off my ear.'

Before she had time to react, Ross had kissed her. The briefest kiss in the world, over practically before it was begun, yet affecting both of them more profoundly than either would ever admit.

'You're amazing,' he said, gazing once more at the painting and shaking his head in admiration. She was wearing apricot lip gloss and he could still taste it. 'And far prettier than Van Gogh. Besides, if you cut off your ear you'd never be able to wear glasses.'

Tessa nodded thoughtfully, realizing that they were both working hard to pretend the kiss hadn't happened. 'Max might do it for me, when he sees this.'

'Don't panic. He has a sense of humour.'

'An extremely well-hidden one.' She looked gloomy and Ross, fighting the urge to kiss her again, reached for his cheque book instead.

'You can't give me that much!' Tessa stared aghast at the cheque in her hands.

'I'm not giving you anything, I'm paying you a sensible price for a bloody good painting.' With an exaggerated sigh, Ross realized that she was going to start being difficult again. Had there ever in the history of the world been a woman more reluctant to accept money and help than Tessa Duvall?

'But we agreed on the price before I started . . .'

'And one hundred and fifty pounds is chicken-feed, Tess. You need to quadruple your prices if you want to attract any serious attention. Cheap paintings are bought by cheap people who just want something to fill in that bare patch of wall over the fireplace. You need to get the real collectors interested. And as soon as they start paying real money for your work they'll recommend you to their colleagues in order to protect their investment. You become covetable, your prices spiral, more and more people jump on the bandwagon . . . and you're made!'

Tessa laughed. Ross was making it all sound so effortless.

'As easy as that?'

'As easy as that.' He snapped his fingers. 'You supply the luxury item and as long as it's well advertised, people will want to buy it. And we are going to make sure,' he added, taking her arm and leading her out of the office, 'that you are very well advertised indeed.'

'Where are we going?' asked Tessa, hesitating. 'I'm supposed to be back at the cottage, refereeing the fight between Dominic and his wife.'

'Maybe she'll strangle him,' said Ross equably. 'Just let them get on with it. We're going to have lunch, to celebrate your imminent success.'

The restaurant he took her to, situated in the centre of Bath, was very glamorous indeed. It was all right for Ross, in his made-to-measure charcoal-grey suit and Dior silk tie, but Tessa hesitated. Faded sweatshirts, cotton leggings and white baseball boots weren't exactly thick on the ground in Zizi's.

'Don't start,' commanded Ross when she opened her mouth

to object, 'or I'll make you pay the bill. Just relax and enjoy yourself. Remember, we're celebrating.'

How Cinderella-ish can one girl get, wondered Tessa, obediently sitting and admiring the glitzy emerald-and-gold décor. Tiffany lamps cast pools of jewelled light upon each table, you could bury your toes in the sumptuous mossy carpeting and the matt green walls were striped with gold-leaf.

'Ever been here before?' asked Ross, not expecting her to say 'yes'.

But Tessa nodded. 'Mmm, dozens of times. I like the way they've done all this, though. Last year's pink and silver was a bit too Barbara Cartland for me.'

Having aimed to thrill and impress Tessa by bringing her here, Ross was instantly outraged. 'Who were you seeing last year? Who the hell could afford to bring you *dozens* of times to a place like this?'

Tessa shrugged and picked up the gilt-edged menu, immersing herself in the blissful luxury of choosing between garlic buttered king prawns and wild mushrooms marinated in red wine and herbs as a starter.

'The wild mushrooms, I think,' she decided, glancing up and finding that Ross was still watching her and waiting for an answer. Mischievously, she added, 'They've always been my favourite.'

'Who?' he repeated with barely concealed impatience. 'Who were you seeing last year?'

'Look,' said Tessa finally, 'not that it is any of your business, but I used to come here three times a week. I worked in the kitchen, washing dishes. Bloody hard work and not very glamorous at all.' She smiled and took a sip of iced Malvern water. 'The money wasn't much but the leftovers were fabulous.'

Ross really should have been a market trader, she thought two hours later. Throughout lunch he had greeted friends and business acquaintances with enthusiasm, introducing them to Tessa and telling each of them that she was a talent to watch out for, a rising star and a marvellous investment. Much in demand for portrait work, she was heavily over-booked at present, but if interested parties contacted Ross at The Grange he would personally ensure that they received priority attention.

Tessa, feeling like a ventriloquist's dummy, smiled and nodded and agreed with every one of Ross Monahan's outrageous lies. Amazingly, people appeared to believe them.

'Will you be charging commission?' she said, when they were finally alone together once more.

His dark eyes regarded her with amusement. 'I'd be happy to accept payment in kind.'

Tessa shook her head. 'Ross, please don't.' Inexplicably a lump came to her throat. Did he have any idea how hard it was for her to remain in control of her emotions when he was being this nice? And what was the matter with her, anyway? She never, ever, cried in public.

Thankfully, it didn't happen. With a rueful grin, Ross spooned dark brown sugar into his coffee and leaned back in his chair. 'Sorry, it just slipped out. I'm nothing but a tart.'

Relaxing, Tessa smiled back at him. 'I know. That's why I want us to be friends. Less traumatic all round. But I am grateful to you for all you're doing. If these people' – she tapped the little pile of business cards with her index finger – 'really are serious about my paintings, it'll make an incredible difference. And I would never have been capable of generating that kind of interest myself.'

Ross, on the verge of remarking that Tessa could arouse his interest any time she liked, bit back the comment and instead tried very hard indeed to think of her as just a friend. Although when all you wanted to do was take your friend to bed, he thought wryly, it wasn't exactly easy.

'I'm merely protecting my investment,' he told her now. 'I've had one or two other ideas as well but they need a bit of planning. In the meantime, tell me how you're getting on. Is your doctor pleased with you? Is everything progressing normally?'

He was slipping into midwife-mode again, Tessa realized with amusement.

'He's ecstatic,' she replied, crossing her fingers beneath the table. Finishing Ross's picture had kept her so busy that she'd had to cancel her last two appointments.

'And you've started ante-natal classes?' he persisted, signalling the waiter for more coffee and ignoring the fact that they were by this time the only remaining customers in the restaurant.

Tessa pulled a face. 'My mother always held the view that antenatal classes were terrible new-fangled inventions, designed by men to make pregnant women look and feel even more ridiculous than they already did. And I agree with her. Besides, I'm going to be so busy that I wouldn't have time for them.' She shrugged. 'Women have managed perfectly well for the last million or so years without the benefit of breathing lessons so I'm sure I'll manage one way or another when the time comes.'

Careful not to rock the boat, Ross behaved like a perfect gentleman when he drove Tessa home. Drawing up at the gate he helped her out of the car and waited while she hunted in her bag for the front-door key. With that expression of total absorption she wore whenever she was lost in concentration, she looked absolutely adorable. Ross was captivated. It was, he decided, all very frustrating to think that if Tessa had been unaware of his past reputation they could have enjoyed a marvellous, rewarding, *normal* relationship. Whereas instead, goddammit, he was forced to act like a caring older brother.

'Thank you for lunch,' she said now, clasping her bag in front of her like a schoolgirl. Glancing at the gentle swell of her stomach he smiled.

'Thank you for my picture.'

Tessa shrugged, feeling suddenly awkward and hunting for something else to say. 'I've enjoyed myself. It's been . . . nice.'

'I know it has.' Ross turned to get back into the car, no longer able to trust himself to maintain a respectable distance between them. Nodding in the direction of the cottage he said, 'I wonder whether your friend would agree. If he's still alive, that is.'

'He'll be alive. His wife adores him. She just can't come to terms with the fact that Dominic has fallen in love with someone else.'

There was an unspoken lesson in there somewhere and Ross knew that it was being aimed at him.

'Well, I'd better get back to the hotel.'

'And I have a few dozen paintings to dash off,' said Tessa with a smile. 'Thanks again, Ross, for all your help.'

Firing the car's ignition, he gave her a farewell salute. 'I'm always kind to pregnant women and children. Particularly,' he added just before he pulled away, 'when the child concerned is my own.'

Chapter 16

Mattie was still worried about Grace.

A fortnight had now passed since that traumatic evening when she had been forced to tell her daughter the truth about Ross Monahan, but she was as far away as ever from discovering how Grace actually felt about it.

She had listened in silence to Mattie's fumbling explanations. The expected tears simply hadn't happened. Mattie, having braced herself for the inevitable outburst of rage, hysteria and shock, had been at a complete loss when, after telling Grace everything, her daughter had fixed her with a gimlet stare and said only, 'Is this the truth?' Whereupon, having received her mother's unhappy assurance that it was, she had risen to her feet, turned and left the room.

And despite Mattie's attempts since then to discuss the situation Grace steadfastly refused to do so. Every morning she left the house at her usual time. Most evenings were spent alone in her room. When Mattie spoke to her about such neutral subjects as food, laundry and her favourite TV programmes, she replied appropriately but seldom initiated conversation herself. Any mention of either Ross or the hotel was greeted with a stony, steadfast silence.

Out of sheer desperation Mattie searched for Grace's diary. She eventually found the charred remains of the cover and a scattering of ashes in the dustbin.

Her daughter's method of dealing with the ghastly bombshell appeared to be by blocking it out of her life. Mattie, so concerned about it that she had shed half a stone, was sure it wasn't a healthy reaction but had absolutely no idea how the situation might be redeemed. It was done – a *fait accompli* – and since Grace refused to talk about it she would have to come to terms with her emotions in her own, intensely private, way.

'Go away,' said Holly briskly. 'You're drunk.'

'Maybe, maybe,' agreed the drunk, leaning against the reception desk and offering her the crimson carnation from his buttonhole. 'But I'd still like to invite you to have dinner with me tomorrow night. After all, you can only say no.'

'Good.' Max was in the vicinity and Holly didn't want to be accused of wasting time again. Busying herself with a pile of mail she said, 'In that case, no.'

'But I'm the best man,' he protested. 'You don't know what you'd be missing.'

'A hangover, probably. Look, you're supposed to be in the ballroom making a speech. I'm supposed to be here, working. Why don't you just leave me alone and go back to the party?'

Holly liked men who were sleek, dark and dangerous-looking – like Max. This one, over six feet tall and built like a rugby player, had a big crooked nose, baggy grey eyes, untamed curly hair the colour of lager and a wide, infectious smile. Looking decidedly ill-at-ease in his morning suit, he was clearly far more of a jeans-and-jersey man. He had a deep, gravelly voice with a slight northern accent. And he was definitely more than a little drunk.

Holly was not smitten.

She watched from beneath her lashes as he shrugged and turned away, heading back towards the ballroom where the wedding reception was in noisy, celebratory progress. It was typical, she thought resentfully, that Max should have missed this shining example of her ability to rebuff a potential time-waster.

Fifteen minutes later one of the bridesmaids, emerging from the ballroom, approached Holly at the desk.

'Could you come with me, please? You're needed at once.'

Perplexed, Holly followed her. When she reached the open doorway three hundred guests broke into enthusiastic applause. To her astonishment, they were all swivelling round in their seats and looking at *her*. Cheers and whistles of approval ricocheted around the room. The best man, standing at the top table, grinned and raised his glass in her direction.

'Ladies and gentlemen, here she is. The woman of my dreams, the woman who broke my heart . . . the woman who refused my invitation to take her out to dinner.'

'He's my brother,' whispered the bridesmaid amid renewed cheers. 'He's very shy.'

Holly, scarlet with embarrassment, could cheerfully have killed him. He was going to humiliate her publicly in order to pay her back and the heavy doors had been closed behind her now, preventing escape. Where the hell was Ross, she thought desperately, when she needed him?

'But I don't take "no" for an answer,' boomed the best man. 'And I'll always resort to blackmail when necessary. So . . . my speech doesn't begin until this stunning young lady changes her mind and agrees to have dinner with me tomorrow night at a restaurant of her choosing.'

Holly had been imagining such a terrifying range of alternatives that her first reaction was one of profound relief.

Her second was to laugh. The man was nothing if not persistent. And if he was offering her a choice of restaurants he must at least have money, if not class.

The wedding guests were waiting. Finally, still blushing, she nodded. Wild applause and vociferous approval greeted her decision.

'Thank you,' said the best man, grinning with satisfaction. 'If you'd be so good as to write down your name and address and your chosen restaurant, my sister will take the details. And now, since I know how very busy you are, you'd better return to your desk. I shall make my long and eagerly awaited speech. And I'll pick you up tomorrow night, at eight-thirty.'

'He probably won't even turn up,' said Holly, prowling in agitation around Tessa's small living room and irritating Dominic to death.

'Probably not,' he replied cuttingly, 'particularly if he's sobered up.'

Tessa, who was busy painting, said equably, 'I think he sounds exciting and I'm sure he'll turn up. Where have you decided to go?'

'Zizi's.' It was one of Holly's favourite restaurants. 'But I don't even know his name,' she added in despair.

'King Kong,' muttered Dominic.

'Well, at least his manners couldn't be as bad as yours,' she retaliated, still hurt and bewildered by his obvious dislike of her and unable to understand how Tess could put up with him. 'Tessa, do you really think I should go? It's bound to be a disaster.'

'Go,' said Tessa firmly. 'You'll have fun. And wear your red silk dress.'

Holly smiled. 'I don't know why I should take your advice when all you ever do is ignore mine.'

'You *ask* me for advice,' her friend pointed out, 'so I give you sensible answers. All you do is try and persuade me to hurl myself into situations which any sane person would avoid like the plague. Besides,' she concluded, reloading her brush with Burnt Sienna, 'I've never asked for this so-called advice. You just blurt it out whenever the mood takes you. Most of the time I don't even listen.'

'Well, maybe you should,' retorted Holly. 'Because Ross really has changed his ways. I know for a fact that he never sees Antonia now. She hasn't even visited the hotel since Christmas night.'

Tessa winced. Dominic had taken great delight in giving her a blow-by-blow account of his recent visit to The Grange and now he was sitting quietly in the corner, pretending to read the racing results and smirking like mad.

'Thanks Holly, but I'm really not interested anyway,' she replied hurriedly, amazed by how much it hurt to say it. 'I don't *want* to have to rely on a man, any man, and I'm perfectly capable of coping on my own. Just as my mother did. OK?'

'Oh great!' said Ross in exasperation. 'That's all I bloody need.'

He grabbed the pile of just-typed correspondence from his desk, but it was already too late. Hot coffee had infiltrated every page and was even now dripping on to the ivory carpet.

'Don't just stand there,' he snapped at the waitress. 'Clear it up. And if you aren't capable of carrying a bloody tray without spilling anything, I don't know why you bothered coming back to work in the first place.'

Grace shot out of the office, locked herself in the toilet and burst into floods of tears. This was worse than any nightmare.

Unable to face Ross and equally incapable of staying at home and being subjected to her mother's endless attempts to find out how she was feeling, she had told her doctor that she was depressed and had managed to obtain a sick note. While Mattie had thought she was working, Grace had been wandering the streets of Bath, sitting alone in cafés full of tourists, meandering through museums and sometimes just sitting in her small car for hours on end, thinking.

She couldn't *stop* thinking. Her mind simply would not stop working, churning endlessly through the chaos and confusion and almost blocking out reality.

Grace, wanting desperately to block out everything, had begged her doctor to give her tranquillizers or sleeping tablets and had received only a stern lecture in return. Looking younger than her seventeen years she had been equally firmly rebuffed by the sales staff of several off-licences. Finally, with the help of a fair amount of make-up, she had managed to find a small supermarket where she could buy vodka without being questioned. If she drank it too quickly she was violently sick, but soon learned that small amounts at regularly spaced intervals effectively dulled the agony and enabled her to at least sleep at night.

It wasn't much, but it was better than nothing.

And now, having finally plucked up enough courage to return to work and to face seeing him again, this had happened. A hefty vodka on an empty stomach hadn't helped, but she certainly wasn't drunk. Knowing that she had to carry on as if nothing had happened – nothing! – she had gritted her teeth and taken the tray of morning coffee into his office.

But at the sight of Ross, so tall and handsome, so glamorous and *exciting*, her hands had started shaking uncontrollably. He radiated an aura of sexuality and success, the effortless charm of someone who could have anything or anyone he pleased. And Grace felt her mind being choked all over again by the hideous vision of Ross and her mother . . . doing it . . . together.

And that was what had finished her off. The tray had dropped to the desk and the coffee pot had tipped over, launching coffee everywhere. On the verge of tears and unable to cope with his anger, Grace had run away.

Now all she had to do was get out of the hotel before anybody saw her in this state.

And find herself another job, preferably working for someone she wasn't going to fall in love with . . . and who wasn't going to turn out to be her father.

Chapter 17

'You look absolutely stunning.'

'Oh, I'm stunned all right,' agreed Holly, adjusting the hem of her carefully pressed silk dress. 'It's the first time I've been taken out to dinner in a Land-Rover.'

Adam Perry had a loud laugh and wasn't ashamed to use it.

'But a Land-Rover never lets you down,' he assured her, his northern accent becoming more pronounced. 'It's a grand vehicle, sturdy and reliable. If it makes you happier, I was going to pick you up in the Rolls but my sister pranged it this afternoon. Ran it into a bus.'

'That makes me very happy indeed,' replied Holly gloomily, peering out into the freezing darkness and realizing that they were heading away from the centre of Bath. 'But where are we going? Zizi's is behind us.'

Adam was unperturbed. 'I changed your mind; we're going somewhere else.'

'Oh God.' Holly put her head in her hands, realizing that the evening was going to be even worse than she'd anticipated. 'I've been hijacked.'

It got worse. Much, much worse.

Her diamond and pearl bracelet, whose rainbow-glitter would have been exotically enhanced by the considerate lamplight at Zizi's, looked like something out of a cracker beneath the harsh glare of fluorescent striplights. Her make-up, no doubt, appeared equally garish. And her generous cleavage in the low-cut scarlet gown was attracting a great deal of unwanted attention from the surrounding truck drivers and homeward-bound commuters.

The Leigh Woods service station on the M4 might be OK for Adam Perry, looking just like a truck driver himself in ancient denims and a blue-and-gold-hooped rugby shirt, but it was all too much for Holly.

'Now look . . .' she began, as he returned to their table – Formica, orange and smeared with ketchup – with two plates of sausage, egg and chips and a pot of tea.

'Oh God,' said Adam, swiftly intercepting her diatribe. 'She's had a sense of humour failure. Holly, I know what you're going to say and I'm disappointed. I really thought, when I first laid eyes on you, that you were a girl with a sense of humour. And now you're spoiling it all by turning all high-falutin' on me. Sweetheart, this is supposed to be fun—'

'But I'm not *having* fun,' she retaliated, unable even to look at him. 'We were supposed to be going to Zizi's and I got all dressed up and now all those horrible men are leering at me . . .'

'And you'd rather be leered at by men in smart suits,' Adam remarked dryly.

To her horror, he opened his wallet. 'You think I'm pulling a fast one, bringing you here instead of taking you to a restaurant that charges for rice by the grain. Well, I am very disappointed indeed. But if you're that concerned about it, put this in your purse and take a friend to bloody Zizi's.' He tossed two fifty-pound notes across the table, one of which landed on Holly's plate. 'That should cover the cost of a couple of omelettes.'

Holly had never been so humiliated in her life. Her eyes filled with tears as she pushed back her chair and stood up.

'I knew I shouldn't have come out with you. I didn't even want to come out with you in the first place but you forced me into it. You're nothing but a pig.'

The Land-Rover caught up with her just as the slip road met the motorway. Holly, shivering so violently that she could barely stand up in her high heels, attempted at first to ignore it.

'For Christ's sake, will you give up the debutante act and get in?' demanded Adam, leaning at a perilous angle across the passenger seat in order to let her know that he meant it. 'And there's really no need to panic, you know. We can never marry. Who would ever take seriously a woman with a name like Holly Perry?'

Holly was furious. She was frozen by the biting northerly wind. She was humiliated and hungry, and her shoes were absolutely killing her.

But at those words she collapsed with laughter and was forced, with the utmost reluctance, to give in.

Zizi's was packed, but the *maitre d'*, who appeared to know Adam well, found them a table. Her diamonds resumed their opulent glitter and her good mood – entirely against her will – was gradually restored.

'I don't know why you're looking so cheerful,' remarked Adam, halfway through their meal. 'You're paying.'

'I didn't take that money you threw at me,' she protested, forking up the last morsel of lobster from her plate.

'In that case the service station will have one happy waitress tonight.'

'Do you really own a Rolls-Royce?'

'Does it matter? Isn't my personality enough?'

Holly smiled. 'I'm not used to people like you. I don't even know what you do . . . or where you went to school.'

'Is that really important?'

She shook her head at his stupidity. 'Of course it's important!'

He shrugged. 'Is it important if I tell you that I grew up in Yorkshire, attended a local comprehensive and was expelled at fifteen for gambling?'

'Did you?'

'Oh, it was no big deal. The mathematics master only split on me because he couldn't afford to pay his debts.'

Holly swallowed hard. This was not what she was used to. 'And now?'

'Now?' Adam grinned, resting his chin on one hand and mocking her incredulity. 'Now I have a chain of betting shops and all over the country there are teachers making me money. I get a huge kick out of it. I didn't even get maths O level and I make more in a week than they do in a year. Isn't that great?'

'Great,' replied Holly, on automatic pilot. It all sounded incredibly seedy to her. Adam Perry was like no man she had ever met before, but like some weird insect one might find floating in one's drink he held a peculiar fascination. She found that she couldn't stop staring at him. And she still couldn't get over the fact that the fastidious *maitre d'* had allowed him into Zizi's in those terrible, faded, practically disintegrating jeans.

When he'd first clapped eyes on her Adam had decided at once that Holly King was an absolute cracker. She had class, which he liked, but it was gaudy class, which appealed to him even more. He couldn't be bothering with the well-brought-up twinset-and-pearls type at all; he wanted a woman who looked like a woman and who wasn't afraid to flaunt her attractions and she certainly knew how to flaunt them to the limit. All he had to do now was figure out a way to break down her reservations, to really get through to her.

'When you finish eating we'll go back to my place,' he said, emptying the last of the Cristalle champagne into his own glass and draining it as if it were Guinness. 'I've got a water bed; you'll love it.'

Holly cast him a contemptuous look. 'I wouldn't share a water bed with you if we were stranded in the Gobi Desert,' she replied in withering tones.

Chapter 18

'You tell me to work,' protested Tessa, attempting to snatch back her palette. 'You *instruct* me to paint until I drop . . . and now you're dragging me away in mid-flow. I bet Michelangelo didn't have to put up with hassle like this.'

'After spending seven years flat on his back painting that bloody ceiling he'd have welcomed a bit of hassle,' countered Ross briskly, handing Tessa her coat. 'Besides, he wasn't pregnant. Pregnant artists require the occasional break from their duties. Not to mention,' he added with an irresistible smile, 'the odd meal.'

A trick. He had played a filthy rotten trick on her, thought Tessa darkly, twenty minutes later. She had only agreed to come out with him because she was hungry and now she was trapped here in this godawful green-and-beige room watching a repulsive film and attracting all sorts of unwanted attention.

Antenatal classes in Bath were evidently glamorous affairs. Glancing surreptitiously around her in the semidarkness, Tessa noted the preponderance of sleek blondes wearing full make-up, the most exclusive, colour co-ordinated exercise clothes and a great deal of scent. Even their matching nail polish was immaculate, she observed, glancing down at her own, habitually paint-stained hands.

She couldn't imagine anything more hideous than being forced to watch a film – of decidedly poor quality – depicting the actual process of childbirth. There was nothing magical about it as far as she could comprehend; she was only thankful that when her own time came she wouldn't be in a position to see it, particularly not in such gruesome, Technicolor detail.

But Ross had her hand clamped rigidly in his own and there was no escape.

Furthermore, she thought with incredulity, he seemed to be paying genuine attention to the horror film and appeared to have no idea at all how much of a stir his presence at the class was causing.

Ross Monahan, however, was not stupid. With a sinking heart Tessa realized that he was presenting her with a *fait accompli*. In her own vague way she hadn't given the matter a great deal of thought, but had somehow assumed that the identity of her baby's father would remain pretty much of a mystery, known only to the small circle of people who were already aware of the circumstances.

Clearly, however, Ross had other ideas. Scarcely anyone now was concentrating on the film as the on-screen drama approached its climax. Slanting glances, some moderately subtle and others downright farcical, were beaming in on them from all angles. Everyone knew about Ross Monahan and no one could quite believe that he was actually here. Tessa, who couldn't believe that either of them was here, slid down low in her uncomfortable chair, slowly closed her eyes and pretended to fall asleep.

* * *

'That was an unbelievably shitty trick to play,' she told Ross later, tearing into a chicken leg and fixing him with one of her sternest looks to show that she meant it.

He grinned quite unrepentantly and helped himself to a mound of garlicky potato salad with the air of a man who knows he is in the right.

'But necessary. And instructive,' he reminded her, gesturing towards the paintings which adorned her sitting-room wall. 'You wouldn't start a new picture without preparing the canvas first, would you?'

'It's not the same,' retaliated Tessa.

'It's exactly the same! If you don't make sure that your pelvic-floor muscles are in trim you could run into all sorts of problems later on.'

'My pelvic-floor muscles,' she informed him sweetly, 'are no concern of yours.'

Ross looked at her. With her customary blonde top-knot falling down, the sleeves of her baggy white lambswool sweater pushed up and both elbows on the table as she stripped the last morsel of chicken from its bone, her angelic good looks were so at odds with her stroppy attitude that he wanted to laugh.

'They could be,' he replied in a matter-of-fact manner. 'If only you weren't so damned stubborn.'

'I'm not damned stubborn. I'm practical.'

'Oh, right!' Sarcasm fuelled his irritation. 'That's why you've spent the last five years struggling to get by as a part-time, small-time painter. Can you at least bring yourself to admit that my ideas for boosting your career have been better than your own or is even that too much to ask?'

'We'll see about that when it happens,' Tessa shot back at

him, annoyed by his attitude. She was grateful for his help so far but she was damned if she was going to allow Ross to hold it over her, bringing it up at every opportunity and demanding grovelling thanks for a debt that could never be fully repaid. 'The only person I've sold to so far is you,' she reminded him, then added scathingly: 'Don't tell me I have to sleep with all your friends before they deign to buy my paintings.'

Ross had been nursing his secret all day, waiting for the perfect moment to spring the surprise. This wasn't how he'd imagined it happening but it was definitely a perfect moment . . . of sorts.

'Sleep with Nico Coletto,' he said casually, 'and I'll kill you.'

The chicken leg dropped with a clatter to Tessa's plate. The anger drained from her face. Ross speared a mushroom and ate it with enjoyment, waiting for her to react.

'What do you mean?'

'I mean he dropped by the hotel yesterday to see me. We're old friends. He happened to notice your painting hanging in my office and liked your style. He's off on tour to the States next week but as soon as he gets back he wants you to paint his portrait.'

'Nico Coletto wants me to paint *him*?' Tessa was dumbstruck. Overcome with awe. Astounded. The publicity would be sensational. And Holly, poor Holly, she thought with a secret smile, would be absolutely lacerated with jealousy when she found out.

'Two grand,' he said, savouring her reaction. 'Upfront. And an extra two hundred if you can finish it in time for his wife's birthday.'

'Two thousand pounds!' Forgetting that she didn't drink, she grabbed his glass and took a hefty gulp of icy white wine. Shaking her head in wonderment she said, 'I don't believe it.'

'Believe it. Now, am I great?' said Ross modestly, 'or am I great?'

Recovering from the shock, Tessa grinned at him. 'Nico Coletto's pretty great himself. And for that kind of money I'd go to bed with him after all.'

'He doesn't screw around,' said Ross quickly. She'd only said it to tease him, he knew, but the very idea filled him with alarm. Jealousy was an emotion to which he was unaccustomed, but Tessa could always rouse it in him, both effortlessly and at will, and the thought of her with another man, particularly Nico, was unbearable. 'He has one of those happy marriages which you refuse to believe exists.'

She shrugged, enjoying herself enormously. 'Oh, I believe they exist . . . for a while. But sooner or later anyone could give in to temptation. And Nico's had his share of adventures in the past . . . who's to say that if the right girl came along he might not—'

'Stop it!' In a rage, Ross snatched back his wine glass and fixed her with his most ferocious glare. 'Just stop it, will you? I set this whole thing up and you haven't had the common courtesy to even bloody well thank me. All I get instead is a run-down of your plan to jump into bed with one of *my* best friends just for the thrill of breaking up a decent marriage . . .!'

Tessa obtained a quiet satisfaction from knowing that she'd made her point, even if Ross was at this moment too furious to see it. He could sleep with all the married women he liked but he couldn't tolerate the idea of anyone being unfaithful to him. Was it really any wonder, she thought with bleak satisfaction, that she refused to allow herself to become seriously involved with him?

'I was joking,' she said now, in reassuring tones.

'Well, it wasn't funny,' retaliated Ross, the fire in his dark eyes only gradually beginning to recede.

Tessa looked suitably penitent. 'I promise not to seduce Nico Coletto.'

'You're damn right you won't seduce him,' he said grimly, circling the back of her hand with the point of his knife. 'Because you'll be chaperoned throughout every sitting.'

'What?'

'Just to make sure,' said Ross, so seriously that she didn't even dare to smile. 'I'm going with you.'

It was something he had planned to do a couple of days ago and which had completely slipped his mind, but as he made his way back to the hotel Ross spotted a small florist at the end of a row of elegantly fronted shops and since there was a convenient parking space outside he pulled into it. Rifling through his wallet for the scrap of paper upon which he had scribbled the girl's address, he almost gave up. It had only been a spur-of-the-moment idea, anyway, engendered by a sense of guilt that was quite out of character for him. But something about her pale, distraught face had got to him and . . . ah, here it was. And if he wasn't mistaken she lived less than half a mile away. Maybe he'd even drop them round to her himself . . .

Mattie, cold and exhausted and weighed down with groceries, paused at the end of the street in order to transfer the heaviest carrier bag from one hand to the other. She was less than a hundred yards from her front door now, and a cup of tea was what she most needed. A warm welcome from a loving, smiling daughter was what she *most* needed, she corrected herself, but she was resigned by now to the fact that such a miracle simply wasn't going to happen. Narrowing her eyes, she peered through the misty twilight, searching for the familiar little blue Fiat which would signify whether Grace was yet home from work.

But the Fiat was nowhere in sight and the parking space outside their small house was occupied by a large, white, expensive-looking car with its headlights blazing and the driver's door left wide open.

It was a Mercedes, Mattie realized as she drew nearer, rakishly parked and with its engine still running.

Then she froze, gripping her carrier bags so tightly that her short fingernails dug into her palms. For even in the semi-darkness it was impossible not to recognize the tall, dark-haired figure moving out of the shadows of her own front porch and climbing back into the car.

It had been eighteen years since she had last seen him, spoken to him, gladly surrendered her virginity to him, waited in an agony of suspense for him . . . and now Ross Monahan was here, in the flesh, outside her home.

Mattie didn't have time to formulate a plan of action. In the brief seconds when she might have moved forward or shouted to gain his attention she remained rooted to the spot, her heart pounding and her mind spinning as pent-up anger and shame and a determination to protect her daughter from further pain welled up inside her like bile.

She heard the roar of a powerful engine as he accelerated towards her. She blinked as the even more powerful dazzle of the headlights blurred her vision. For a second, dizzied by confusion and the intensity of her emotions, Mattie swayed. Almost without realizing it she stumbled forwards, off the edge of the pavement and into the path of the oncoming car.

He had to swerve sharply to avoid her. For a split second, in the reflected orange street lighting, she glimpsed his face, saw again the so-familiar glittering dark eyes, chiselled cheekbones and sensual, narrow mouth.

No doubt he was at this moment cursing her for her stupidity, cursing the absent-minded housewife who didn't even have the wits to look both ways before she crossed the road. And she had no doubt, too, that in less than twenty seconds he would have put the incident, the minor irritation of having to swerve to avoid a clumsy woman weighed down with shopping, completely out of his mind.

But that was the great difference between them, thought Mattie, turning to watch the Mercedes as it sped off down the main road and breathing in the last, lingering exhaust fumes. She hadn't forgotten. She would never forget. And one day Ross Monahan was going to learn that some people needed to be treated with a little more respect than he had been prepared to give them.

The bouquet, of perfect pink roses and deeper pink carnations amid a froth of white baby's breath, was propped against the front door. When Mattie bent to pick it up the glossy cellophane wrapper crackled and a trickle of water from the protruding damp stems ran down the inside of her wrist. The small white envelope stapled to the top of the wrapper was addressed to Grace.

Once inside the house, Mattie realized how badly she was shaking. She had to sit down at the kitchen table and draw several deep breaths before opening the envelope.

'*I'm sorry,*' the note inside read, '*I shouldn't have blown my top. Get well – and come back – soon. Ross Monahan.*'

You bastard, thought Mattie with tears in her eyes as she shredded the note into a dozen pieces.

Bastard, she thought as she stuffed the pieces into an almost empty coffee jar and pushed it into the bottom of the kitchen bin.

Bastard, she thought furiously, ripping the cellophone away from the flowers and inhaling their sickly perfume. The bouquet was too large to dispose of in one go; she would have to separate it and wrap each section in newspaper.

'Bastard,' she said aloud as she dropped the newspaper-wrapped parcels into the dustbin and emptied the messy contents of the kitchen bin over them for good measure.

She would protect Grace from that selfish, conceited, careless bastard of a man, she vowed as she replaced the lid of the dustbin with a crash. If it killed her.

Chapter 19

Holly, flicking through the newspaper, found what she was searching for and perched on the arm of the chair in order to discover her destiny in comfort.

'I'm going to have problems with my financial situation but will otherwise enjoy a day filled with pleasure and fun,' she announced in theatrical tones for the benefit of her fellow workers, taking their early break in the restroom. 'What utter rubbish! I've never had a financial problem in my life and how the hell am I supposed to enjoy a day filled with pleasure and fun when I'm stuck here on a sixteen-hour, double-sodding-shift?'

'Mrs Polonowski's a fortune teller,' supplied Lucy, one of the young chambermaids. 'She read my tea leaves the other week and told me that I was going to get engaged to a handsome man. Well, that very night,' she went on, with mounting excitement, 'I met Derek down at the Red Lion. And the next day I found that diamond ring inside one of the pillowcases in Room Six . . .'

Holly recalled the ring, a spectacular square-cut yellow diamond belonging to an equally flamboyant Australian opera singer who had created merry hell when it had gone missing and who had given Lucy a fifty-pence reward for finding it. The connection, she felt, was on the fragile side but the bit about the handsome man was definitely promising. That kind of fortune telling was right up Holly's street.

Rosa Polonowski, who worked as a washer-up in the hotel kitchens, needed little persuasion to be lured away from her sink for a quick cup of tea and a spot of impromptu palmistry in the rest-room. A garrulous lady in her late sixties who had arrived in England after the war, she had steadily increased her command of the English language during twenty-five years of fortune telling with a travelling fair. No longer Madame Rosa, she continued nevertheless to employ her talent; it was a sure-fire way to make new friends and if those new friends were thoughtful enough to reward her for her trouble with a glass or two of sweet sherry, so much the better.

She took her time over Holly's hand, holding it between her own gnarled fingers and admiring the elegant watch which adorned her wrist.

'You are lucky girl,' she said in her heavily accented English. 'So lucky, you will have much happiness. But zer is problem, my darling. Bik problem for you with ze men.'

You're telling me, thought Holly with a faint smile, but she said nothing.

'Bik problem to decide which man you choose,' continued Rosa Polonowski with a beady glance up at Holly's face. 'Two bik men, one dark and one fair. So different and yet both in secret loff for you. Ze dark one, he never smile. A true dark horse, you understand. One dark horse and one bik brown bear, see. And when you have made your choice you vill be so happy. You haf children, two children, and much good health.'

Holly, so excited by now that she could barely speak, whispered, 'But which one do I choose? The dark one? Is he really in love with me? Is he the one I'm going to marry? My God, I can't believe it!'

Rosa Polonowski forbore to mention that she hadn't said anything about any marriage. She patted Holly's hand and smiled, revealing incredibly crooked teeth and a great many gold fillings.

'Zat I do not say. You haf your own choice to make. You clever girl. You make good choice, I know.'

'Oh, Mrs Polonowski,' cried Holly, quite overcome by the thrilling possibilities. 'This is incredible. And everything you've told me is absolutely right, only I didn't know – I couldn't know – that he was already in love with me. But now that I *do* know . . .'

'Holly, what the bloody hell do you think you're doing in here?' roared Max, erupting into the room like a thunderstorm and scaring the wits out of almost everyone there. Only Holly, mesmerized by Mrs Polonowski's stunning revelations, didn't react. With renewed fury, Max grabbed her hand – the very hand which had just revealed her starry future – and yanked her unceremoniously off her stool.

'For Christ's sake,' he barked, shoving her towards the door. 'There's a queue of guests at reception, the phone's going wild and your coffee-break ended fifteen minutes ago, so will you take that inane smile off your face, pull yourself together and get back to bloody work? If this happens again,' he added fiercely, 'you're going to lose your job.'

He loves me, thought Holly, still in a daze. He's tall and dark and he never smiles but that doesn't matter. Because now I know that Max Monahan, beneath that dark, terrifying exterior, really does love me . . .

Antonia stared moodily out through the drawing-room windows at the rainswept drive, along which Ross no longer drove. She could have screamed at the thin, blond stranger who had interrupted their reunion in the swimming-pool; since then, she had hung around the hotel like a goddam groupie and had been cut dead by Ross every time. And the pain-in-the-neck fact was that the more he ignored her, the greater her fascination with him grew.

Bored and fractious, she slumped down lengthways across the pale yellow, silk upholstered sofa and picked up the newspaper Richard had left behind, folded open as usual at the boring financial section. For several seconds the only sound in the room, apart from the slow, echoing tick of the grandfather clock, was the rustle of irritably turned pages. Abruptly, the rustling stopped. Ross's name leapt out of the gossip column like an explosion. Scanning the lines, Antonia experienced actual physical nausea as she read the sycophantically worded article proclaiming his impending fatherhood and his apparent devotion to the blonde artist, Tessa Duvall, with whom he had attended antenatal classes in Bath.

Dropping the newspaper to the floor, Antonia gazed once more at the deserted driveway. So the girl had been smart enough to get herself pregnant, she thought, closing her eyes and imagining the unfashionably dressed blonde with her revolting, disfiguring bulge. And so far, it appeared, Ross was humouring her, presumably revelling in the excitement of impending fatherhood.

But Antonia knew him too well to be seriously disturbed by what she had learned. Ross might have fallen prey to the apparent novelty of the situation but the reality would soon pall, of that she had no doubt. Ross simply was not cut out for that kind of commitment. It was a shock, she concluded as the nausea slowly receded, but not a terrible shock. It wasn't something to worry too badly about, simply because she knew Ross too well. In a few months, decided Antonia with smug satisfaction, he would be hard pushed to even remember the little tart's name.

Mattie didn't know whether to be relieved or angry when she'd finished reading the article in the newspaper.

She felt sorry for the pregnant girl, of course. Tessa Duvall, blonde artist, didn't know what she was letting herself in for. Mattie wondered whether she had done it deliberately, hoping that Ross would in turn offer to marry her.

But the news about the baby wasn't going to be easy for Grace to come to terms with, either. Coming as it did on top of everything else, her sense of loss could only be heightened, and who knew how she would feel, having to watch and listen to Ross extolling the virtues of fatherhood?

Since she steadfastly refused to change her job and move away from the hotel, however, there seemed to be nothing more that Mattie could do to help her.

'You're famous,' crowed Holly, waving the paper in Tessa's face. 'Look, they've even spelt your name right. What a shame there isn't a photo.'

'Of me, flat on my back with my legs in the air?' Tessa raised her eyebrows. 'Now that *would* put people off their food. I knew something like this would happen,' she went on, loading her brush with yellow ochre and applying it with quick, deft strokes to the canvas. 'Ross must be regretting it now.'

'It was Ross who showed me the article. He's been reading it to everyone. Tess, he's as proud as . . . as a new father!'

'Don't worry,' said Tessa, concentrating on her painting. 'The novelty will wear off. He'll be back to normal soon enough.'

'You should get Rosa Polonowski to read your palm,' said Holly smugly, having already regaled Tessa at length with the details of her own dazzling future.

'She wouldn't be able to see it,' Tessa retorted, holding up her hands. 'My destiny is well and truly sealed. By paint.'

Grace wouldn't have seen the article in the gossip column if she hadn't bumped into Sylvie Nash that lunchtime in a coffee shop in Bath.

'Grace, how are you?' exclaimed Sylvie, her arms entwined around her boyfriend and her short black skirt hitched up to reveal a great deal of tanned thigh. 'Heard the latest about Ross?'

Sensitive to the name and swallowing hard, Grace shook her head. 'No, what?'

'It was in the paper today. He's going to be a daddy! Lucky baby,' said Sylvie, who liked to keep her jealous boyfriend on his toes. She pouted and smiled at Grace. 'Imagine having Ross Monahan as a father.'

'Imagine,' echoed Grace automatically, moving towards the door. Desperation gripped her. She needed a drink, fast. And a copy of whichever newspaper had printed the news.

'She's a funny little thing,' murmured Sylvie as Grace sidled out of the café. 'So quiet. She still doesn't look well, does she?'

'The quiet ones are the worst,' replied her boyfriend with a smirk. 'I bet I could cheer her up, put a bit of colour in her cheeks.'

'Just try it,' retaliated Sylvie, bristling with jealousy. 'And you'd find out what it feels like to have *real* colour in your cheeks.'

Chapter 20

'My God,' shouted Holly, above the incredible noise of whirling propellers as the helicopter circled high above the racecourse. 'I can't believe how *big* it is!'

'Ah, those words,' said Ross with a grin. 'Music to my ears . . .'

Holly burst out laughing and Max stared pointedly out of the small side window, ignoring their ribaldry and wondering – not for the first time – how such a special and long-awaited day could have so rapidly deteriorated. What else, he ruminated, could go wrong now?

But that didn't even bear thinking about. Crazy Daisy, the all-black five-year-old with a mercurial temperament and all the determination of a crusader, meant the world to him. If anything should happen to her during the course of this afternoon's big race he didn't know what he would do.

He had hired the helicopter, a gleaming red-and-white, ludicrously expensive Bell Jet Ranger, for Francine and himself. When she had contacted him last week all the old feelings had resurfaced. She was returning to England for a few days, she had told him, her husky, accented voice shimmering over the phone line from Normandy, and yes, she would adore to attend Ascot with Max to watch his horse competing in the race for the prestigious Amerson Cup.

And then, the day before the race meeting, he had received not a phone call but an impersonal fax from Francine, bluntly informing him that she would not, after all, be able to come to England. Just that. No excuses, no apologies. He could only presume, bitterly, that some other suitor had arrived on the scene dangling a larger and more interesting carrot with which to entice her away.

Hiding his disappointment, he had invited Ross to go with him instead. Ross, upon learning that the helicopter was a five-seater, had promptly said, 'That's great, we'll take Tessa along with us.' And then, for some reason Max couldn't fathom, Holly King had managed to weasel her way on board and his carefully planned outing *à deux* had disintegrated completely. Holly kept prattling on about some fortune teller and the vital importance of dark horses. She prattled on, full stop. Her ridiculous outfit, with its geranium-red lace and gravity-defying matching hat, may have been suitable for Ladies' Day, but for a race meeting in blustery March it was ludicrously inappropriate.

It was all bitterly disappointing. Max wished, now more than ever as they began their noisy descent, that he had driven up to the meeting instead. Alone.

But when the helicopter finally came to rest on the wind-flattened grass and the doors slid open, even Max's sense of irritation was banished. The electric atmosphere of Race Day and the buzz of excitement and adrenalin were irresistible. Ross lifted Tessa down and Max turned to help Holly, who was teetering on the step in scarlet high heels. At least her overpowering scent would be diluted now that they were out in the open air, he thought with amused resignation, although in that dress there wasn't a hope in hell of losing her in the crowd.

Hanging on to Max, Holly jumped. By the time her feet touched the ground her ruffled skirt was up around her waist, exposing emerald-green French knickers, pale, plump thighs and bright pink suspenders.

Holly was out to impress Max but she hadn't planned on going quite this far. Not so soon, anyway. With a shriek of embarrassment she tugged her dress down to her knees and almost fell over because her heels had sunk into the soft ground. Ross roared with laughter.

'If you were a gentleman you'd lend her your shoes,' protested Tessa.

'If Holly were a lady,' Ross countered, 'she wouldn't own a flamingo-pink suspender belt, let alone wear one.' Winking at Holly, he added, 'In public.'

Over a light lunch in the Arundel Restaurant, at the east end of the grandstand, Max's mood continued to improve. He had been to visit Crazy Daisy, who was on great form, and whom the good-to-soft going suited to perfection. Ross was chatting to an old college friend and getting stuck into the Bollinger, and Holly and Tessa were poring over the racing pages of the *Sporting Times*, studying form and pretending to know what they were talking about. Holly, who was still obsessed with dark horses, wanted to put a tenner each way on Black Monday in the first race. Tessa, listing her own prospective winners, was taking more notice of the colours of the jockeys' silks than of the horses' prowess. Pink and lilac, to match her own oversized striped blazer and loose top and trousers, featured heavily among her selection. Women, thought Max with exasperation, had a bizarre logic all their own. Particularly Tessa Duvall. He still hadn't made up his mind about her at all.

* * *

Tessa, despite her earlier misgivings, was also enjoying herself. When Ross had invited her to make up a threesome with Max and himself she had laughed aloud at the absurdity of the idea. An uneasy truce was one thing but Max – whom she suspected was more taken with Francine Lalonde than he let on – hadn't been in the sunniest of moods since his return from Amalfi. His occasional barbed comments and cynical looks served as a reminder of what he really thought of her.

But even as she had been ticking off on her fingers all the reasons why her presence at the races would ruin everyone's day, Holly had interceded.

'But it's fate, Tess!' she'd exclaimed, grabbing the sleeve of Ross's jacket in her excitement. 'Don't you see? When Rosa Polonowski talked about my dark horse I didn't even know that Max had bought Crazy Daisy. And it's doubly significant because Max is *my* dark horse . . . oh Tess, it could change my whole life. We have to go!'

'We?' queried Tessa, glancing across at Ross and marvelling at Holly's nerve. But Ross, recognizing that Tessa would go if Holly went with them, agreed at once.

'No problem,' he said, grinning at Holly. 'It's a five-seater. And you have the day off anyway. That's settled then.'

Tessa frowned. 'But won't . . .?'

'Leave Max to me,' said Ross, blithely ignoring the prospect of his brother's wrath. 'I'm sure he'll understand when I tell him that it could change his whole life.'

After lunch they made their way through the crowds down to the ground floor where the betting shops were situated. Tessa was shocked when she heard Ross placing his bets. She was putting a pound on each horse and he was pushing piles of tenners across the counter, joking with the cashier and stuffing the betting slips into his back pocket as casually as if they were bus tickets.

And he knew so many people, she thought in bemusement. They'd only arrived an hour and a half ago and already he'd bumped into a dozen or so old friends and acquaintances.

They simply led different lives, she reminded herself as they headed off to watch the first race. Different lifestyles, different values. And because of those fundamental differences they could never share a real relationship.

So it was sad, but hardly a revelation. Vowing not to let it spoil their day she allowed Ross to take her hand and guide her towards the crowded staircase.

'Pregnant woman,' he announced, so that all around him could hear. 'Come on, make way for the pregnant woman. Take deep breaths, darling, and time those contractions. And, for heaven's sake, try not to give birth during the race.'

Crazy Daisy was running in the third race of the afternoon. Having won only one race so far this season she was considered to be pretty much of an outsider at 66–1. Max, behaving like an anxiety-ridden father, told anyone who would listen that while, of course, she wouldn't win, there was always a chance that she might be placed. When Colin Eames, Daisy's trainer, visited them briefly in their box high above the grandstand, he whispered to Tessa that she should put her money on Hard as Nails, the 7–4 second favourite.

'But surely Daisy has a chance?' said Holly loyally. She had gone mad and bet twenty pounds to win on Max's all-important dark horse, as well as a tenner each way on Secret Desire in the second race.

'Every horse has a chance,' replied Colin diplomatically. 'But don't hold your breath. The going might suit Daisy but she hasn't had the experience over three miles. We're just hoping she has a good race today, that's all.'

When Max told Tessa for the tenth time that Daisy was a great little horse but that they mustn't expect her to win, she almost felt sorry for him. With his ashen face and unsteady hands he looked as if he was suffering from a bad case of stage-fright.

'And bloody Holly's not helping at all,' he complained. 'She's convinced that Daisy's going to win.'

'Have another drink,' urged Tessa, swiping a half-empty bottle from Ross's grasp and refilling Max's glass. 'Owning race horses can damage one's health, it seems. And calm down, Max. It's not as if we're going to refuse to speak to you if Daisy finishes last. We're supposed to be having fun.'

The first race was fun, for Tessa at least. The sun came out, the huge crowd roared the horses round the course and amid a crescendo of cheers, groans and wild applause the evens favourite, a big grey called Derelict, stormed past the finishing post, his jockey a blur of pink and white on his back.

Tessa won two pounds. Holly's choice, Black Monday, was seventh. Ross lost fifty pounds on a chestnut mare who tipped her rider neatly into the water at the third.

Holly was having a fabulous time anyway. It didn't matter in the least that Black Monday hadn't won – as far as she was concerned it simply proved that Daisy would. And she revelled in her role of professional cheerer-upper, reassuring an increasingly jittery Max that in no time at all he would have his hands on both the Amerson Cup and the vast winner's cheque that went with it. With her hat firmly secured by half a dozen hat pins and her skirt remaining decorously around her knees, Holly was convinced that she looked like a real racehorse owner's girl-friend. Ascot, she decided, was her kind of place.

At that moment an ear-splitting whistle pierced the air, closely followed by a flying champagne cork which, having been lobbed with unerring accuracy, bounced off the wide brim of her hat and dropped neatly into her cleavage.

'Goal!' roared a voice, amid much male laughter. 'Hey, Holly! I've lost my cork. Can I come up and look for it?'

Snatching the offending missile from its resting place and blushing so hard that she clashed with her hat, Holly moved away from the balcony. Damn Adam Perry and his big mouth! How *dare* he humiliate her like this? And how could he take such noisy delight in doing so?

'Nice friends you have, Holly,' murmured Max, glancing over the edge of the parapet at the crowds below. 'Who is he, a boy-friend of yours?'

'No, he is not!' she spluttered. 'He's an ill-mannered pig. I wouldn't go out with him if he were the last man left on the planet.'

'Mmm,' said Max mildly. 'Well, he's blowing kisses in this direction and I don't think they're meant for me.'

'He's revolting,' replied Holly dismissively, snatching up her racing guide and pretending to study it.

'Well, I think he's coming up to see you anyway.'

'Oh my God!' she cried, mortified. If Adam Perry wrecked her big chance with Max she'd kill him with her bare hands.

How he managed to get past security she didn't have a chance to find out. Thirty seconds later Adam swaggered into their private box, lifted Holly off the ground and hugged her so hard she thought she'd burst out of her dress.

'Holly, look at you! What a sight for bloodshot eyes! And fancy bumping into you here. Hi,' he added, turning to the rest of them and flashing a grin in Tessa's direction. 'Adam Perry. Nice to meet all of you. I'm the one Holly's going to marry,' he continued blithely, 'just as soon as I get my name changed by deed poll. By this time next week I'll be Adam Day and then pretty soon after that this gorgeous girl, for better or for worse, will be—'

Seeing the shame and loathing in Holly's eyes, Max cut in. 'Actually,' he said, his tone pleasant but firm, 'the lady is with me. And she'll be with me next month . . . and the month after that . . . so if I were you I'd shelve the wedding plans. If anyone is getting married it's Holly and myself, OK?'

Ross, whom Adam Perry couldn't see, was struggling to control his laughter. Tessa held her breath, praying that nothing awful would happen. Holly, released from Adam's bulky grasp, almost fainted.

But Adam, instantly contrite, reached for Max's hand and shook it. 'I'm sorry, truly I am. I had no idea that Holly was . . . involved. I do hope I haven't offended anyone.'

'Not at all,' replied Max smoothly.

Adam shrugged and looked relieved. 'Well, I'd better return to my party. You're a lucky man, if I may say so. Holly's a wonderful girl. Far too good for the likes of me anyway.' Then he flashed another grin, encompassing them all. 'But one can always hope. Maybe one day I'll get lucky and find myself a girl as gorgeous as this one. Goodbye then, Mr . . .'

'Monahan,' said Max, shaking his hand once more.

'Mr Monahan,' said Adam, nodding his head in recognition. 'Of course. And Holly,' he added, turning to her, 'once again, I am sorry. Maybe next time we bump into each other you'll be Mrs Monahan. Anyway, I hope you'll be very happy together.'

'I'm sure we will,' said Max, smiling at Holly and giving her arm a gentle, affectionate squeeze.

Holly, unable to speak at all, merely nodded.

The second race passed her by in a blur. She didn't even realize her horse had won until Tessa prised open her fingers and extracted the screwed-up bundle of betting slips.

'Tess, I can't believe it,' she whispered, gazing at Max's broad back as he leaned against the parapet.

'Neither can I,' said Tessa, flattening out the crumpled winning slip with the heel of her hand. 'Secret Desire, a tenner each way . . . at twenty to one . . . that's over two hundred pounds!'

Holly smiled to herself. Tessa, always so down to earth and practical, simply didn't understand. But it was really, really happening at last. Her whole life was about to change, just as Rosa Polonowski had predicted . . .

Chapter 21

By the time the horses were lined up at the start for the Amerson Cup, Max was chain-smoking. He'd watched Crazy Daisy racing before, of course, but this was different, her first really big race, and he'd never felt so wound up in his life. He knew she didn't have a chance of winning but still ... it was impossible not to imagine that maybe, just maybe, by some outrageous miracle ...

'She's beautiful,' said Tessa, at his side. She was peering through binoculars at the line-up, her expression intent, her swollen stomach resting lightly against the stone parapet. '*And* your jockey's wearing a pink cap. They can't fail.'

'She won't win,' repeated Max automatically. 'I just want her to have a good race. I just hope that—'

'Well, I want her to bloody well win,' declared Ross, coming between them and taking over the binoculars. 'And our staff will be pretty pissed off if she doesn't,' he added with a grin, 'seeing as I've put next month's salaries on her.'

Seconds later they were off. Holly, having recovered her voice, yelled until her lungs were burning. Tessa clung on to Ross. At the end of the first circuit Crazy Daisy was lying in tenth place and the field was beginning to spread out. Max, scarcely able to watch, held his breath as one of the leaders fell at the ditch. Daisy's jockey pulled her over to the left just in time to avoid ploughing into the fallen horse. She cleared the water jump, edged past two more contenders and kicked out her heels as she charged over the next fence. Daisy was enjoying herself, which was more than he was. With Ross and Holly now yelling together, urging Daisy on, Max closed his eyes for a second.

'Max, look!' gasped Tessa, grabbing him. 'She's over-taken Hard as Nails! She's *flying*!'

Desperately in need of another cigarette but knowing that he wouldn't be capable of lighting one, he gripped the edge of the parapet. Another fence was cleared . . . then another . . . and now Daisy was lying in fourth place with only three furlongs to go.

'COME ON DAISY!' screamed Holly above the tremendous roar of the crowd, and suddenly Max found himself clutching her hand. Glancing down, he saw that he had been squeezing it so tightly that her fingers were blue.

But now he really couldn't bear to watch the race. If he looked up, Daisy would fall. The crowd's screams were deafening, Holly was leaping up and down beside him and the horses were approaching the final fence.

'She's gaining on them,' said Tessa in wonder. Seconds later, realizing that Max was still unable to watch, she said, 'They're over the last and she's overtaken the favourite. Max, you have to see her!'

He straightened up, narrowing his eyes and focusing on the horses as they stormed up towards the finish. Daisy was lying in third place, a length behind the second and a length and a half behind the leader. And even as he realized that he couldn't yell, couldn't utter a single sound, she accelerated again, her timing perfect, her black tail flying . . .

The crowd went wild. Holly, ripping off her hat, hurled it into the air and didn't even see it as it cartwheeled down towards the spectators below. She was in Max's arms, hugging him, being hugged in return and so overwhelmed with happiness that she almost wept.

Then Max, in a daze, was kissing Tessa and Ross was uncorking a magnum of Bollinger which Max hadn't even known he'd bought.

'To darling Daisy,' pronounced Ross, handing them each a too-hastily filled glass and lifting his own into the air. 'Another ten feet and she would have won. But second place is more of a miracle than any of us really dared hope for. To Daisy,' he toasted, and they all clinked foaming glasses. 'God bless her and all those who had an each-way bet on her. I don't know about the rest of you,' he added, pulling Tessa to his side and dropping a kiss on the tip of her nose, 'but I've just won eight and a half thousand pounds.'

'We have to go and see her,' said Max, his hand shaking dreadfully as he put down his glass. Semi-drunk on elation and Bollinger he looked down and found that somehow his arm had found its way around Holly's waist. 'Coming with me?'

Holly, her stomach sucked in and her entire being focused on the glorious sensation of Max's fingers actually touching her midriff, vowed to go on a diet. She could smell his aftershave, feel his warmth. She could almost swear that those were actual tears in his dark eyes.

'We'll all go,' declared Ross, grabbing Tessa's hand. 'I want to see her as well. But I have to warn you,' he added with a wink in Max's direction, 'I've fallen in love with that horse. If Crazy Daisy asks me to marry her I'm going to accept.'

Realizing that she didn't feel quite right but not knowing what was wrong, Tessa was keeping her dilemma to herself. It had been a wonderful day, the realization that Max was actually human had been a gratifying one, Holly was so ecstatic she was practically on another planet and Ross had been in tearing spirits, fussing over her, making her laugh and doing his best to ensure that she was enjoying herself.

But she sensed now that his patience was beginning to wear thin.

It wasn't easy, thought Tessa, pretending to have fun when everyone else was getting plastered and you were stone-cold sober. It was even harder when they were celebrating and you were wondering why – after six marvellously trouble-free months – you should suddenly be experiencing a dull, aching sensation in the pit of your stomach. She was no garage mechanic but it felt exactly as if her big-end had gone.

'I'll wait here,' she told Ross, as Holly and Max left the box. He looked blank. 'Tess, you can't! We're going to see Daisy. She's just run the race of her life.'

'And you've fallen in love with her,' said Tessa, attempting to make light of the situation and failing utterly. 'Maybe I'm jealous. Look, I just want to stay here. I'll see you when you get back.'

'Are you OK?' he asked, concerned but at the same time struggling to suppress a niggling irritation. He'd worked so hard to make the day a good one for Tessa and now she was throwing it back in his face and looking merely bored. When she assumed that closed expression which so annoyed him he knew that she was shutting him out, and that the happy, carefree intimacy between them had been lost.

'I'm fine,' she retaliated shortly.

'Right,' said Ross, turning to leave. 'We'll see you later. Don't have too much fun on your own, will you.'

Holly guessed that something was wrong as soon as she spotted Ross and Colin Eames' daughter standing together in a far corner of the yard. She didn't know what they were discussing but there was a lot of universal body language going on which needed no explanation. Rachel Eames, a nubile nineteen-year-old, was tossing back her thick black hair, licking her pale lips and touching Ross's arm for emphasis every time she leaned forward to whisper in his ear. Ross was making her laugh. Neither of them was taking a blind bit of notice of Daisy, who was high-stepping jauntily around the stable yard in her white blanket, enjoying all the attention being paid to her by Max, Colin Eames, her stable lad and other assorted well-wishers.

Emboldened by alcohol and by her own happiness, Holly made her way – somewhat unsteadily in her high heels – across the cobbled yard.

'A private word, if you wouldn't mind,' she said, addressing Ross but managing at the same time to cast a supercilious glance in Rachel Eames' general direction.

'You have that crusading look about you,' remarked Ross, when they were alone. He wasn't smiling now.

'So what's up?' she countered. 'Bloody hell, Ross, why do you have to *do* it? What are you trying to prove?'

His dark eyes narrowed. 'We were only talking.'

'Bullshit,' replied Holly flatly. 'You were deliberately flirting with her. And where's Tessa?'

'Couldn't be bothered to come,' he drawled. 'Just not interested enough to make the effort. And you don't need me to remind you how stubborn she can be when—'

'She's pregnant, for heaven's sake!' exploded Holly. 'Maybe

she's tired. Has that small possibility even occurred to you or have you been too busy chatting up other women to think about it?'

Ross shot her a look of sheer disbelief. 'We are talking about the same Tessa Duvall, are we? My God, she's as strong as an ox! She walks for miles, rides that bloody bike of hers everywhere and *refuses* to borrow my car . . . she's got more stamina than I have. Holly, Tessa is simply bored.' He gestured in despair towards Daisy and her circle of admirers. 'I wanted her to have such a great time today. I wanted to show her the kind of lifestyle she could have with me. Any normal female would be impressed . . . aren't *you* impressed by all this?'

It was a plea for reassurance which Holly was unable to resist. Ross wasn't used to being given a hard time and he was at a loss to know how to deal with it. And although she wouldn't dare tell him so, it rather suited him.

She smiled, then shivered. The pale sun was disappearing behind a bank of dirty grey clouds and a light breeze was blowing. 'Tessa *has* enjoyed herself. It's been a marvellous day. But she is pregnant and pregnant women sometimes need to take it easy. It helps,' she said sternly, 'if their male companions show a bit of consideration. Storming off and chatting up the first girl they come across doesn't solve anything. Neither,' she added casually, 'does taking their phone number.'

Ross grinned. Holly wasn't a bad old thing. She certainly wasn't slow, either. Removing his dark blue blazer and draping it around her shoulders, he pulled a crumpled racing slip from the top pocket and tucked it into Holly's palm.

'She gave me her number,' he said, his good temper restored. 'But don't worry, I wasn't going to use it.'

'I know you weren't,' Holly replied complacently, shredding

the slip of paper and watching the pieces scatter like confetti in the breeze. 'She wasn't your type.'

'In that case, we'd better be heading back,' said Ross with a rueful smile. 'Or my type will be wondering where we've got to.'

By the time they had watched the video re-run of Crazy Daisy's magnificent race in the Pall Mall bar, hedge-hopped by helicopter to a restaurant bordering Windsor Great Park and enjoyed a noisy, celebratory meal, it was nine o'clock. The dull ache in Tessa's stomach had disappeared. Putting her feet up and resting quietly for twenty minutes had done the trick and it hadn't even been necessary to mention its existence. Neither had she needed to apologize to Ross for her abruptness earlier; on returning to the box with Max and Holly, he had squeezed her hand briefly, murmured, 'My fault. I'm sorry,' and gazed at her with such longing that for a second her knees had threatened to buckle.

'It wasn't your fault, it was—' she had begun to say, but Ross placed his finger against her lips, stopping her.

'Ssshh. I don't often apologize. Make the most of it while you can. Besides, I have great news.'

'What?'

'I asked Daisy to marry me.' He paused. 'She turned me down. Said I wasn't her type.'

'You poor man!' exclaimed Tessa. 'But why is that great news?'

Ross winked. 'Well, it means I'm still single, available and open to offers . . .'

'The best day ever,' sighed Holly, when she and Tessa were at last alone together in the Ladies' cloakroom. 'Tess, can you believe the difference in Max?'

Tessa, pushing a comb through her windswept hair, said, 'You mean he's sawn off his horns?'

'I mean he's actually being nice to me,' said Holly with pride. Puckering her lips she leaned towards the mirror and applied a generous layer of bright scarlet lipstick. 'More than nice. He told Adam where to get off, didn't he? When he said we were going to be married I almost fainted.'

'Don't get too carried away,' warned Tessa gently. 'He only said that to get you out of an awkward situation.'

But Holly, spraying scent down her cleavage and in a wild circle around her head, was undeterred. 'Ah,' she countered triumphantly, 'he only *thinks* he said it to get me out of an awkward situation. Deep down, he means it. He just doesn't know it yet!'

They were halfway home when Tessa was seized by the first wave of pain. Real pain this time, clawing at her stomach and taking her so much by surprise that she cried out.

'Sorry,' said Ross, assuming that he had accidentally stuck his elbow into her ribs. Then he saw that her hands were clutching her stomach, and that her eyes were closed. 'Tess, what's wrong?' he said urgently, but she shook her head.

'I don't know. It hurts . . .'

'Jesus! Max, we've got to get Tessa to a hospital. Tell the pilot to land. Where the hell are we, anyway?'

Holly, biting her lip, put her arm around Tessa. Max, swivelling round in the front seat, saw the pain etched into her face. She was deathly pale and trembling, shocked by the suddenness of the onslaught and no doubt worried sick by the thought of what it might mean.

But as the pilot pointed out, there was no point in making an unscheduled landing. They were twenty minutes from Bath and they could land in the grounds of the Royal United Hospital. All Tessa could do until then was grit her teeth and hang on. And pray that the pain didn't get any worse.

The remainder of the journey was in sad contrast with their joyous mood of earlier. Ross held Tessa in his arms, his murmured reassurances punctuating an otherwise tense silence. Holly, who never bit her nails, chewed them down to the quick. Max stared out of the window, scanning the black landscape dotted with lights and despising himself for wondering whether – in the long run – a miscarriage now might not be a blessing in disguise.

When they finally landed in the centre of a cricket pitch adjacent to the hospital Ross lifted Tessa gently down from her seat. Max and Holly, at Tessa's request, were to return to the hotel, where Ross could contact them as soon as there was anything to report.

'Don't worry,' said Tessa, attempting to reassure them. 'I'm sure everything will be fine.'

'I know it will.' Holly kissed her, smiling with a confidence she didn't feel.

'I'll phone,' said Ross briefly and turned towards the hospital, carrying Tessa.

'Your jacket will be ruined,' she said weakly. 'I can feel it. I'm so sorry.'

'My God,' he replied, gazing down at her and willing everything to be all right – for he too could feel the sticky warmth of lost blood against his arm – 'you've said some stupid things in your time, Tessa Duvall . . .'

Chapter 22

'You'd think we were expecting Elizabeth Taylor,' grumbled Sylvie as she handed over to Holly at the end of her shift. 'I've never seen Ross in such a bossy mood – and that's saying something! Your friend Tessa must be hot stuff.'

'She's pretty fragile stuff at the moment,' said Holly, glancing at the list Sylvie was leaving her and seeing that as usual she was being stuck with all the ultra-boring tasks which Sylvie never seemed to have time to get round to doing. 'And she didn't want to stay here but Ross insisted. She has to have complete bedrest and there's no way she could do that at home. Ross and I ganged up on her and made her see that this was the only sensible solution.'

'Mmm,' sighed Sylvie. 'I must say, I wouldn't kick up too much of a fuss. I can think of worse things than lazing around in bed and being waited on hand, foot and finger by Ross Monahan.'

Tessa couldn't. By the end of her first day at The Grange she realized that she was in danger of being driven completely crazy. If she hadn't been so acutely aware of the need to stay in bed she would have run away. And, most frustrating of all, she couldn't even scream at Ross because he was doing it all for her.

There were flowers everywhere, great bowls of carnations in a dozen shades of pink, overpoweringly scented white roses and tall vases of blue iris.

There were jugs of fresh orange juice, baskets of fruit, piles of glossy magazines, virgin pads of thick drawing paper, boxes of pencils – 3H to 5B – and a Sony Walkman.

There was a huge colour television, a video recorder and a stacking stereo. With tapes.

There was a telephone, as well as a little button beside the bed which she only needed to press in order to summon assistance from downstairs.

And downstairs there was a chef who, at the drop of a hat, would prepare for her whatever light but nutritious meal might take her fancy.

It was all very luxurious, and extremely nice.

But there was also Ross, and she wondered why on earth he'd thought she would ever need the little bedside button, because he was always *there*. Hovering. Asking her how she was feeling. Pouring her yet another glass of unwanted orange juice. Squashing her feet every time he sat down on the end of her bed. And getting on Tessa's nerves to a serious degree.

The hotel, presumably, was managing to muddle through without him, although she had only his word for that. Now, in his faded denims and pale pink sweatshirt, he was lounging in a chair beside her with his long legs stretched out before him, seemingly happy to spend the rest of the evening doing nothing more businesslike than the crossword.

This, she decided, was even worse than being in hospital, where there had at least been the distraction of bustling nurses, fellow patients and a gregarious Irish cleaner by the name of Fidelma O'Feharty, who had made no secret of her admiration for Ross.

Being the subject of his undivided attention, however, was downright exhausting. Ross was watching over her more closely than any kidnapper. And Tessa, who hated any kind of fuss, simply wanted to be left alone.

'I'll have a word with him,' said Holly bravely, the following morning. Ross, having been forced downstairs to keep a long-standing appointment, had left Holly in charge of the patient. He was, he assured her, only a button-press away. 'But you *do* have to rest,' she added, 'and he's only trying to help.'

'Extremely trying,' murmured Tessa with a wry smile.

'But if he doesn't take any notice of me – and he doesn't normally – you'll just have to lie back and suffer his unwanted attentions like a lady. And be grateful,' Holly added seriously, 'that at least the baby is all right.'

'I know, I know. I am grateful,' said Tessa, tipping her fruit juice – pineapple, today – into the nearest flower vase. 'And Ross has been wonderful. It was so reassuring, having him there at the hospital during those first few days. I don't know how I would have coped without him.' She paused, pushing her hair away from her face and staring pensively at her bare toes. 'But that's half the trouble, don't you see? He's making himself indispensable and I'm beginning to rely on him. I mean *really* rely on him, and it scares me.'

'Well?' demanded Ross, bursting into the room an hour later. 'What the bloody hell have you been telling that bitch downstairs?'

Tessa's heart sank as he hurled his jacket in the direction of the nearest chair, ripped off his tie and landed with a furious thud on the end of the bed. She managed to move her feet away just in time.

'I only—'

'You told her that I was suffocating you,' he interjected icily.

It was just as well, thought Tessa, that Holly hadn't chosen a career in the diplomatic corps. Not wanting a full-scale argument – she was, after all, supposed to be keeping her blood pressure down – she reached out and touched Ross's arm. 'I'm sorry, I didn't mean it to sound like that. But you're doing everything for me and I'm used to looking after myself. It seems weird, that's all.'

Ross relaxed slightly, his expression softening. 'Right now,' he said, 'you need looking after. OK, maybe I've been going over the top a bit, but I've never done this kind of thing before. And I do *like* looking after you,' he added with a crooked smile.

'I like it too,' said Tessa weakly. All of a sudden the tensions and fears and muddled emotions of the past ten days appeared to be catching up with her. She thought she might burst into tears. Her defences were crashing down around her, no longer under her own control. She didn't have the energy to concoct excuses and was too exhausted to lie. 'I like it,' she repeated slowly, her vision blurring as tears welled up in her eyes. 'And that's why I'm afraid.'

Ross, touched beyond words by her admission and by her vulnerability, moved towards her. He drew Tessa into his arms just as the first tear slid down her cheek. And, exerting superhuman control, he confined his kisses to her forehead and temple. Only when she had finally stopped crying did he lift her face to his and brush his mouth lightly against her parted lips. And when he felt Tessa responding, her fingers splaying against his shoulders and her body shifting slightly in order to fit more closely against his own, he felt as if he had won a great battle. That indescribable magic was still there, as he had known it would be, but now at last he had succeeded in proving to Tessa that it still existed. And that it was too precious and too important to ignore.

'I've never done that before,' he said, minutes later. Tessa was still curled up beside him, but in deference to her blood pressure – and his own – she was sipping a glass of grapefruit juice and he had poured himself a small Scotch.

She glanced up at him in disbelief. 'Done what?'

'Kissed someone. Like that.' He paused, then grinned. 'Knowing that my intentions were entirely honourable.'

Tessa patted his hand. 'You poor thing. All that effort and no end result. Here you are, in bed with a celibate. Life's really a bitch, isn't it?'

'Don't be flippant,' said Ross, hurt. 'It's not like that at all.'

'Novelty value, then.' Tessa forced a wan smile, knowing it to be the truth. 'Don't worry, it'll soon wear off.'

'Why can't you take me seriously?' he demanded, putting down his tumbler of Scotch and forcing her to meet his gaze. 'It's not novelty value at all.' He paused for a moment, his dark eyes quite serious, his heart racing. 'Nothing's changed. I still love you. And I still want you to marry me.'

This time, Tessa didn't laugh. This time it wasn't so funny. She was beginning to feel that the harder she struggled to retain her independence the more determined Ross became to take it from her. And right now she didn't know whether she had the strength of will to keep fighting for it.

She was no longer even sure that what she had been doing was right. How many girls, after all, would reject a man like Ross? He radiated charm, was devastatingly attractive and a spectacular lover. He was successful. And wealthy. And he could make her laugh.

And the more Tessa tried to tell herself that such a relationship couldn't possibly last because he was also by nature capricious, easily bored and a notorious womanizer, the more effort he put into disproving it. He had been unfailingly kind and patient with her, had behaved like a model father-to-be and – as far as she was aware – was showing absolutely no interest at all in other women.

Very soon she would have no grounds for reasonable argument left.

'You know,' said Ross slowly, 'this habit of yours of not replying when I ask you to marry me isn't exactly doing a great deal for my morale.'

'Ah.' Tessa smiled up at him. 'But it's doing wonders for mine.'

'And?'

She shrugged. 'Can't we just see how things go for a while?'

'Is that a yes,' demanded Ross impatiently, 'or a no?'

'It's a let's-just-see-how-things-go-for-a-while,' Tessa replied in soothing tones.

He raised his eyes to the ceiling in an attitude of despair. 'Ever thought of becoming a politician?'

Ross had been intending to take Tessa's lunch tray upstairs to her himself, but Holly had intercepted him at the foot of the staircase. She was putting a call from Florida through to his office and it couldn't wait.

'Here,' said Ross, pushing the loaded tray into Grace's hands as she sidled past him. More withdrawn than ever, she hadn't even thanked him for the flowers he had delivered to her doorstep. Her pale face wore a permanently haunted expression and she still looked decidedly unwell. 'Can you take this up to Tessa? She's in suite twelve.'

As if Grace didn't know.

'Come in,' called Tessa, when Grace tapped on the door. 'Oh, wonderful! How kind of you. Here, let me just clear this mess out of the way . . .'

Disarmed by Tessa's smile and by her energetic attempts to gather together the untidy pile of sketches spread around her on the bed, Grace overcame her shyness.

'You shouldn't be doing that.' Placing the tray on the bedside table, she took over, picking up the sketches and pausing to admire one of Holly. 'It looks just like her.'

Tessa lay back against the pillows and admired the girl's slenderness. She'd found herself becoming increasingly envious, recently, of people with waists.

'If you've got ten minutes to spare, I could do you. Now that I'm in exile up here I'm running out of subjects. Are you dreadfully busy downstairs?'

They were, but Grace couldn't resist the unexpected invitation. Helplessly obsessed with Ross Monahan, she was also wildly curious to discover as much as possible about those close to him. And if Tessa wasn't close, she didn't know who was.

'Your lunch . . .' she began, but Tessa dismissed the hesitant protest with a careless wave of her pencil. 'Cold salmon and green salad. I can't afford to get much fatter; I look like a Buddha as it is.'

Grace didn't think she looked like a Buddha. The room was warm and Tessa was sitting on the bed rather than in it, her legs stretched out in front of her. She wore a long white T-shirt and her blonde hair hung loose around her shoulders. The sunny room was filled with flowers, Tessa's eyes were friendly and her smile warm as she gestured to Grace to sit down. Grace, who had wondered whether she might hate this girl – Tessa had, after all, experienced in reality what she had fantasized over for months – was completely won over.

'Mr Monahan was going to bring you your lunch,' she said, seating herself nervously on the edge of the squashy chair. 'But he had to take a phone call.'

'Thank goodness,' exclaimed Tessa, only half-joking. 'I've sketched him at least half a dozen times in the past two days. You make a nice change. Could you turn your head slightly to the left? That's perfect.'

In her new position, Grace was able to see the pile of earlier sketches. Reaching across, she pushed aside the top two and picked up the third. Ross, his mocking, mesmerizing, thickly lashed dark eyes alight with amusement, regarded her with an affection that she herself had never experienced. Grace felt her heart hammering in her chest. It wasn't easy to breathe normally. Unable to remain silent, she said, 'He's handsome.'

'Tell us something we don't know,' said Tessa, pulling a wry face and concentrating on Grace's cheekbones. 'No, don't tense up. Sit back and relax.'

Mesmerized by the likeness of Ross, Grace said, 'My father was very handsome, too.'

'Was?' queried Tessa gently. 'What happened to him?'

A faint, sorrowful smile touched the corners of Grace's mouth. 'He's dead.'

'Mine too.' Tessa, working to capture the sad, sweet smile, spoke in matter-of-fact tones now, anxious not to provoke an outburst of tears. 'You can keep that if you want,' she added, seeing that the girl was still clutching the charcoal sketch of Ross. 'You could pin it up in the coffee room and throw darts at it whenever he gets too bossy.'

'For Christ's sake,' said Ross, bursting into the room five minutes later and casting an icy glare in Grace's direction. 'The restaurant's bursting at the seams with customers waiting to be served. What the hell do you think you're *doing* up here?'

'Don't get stroppy,' said Tessa, putting the finishing touches to her sketch. 'And don't shout at Grace, because it's my fault. I asked her to stay.'

'I'll shout at whomever I like,' he retaliated, but with less irritation now. 'It's my hotel.'

'I'd better go,' said Grace hurriedly. Her face was pink, her fingers agitated. Tessa winked at her and handed over the completed sketch.

'Don't worry, I won't let him take it out on you.'

'Thank you.' Grace gazed at the portrait, skilfully executed and capturing her likeness with astonishing accuracy. Rising to her feet, she glanced nervously at Ross and then once more at Tessa's swollen stomach. As a child she had always longed for a brother or sister. Now, bizarrely, she was getting one.

'Come on, come on,' sighed Ross, not bothering to conceal his impatience.

She had always wanted a father, too.

'Sorry, Mr Monahan,' whispered Grace.

'Thanks for sitting for me,' called out Tessa.

Ross frowned. 'You shouldn't encourage her,' he said, when Grace had closed the door behind her. 'She's always taking time off. There's something odd about that girl. I don't trust her at all.'

Chapter 23

They had been lucky; the weather conditions were perfect. A pale sun lit up an even paler sky and a mist hung low over the ground. The dozen or so hot-air balloons in various stages of inflation littered the field behind The Grange, their gaudy fairground colours at odds with the deadly serious expressions of those whose task it was to get the fickle creatures airborne. Tanks of liquid propane gas were checked, sandbags hauled into position, crown ropes tested and potential wind speeds anxiously calculated. For those who were prepared to pay for the privilege, travelling in a hot-air balloon was nothing more than fun, expensive but exhilarating. Those who owned them worked hard to keep it that way.

Antonia couldn't care less how the balloons stayed up; she just enjoyed the ride. Particularly since she had managed to wangle this flight with Ross.

Shoving her cold hands into the pockets of her ski jacket, she leaned back against the bonnet of Richard's bronze Audi and surveyed the two of them from a distance as they checked the security of the mooring ropes currently holding down the green-and-blue striped Nizo balloon, whose ownership was shared between Richard and a disappointingly ugly Frenchman named Maurice Bertrand.

Just watching Ross made Antonia feel better, more alive. In his pale denims and a white padded jacket, with his black hair curling over the collar and his hands resting casually on his lean hips, his desirability took her breath away. She had to get him back.

'You're looking well,' she told him an hour later, when they were finally airborne. The gas-jet roared as Maurice, his face mottled with cold, checked the dumping rope and consulted his compass. Totally wrapped up in the business of flying the balloon, he would pay no attention to whatever Antonia said. 'It can't be easy for you,' she added, keeping her voice low and moving closer to Ross.

'What can't be easy?' He wasn't looking at her. His dark eyes scanned the horizon. Below them, rows of toy-town houses the colour of bleached sand curved into the hillside. With the gas-jets closed, the silence was incredible. They were floating high above the city and the sensation, thought Antonia, was mind-blowingly erotic.

'It can't be easy for you,' she continued patiently. 'There's poor old Tessa, confined to bed and off-limits. Don't you find it ... frustrating?'

'Not in the least,' replied Ross with irritating cheerfulness. It was a blatant lie but he'd guessed at once what Antonia was up to and had no intention of playing along with her game. He wouldn't give her the satisfaction, any kind of satisfaction ...

'You surprise me.' Antonia blew on her hands in an attempt to warm them and thought how much nicer it would be to slip them beneath Ross's cashmere sweater. 'I've never thought of you as the celibate type.'

'Well, there you go,' he said complacently. 'I'm full of surprises.'

'You certainly were last year.' Glancing over her shoulder at

Maurice, Antonia lowered her voice still further. 'The last time we went up in this balloon together we joined the quarter-mile-high club. Don't you remember, darling?'

He smiled, quite impervious now to her unsubtle methods. 'You may have joined it last year. I was a founder member.'

'And you can't expect me to believe that you've changed,' she murmured, edging closer still. 'Ross, it's not natural! I know it's not poor Tessa's fault but she can't give you what you need, and since Richard did his back in the other week we haven't—'

'If I were you,' interrupted Ross briskly, 'I wouldn't keep calling her "poor Tessa". She's fine, the baby is fine and we're both very happy. And since I'm not terribly interested in hearing about your disrupted sex life, maybe you could give it a rest. Look,' he pointed below them, to a lone vehicle traversing a winding, tree-lined lane, 'there's Richard in the Land-Rover, heading towards Lansdowne.'

'Oh, sod Richard,' declared Antonia moodily. 'All he seems to do these days is complain about the amount of money I spend on clothes. If he only knew how much they really cost . . .'

'And how frequently you take them off,' he remarked, unable to resist the jibe.

This trip wasn't turning out as Antonia had planned. Thoroughly rattled, she turned and glared at him. 'Moralizing now? Ross, it really doesn't suit you.'

He shrugged, unconcerned.

'I give it two months. No,' she amended ruthlessly, 'six weeks.'

'Give it as long as you like,' said Ross with undisguised amusement. 'Just don't bother me. Last year was fun but that's all changed now. I'm going to marry Tessa.'

By this time even Maurice had to be listening but Antonia no longer cared. As her control slipped, her voice rose. The sudden whoosh of the propane gas-jets couldn't disguise her mounting agitation. 'Christ, that girl's clever! Don't you see what she's doing to you?'

'Since I can't very well shove you out of this basket,' he said, his dark eyes regarding her with bored detachment, 'I assume I'm going to find out anyway.'

'It's the oldest trick in the book!' screeched Antonia, bursting with the desperate unfairness of it all. 'She's got nothing, you've got everything. She deliberately got herself pregnant and then played hard to get. My God, anyone can pull a stunt like that . . . *I* could have done it!'

This was too much. It also bore a dangerous similarity to Max's own cynical interpretation of events. Ross, close to losing his own temper now, longed to shake Antonia until her teeth rattled. Instead he gripped the rim of the rough wicker basket so tightly that his knuckles turned white. 'You *could* have done it,' he agreed grimly. 'That's what's so scary, and I just thank God that I met Tessa in time. Women like you,' he added with deliberate cruelty, 'are a walking advertisement for condoms.'

'And you're a fucking hypocrite,' Antonia hissed back at him, pale lips narrowing to an ugly line. 'Because it won't be long before you're buying them wholesale. And you won't be using them up on Tessa Duvall, either.'

Chapter 24

Every year at the end of March the Royal Academy invites artists to submit works of quality for possible inclusion in their Summer Exhibition. Every year, roughly twelve thousand paintings are paraded – at dizzying speed – past the line-up of judges, venerable members of the Royal Academy who appraise, reject and finally select between fifteen hundred and two thousand of those paintings for show at their world-famous exhibition. Those lucky artists whose work is accepted gain tremendous kudos; the prestige, publicity and general public interest is far reaching. The plethora of talent scouts, working on behalf of both discerning private buyers and the top galleries in Europe and the States, scrutinize each painting, assessing its artist's talent and commercial viability. No one wants to miss out on the possibility of discovering another Hockney, Annigoni or Cook. A successful showing at the Academy's Summer Exhibition can, quite literally, change an artist's life.

Max, skimming through the *Telegraph*, only paused to read the article because the novel he was currently working on included an arts scam involving a crooked dealer and a drugs-crazed forger. Such information was always worth knowing and might prove useful.

Ross, picking up the abandoned newspaper at lunchtime and finding it folded open at the appropriate page, read the article with far greater interest. The business of parading the paintings past a row of judges appealed to his sense of humour; it sounded like Miss World minus the swimsuits. Ross didn't know a thing about the art world but even he had heard of the Royal Academy. Anyone could submit up to three paintings. The boost to a struggling artist's career, should his or her work be chosen, could be monumental.

Swivelling around in his chair he gazed up at Tessa's painting, his dark eyes thoughtful. He'd never before experienced the dilemma of being in love with a girl who refused to take their relationship seriously because he had too much money. As far as Tessa was concerned, his wealth and her own lack of it formed an insurmountable barrier between them. Her stubborn ideas drove him to distraction. And he had absolutely no intention of giving his money away, even for Tessa. Spurning his admittedly luxurious lifestyle in order to live in bliss and poverty with a beautiful, obstinate fellow-pauper wasn't his style at all.

The only sensible solution, therefore, seemed to be to drag Tessa, kicking and screaming no doubt, out into the real world where money counted just as much as love.

And by great good chance, observed Ross with a smile, the dear old members of the Academy were to commence their judging tomorrow.

Holly hadn't lost faith for a single moment in the powers of Rosa Polonowski but she was having trouble controlling her impatience.

Neither would she have dreamed of blaming Tessa for so drastically altering the course of events on their way back from Ascot the other week. A threatened miscarriage was a threatened miscarriage after all.

But Holly still couldn't help feeling disappointed that such an idyllic day had ended so uneventfully for Max and herself. The dreamed-of inevitable conclusion to that idyll had been wiped out. Lost. And so far failed to show any signs at all of rematerializing. Ground gained so dramatically had been lost and she was back just where she started, with Max behaving as if that blissful day – and their miraculous closeness – had never even happened.

It was all fate, of course. She knew that. What would be would be and Max was simply taking his time in coming to terms with the realization that there was no escaping their shared destiny. She knew that too. But it was still bloody exasperating, having to wait so long for it to finally happen.

And it didn't make matters any easier, having people like Adam Perry around to stick their clumsy great oars in.

When Holly had applied for the position of receptionist at The Grange, Ross had informed her that her duties would be challenging and varied and she had replied cheerfully that she thrived on variety and challenge.

Somehow, though, she had never envisaged herself crawling around the foyer on all fours in search of a contact lens while its erstwhile owner languished in a chair sipping gin and tonic and making no attempt whatsoever to join in.

Adam, his arms full of flowers, paused to admire Holly's delectable bottom as she shuffled backwards in response to the other woman's suggestion that 'it' might be nearer the doors. Her curvaceous thighs were clearly outlined by the thin material of her crocus-yellow skirt and when she leaned forward he caught an enticing glimpse of white stocking tops and pale flesh.

It did a man a power of good, he thought, to be presented with

201

such a wondrous sight on a grey Tuesday morning. Holly was, quite simply, gorgeous.

Sensing that someone was standing behind her, Holly glanced over her shoulder and swore quietly. Then, realizing that Adam Perry had been ogling her rear view and wasn't even attempting to do so with any subtlety, she raised herself on to her knees and glared at him.

'What are you doing here?' she snapped, further irritated by his stupid grin. 'I'm busy. And I don't want your stupid flowers, either.'

'They aren't your stupid flowers.' The imperturbable grin widened as she struggled to her feet, allowing him another brief glimpse of stocking top in the process. 'So you're spared the trouble of hurling them into the nearest bin.'

Doubly embarrassed now, Holly concentrated on her hair, which had worked free of its restraining combs.

'What about my contact lens?' demanded the woman in the armchair, tapping long magenta fingernails irritably against the side of her glass.

'I'm sorry,' said Holly. 'It's lost.' Then she squealed as Adam moved towards her, shifting his cellophane-wrapped bouquet beneath one arm and reaching towards her breasts with his free hand.

Before she even had time to slap the offending hand away, his huge, rugby player's fingers had brushed her left nipple. A fraction of a second later, his forefinger and thumb forming an O which exactly matched the shape of Holly's mouth, he said, 'Lucky contact lens.'

The all-important little circle of plastic was transferred from finder to grateful owner. Holly was forced to swallow her outrage, along with the urge to slap Adam Perry's horrid smirking face. Gathering her dignity and brushing carpet fibres from her knees, she retreated behind her desk and busied herself with a pile of invoices.

'No rock, then,' remarked Adam conversationally, leaning across the desk and peering at her trembling hands.

'I beg your pardon?'

'You aren't engaged to be married to the magnificent Max.'

'Not yet,' replied Holly icily, praying that Max wouldn't choose this moment to storm into reception and bawl her out. With a meaningful glance at the bouquet Adam was carrying, she said, 'May I help you?'

'More than you could ever imagine,' replied Adam in mournful tones. 'But since you are otherwise engaged – well, nearly – maybe you could point me in Tessa's direction. The flowers,' he added with insincere apology, 'are for her.'

'Suite twelve. Second floor,' replied Holly, somewhat miffed. She hadn't imagined for a moment that Adam might be here to see someone else. 'But why? You hardly know her.'

'I met her at Ascot,' he said. 'I liked her. I was sorry to hear about what happened. She's OK now, though?'

Holly forced herself to relax. She didn't, after all, even like Adam Perry. And a couple of dozen red roses was so typical of him. No imagination, no subtlety . . .

'She's fine. Bedrest. Shall I phone through and tell her you're here?'

'No need.' Shaking his head, he flashed that infuriating grin once more. 'You know me, darling. I do like to take people by surprise.'

* * *

'How lovely!' exclaimed Tessa, genuinely touched by Adam's gesture. Despite Holly's violent reaction, Tessa had taken an instantaneous liking towards the big, sandy-haired man now fitting himself with care into the chair beside her bed.

'I'm just glad to hear that you and the baby are OK,' said Adam in his easy, forthright manner. 'And I know that Ross is taking excellent care of you, but if there is anything you need . . .'

'I have more than I need,' she protested, gesturing towards the television and video, the stacks of books, the newly installed bedside fridge. 'I'm being spoiled rotten, but thank you for the offer. How are you, anyway?'

'Madly in love,' he replied soulfully. 'Is Holly really going to marry Max?'

If she has to put him in a straitjacket and push him up the aisle in a wheelbarrow, thought Tessa, but wisely forbore to say so. Instead, choosing her words with care, she shrugged and said, 'If everything goes according to plan.'

'She's pretty strong-willed. I don't suppose she's the kind to change her plans?'

'Stubborn as a mule,' said Tessa, feeling sorry for him. Knowing that Holly was making the wrong choice didn't help matters. She and Adam could have been wonderful together, if only she'd give him a chance to prove himself to her. Adam was real, Max a fantasy. One day, probably when it was too late, Holly would realize that.

'I don't have any chance at all, then.' He stared down at his hands, the huge fingers interlacing like those of a smoker who knows he mustn't light up. Then the laughter lines around his eyes deepened as he dredged up a self-mocking smile. 'I'm a big boy, Tessa. You can tell me. Cruel to be kind and all that . . .'

'You really shouldn't be asking me,' began Tessa slowly, picking up a pencil and twiddling it between her own fingers in order to distract her mind from what her mouth was about to say. 'But sometimes it's easier to see other people's mistakes than to recognize one's own, and I do think she's making a mistake. At the moment she's too besotted to think clearly but eventually . . . maybe . . . she'll realize that Max isn't what she wants after all. And then . . .'

'You really think there might be a chance then?' he said, as eagerly as a small boy.

'Possibly a slim chance,' she replied in guarded tones. 'And I mean very slim, so don't hold your breath.'

Adam beamed. For a second she thought he was going to hug her. 'Sweetheart, you are an absolute tonic. I knew I could count on you. Between the two of us we'll bring her to her senses—'

'A *slim* chance,' repeated Tessa sternly, but Adam's irrepressible grin had reasserted itself.

'Hey, they're my favourite kind! How about a small side-bet now? Thirty-three to one that I get the girl in the end!'

Chapter 25

'You see, I'm holding a small dinner party,' said Holly, trying desperately to make it sound as if she did this all the time. Since Max wasn't showing any signs of asking *her* out she had decided to do the sophisticated, *Cosmopolitan* thing and practise a spot of role-reversal. Any man with an ounce of good breeding wouldn't dream of turning down such an invitation, according to the magazine she'd been furtively reading under cover of the reception desk. 'Just a few friends, wonderful food and some rather special wine I've been saving . . .'

Max, up to his eyes in work, hadn't had time to read *Cosmopolitan*. Without even glancing up, he said, 'That's very nice of you, Holly, but I'm afraid I can't make it. Sorry.'

'Why not?' wailed Holly, the careful veneer of sophistication crumbling in an instant. 'Bloody hell, Max, I haven't even *told* you yet when it is!'

This time he did look up, his dark brown eyes surveying her with world-weary amusement while his mind continued to concentrate on the intricacies of the plot he was in the process of formulating.

'When is it?'

'Thursday,' said Holly, twisting her fingers into knots behind her back. Then, seeing him hesitate, she blurted out, 'Or Friday. Whichever suits you best.'

'Sorry,' repeated Max, returning his attention to the

fluorescent-green screen of his word processor. 'I'm afraid I really can't make it. Pressure of work,' he added, tapping the screen. 'I need to put in a bit of overtime.'

'You never work overtime,' she argued accusingly. 'You put in a few hours a day and take time off whenever you feel like it.'

Max, so engrossed in this new project that he didn't even realize the extent of her wounded pride, simply shrugged. How could he be expected to waste his time with boring dinner parties when the screenplay to end all screenplays was on the verge of being born? Besides, the sooner it was completed the sooner he would win back the love and undying gratitude of Francine . . .

'I have to work,' he said firmly. 'This is important.'

To her eternal shame, Holly felt tears burning at the back of her eyes. Having read the plot outline on the VDU she had already guessed the reason behind Max's sudden, all-consuming desire to immerse himself in this new project. He was clearly still besotted with Francine Lalonde, with whom she could not even hope to compete. It was cruel, frustrating and quite, quite unfair.

'Of course it's important,' she said, biting her lip as she struggled to keep control. Turning to leave, she said, 'I only hope it's as important to her as it is to you.'

'It is, it is,' said Max happily, so wrapped up in his own thoughts and plans that it didn't occur to him to question Holly's oblique reference to Francine. 'Don't worry, Holly. Everything's going exactly according to plan.'

As he handed Tessa's painting over to one of the porters, Ross felt uncomfortably as if he were abandoning a newborn baby on the steps of some hospital.

The Royal Academy was buzzing, as crowded as Harrods on the first day of the sales. The fact that almost everyone was hauling bloody great paintings around with them didn't help, either.

'Take good care of it,' said Ross, slipping the man a tenner, and the porter winked.

'Don't you worry, guv. I'll treat it like one of me own.'

After a long lunch with his old friend Nico Coletto and an expensive couple of hours touring Regent Street and the Burlington Arcade, Ross returned to the Academy. Faces which had earlier been alight with hope, now bore the strain of rejection. Stoicism vied with downright disappointment. The lucky few whose works had been accepted were obviously keeping quiet about it. No one, as far as Ross could make out, was actually smiling. It was by sheer chance that he encountered the same brown-coated porter in the midst of the crowds thronging the entrance hall. The porter, clearly unconcerned by the sombre atmosphere, greeted Ross with a jubilant thumbs-up and a broad grin. 'Brilliant, mate. You're in.'

Ross, though pleased, was not surprised. He hadn't doubted for a second that Tessa's work was worthy of showing. It hadn't needed a pencilled 'This way up' on the back like the one being jostled irritably past him at this moment.

'That's great,' he said, wondering whether the porter would be expecting a further tip to deliver the painting back to him. 'Am I supposed to collect it myself or do you do that for me?'

The man looked at him as if he were crazy. 'Blimey mate, where you been all your life? New to this, are you? It stays here now, until the exhibition.'

'Bloody hell, you're joking!' declared Ross. The whole idea had been to smuggle Tessa's painting up here while she was bed-bound and to have it safely back in place before anyone noticed it was missing. He had planned on bringing her up to London for the day in order to view the Summer Exhibition and allowing her to discover her own work hanging here.

Damn, he thought irritably. Now he'd have to think up some excuse for the fact that the picture had gone AWOL.

'Forgive me,' said Dominic, 'for not believing you last time when you told me you were famous.' Pausing in the doorway, he bowed. Tessa giggled.

'How did you know I was here?'

'Read it in the papers, of course. You're getting more press coverage than the Royals at the moment. So I thought I'd come and see whether you still deign to mix with us lesser mortals.'

'I *love* mixing with lesser mortals,' she assured him as he limped over to the bed and gave her a hug. 'Especially you. Sit down and tell me all the gossip. How are things going with all the women in your life?'

Dominic pulled a face. 'Why do you suppose I'm here? My wife threw me out. Marina left me. Josie,' he added in disgust, 'ran off with an extraordinarily untalented painter from St Ives.'

'You're all alone?' gasped Tessa with mock dismay. 'Is there no justice in this cruel world? However will you cope?'

His sky-blue eyes regarded hers with soulful stoicism. His tanned fingers stroked the insides of her slender wrists. 'I shall bury myself in my work,' he replied mournfully. 'And embrace celibacy. Maybe in time – seven or eight years say – I might meet another woman with whom I could consider sharing my life, but until then . . .'

'Please!' exclaimed Tessa. 'You'll have me in tears next. This is heartrending stuff.'

'My heart has never been so rended,' Dominic assured her, his expression tragic. 'I need comfort, I need understanding. I need to know that my true friends still care about me. I need—'

'Don't tell me,' intercepted Tessa shrewdly. 'Let me guess. A roof over your head.'

'Not only incredibly fat,' he replied with a dazzling smile as he ran his hand lightly over her swollen stomach, 'but incredibly kind. I knew you wouldn't let me down. Oh yuk, it kicked me!'

'I'm turning into an old spinster,' declared Holly on Friday afternoon. 'All my friends are paired up. You,' she pointed accusingly at Tessa, 'are laid up in that damned bed and all I've got to look forward to on my precious night off is a frozen curry and *Coronation Street*.'

'You hate *Coronation Street*,' said Tessa patiently. It didn't appear to have occurred to Holly that she, too, might be bored, stuck in bed for the third week running with only an occasional foray into the bathroom for excitement. When Holly was upset she liked the world to really know about it.

'Exactly!' Snatching a peach-tinted carnation out of a nearby vase, Holly began agitatedly shredding petals all over the bed. 'He loves me not, he loves me not, he loves me not! What am I supposed to do, Tess? Take up evening classes in knitting?'

'There's always Adam,' suggested Tessa hesitantly, realizing that her timing wasn't brilliant, but risking it anyway.

Holly jammed the headless carnation stalk back into the vase and rose to leave. 'For heaven's sake,' she snapped. 'I'm not that desperate.'

'In that case,' said Tessa with a wry smile, 'tell me tomorrow what happens when Mike Baldwin finds out about Deirdre's sex change.'

'Christ, that cottage is isolated,' complained Dominic half an hour later.

'I'm sorry,' said Tessa, suppressing a sigh. 'Why don't I pop down there now and build a few pubs and houses around it?'

Sensing her irritation, he smiled. 'I know, I know. I'm an ungrateful sod. It's just that I'm hopeless on my own. Last time you were there.'

'And now I'm here. If I moved back to the cottage,' she added slyly, 'you'd have to wait on me hand and foot. *And* do all the washing up.'

Dominic, recognizing the dig, pulled a face. 'OK, so I'm not the world's greatest nurse. But Tess, I don't know anyone in Bath and I'm so *bored* . . .'

'I want you to know that this was Tessa's idea, not mine,' announced Dominic without preamble. 'So don't go getting any funny ideas.'

Holly, not in the sunniest of moods, glared at him. Sarcasm and abuse from yet another disinterested male was just what she needed right now.

'Don't flatter yourself,' she said irritably. 'Just shut up and get on with it.'

Dominic pulled a face. 'Charming. OK, Tessa mentioned the

fact that you were bored and lonely. I simply thought you might like to go out somewhere tonight.'

'With you?' said Holly, her eyebrows lifting in disbelief.

'According to Tessa,' said Dominic, his own expression deadpan, 'no one else is interested.'

'I also told her that I wasn't desperate,' she retorted smartly.

'So is it yes or no?'

For a micro-second, *Coronation Street* exerted its pull.

'OK then,' said Holly, knowing she would live to regret it.

Dominic looked triumphant. 'Is that a yes or a no?' he repeated, taunting her now.

'Don't push it, smartass, it's an OK.'

Chapter 26

After years of being caught out by women, Ross imagined himself to be a pretty accomplished liar. When confronted with the evidence he stuck rigidly to his motto: deny, deny, deny. And until now it had served him remarkably well. Lying was easy. Stick to your guns for long enough and everyone runs out of arguments in the end.

Lying to Tessa, however, was a different matter. She didn't argue, for a start. And if she doubted the truth of what he was saying, she gave no sign of it.

The problem for Ross was that the more readily she accepted his explanations the more convoluted they became.

'And since Nico's convinced that this friend of his will be interested in your work,' he said, elaborating still further, 'he asked me if he could borrow your painting.'

'Fine,' said Tessa cheerfully. 'And it isn't my painting any more, anyway. It's yours.'

'Yes, well . . . this friend is over in the States at the moment, even Nico doesn't know when he'll be able to get back. But as soon as he does, and sees your – my – painting, he'll return it.'

'Good. Ross, d'you think you could pass me the book that's on top of the chest of drawers over there?'

'It might take a couple of months,' he said warily.

Tessa tilted her head to one side. Speaking slowly and clearly, she said, 'It's a library book. It'll be overdue by then. Couldn't you get it for me now?'

'I meant the painting,' said Ross, still edgy.

'I'm bored with this story,' shouted Tessa, hurling a cushion at his head. 'Do whatever you like with your painting. Just pass me that bloody book.'

After a decidedly rocky start, the evening had turned out far better than either Dominic or Holly had imagined possible.

Since Dominic was without transport, Holly had picked him up from Tessa's cottage. Determined that he shouldn't think she was out to impress, she had taken care to dress as casually as possible in a very plain, sage-green cotton shirt worn over darker green Fiorucci jeans. Minimum make-up, minimum perfume and a decidedly offhand manner completed the outfit. Dominic, realizing at once what she was up to, took enormous pleasure in outdoing her in every department. His own creased black sweatshirt and torn denims were genuinely old, he wore no make-up and as far as offhandedness was concerned, he was unbeatable.

But verbal sparring could only pass the time for so long. After a couple of drinks in a tiny, candlelit wine bar in the centre of Bath, Dominic managed to break through Holly's mile-high defences long enough to discover – to his amazement – that she enjoyed listening to live jazz.

He was even more astounded, three hours later, to find out that she could not only dance rather well, but that she possessed more stamina than the All-Blacks. With her red-gold hair flying, her cheeks flushed and her hips swaying, she monopolized the dance floor, exchanged good-natured banter with the band and danced a succession of partners into the ground.

And since all that exercise in such a hot, smoky cellar made her incredibly thirsty, she also had a great deal to drink.

'Pizza,' she said finally, collapsing beside him and finishing off his pint of lager. 'I must have pizza. There's a great restaurant just around the corner from here.'

'Good,' replied Dominic. 'God knows how I'm going to get home tonight, because you certainly can't drive. You're drunk.'

'I'm enjoying myself,' said Holly, sounding surprised. 'And I was so sure I wouldn't. Isn't life strange?'

'Bizarre,' agreed Dominic, keeping a straight face and deciding that Holly wasn't so awful, after all. 'But I still don't know how I'll get home.'

She gestured airily with his empty glass. 'No problem, you can stay with me. My flat's not far from here.' Then she grinned and gave him a nudge that nearly sent him flying. 'But I don't want you to get the wrong idea. I'm talking about a bed for the night, nothing steamy.'

'My sentiments entirely,' agreed Dominic, profoundly relieved. Taking her arm, he pulled her to her feet. 'Now, pizza. If you don't eat something soon you'll be out cold.'

Dominic had never thought of Holly as attractive, however he was prepared to admit that there was something about her which would undoubtedly appeal to other men.

And now that they were back at her flat and he had consumed the best part of a bottle of Barolo, he was also able to concede that she really wasn't looking bad at all. That pale green shirt suited her and the fact that another button had just popped undone only added to its appeal. A lifelong devotee of slender women with small breasts and narrow hips, Dominic wondered what it would be like to make love to someone like Holly, all extravagant curves and pillow-softness.

'What?' she demanded, reaching past him for a second slice of pizza Margherita.

Dominic smiled. 'I was wondering what you . . . felt like.'

Holly was feeling deliciously reckless. She'd had enough of being ignored by Max, she badly needed an ego-boost and she wasn't so drunk that she hadn't realized what was going on in Dominic's mind. Maybe a one-night stand was just what she needed, after all.

Dropping the pizza back down into its box, she stretched out across the settee and returned his smile.

'I think,' she said slowly, 'I feel like another glass of wine.'

'You'll regret it in the morning.' Dominic refilled her glass anyway, brushing his fingers against the inside of her wrist as he handed it to her. The pale skin was silky, deliciously warm and apricot-scented.

Max didn't appear to want her, not at the moment anyway. Holly, who was lonely and who craved affection, set aside the glass and leaned forward, reaching out to touch Dominic's own brown hand. As she watched their fingers curl together she said softly, carefully, 'Don't worry, I never regret anything in the morning.'

'No, I sold it last week.' Ross, speaking on the phone, didn't even acknowledge Grace's timid sideways entrance into his office. Out of sheer habit, he swivelled around in his chair in order to gaze at Tessa's painting and instead encountered bare wall. Frowning, he swivelled back again. 'Well, they saw it, liked it and made me an offer that only a madman would refuse.

I hadn't planned on selling it, but a profit's a profit, after all.'

He transferred his frown to Grace, who was taking an extraordinary length of time to clear away two empty coffee cups. Harry Bradford, who had set his heart on buying Ross's boat, was still expressing his disappointment and trying hard to find out exactly how much Ross had sold it for. Ross, enjoying himself, neatly evaded him at every turn.

'Sentimental value? Of course it had sentimental value,' he exclaimed, leaning back and pushing his fingers through his gleaming dark hair. 'But we *are* businessmen, Harry. You know how it is . . .'

'I didn't realize that Mr Monahan had sold your painting,' said Grace when she took Tessa's evening meal up to her an hour later.

Tessa, startled, said, 'Neither did I. Are you sure about that?'

'I heard him talking on the phone. He said he'd sold it last week because someone had made him an offer he couldn't refuse,' relayed Grace, who had wondered at the time why the picture – which she liked a lot – had vanished from the office. Wearing an indignant expression, she added, 'He also said that it had sentimental value but that he was a businessman and money came first. I thought he would have told you, though.'

'Maybe he didn't want to hurt my feelings,' said Tessa, recalling the string of garbled excuses he had come up with and trying hard not to feel hurt. It was Ross's painting and – as she had so impatiently told him at the time – he could do whatever he liked with it. She was disappointed, nevertheless, that the prospect of making a quick profit had meant more to him than the pleasure of owning a piece of work which he had, after all, commissioned for himself in the first place. It was yet another ill-timed, jolting reminder of the vast differences between them.

'Well, I think it was a rotten thing to do,' declared Grace self-righteously.

So do I, thought Tessa. But I'm damned if I'll let Ross realize quite how much it bothers me.

'You'll have to stop talking for a few minutes now,' she said, flexing and unflexing her right hand and easing herself into a more comfortable position. 'I'm concentrating on your mouth.'

Nico's dark green eyes narrowed with amusement. 'In that case,' he countered, 'I shall concentrate on your legs.'

'I wouldn't bother.' Tessa pulled a wry face. 'They're not a pretty sight. Honestly, I didn't know it was possible to *get* so fat.'

Nico grinned. 'You'll shrink back afterwards. And I like looking at pregnant women, anyway. What are you now, seven months?'

She nodded, working to capture that famous half-smile. Ross had been right; any worries she might have had about painting Nico Coletto had been banished within minutes of their first meeting. His easy charm and complete lack of showbusiness egotism had disarmed her totally. He was funny, thoughtful, wonderfully easy to talk to and quite clearly devoted to his wife and family.

'Camilla was huge at seven months,' he added reassuringly. 'She looked gorgeous, but she kept saying she felt like an elephant seal. I could only take photos of her if she didn't know it was happening.'

Instead of reminding Nico that he was supposed to be keeping quiet, Tessa said curiously, 'Were you there with her when she was actually having the baby?'

'Of course I was.' Nico looked surprised. 'I wouldn't have missed it for anything. And it was absolutely fantastic,' he went on with genuine enthusiasm. 'I couldn't believe it was really happening . . . one minute there was this vast lump inside Cami's stomach and moments later they were putting a real live baby, our own *daughter*, into my arms.'

Tessa paused, her paint brush in mid-air. 'It sounds nice.'

'Sweetheart, it's miraculous. You just wait until it's your turn.'

'The trouble is,' she admitted with reluctance, 'Ross wants to be there and I'd rather do it on my own.'

'No, you wouldn't,' declared Nico flatly. 'You just think he'll find it a turn-off. Camilla's first husband wasn't with her when she had their two children, but I insisted on being there when Katrina was born . . . and in the end she was glad I was. Look,' he went on eagerly, 'we can phone her now if you like; you can speak to her and she'll tell you how she felt about it.'

'No, no,' protested Tessa, knowing when she was beaten. 'I'll take your word for it. And now,' she added with renewed determination, 'you really do have to shut up for five minutes, otherwise we'll be here until midnight.'

When Tessa had moved back home a week earlier, no longer sentenced to bedrest and anxious to see what kind of a tip Dominic had made of the cottage, Ross had made no secret of his dispproval.

But since he wasn't able to change her mind – she was still as infuriatingly obstinate as ever – he was forced to do the next best thing and keep as close an eye on her as possible without letting her realize that he was doing so.

'Look out,' said Tessa, glancing through the kitchen window and checking her watch. 'Quick, cover up that escape hatch and hide the shovels. Herr Kommandant's making his evening patrol.'

'And bringing us a Red Cross parcel,' observed Dominic, coming up behind her. 'Great, I hope it's smoked salmon again.'

'Hi.' Ross, entering the cottage, dropped a casual kiss on Tessa's temple and managed to ignore Dominic completely. 'Just thought I'd pop over and see how you were doing. How did it go with Nico?'

'Fine.' Tessa smiled. At least Ross hadn't insisted on staying with her throughout the sitting, as he had initially threatened to do. 'I liked him. I felt awful about not being able to travel up to London, but he said it wasn't a problem at all. He's working on an album with some musician friend who has a recording studio near here, apparently, and he's going to fit the next couple of sittings in with that.'

Despite their differences, Ross and Dominic exchanged a brief, despairing glance. Only Tessa, surely, could call Peter Gabriel 'some musician friend' without even realizing who he was.

'Well, let's see how it's going,' said Ross, turning towards the easel set up in front of the living-room window. 'Jesus, Tess! You can't do that to him. Nico will flip his lid when he sees this!'

Tessa looked worried. 'It's only an initial impression,' she protested. 'I always rough out the first sketch in brown. But don't you think it's like him?'

Dominic, who had executed in less than ten minutes the bizarre, barely recognizable caricature of Nico, had to turn away in order to hide his smile. Tessa, looking absolutely distraught now – there were even real tears glistening in her emerald eyes – clung on to Ross's arm and glanced up at him for reassurance.

'You like it really, don't you?'

'No, I bloody well don't!' he declared flatly. He was, after all, the one who had bulldozed Nico into having his portrait painted by Tessa. And not for peanuts either. 'It looks like a cartoon drawn by a retarded monkey.'

'It's neo-impressionistic abstract Dadaism,' said Tessa in a small voice. 'It's adventurous.'

'Tess, it's fucking awful,' said Ross urgently. 'Look, you have to ditch this and start again, right away. Nico needn't even know. He hasn't seen this yet, has he?'

She shook her head, a single tear trickling down her cheek. 'He wanted to wait until it was finished.'

'Thank God for that.'

'So *you* don't like it,' she murmured huskily. 'But you've told me a dozen times that you don't understand modern art. Who knows, maybe Nico will absolutely love it.'

'Trust me,' he replied, his tone grim. 'He'll hate it.'

Tessa shrugged. 'In that case, he could always sell it.'

But Ross didn't bite. Pushing his fingers distractedly through his hair, he said, 'I don't believe this. For heaven's sake Tess, tell me you aren't serious.'

'OK,' said Tessa, winking at him. 'I'm not serious.'

He stared at her. 'You're joking!'

'Oh no,' she said with a slight smile, 'I'm quite serious about not being serious.'

Chapter 27

A fortnight and two further sittings later, Tessa finally completed the portrait. She spent the next week lazing in the garden, turning a pleasing shade of golden brown and praying that the paint would be dry by Saturday.

After several days of torrential rain the previous week, the weather had improved dramatically. Now, on the first of June, a brilliant sun hung in a cloudless, cobalt-blue sky and Tessa's sunglasses, slippery with Ambre Solaire, kept sliding down her nose. Her huge stomach was very brown indeed but since she was unable to lie on her front her back was several shades paler. Dominic, who didn't have this problem, had fallen asleep with his face buried in a cushion, unaware that Tessa had cut the Batman logo out of newspaper and placed it carefully between his shoulder blades.

It was hot. Sighing with lazy pleasure, she closed her eyes and contemplated Saturday's party. Nico, Camilla and their four children, together with Nico's two glamorous sisters and their own large families were descending upon The Grange in order to celebrate Camilla's birthday. Nico had insisted that Ross and Tessa should join them and she knew that he and Ross between them had organized a small amount of press publicity prior to the party, in order to promote her own work. It was all very exciting, not to mention nerve-racking. She didn't have a clue how she would react when she found herself face to face with real-live journalists.

A moment later her mobile rang. Tessa, still not used to it, leapt a mile and cursed the day that Ross had bought it for her. Apart from never having been able to afford the luxury of a telephone she had always enjoyed the sense of being incommunicado, but Ross had insisted that she have one as a condition of her release from the hotel.

'You're pregnant, for heaven's sake,' he had told her, as if she hadn't noticed. 'You can't live in solitary confinement.'

'I've got Dominic,' she had retaliated, and Ross had given her a look that said it all.

'And I've got an appendix,' he had replied in withering tones. 'But that doesn't mean it's of any use to me.'

Finding the phone at last, buried beneath the *Daily Mail* and an empty Maltesers packet, she punched the button and said, 'Hello, Ross.'

'I could have been anybody,' he told her reprovingly.

'But you and Holly are the only people who know I'm on the phone,' she said, lying back in her deckchair and surveying the garden. It was badly in need of attention but, as with her uneven tan, there was little she could do about it at present.

'I could have been Holly,' he remarked, adding, 'God forbid.'

'I'll tell her you said so.'

'Actually I have something to tell you.' His tone altered abruptly, became serious. 'Tess, I'm afraid it's disappointing news.'

'Disappointing news?' she echoed, unable to imagine what it might be. 'Ross, tell me.'

'I've just heard from Nico. He asked me if you'd mind very much if he didn't buy the painting after all.'

Tessa's mouth went dry. 'What? Why, what's wrong with it?'

223

'I'm sorry, sweetheart. I know it's a bit of a blow. He didn't like to say anything at the time, but he really feels that it makes him look too old.'

'He doesn't want it?' She stared helplessly at the crumpled, discarded copy of the *Daily Mail*. Her horoscope had warned her to prepare herself for a disappointment, but she didn't believe in horoscopes. 'What about Saturday?'

'All off I'm afraid.' The note of sympathy in Ross's voice was clearly evident. 'Well, they're still holding the party here at The Grange and he says we're still welcome to join them, but I've told him to stick his lousy invitation. And I've cancelled the photographers, of course.'

'Oh Ross, this is awful,' said Tessa shakily. 'I really thought he liked the portrait.'

'Sweetheart, you know what these rock stars are like,' he said consolingly. 'They just don't have any appreciation of real talent. When he told me that his nine-year-old son could have painted a better likeness I realized that he had absolutely no idea of—'

'He said *that*?' she shrieked, ripping off her sunglasses and hurling them into the nearest flowerbed. 'You're kidding!'

'Yes,' said Ross happily. 'I am.'

'It's wonderful!' exclaimed Camilla, seeing her husband's portrait for the first time. 'Tessa, how can you paint like that? You've caught his personality exactly.'

'I know.' Nico, putting his arm around his wife's slender waist, winked at Tessa. 'I'm an ugly son of a bitch, aren't I?'

Camilla, accustomed to his sense of humour, ignored him. 'And that smile,' she enthused, moving closer. 'Darling, it's so *like* you!'

'You don't think it makes me look old?' he asked, managing to keep a straight face for an entire second. Then, with a sideways glance at Tessa, he burst out laughing. 'Sorry, Tess. Ross told me everything. I still can't believe that you really fell for it, though. You already knew how great I thought the portrait was.'

'I suppose it was a combination of my fragile ego and the thought that you were just being polite,' said Tessa, with a rueful grin. 'Finishing a painting is a bit like having a baby; you don't want anyone to tell you it's ugly.'

'And speaking of ugly babies,' said Nico cheerfully as Ross approached them with Katrina in his arms. 'Give me back my daughter, Monahan. Trini, come and give your daddy an enormous kiss.'

'Daddy,' beamed Katrina, flinging a chubby brown arm around Ross's neck.

'Trini, sshh!' remonstrated Nico. 'There are reporters present. Ross isn't your daddy, *I* am.'

'I'm just grateful that she looks like Nico,' Camilla told Tessa, as Nico swept his beautiful daughter into the air. 'She's dreadfully indiscriminate. As far as she's concerned, every man she sees is Daddy and the effect can be electrifying.'

'She certainly gave Rod Stewart a scare last week,' recalled Nico with a broad grin. 'Hey, Trini! What do you think of this then? Who is it?' Swinging her around, he pointed her in the direction of the portrait. Katrina's huge green eyes focused with interest upon the likeness and a moment later she let out a shriek of delighted recognition.

'Who is it, Trini?' prompted Nico proudly.

'Mummy!'

* * *

Tessa was grateful to Nico for his reassuring presence at her side while she underwent the ordeal of answering questions from the three journalists chosen to interview her. With his easy camaraderie and expertise, he helped her to relax as they posed in front of the portrait for photographs. As far as he was concerned, of course, it was just another brief encounter with the Press, thought Tessa, admiring his effortless repartee and wishing that her pulse would slow down to something approaching its normal rate. But it was her first real experience in this field and she was only too aware that they were far more interested in her unborn child than in the portrait.

The air in the library was cool, however, which helped. Through the long windows she could see the rest of the party beginning without them, thirty or forty of Nico's friends and relatives enjoying themselves outside on the sunbaked, flower-strewn terrace. She wished she could join them.

'So the baby's due in five weeks, Tessa,' said the journalist from the *Express*, her smile conspiratorial. 'Tell me, do you and Ross have any marriage plans lined up?'

'Sadie, please,' intercepted Nico, before Tessa could even formulate a reply. 'We're here to promote Tessa's career. She's a marvellously talented artist; isn't that enough for you?'

'Marrying Ross Monahan could be construed as a marvellous career move,' parried Sadie Labelle, directing a coquettish smile in Nico's direction. 'Not to mention a pretty desirable proposition in its own right. Many have tried before now, after all.' Extending her smile to include Tessa, she added, 'And I must say, I wouldn't say "no" to him myself.'

'Ross would never tangle with an old dog like you,' said Nico cheerfully. 'There are limits, Sadie.'

Sadie arched pale, elegantly plucked eyebrows in Tessa's direction. 'Ignore him, dear. Nico's sense of humour is bizarre to say the least. Why don't *you* tell me what your immediate plans are?'

Tessa, straightfaced, said, 'Well, I'm going to have a baby.'

'And will you and Ross marry, or is he happy to father an illegitimate child?'

Sadie Labelle was famous for her hard-hitting personality pieces and ascerbic manner. Her controversial method of questioning frequently resulted in lost tempers and heat-of-the-moment indiscretions. Tessa smiled, forcing herself to relax.

'He's happy to father a child,' she replied sweetly. 'Neither of us wants to get married just for the sake of it.'

'So you didn't plan this with the deliberate intention of trapping him into marriage?'

Tessa, refusing to bite, shook her head. 'I didn't plan anything. I never do.'

'But a child needs security,' persisted Sadie. 'Without Ross, your situation would be difficult to say the least, whereas if you were married to him you could have everything you've ever wanted. Or could it just be that Ross hasn't asked you to marry him?' she concluded archly.

'It could be,' said Tessa, her own expression thoughtful. 'But on the other hand it could also be due to the fact that I'm already married.'

'Why didn't you just tell them that we *were* getting married?' asked Ross an hour later, his eyes shielded behind dark glasses but his tone truculent. Sadie Labelle wasn't going to take too kindly to the fact that Tessa had lied to her. Besides, he didn't want people to start wondering whether there might not be some deep dark reason why Tessa chose not to be his wife.

'Don't nag, Ross. She annoyed me, that's all.' Tessa stretched out in the white, wrought-iron chair and shook back her hair. 'She wasn't the least bit interested when I was talking about my work. At least the others bothered to listen ... just. And Nico thought it was funny, anyway.'

'Nico can afford to think it's funny,' he replied grimly. 'But you may have blown a great chance. Sadie Labelle can be a bitch, Tess.'

'Don't worry,' said Tessa, kicking off her flat, pale pink shoes and grinning at him. 'So can I.'

Chapter 28

When Ross turned up at the cottage two days later he was less than amused to discover Tessa, wearing only a sunflower-yellow bikini, submitting with a smile on her face to a dubious-looking back massage from Dominic.

'If I were you,' he said, his tone dangerously cool, 'I'd leave her alone.'

'If you'd left her alone in the first place,' replied Dominic equally smoothly, 'she wouldn't have backache now.'

Tessa sighed. Her back really was hurting and the last thing she needed at this moment was a battle of wills between two men who didn't trust each other an inch.

Ross threw his jacket over the nearest chair and dropped his car keys on to the coffee table. 'I've come here to speak to Tessa. Alone.'

'Suits me,' said Dominic with a careless shrug. 'I was just leaving anyway.'

'He should have left weeks ago,' stormed Ross ten minutes later as he watched Dominic saunter down the lane. 'That's something else we have to have a serious talk about.'

He didn't doubt for a moment that he was right to distrust Dominic. Tessa had always been ludicrously unaware of her own desirability. As her pregnancy had advanced she had made constant fun of her figure; to hear her talk one would imagine her to be grotesquely overweight.

But she was not. She still carried herself with uncontrived elegance, her long legs were as slender as ever and the recently acquired tan only served to accentuate the dazzling colour of her eyes. Her sunkissed blonde hair, freshly washed and rippling past her brown shoulders, smelled of shampoo and her once small breasts, having miraculously blossomed with pregnancy so that they spilled over the top of the flimsy yellow bikini, were equally tanned.

In fact, thought Ross with a fresh surge of jealousy, the tan was far too all-over for his liking. Having long ago recognized certain inescapable similarities between Dominic Taylor's character and his own, he was only too well aware of the dangers that entailed. Tessa might not realize how delectable she was looking but Dominic was another matter altogether.

It was definitely time, Ross decided, to put his foot down.

Tessa, meanwhile, was carrying a tray out into the garden. Ice cubes clinked, a lone bee droned. It was going to be another stunning day . . . or it would be, she thought, if Ross would only take that mutinous expression off his face.

'I'm not going to argue with you about Dominic,' she said, as he followed her outside. Choosing a perfect ripe strawberry, she popped it into her mouth and offered him the bowl.

'Good,' he said briskly, shaking his head and lighting a cigarette instead. 'In that case, boot him out.'

'Ross, he's a *friend*. You're being unreasonable.'

'No, I'm not,' he countered. 'He's the one who's being bloody unreasonable. Apart from the fact that there isn't room in this cottage to swing a cockroach, and apart from the fact that you're about to have a baby – though God knows where you think you're going to find the space to put it – it just isn't *decent*.'

'Dear me,' said Tessa idly as she bit into another strawberry. 'Whatever will the neighbours think?'

'Exactly!' Ross flung his barely smoked cigarette into the centre of a clump of dusky-pink hydrangeas. 'And it isn't funny, either. When you're expecting *my* child you have to take these things into consideration. Jesus,' he fumed, 'don't you realize what someone like Sadie Labelle could make of this if she wanted to?'

'Yet the fact that you've been screwing yourself stupid for the past fifteen years is perfectly OK?' demanded Tessa, her own temper beginning to rise now.

'That's different,' he replied dismissively. 'And you know it. Look,' he went on a moment later, his tone softening in an attempt to defuse the situation, 'I'm only saying all this because I'm concerned about you.'

'No, you're not, you're concerned about *you*,' Tessa retaliated bitterly. Her back was still aching and she simply wasn't in the mood to placate him. 'Just because two people of the opposite sex happen to like each other doesn't automatically mean they want to have sex with each other. I realize that this is an alien concept to someone like you but you have to understand. Dominic and I have been friends for years and if he wants to stay here, he can. And what's more,' she added in dismissive tones, 'I don't give a toss about what anyone else might think.'

'So, you're happy to live with him but not with me.' Right now, Ross could cheerfully have strangled Dominic. Thank goodness he'd had the sense to leave. 'How can you let him touch you, Tessa? You know damn well what he's like.'

'He's like you,' she replied, her green eyes glittering

with derision. 'And you'll just have to take my word for it when I tell you that our relationship is platonic. But if you don't believe me, maybe the fact that I'm eight months' pregnant might—'

'You aren't going to be pregnant for much longer,' Ross cut in. 'What's going to happen, after the baby's born? He's not bloody well staying here then!'

Tessa and Dominic had discussed the matter weeks ago and it had been agreed that as soon as the baby arrived Dominic would return to Cornwall. His wife, the long-suffering Suzanne, had disappeared off to the States to visit her family and their home was standing empty, awaiting Dominic's return. But since Ross had no right to lecture her like this she was damned if she was going to tell him so.

'Of course he is,' she said airily. 'There's plenty of room. Back in the nineteen thirties this cottage was occupied by a farm worker and his wife and their three children.'

'That's obscene,' declared Ross, lighting another cigarette and glancing at his watch. He had a meeting to attend in London at two o'clock and it was already almost noon.

'No,' said Tessa sharply. 'It's your attitude to the kind of lifestyle necessary in order to enjoy oneself that's obscene. This is my home, I'm happy here and I don't happen to need five-hundred square feet of living space all to myself to prove it. My God,' she exploded, no longer able to keep her thoughts to herself, 'you have absolutely no idea how privileged you are, and how different *we* are! You live in your ivory bloody tower' – she gesticulated wildly across the valley in the direction of the hotel – 'and spend money like tap water . . . didn't you even realize how I felt when we went up to Ascot? There you were, betting more on a single horse race than I'd ever earned in a fortnight. That's how different we are!' she concluded icily. 'And that is what is truly obscene.'

At that moment Ross almost hated her. He had come here today with the intention of finally persuading her to marry him – or at least to live with him – and been confronted instead with the sight of her and Dominic together, practically in flagrante delicto. Furthermore, the bad-tempered bitch had succeeded in swinging the conversation around in order to launch an unforgivable attack on him, his morals and his own hard-earned wealth.

'I buy you things with my despicable money,' he reminded her, his voice a dangerous monotone.

'But I don't *want* you to buy me things!' yelled Tessa. 'I don't *need* your things. Which particular things are you talking about anyway?' she demanded, reaching down and grabbing the silver mobile phone from beneath her deckchair. 'This? This is how much I need your bloody things!'

The phone crashed against the garden wall and went 'ting'. Tessa watched with satisfaction as the silver case smashed, ricocheting into the air and falling into the midst of a dense patch of drastically overgrown forget-me-nots. The fact that she didn't normally go in for such melodramatic gestures only added to her pleasure; Ross's face was an absolute picture.

'You are an ungrateful cow,' he said slowly, flicking his car keys from one hand to the other. There was clearly no point in staying while she was in this kind of mood. Right now, Dominic was welcome to her. 'I'm leaving.'

'Hooray,' said Tessa with vicious sarcasm. 'Got the message at last.'

Ross cast her a final despairing glance. 'Too right I have,' he drawled, furious with her for proving once again that she had the ability to ruin everything. 'And when the baby's born, I don't want you and darling Dominic to worry too much about hurting my feelings. I was never cut out to be a godfather anyway.'

The uncomfortable ache metamorphosed into real pain an hour later. Tessa bit her lip and attempted to ease herself into a more comfortable position in the deckchair. The sun was beating down now and her upper lip was drenched with perspiration. Too late she recalled why she had never smashed glasses when her temper was aroused. They needed sweeping up afterwards. Similarly, a broken phone was a broken phone; all of a sudden it was no longer there when you needed it.

And as the pain intensified she knew that she had never needed a telephone more urgently in her life.

'I asked him how Tessa was and he practically bit my head off,' said Sylvie Nash, distinctly put out by the rebuff. 'He was in a terrible mood.'

'Poor Ross,' said Antonia sympathetically, lounging against the reception desk and thinking fast. 'And he's had to drive up to London?'

'He has a meeting scheduled for two o'clock,' Sylvie told her, consulting the photocopied list in front of her. 'At the Ritz. He's going to be late as it is and I doubt whether he'll be back before eight o'clock this evening. Was it something urgent?'

'Oh no,' Antonia assured the blonde receptionist, at the same time thinking that if she had her way Ross wouldn't be back that night at all. 'Don't worry, I'll give him a ring tomorrow.'

'Maybe he'll be more cheerful then, anyway.' Sylvie's talent for idle chatter was legion. 'I can't think why he should have been so stroppy earlier. He and Tessa must have had some kind of row.'

Frustration strikes, thought Antonia happily, already planning what she would use as an excuse when she phoned Richard. Thank goodness she'd had her hair streaked yesterday. And she could wear that new, ludicrously expensive Paul Smith dress with nothing underneath. This time Ross wouldn't be able to turn her down.

'I'm sure he'll be more cheerful tomorrow,' she assured Sylvie with a complacent smile. 'In fact, I can almost guarantee it.'

By two o'clock Tessa was in a state of genuine panic. There was no doubt at all now that this was the real thing and that her predicament was serious. Her waters had broken, gushing warm liquid down her thighs, and the contractions were becoming stronger and more prolonged. Having clumsily retrieved the mangled phone from the flowerbed and discovered that it really was as useless as she had feared, she managed to drag a deckchair as far as the front gate so that she could at least sit in it while waiting for someone – anyone – to come along the narrow lane. But the sun continued to blaze down, her entire body was drenched with sweat and the only living creature to put in an appearance was a lone rabbit, bouncing across the field opposite.

Reaching the main road at the end of the lane was by this time a physical impossibility. Lying out in the sun was almost as unbearable, but if she crawled indoors she ran the risk of missing her only remaining hope, a passing car.

Closing her eyes and silently cursing her stupidity, she

clutched her taut, pain-wracked stomach and wondered whether she would be capable of giving birth on her own. Dominic, she knew, wouldn't be back for hours. The deserted lane remained deserted. By smashing the phone in a mindless moment of anger she could well have endangered her baby's life, maybe even her own. Out here, in this sunny garden, they could both die. She gasped as another vice-like spasm of excruciating pain gripped her. The need to push was becoming overwhelming now but she knew she mustn't do so. All my own fault, thought Tessa despairingly, her bare heels digging into the sun-dried grass beneath her. How could I have been so *stupid* . . .?

Sylvie, not knowing how to deal with the man on the phone, passed the call on to Max. He, unamused at being disturbed, was even more annoyed when he eventually realized that the caller wanted Tessa.

'She's no longer staying here,' he replied curtly, not wanting to lose the thread of the particularly tricky scene he was working on. 'And I don't have her mobile number but I'm sure you can get it from reception.'

'But you are Mr Monahan,' persisted the man. 'We were instructed to refer any correspondence directly to you.'

'I'm not that Mr Monahan. He's unavailable for the rest of the day.' Max frowned at the VDU and silently mouthed a line of dialogue, wondering whether it really worked.

'In that case I shall have to contact Miss Duvall,' said the voice with fastidious disapproval. 'Thank you so much for your help.'

Less than five minutes later, Max's phone rang again.

'What?' he barked with mounting impatience.

'I'm very sorry to have to trouble you again, Mr Monahan, but Miss Duvall's mobile phone is currently out of order. Since this is a matter of some urgency I wondered if there were any other way in which she might be contacted.'

By this time Max's concentration had been well and truly shattered. Screenplays were ten times more difficult than novels and if it weren't for Francine he would never have persevered with this one. But he needed a break and he supposed he could always drive over to Tessa's cottage. It would be his good deed for the day.

'Give me your number,' he said, less irritably this time. 'I'll make sure she phones you this afternoon.'

'That's very kind of you,' replied the caller, his own tone correspondingly warmer. 'If she could call me back any time before five?'

Good, thought Max, glancing at his watch. He could have a quick swim first. And then maybe something to eat before he set out . . .

Chapter 29

The only way Ross was able to control his anger was by immersing himself in the business to hand. Having driven up to London at lunatic speed – if any police patrol cars had been around they certainly hadn't been able to catch up with him – he had arrived at the Ritz in a foul mood, his mind churning with replays of the dreadful argument with Tessa and with the insults they had flung at one another.

But good businessmen didn't allow their private lives to disrupt their work. That was the way to slide downhill, fast. Forcing himself to forget Tessa for a couple of vital hours, Ross smiled and shook hands with the gathered executives, made pleasant preliminary small talk until the meeting was declared open, then concentrated on the matters under discussion with such all-consuming intensity that time, miraculously, really did fly.

At first she thought it must be a mirage induced by heat, pain and sheer desperation. A dark grey, matchbox-sized car far away in the distance with a white dust-cloud kicking up behind it appeared to be heading towards her. Panting noisily she managed to pull herself up on her elbows to see the mirage more clearly. As it approached she was able to make out the roar of a powerful engine amid the dizzying thud of her own pulse drumming in her ears. It really was a car. All she had to pray for now was that the driver, upon seeing her, would stop.

Tessa, by this time exhausted and on the point of collapse, didn't have the energy for tears when the car screamed to a halt at the roadside. For a confused moment she thought it was Ross. When Max leapt out of the car and said, 'Jesus Christ!', her confusion mounted and she shook her head in bewilderment.

'What did you say?' demanded Max, his voice echoing strangely as he leaned down and scooped her up into his arms.

'Wr . . . wrong brother,' murmured Tessa, closing her eyes and clutching at his shoulders with sweat-soaked fingers. A moment later she felt herself being deposited in the back of the car, just as another agonizing surge of pain pressed down into her spine. Gripping Max's hands, she bit her lip and forced herself not to scream. When the contraction receded she opened her eyes once more, pushed her wet hair away from her forehead and managed a wry, barely discernible smile. 'But under the circumstances,' she added weakly, 'you'll do.'

'Well, well,' said Antonia softly, knowing at that moment that she had won. If Ross, upon seeing her, had veered away . . . well, then she would have lost.

But he had not, and victory – pleasurable victory – was hers. Crossing her tanned legs so that the slippery silk jersey edged up another couple of inches, she allowed her mouth to curve into a conspiratorial smile. 'What an amazingly small world we live in. Ross, how are you?'

'You shouldn't be sitting alone like this in an hotel foyer,' he remarked bluntly, stalling for time but realizing even as he did so that there was no point. For all his harsh words to her in the past, Antonia knew him too well to be fooled.

Her dark blue eyes widened in mock alarm. 'You mean I could be picked up? Propositioned? By a tall, dark stranger? My God, what a terrifying prospect!'

'It is,' said Ross, slowly nodding his head, his own dark eyes taking in every detail. 'Particularly for the tall, dark stranger.'

This time Antonia threw back her head and laughed. The midnight blue jersey obligingly slid sideways to reveal a little more cleavage and he caught a waft of her familiar heady perfume.

'In that case,' she replied, 'maybe it's just as well that I bumped into you instead.'

'Maybe,' said Ross, though he seriously doubted it. What he should do and what he knew he was about to do were two different matters entirely and it was more than likely that he would live to regret it. The trouble was, right now he simply didn't care. Glancing across the sumptuous peach-and-grey foyer and abandoning the pretence, he said, 'Wait here and I'll book us a room.'

In reply, Antonia opened her clutch bag, removed a key and dangled it in front of him. With a small, triumphant smile she murmured, 'Great minds think alike, darling. I already have.'

Unable to resist taunting him, she slipped out of her dress and said, 'Don't you feel guilty?'

She had chosen just the right moment in which to ask him. Unbelievably aroused by her unexpected nakedness, Ross dismissed the question with a slow shake of his dark head. No matter how hard he had tried, Tessa had persisted in believing the worst of him, doubting his motives at every turn and refusing to even consider the possibility that his feelings for her might be genuine. He had worked so hard to show her that he had reformed – never before had he lavished even a fraction of the attention he had given her on any other woman – but so determined was she to protect her goddamned independence that it had been nothing but a waste of time. He had offered her the world and she simply hadn't wanted it.

As far as Ross was concerned now, he deserved a little fun. It was, he thought, only fair. And long, long overdue.

'I don't believe in feeling guilty,' he told Antonia, moving towards her and running his fingers lightly between her golden breasts. 'It's a waste of time.'

Aching for him to pull her into his arms, she said, 'I think we've wasted enough time already. How long has it been now, Ross? Six months?'

He grinned. 'You tell me.'

She knew, of course. Five months and sixteen days, give or take a few hours. But since she had no intention of letting him know quite how obsessively she had been counting the weeks, she reached up instead and loosened his tie, letting it fall to the floor, then returning her attention to the buttons of his white linen shirt.

'Well?' he demanded, when she didn't reply.

'So long,' said Antonia finally, as the last button came undone, 'that I've almost forgotten what to do.'

And then, at last, he removed his shirt and drew her towards him, his dark eyes glittering with desire and his erection pressing against her flat, taut stomach. His hands slid from her shoulders, tracing the contours of her slender waist and narrow, almost boyish hips. She quivered in delicious anticipation, her own fingers finding the cold metallic rectangle of his belt buckle, her entire body tingling with helpless longing.

'Ah,' said Ross, a few minutes later, as Antonia pulled him down on top of her, her legs curling around his waist, 'I knew you'd remember in the end.'

They made love with a fury and desperation heightened by long months of abstinence. True to his word, Ross didn't allow the niggling presence of Tessa in his mind to worry him. Here was someone instead who desired him physically and didn't complicate matters by wondering whether or not it was the right thing to do.

Furthermore, Antonia's uncomplicated enthusiasm for his body was doubly welcome because he knew that she was smart enough to keep sex and emotions well apart. What they shared was nothing more than healthy, no-nonsense lust and the ability to give each other enormous pleasure.

And what, he thought as she climbed on top of him and expertly insinuated herself into position once more, could possibly be wrong with that?

Chapter 30

'She's in the final stage of labour, the baby won't be long now,' pronounced the midwife, handing Max a paper cap and a crumpled green hospital gown as she spoke. 'You'll have to put these on if you're coming into the delivery room.'

'Absolutely not,' declared Max, horrified. Thrusting the gown back at her, he shook his head for added emphasis. 'I'll stay in the waiting room, thanks.'

The midwife, who thoroughly disapproved of men who casually impregnated their partners but who couldn't even be bothered to witness the miracle of birth, fixed Max with an icy glare.

'Now, now, Mr Monahan. You really should be thinking of your poor wife. Don't you think she'd prefer to have you with her, giving her encouragement and helping her through this? Of course,' she added with a hint of scorn, 'if you're worried that you might faint—'

'Wrong Mr Monahan,' said Max wearily, for the second time that afternoon. 'I'm not the father, just the chauffeur. And I can promise you that the last thing in the world Tessa would want is to have me in there with her, mopping her brow.'

After seventeen years of midwifery, nothing fazed Molly Richardson. 'In that case,' she replied briskly, 'you may wait in the waiting room. Is the prospective father likely to turn up shortly?' she enquired, glancing at the watch pinned just above her left breast. 'Because we won't be able to wait for him, I'm afraid.'

'He's at a meeting in London. He . . .' Max's explanation was interrupted at that moment by a muffled shriek from inside the delivery room, followed by a short, sharp epithet quite unsuitable for young ears.

Molly Richardson smiled and moved towards the door. 'I'd better get back inside. As I said, not long to go now.'

Holly was overjoyed when she picked up the phone at home and heard Max's voice. Within the space of two seconds her imagination had succeeded in conjuring up at least half a dozen fantasies, each of which concluded with a trip up the aisle, bridesmaids in ruffled, rose satin dresses and everlasting bliss.

'Max, how nice,' she managed to say at last, so overexcited that the phone almost slipped through her fingers. And thank *goodness* she'd stayed at home this afternoon instead of trailing around the shops . . . although if he wanted her to have dinner with him this evening she'd have to rush out and find something stunning to wear . . . if that slightly too-tight, emerald-green dress with the boned bodice and wonderfully scalloped hemline was still there, she could buy that and simply not breathe . . .

'I thought you'd better know that Tessa's about to have the baby,' announced Max curtly. 'She's in the delivery suite right now, but when it's over she'll go to Deverell Ward.'

'Tessa's having the baby?' repeated Holly idiotically. The words were so far removed from her glorious fantasies of just a few moments ago that she had trouble digesting their meaning. 'Is it a boy or a girl?'

'The damn thing hasn't been born yet,' exclaimed Max,

exasperated by her stupidity. 'My God, why Ross ever agreed to employ you is beyond me!'

Stung by his brutal words, Holly snapped back: 'Maybe I'm great in bed.'

'You'd have to be spectacular,' he said witheringly, 'to compensate for such a chronic shortage of common sense. Now, are you coming down here or not?'

At last, thought Holly, fighting back tears. The invitation she'd been waiting for, for so long.

'Of course I am,' she said indignantly, wiping her eyes and glaring into the receiver. 'Tessa's my best friend.'

If Holly hadn't known better, she might have suspected that Tessa and Max cared for each other more deeply than either of them had let on.

How, she wondered, could Max be such a bastard one minute and so wonderful the next?

The moment when the midwife had come into the waiting room and informed them that Tessa had given birth to a beautiful baby daughter had been the moment Max had done his Jekyll and Hyde bit and now here he was, gazing in adoration at the bundle in Tessa's arms and acting for all the world like a besotted new father. For heaven's sake, he'd even kissed Tessa on the check and given her a gentle, congratulatory hug. Holly's only consolation at the time had been the look of stunned disbelief on Tessa's face as he did so.

'You really don't have to stay, Max,' said Tessa, looking up at the clock on the wall. It was almost eight-thirty in the evening. 'You've been here for hours and I know how busy you are.'

'No problem,' he shrugged, brushing the tip of the baby's

nose with his finger and smiling triumphantly as the dark, Monahan-shaped eyes opened in bemusement. 'Look at her. She's beautiful.'

'Ah,' said Tessa wickedly. 'But are you sure she's Ross's daughter?'

Max had the grace to look ashamed. 'I didn't ever really doubt it, you know. I was merely exercising a bit of caution on my brother's behalf.'

Until that moment, Tessa hadn't mentioned Ross. Now she smoothed the baby's sleek black hair and said, very casually, 'Is he at the hotel?'

Max shook his head. 'He wasn't back when I phoned earlier. I've left a message for him – I'm sure he'll be here soon.'

'He may not be. We had a bit of an argument this morning. A hell of an argument,' she corrected herself sadly. 'And now he's missed all this.'

'Everyone has arguments,' said Holly, sensing how upset Tessa really was and hurrying to reassure her. 'It's just bad timing. And you didn't want him to be in there with you while you actually had the baby anyway, did you?'

'Just as well.' Tessa shrugged, assuming a nonchalance she didn't feel. No one had warned her that it would be like this; an avalanche of muddled emotions warring within her, this massive surge of love welling up from nowhere so overwhelming that she didn't know quite what to do with it. All of a sudden, Ross's absence seemed so tragic, so desperately sad that she wanted to burst into tears. Cuddling the baby, her own baby, she bent her head and allowed her hair to fall forward, concealing the desolation in her eyes.

'Maybe we should leave,' said Holly, leaning across and

putting her arms around her. 'Visiting time ends in ten minutes anyway. If your phone's broken, I'd better drop in at the cottage and let Dominic know what's happened. He'll be worried.'

'Would you?' said Tessa gratefully. Ever since Holly's one night out with Dominic – about which they had both been spectacularly unforthcoming – Holly had tended to avoid visiting Tessa whenever she knew Dominic would be there. 'And could you pick up a toothbrush and a couple of nightdresses?' She managed a wan smile. 'I was pretty under-dressed when I got here.'

'Do you want me to give you a lift?' asked Max, addressing Holly and sounding more friendly than he had all afternoon.

'Oh yes, please.' Maybe this would be her big chance, an awfully long time coming but worth every minute of the wait. She gave him a dazzling smile, perking up instantly.

'Sorry, I forgot.' He tapped his forehead and pointed to her car keys protruding from her open handbag. 'You have your own car here. Well, you can pick up Tessa's things and I'll head back to the hotel. And don't worry,' he added, turning to Tessa with a reassuring wink, 'as soon as Ross gets back he'll be over to see you, I can guarantee it. Just don't be surprised if he turns up at three o'clock in the morning – you know how these business meetings can drag on.'

Ross's business meeting had certainly dragged on. He didn't turn up at all that night, although Tessa's heart skipped a couple of beats each time she heard hurried male footsteps echoing along the corridor outside the ward. At four-thirty in the morning, exhausted but quite unable to sleep, she eased herself cautiously out of bed and padded barefoot down to the nursery. The night sister found her standing over the baby's cot with tears streaming down her face.

'There now dear, plenty of new mums feel like this after all the excitement's over.' She put a reassuring arm around Tessa's quivering shoulders. 'We'll have a word with the doctor in the morning if you're still feeling a bit weepy then, shall we?'

By breakfast time Tessa no longer knew whether to laugh or cry. Three of her fellow patients and two nurses had told her how lucky she was to have such a handsome loving husband. Maisie Naylor, the forty-year-old occupant of the bed next to hers, slurped her lukewarm tea with enthusiasm and said loudly, 'Course, my Jack don't 'ardly bother comin' to see me no more, not after eight kids. But your old man, I seen 'im last night and me eyes near as dammit dropped out of me 'ead. What a looker 'e is! And don't your little'un take after 'im. Just my bleedin' luck,' she added gloomily, 'to 'ave eight kids and all of 'em the dead spit of my Jack, poor little buggers.'

Back at The Grange, Max called directory enquiries. Ross could have spent the night anywhere but it was just possible that he had taken a room at the Ritz.

When the phone rang at nine-fifteen in the morning, Ross rolled over and buried his head beneath the pillows. A surfeit of sex, two bottles of Gevrey-Chambertin and little more than three hours' sleep were taking their toll.

Satiated and smiling, Antonia picked up the receiver.

Five seconds later she tapped his bare brown shoulder. 'For you.'

'You stupid bastard,' snapped Max. 'What the hell do you think you're doing?'

'You're the writer,' Ross retorted, lying back and clutching his forehead as the full force of his hangover struck home. 'Use your imagination.'

'I don't need to. Christ, you must be out of your mind.'

'Don't panic, I'm over the age of consent.' Ross, thoroughly put out by Max's self-righteous tone, was tempted to slam down the phone. 'What the hell's wrong with you, anyway? Has The Grange burned down or is it something more serious, like the fact that you obviously didn't get laid last night?'

'Oh, nothing important,' said Max disgustedly. 'Tessa had the baby, that's all. I know it's crazy, but I actually thought you might have wanted to know.'

Chapter 31

'So was *that* one the father?' demanded Maisie Naylor, when
Dominic was safely out of the ward. She looked at first perplexed,
then gave Tessa an enormous wink. 'Or does 'e just think 'e
is?'

'Neither.' Despite her churning anxiety, Tessa managed a faint
smile. She didn't know what she would have done without
Maisie's outrageous patter to enliven her morning. 'He's a friend.'
It crossed her mind to add that Dominic was the man she lived
with but Maisie would find such thrilling news hard to keep to
herself and Max had already warned her that the Press would be
sniffing around as soon as they heard about the birth of Ross
Monahan's daughter.

Quite suddenly, Ross's arguments – which she had always so
flippantly dismissed – had acquired real credibility and she was
forced to admit to herself that he had been right all along. The
prospect of scurrilous gossip in the papers appalled her now. Her
baby, so new and innocent, had to be protected from such
rubbishy speculation.

It was already eleven o'clock and there was still no sign of
Ross. Tessa fought back fresh tears; she had never needed to see
him so badly in her life and despite Max's reassurances she
couldn't help fearing the worst. His parting shot yesterday had
been pretty equivocal. Maybe he really didn't want anything
more to do with either the baby or herself.

* * *

When Ross burst into the ward at eleven-thirty he found Tessa's bed empty. Having built himself up for this moment, the sense of anti-climax was crushing to say the least. Hastily, he averted his eyes from the woman in the adjacent bed who was breastfeeding her own infant. She, however, appeared unconcerned by his presence.

'It's you, innit,' she crowed delightedly.

'I beg your pardon?'

'You're 'im!' declared Maisie, shifting her frantically suckling baby from one enormous breast and locking it into position on the other side. 'And about bleedin' time an' all.'

'Where's Tessa?' said Ross, praying that nothing terrible had happened. 'Is she all right? And where's the baby?'

'We're here,' said Tessa quietly and he swung around, his pulse racing, to find her standing behind him with the child in her arms.

For a moment Ross was lost for words. The rest of the ward had gone quiet; everyone – even the nursing staff – was watching with avid interest. Never in his life had he felt so on-display, so uncertain of his reception . . . and so very, very guilty.

'Tess, what can I say?' He shook his head, searching for the right words. 'I'm sorry. I can't tell you how rotten I feel—'

'Sshh,' murmured Tessa, her eyes glistening with tears. 'I'm sorry too. It was a silly argument and I was as much to blame as you were. I'm just glad you're here now.'

And, cradling their sleeping daughter to her chest, she stretched up and kissed Ross on the very corner of his mouth.

Sagging with relief, he put his arms around her and drew her towards the bed, at the same time gazing down at the dark-haired baby in her arms.

'Can I hold her? Is she OK?'

'She's fine,' Tessa assured him with a smile, taking care to support the tiny head as she handed their daughter over to him, then easing back the snowy blanket so that Ross could see the perfectly replicated Monahan features for the first time. 'We're both fine, thank heavens. Although,' she added wryly, 'I suppose I really should thank Max.'

'It was my fault.' Ross, unable now to tear his eyes away from his beautiful daughter, shuddered to think how narrowly disaster must have been avoided. If anything had happened to Tessa and the baby while he had been in London . . . with Antonia . . . he didn't know what he would have done.

But Tessa, consumed with her own guilt, couldn't bear him to take the blame.

'It wasn't,' she said urgently, her eyes filling once more with tears of shame. 'You were right and I behaved like a spoilt bitch. And if I hadn't smashed the phone—'

'Don't,' commanded Ross, kissing the top of her head and no longer caring that they were being watched. 'Jesus, this lot could give the KGB a run for their money. I'm going to get you moved to a private room.'

'Absolutely not,' declared Tessa. 'I like it here. They're only taking such an interest because they think Max is the father and they're wondering who on earth you are.'

'Bloody cheek!' exclaimed Ross, outraged. And at that moment the baby awoke, opening long-lashed navy-blue eyes and gazing up at him with sleepy bemusement. The expression on her face said so clearly 'who the hell are you?' that both Ross and Tessa burst out laughing.

'There's something else you haven't told me,' he said, moments later.

'What?'

'My daughter's name.'

Tessa smiled. 'Olivia.'

'Ladies and gentlemen,' announced Ross, raising his voice and addressing the ward in general. 'I'd like to introduce you all to Olivia, my daughter. My name is Ross – repeat, Ross – Monahan and *I* am Olivia's father.'

Amid the ensuing laughter and applause – for everyone had felt sorry for Tessa the night before – Maisie Naylor added her own verdict of approval. Eyeing Ross with evident pleasure she said cheerfully, 'And if you ever fancy another one, my darlin', I'd be only too 'appy to oblige . . .'

'Antonia, we have to talk.'

'Only talk?' she protested lightly, attempting to gauge Ross's mood and crossing her legs with deliberate slowness. 'Sweetheart, we have the whole evening ahead of us. And talking sounds so dull!'

'Stop it,' said Ross, his tone firm. Bitterly ashamed of his behaviour earlier in the week, he was determined now to make Antonia understand that it really was all over between them. 'Look, you must realize what I'm going to say. Tessa and the baby mean everything in the world to me and I'm not going to risk losing them now. I've been an idiot in the past but this time I'm serious. I love Tessa, I adore Olivia and I only hope you can respect that.'

253

Antonia lit a cigarette, swallowing her disappointment and concentrating hard on the blue spiral of smoke drifting lazily towards the ceiling. When Ross had contacted her and asked her to meet him tonight she had suspected as much but a part of her had still hoped that their affair could continue.

'I see,' she said thoughtfully, her dark blue eyes gazing just past him. 'Allow me to put it in a nutshell, darling. You're a dramatically reformed character and you want to make sure I keep my mouth shut. Is that it?'

Ross sighed. He couldn't afford to antagonize Antonia, yet at the same time he found it difficult to believe that she was really taking it this calmly.

'I suppose so,' he said at last. 'I know I've been a bastard but this means so much to me. I want you to understand just how important it is.'

'Of course I understand,' said Antonia warmly. 'I have feelings too, don't I? I remember how important you were to me, for instance.'

Ross shot her a wary glance and she laughed. 'Don't look at me like that, darling. I used the past tense, didn't I? What I'm trying to say is that you and I had a marvellous affair. At the same time we both respected the fact that I was married to Richard. Being discreet about it was all part of the fun.'

Ross nodded agreement, since that was what Antonia appeared to expect him to do, although inwardly he couldn't help remembering that discretion hadn't always been one of Antonia's major virtues.

'We're both civilized adults,' she continued, stubbing out her cigarette and relaxing once more in her chair. 'And of course I appreciate your current dilemma. So please don't give it another thought, Ross, because I shan't breathe a word about our recent . . . adventure . . . to anyone.' She paused, brushing her index finger against her mouth in a thoughtful fashion. 'But you do have to promise me one thing.'

His heart sank. He thought it had all been too good to be true.

'Go on,' said Ross, bracing himself for whatever lay ahead.

'Don't tell me it's over between us,' said Antonia simply. 'I couldn't bear to think that we'll never make love again. I want to believe that just maybe, one day – if it doesn't work out between you and Tessa – you might come back to me.'

Ross, expecting hideous blackmail at the very least, was so relieved he could have hugged her.

'You've got it,' he assured her, safe in the knowledge that such an occasion would never arise. 'And Antonia, thank you for being so understanding. I do appreciate it.'

'Good,' she said, with brittle lightness. 'And don't forget, darling. Whenever you do decide to come back, I'll be waiting for you.'

'Hello!' said Tessa, disguising her surprise with a smile. 'How lovely to see you again. Did Ross send you over with those?'

Grace, hovering uneasily at the foot of the bed, turned pink. 'No . . . no, they're from me, actually. I remembered how much you like white roses . . .' Her voice trailed away as she spotted the lavish blooms spilling out of the tinny vases on Tessa's bedside cupboard, creamy white roses of infinite perfection, far superior to her own.

'They're beautiful,' said Tessa firmly, burying her face in Grace's roses and breathing in their scent. 'And they smell absolutely gorgeous! How kind of you, Grace. Come on, drag that chair over and sit down. Catch me up with all the gossip Ross doesn't know about . . . oh, how awful of me, you haven't come here to gossip, have you? You want to meet Olivia!'

As Tessa slid out of bed, crossed to the wheeled crib and carefully lifted the baby from its cocoon, Grace pushed her carrier bag under the chair and took a deep breath. The compulsion to see her half-sister had been overwhelming but now that she was actually here she could scarcely believe her own daring.

'Here she is,' said Tessa proudly, and the next moment Grace was holding Olivia in her lap, gazing into eyes so like Ross's that she almost expected the baby to issue a demand for fresh coffee. At once.

'She's perfect,' said Grace, blinking back tears. The baby, needless to say, didn't resemble her in any way at all.

Tessa smiled. 'She looks exactly like Ross.'

'Yes.'

'You know, I can hardly believe she's really here at last. Ross can't keep away – he's absolutely bowled over by her. He can't get over the fact that he's a father.'

'Yes,' repeated Grace tonelessly, as she cradled the child in her arms. 'It must feel incredible. Like nothing else on earth.'

Chapter 32

If it had taken a great deal for Grace to pluck up enough courage to visit Tessa and Olivia at the hospital, it was nothing in comparison with the effort of will required by Mattie when she had set out that evening.

Now, having found herself a seat in the crowded bar of the Charrington Grange Hotel, she ordered a large gin and tonic and allowed herself ten minutes in which to gather her non-existent composure.

But the time had come to confront Ross Monahan at last. Ostrich-like, she had done nothing and simply prayed that matters would somehow sort themselves out. Having persuaded herself that Grace's uncommunicativeness was a sign that she was dealing with the bombshell in her own characteristically silent manner, Mattie had concentrated instead upon urging her daughter to get out more, to take up new interests and make new friends. Passively, Grace had agreed and Mattie had heaved a sigh of relief.

Sipping her gin and tonic now, and willing her hand not to shake, Mattie suppressed a shudder as she recalled yesterday's chance meeting in the supermarket with Barbara Newcombe, who lived for salacious gossip and whose own dull family were a source of constant disappointment to her.

But Babs Newcombe's loudly whispered and triumphantly proclaimed comments had turned Mattie's stomach. Evidently, Grace had been seen – not once but twice – very much the worse for wear. On the first occasion Babs herself had spotted her drinking straight from a vodka bottle on a bench in Bathampton Park. The second time her daughter had come home and reliably informed her that Grace, sprawled out on the grass in the same park, had been holding an unintelligible conversation with a pigeon.

'I felt it was only my duty to tell you,' Babs had concluded happily. 'My Tracey was shocked of course, but then she's such a good girl, never been any trouble at all.'

'Oh yes, you're lucky,' agreed Mattie, numb with shock and at the same time suppressing the urge to hurl a can of mixed vegetables at the smug, smiling face looming before her. 'And now that she's stopped mixing with that crowd of glue-sniffers who hang around the underpass her complexion is *so* much better . . .'

But, of course, a thorough search of Grace's bedroom that evening had produced the damning evidence she so desperately hadn't wanted to find. At the very back of the wardrobe, hidden inside a shoebox, was a three-quarters full bottle of Smirnoff. At that exact moment, Mattie knew that something had to be done.

Richard Seymour-Smith, on his way to the bar, didn't notice Mattie sitting alone at a table for two. His mind was taken up with what he imagined his wife might be up to right now.

Having returned unexpectedly early from a meeting in Birmingham to find Ross's car parked outside the house, Richard had driven smartly away again and headed for The Grange where he could at least have a few quiet drinks safe in the knowledge that his wife's lover was fully occupied elsewhere.

But the drink didn't appear to be doing its job tonight. As he paid for his fourth Scotch he reflected that he was still completely sober. The edges weren't even faintly blurred and the remorseless sense of humiliation was still as strong as ever.

His co-ordination failed him, however, as he made his way back towards his table. With his drink in one hand and a cigarette in the other, he was unprepared for the sudden movement of a chair being pushed back as its occupant rose to leave. Caught momentarily off balance and taking care not to spill his Scotch, Richard didn't even realize that the lighted tip of his cigarette had come into contact with human flesh.

Mattie shrieked, jerking instinctively away from the sudden searing pain and almost knocking over her own drink. But it was too late; the damage was done. The burn on her upper arm would heal within a week – she wasn't a bit bothered about that – but her one and only decent dress was without doubt ruined beyond repair.

Richard was mortified. Apologizing profusely, breaking out in a film of perspiration as he realized how much unwanted attention he was receiving from surrounding tables, he dabbed hopelessly with his handkerchief at the scorched material. His glasses slipped down his nose as his anxiety intensified.

Finally, gently – and because he was getting in everyone's way – Mattie caught hold of his arm and managed to persuade him to sit down opposite her.

'Please don't worry,' she said, a sympathetic smile warming her face. 'It was an accident. And I'm sure I'll be able to mend it, anyway. It's only a little hole.'

Although still agitated, Richard was by nature an observant man. The dress, he realized at a glance, was neither new nor expensive yet the woman was prepared to take the trouble to try and repair it herself – unlike Antonia who would have gone home and chucked it in the nearest bin. Furthermore, whereas Antonia would have screamed abuse and demanded immediate compensation, this woman was reassuring him, playing down the situation and not even mentioning the burn on her upper arm, which had to be painful.

'I can't tell you how sorry I am,' said Richard, fumbling for his wallet and pulling out a sheaf of ten pound notes. 'Please, you must allow me to reimburse you . . .'

'Oh, stop it!' exclaimed Mattie, pushing his money away and laughing out loud. 'I couldn't let you do that. This old thing is on its last legs anyway.'

But, Richard noticed, the pale pink cotton dress was immaculately pressed and obviously well cared for. Attacked by a fresh wave of guilt – he was by no means an expert but he was pretty sure that a cigarette burn couldn't even *be* repaired – he thrust a handful of notes into the woman's hand.

'I won't take any money!' persisted Mattie, pushing them back at him and still smiling. 'Besides, whatever will people think? Everyone's going to assume I'm a prostitute now!'

'God, I'm sorry,' muttered Richard, aghast. His glasses slid down his nose once more and he shook his head in embarrassment.

'Look, if it would make you feel happier you can buy me a drink,' Mattie said kindly. She glanced at her watch and grimaced. 'I was supposed to be seeing someone but I could do with a bit of Dutch courage anyway, before I do.'

'You're meeting someone here? Won't he mind if he sees me sitting with you?'

'It's not that kind of date,' replied Mattie, her smile draining away as she remembered the purpose of her visit. 'Actually, I wanted to speak to the hotel manager, but I don't even know if he's on duty this evening. I suppose I should have made an appointment but I didn't think—'

'He's not here,' said Richard, the muscles at the sides of his mouth tensing with renewed regret. He liked Ross; he just wished Antonia didn't like him too.

'Oh,' said Mattie, slumping back in her chair. It was like dreading a visit to the dentist then being told at the last minute that your appointment had been cancelled. She didn't know whether to feel disappointed or relieved. 'You're quite sure? He's definitely not in the hotel?'

She had a sympathetic face, thought Richard, and such a soft, reassuring voice. She would understand.

'I'm quite sure,' he replied evenly. 'You see, at this very moment he's probably in bed. With my wife.'

He was such a nice man, thought Mattie two hours and several drinks later. She hadn't realized that nice men still existed.

She had been careful, of course, not to unburden herself as he had done, explaining only that she was concerned about her daughter and that she had hoped Ross might be able to reassure her that all was well at work.

Mostly, however, they had talked about each other. Following his initial 'confession' – for he persisted in taking the blame for his wife's infidelity and refused to admit that either Antonia or Ross might be at fault – Mattie had steered the conversation around to him. Within a short time she had learned about his upbringing in the sleepy Yorkshire dales, his schooldays in Leeds, his scholarship to Oxford and his subsequent career in accountancy. She learned too of his love for classical music and Duke Ellington, for Chinese food and real Yorkshire puddings, for wildlife and hot-air ballooning, for the writing of Anthony Trollope and H. E. Bates . . .

'You're making me do all the talking,' he said finally, leaning back and giving her a wry look. 'How do you *do* that?'

'Truth drug,' said Mattie with a shrug. 'I slipped it into your drink when you weren't looking.'

'I'm not used to talking so much. Not about myself, anyway.'

'I'm interested,' she replied truthfully. 'I love listening and finding out about other people's lives.' She smiled and took an appreciative sip of her drink. 'Probably because they're almost always more interesting than my own. I suppose I'm just plain nosey.'

Richard thought she was wonderful. He had never felt so comfortable, so completely at ease in his life. And the more he looked at Mattie the more she appeared to metamorphose from a slightly overweight, tired-looking housewife without particular distinguishing features into a charming, sparkling-eyed, some-how younger woman with an irresistible smile and a voluptuous figure which suited her down to the ground. It was so wonderfully appropriate to her warm personality that he couldn't imagine her being thin.

'Now it's your turn,' he said, leaning across the table towards her. 'Tell me all about your life. I want to know what *you* like.'

'I'm not like you, for a start,' replied Mattie, with a self-deprecating shrug. 'I'm not an intellectual, I haven't been up in an aeroplane – let alone a hot-air balloon – and I've never even eaten proper Chinese food, only chicken chop suey from our local takeaway.'

'So those are the things you haven't done,' said Richard gravely. 'Tell me what you enjoy doing.'

'I like watching old films,' she said, cupping her chin in her hands and gazing dreamily into the distance. 'Fred Astaire and Ginger Rogers, Bing Crosby and Grace Kelly, that kind of thing. I adore fresh cream cakes. And bonfire night. And managing to complete the crossword puzzle in the *Express*. And I'm addicted to trashy novels, the romantic kind where you know it's all going to work out in the end. I love happy endings.' Then she flushed, realizing how silly and trite she must sound. 'So there you are,' she concluded, flapping her hand in an awkward gesture of dismissal. 'I did warn you that I wasn't an intellectual.'

'You're a romantic,' replied Richard, gazing at her with sheer pleasure. 'It's nothing to be ashamed of. And if you didn't like happy endings you wouldn't be human.'

The meeting with Antonia had been difficult but Ross had made up for it by spending the second half of the evening far more pleasurably, with Tessa and Olivia. Convinced now that nothing more could go wrong between them he was in an extremely good mood.

As he drove up the gravelled drive to the hotel entrance he observed two people climbing into a waiting cab. The lights were dim, but he could have sworn that the person helping the woman into the back seat of the taxi was Richard Seymour-Smith.

But by no stretch of even the wildest imagination could the woman with him be mistaken for Antonia . . .

'I can't believe we're really doing this,' whispered Mattie, terrified that the taxi driver would overhear.

'Sshh.' Richard didn't want her to start voicing doubts. He placed his hand over one of hers and gently squeezed it. 'Tell me what else you like. I want to know.'

She giggled. They were both slightly drunk but nicely so. 'Long baths, long hot bubble baths after a hard day at work. And listening to *The Archers* on Sunday mornings . . . oh, it's no good! You're trying to distract me and you mustn't. We really *shouldn't* be doing this.'

'We haven't done anything yet,' Richard reminded her, secretly astounded by his own daring.

'You know what I mean,' said Mattie, shaking her head. 'This is terrible. I'm supposed to be trying to sort out my daughter's problems and here I am, tipsy myself. What sort of mother am I?'

'I'm sure you're a wonderful mother.' Richard spoke in low, reassuring tones but she shook her head once more, with such vigour that her breasts jiggled enticingly against his sleeve.'

'I'm a disgrace.'

Terrified that she was about to change her mind, Richard said – very firmly this time – 'No, you are not.'

'Of course I am! Apart from anything else, you're a married man.'

During his evening with Mattie, Antonia's infidelities had faded into misty insignificance. Now, thought Richard, they seemed a positive godsend.

'It doesn't count,' he declared triumphantly, 'when the man is being cheated on by his own wife.'

'Oh.' Mattie smiled into the darkness. She hadn't seriously intended changing her mind anyway but absolution, she decided dizzily, was a marvellous thing. 'Good. But we must stop at my house first. I have to make sure that Grace is all right.'

Richard, praying that she would be, patted Mattie's hand and said, 'Of course.'

*   *   *

Grace was in fact in a surprisingly good mood. Visiting Tessa and the baby in hospital had provided her with a feeling of secret importance which had cheered her up immensely. And since she had felt in no need of a drink she hadn't yet discovered the fact that her secret vodka supply had disappeared.

She looked up from the television and smiled when Mattie arrived home and was immediately intrigued by the expression – a mixture of guilt, elation – and surprise – on her mother's face. It was exactly how Holly King always looked when, once in every blue moon, Max deigned to be nice to her.

Mattie, whose first act upon returning home was invariably to toss her handbag on to the dining table and collapse into her favourite chair, hovered in the centre of the room and clutched her bag to her stomach like a hot water-bottle.

'Hello, darling! How are you?'

Grace, who favoured vodka herself because it was odourless, realized that her mother was speaking through clenched teeth in an effort to hold in the gin fumes. She sounded like a very bad ventriloquist.

'I'm fine, Mum. Would you like a cup of tea?'

Grace stood up, preparing to move towards the kitchen. Mattie edged guiltily sideways.

'No, no. Er . . .' At least Grace was sober. Thank God. 'Um . . . actually, I'm thinking of popping out again. You see, Pam and I bumped into someone tonight . . . Janie Collins . . . she's an old friend we haven't seen for years, and she's invited us both back to her house. So I thought . . . if it was all right with you . . . I might stay there overnight and Janie can drive me back tomorrow morning.'

Well, well, thought Grace, managing to keep a straight face. Mother's got herself a man! And about time, too.

'That sounds sensible,' she said, dropping easily into her chair. 'That's fine.'

'Are you sure?' said Mattie, sounding even more like a teenager than ever. 'Do you think you'll be all right on your own? I wouldn't have agreed to go, but Janie was so insistent.'

'I'll be perfectly OK, Mum. Really. I hope you have a lovely time with Janie and Pam.'

In a rush of gratitude and relief, Mattie forgot the gin fumes and leaned over to give Grace a kiss. 'Oh, thank you, darling.'

'Don't forget, Mum,' said Grace, just before the door slammed.

Mattie's face, bright-eyed and pink-cheeked with anticipation, reappeared around it. 'Forget what?'

'Your toothbrush.'

'I *still* can't believe that we're actually doing this,' sighed Mattie, tucking in her stomach as Richard ran his left hand over the mound of soft flesh. If he had told her how pleasurable he found her plumpness she would never have believed him. 'I can't believe that we are here, that we checked into this hotel as Mr and Mrs Robinson and that—'

'That it could be so perfect?' suggested Richard, inhaling her sweet scent and kissing her shoulder. A moment later she winced and he realized that his chin was brushing against the angry red cigarette burn he had inflicted earlier. 'Sorry, sorry. Does it hurt dreadfully?'

'It hurts wonderfully,' said Mattie, reaching for him. 'And I can't tell you how glad I am that it happened. I know we women aren't supposed to say such things, but I really think

266

this has been the most marvellous night of my life.'

'Really?' whispered Richard, overwhelmed with pride and pleasure. Having never before been unfaithful to Antonia he was beginning to understand now what had drawn her to Ross. Adultery, he reflected, was more fun than he had ever imagined possible.

Pushing the distant memory of her one night with Ross Monahan firmly to the back of her mind, Mattie nodded, burying her face against his chest. Ross didn't count; the marvellousness of it had been too one-sided. Whereas lying here with Richard was a different matter entirely; even though they had only just met she sensed that their feelings for each other were mutual.

And as if reading her mind, he said with a trace of urgency, 'Mattie, I want you to know that I'm not doing this to pay back Antonia. I didn't drive over to The Grange tonight with the intention of picking up a woman . . . a total stranger . . . and persuading her into bed with me. I've never done anything like that in my life, believe me.'

'I do believe you.' Smoothing the worried frown lines from his forehead, she marvelled afresh at his ability to make her happy. And he wasn't just a tremendously *nice* man, either. In his charcoal-grey businessman's suit Richard epitomized everyone's idea of a sober accountant but here, now, without clothes and minus those serious spectacles he was a desirable man with a lean, if not overly muscular, body, gentle hands and seductive grey eyes. To Mattie's surprise and delight, he was also spectacularly well endowed. For the life of her she couldn't imagine why Antonia should ever want to stray from such secure and loving arms and tangle instead with someone as mercurial and undependable as Ross Monahan.

'Where are you going?' Richard reached for Mattie's arm as she swung her legs over the side of the bed.

'I'm thirsty. I thought I'd get a glass of water from the bathroom. Or there's a machine here,' she exclaimed, delighted by the discovery of such unaccustomed luxury. 'I could make us both a cup of tea.'

Hauling her back into bed beside him, Richard smiled and picked up the phone. 'Don't move, this is a special occasion. Hello? Room service, please. I'd like a bottle of Bollinger sent up to Room Forty-two.'

He wasn't wildly experienced in such matters, but he wouldn't mind betting that their room number was compatible with Mattie's splendid bust measurement.

His eyebrows lifted in disbelief as the receptionist informed him that it was three-thirty in the morning, and that room service ceased to operate at midnight.

'But that's terrible!' he exclaimed, winking at Mattie. 'If I'd known this was the case we would have stayed at the Charrington Grange. I know for a fact that they cater for their guests' *every* need.'

'Well, I'm glad,' said Mattie happily, leaning across him and switching on the Teasmade. 'I'd rather have a nice cup of tea anyway.'

At their respective homes, Grace wondered who her mother's new man might be and hoped he was nice, while Antonia lay awake for hours thinking about Ross and sparing only a few fleeting seconds in order to wonder why Richard hadn't returned from Birmingham that evening as he had said he would.

Chapter 33

The centre of Bath was crowded with tourists and having to continually zigzag her way past them had exhausted Holly almost as much as the actual business of shopping.

But bingeing on clothes was one of her most pleasurable vices and when she finally collapsed into a seat outside one of her favourite pavement cafés, just around the corner from the Pump Rooms, the sight of her glossy pyramid of carrier bags – and the thought of their sinfully expensive contents – more than made up for the fact that the soles of her poor feet were actually burning with pain.

Five minutes later, as she was demolishing a plate of blueberry cheesecake, she spotted Adam Perry rounding the corner, apparently making his way towards the wine bar across the road. Grabbing her RayBans and hastily shoving them on to her face, Holly ducked her head and tried to make herself smaller. If only that troupe of camera-happy Japanese would move a couple of feet further to the right – and maybe grow a little taller while they were at it – she would be safe.

But they didn't and she wasn't. The next thing she knew Adam was yelling, 'Hey, gorgeous!' and waving his arms so vigorously that he almost sent a small, spectacled visitor from Japan sailing into the fountain.

Cringing, Holly squeezed out a smile and put down her fork. She would be polite, she decided; maybe allow him to buy her a coffee and chat for a few minutes, then make her excuses and leave.

But Adam, it seemed, had other ideas. Pink with indignation, she watched him turn and head towards the wine bar, one hand jauntily dangling his car keys as he strolled across the square.

Bloody cheek, thought Holly, outraged, and to cover her embarrassment she snatched up her fork once more, digging into the remains of the cheesecake. Who the hell did Adam Perry think he was, anyway?

'And she even smells gorgeous,' proclaimed that familiar male voice two minutes later. Holly, who hadn't noticed his return, jumped a mile as he planted a noisy kiss on the back of her neck. Once again, of course, he had managed to make her the unwanted centre of attention. Even the pigeons, it seemed, were watching with amused interest.

'Sit down,' she hissed, and he roared with laughter.

'I bet you're wondering where I'd got to! Did you feel snubbed? Well, not to worry, angel, I'm here now. Just had to pop across the road and let some friends know I wouldn't be joining them after all. Now that I'm free I can take you somewhere stupendous for lunch.'

He looked so incongruous among the delicate, touristy prettiness of the courtyard. Even the small white chair seemed scarcely capable of bearing his great weight. Holly, taking in the bizarre combination of a strawberry-pink cashmere sweater, creased white cricket flannels, unruly hair and brown, highly polished Gucci loafers, silently marvelled at the man's ability to humiliate her at every turn, and to take such obvious delight in doing so.

'I'm sorry,' she said evenly, 'but I'm afraid I have other plans. Will you leave those *alone*?'

But Adam was already delving into the first of the glossy carriers. And naturally, he had to pick on the Janet Reger bag.

'Holly, this is some serious shopping you have here. I say . . .!'

The French schoolgirls at the next table dissolved into giggles as he held aloft a pair of diaphanous, midnight-blue briefs and matching lacy bra. 'These are absolutely splendid! Very, very seductive—'

'Stop it!' Snatching them from his hand and stuffing them back into their bag, Holly reflected that it could have been worse; hidden in the bottom of the Marks & Spencer carrier was a super-strength panti-girdle. If he had waved that around she really *would* have been embarrassed . . .

'Cancel them.'

'What?'

Adam grinned. 'Those boring old "other plans" of yours. It's a beautiful afternoon and I really think we should spend it together. You could wear your new undies and I could slowly undress you . . . mentally, of course.'

He really was impossible. Holly shook her head. 'I don't want to change my plans. Ross is bringing Tessa and the baby home from the hospital today and we're having a small welcoming party at the cottage.'

'But that's great!' said Adam, undeterred. 'We can go together. On one condition.'

Caught off-guard by the fact that he had so blithely invited himself along, Holly said helplessly, 'What?'

He patted her knee. 'That you wear those delicious new undies, of course.'

* * *

Somebody up there had to be in cahoots with Ross, thought Tessa suspiciously. Never a party person, the size of her home had always seemed perfectly adequate. Well, small but adequate.

This afternoon, however, her poor cottage was struggling to cope with what seemed like an invasion of well-wishers and Ross was wearing an 'I-told-you-so' expression that was all the more irritating because it was entirely justified.

'I want her to come and live with me,' she heard him saying to Holly as she squeezed past in an effort to reach the tiny kitchen, 'but she's so bloody stubborn . . .'

'But don't you live in the hotel?' queried Adam, who took up as much space as three normal-sized people. 'Whoops, breathe in, everyone; recently pregnant woman trying to get through.'

They're all in league against me, thought Tessa. Ross must be loving every minute.

'I've *told* her,' he was explaining now with exaggerated patience, 'that I'd buy us a house . . . something that's a decent size . . . but she won't even discuss it. Did you hear that Hunter's Lodge was going up for auction next week, Adam?'

'Beautiful place!' declared Adam expansively. 'I knew the previous owners, stayed there a few times. Fabulous views, six bedrooms and a swimming-pool.'

It was a conspiracy, thought Tessa darkly as she battled her way back past them. She loved her cottage – every dear little square foot of it – and if Ross thought he was going to win her over with six totally unnecessary bedrooms and a pool he was going to have to think again.

'Tess,' said Max, who was holding Olivia and bending his head in order to navigate the low beams of the sitting room, 'could you get me a cloth from the kitchen? She's just thrown her lunch up over my shirt.'

'Oh, here we go again! Hold your stomachs in,' boomed Adam, as Tessa edged past them once more. 'Ross, how much is Hunter's Lodge expected to go for? Jesus, this cottage is small, I've seen bigger hamster cages . . .'

'All right, all right!' said Tessa, realizing that she could no longer tolerate such unashamed barracking. 'You should all be ashamed of yourselves . . . but I give in.' Turning to look at Ross, she said, 'I don't know what we'll do with six bedrooms but if you've really set your heart on it . . .'

Holly hugged her. Ross, unable to believe that he had finally won, gave Tessa a rapturous kiss. Adam, raising his glass of champagne and brushing it against Olivia's curled fist, said, 'I don't know what you'd do with six bedrooms, sweetheart, but if I were in your shoes' – and he grasped Holly enthusiastically around the waist as he spoke – 'I know *exactly* what would be uppermost in my mind.'

'Pervert,' said Holly, swigging the last of her drink and hoping that they might at last be allowed out into the garden. Ross had insisted that they all stay inside and make themselves as large and inconvenient as possible.

'It's not perverted,' said Adam, pinching her bottom. 'It's human nature, mutual attraction, *chemistry* . . .'

Hunter's Lodge was acquired with almost indecent haste as Tessa had known it would be. Ross, disposing effortlessly of all other interested parties, had outbid them as only a truly determined buyer could outbid and the opposition had shrivelled and died before Tessa's very eyes.

'It's ours,' he told her, hugging her. 'We have a proper home for Olivia. And now, can you think of any reason . . . any reason at all . . . why we shouldn't get married?'

It was the silliest reason in the world and Tessa despised herself for even thinking it but one niggling doubt still remained. For despite everything Ross had done for her – and despite everything he meant to her – she hadn't been able to forget the fact that he had commissioned her to do a painting, apparently been more than pleased with the result, yet had then calmly sold it for a profit as if it had had no more sentimental value than a bunch of BT shares.

'What?' he said now, studying her expression. 'Tell me.'

Tessa shook her head. She *was* being silly. Buying and selling and making money in the process was what businessmen did and if she was going to make a decent living from her painting she had to come to terms with that fact. She would have to learn not to take such transactions as a personal slight.

'Really, it's nothing.'

Ross gave her one of his looks. 'If it's stopping you from agreeing to marry me,' he said evenly, 'then it's something. And there's no point in clamming up now because I'm not going to give up until I find out what it is.'

Knowing that he was nothing if not persistent, Tessa sighed and said quickly, 'You sold the painting I did for you.'

For a moment he was caught off-guard. She saw guilt and a hint of amusement flicker in his dark eyes and knew that he was going to try and joke his way out of it.

'Who told you?'

'It doesn't matter,' she said, because there was no need to involve Grace in the situation. 'I just know. And I also know that it shouldn't bother me . . . but it does.'

He was half-smiling now, taking her hand and squeezing it in a conciliatory manner. 'Sweetheart, I haven't sold it. I told you what happened – Nico wanted to borrow it to show some friends. It's at his house in London.'

'Stop it,' said Tessa despairingly. 'Don't you understand that this is what I can't bear? I don't want you lying to me.'

'But Tess . . .'

'And if you *are* going to lie,' she continued with a trace of bitterness, 'you really should organize your alibis a little more thoroughly. When Nico and his wife came down to The Grange I asked Camilla if she liked the painting. She didn't even know what I was talking about.'

Chapter 34

'I thought you said your aunt lived in Bloomsbury,' said Tessa, as they drove down Regent Street towards Piccadilly Circus.

Ross grinned. He was enjoying himself immensely. Since inventing Aunt Dorothy twenty-four hours earlier – a retired orthopaedic surgeon in her late sixties with a formidable demeanour, a glass eye and rapier wit – he had become quite fond of the old bat.

'She does, but she insisted upon taking us out for lunch at this new restaurant she's discovered in Old Bond Street. We're meeting her there.'

This was the first Tessa had heard of it. Twisting round, she glanced at Olivia, happily asleep in her cot on the back seat. 'I hope the restaurant doesn't mind babies.'

'We're Aunt Dorothy's guests,' said Ross. 'They wouldn't dare.'

'We'll be just around the corner from the Royal Academy,' she remembered, as they approached Swallow Street. 'Oh, Ross . . . it's the Summer Exhibition this week. Do you think we'd have time afterwards to pop in for half an hour? I'd love to see—'

'Sorry, Tess.' He shook his head and grimaced. 'Aunt Dorothy isn't interested in art. Far too frivolous. But if she offers to give you a guided tour of the Science Museum you'll know she likes you.'

'Terrific.' She sighed as they sailed past the Royal Academy, its entrance bustling with visitors. Aunt Dorothy sounded positively terrifying. For the life of her she couldn't imagine why Ross was so keen for her to meet this aged relative whom until yesterday he had never even mentioned.

Luckily, finding Tessa in an advanced stage of labour had concentrated Max's mind to such a degree that he had completely forgotten to tell her about the phone call from the Academy. Even more luckily, when he *did* finally remember, he had told Ross rather than Tessa and Ross had been able to deal with the problem of the chipped frame. So much, he had thought wryly, for the porter pocketing his tip and assuring him that the painting would be treated with nothing but tender loving care.

But the painting, Tessa's painting, was at this moment on display at the Academy and here they were now, practically on the doorstep. Glancing at his watch, Ross said, 'Well I can't see Aunt Dorothy's motor bike anywhere, so maybe we will have time for a quick look at the exhibition after all. Just for a few minutes.'

Thankfully, he had the foresight to take charge of Olivia once they were inside. Whizzing Tessa past the first gallery, he paused at the entrance to the second and said, 'These look more interesting.'

And if Tessa had been holding Olivia there was a faint chance – just the very *faintest* chance – that she might have dropped her.

At first she genuinely thought she was hallucinating. Then, as the crowds jostled around her, she thought that by some million-to-one shot somebody else must have painted a picture so similar to her own that from this distance it looked practically identical.

She moved towards it like a sleep-walker, her fingers tightly clenched at her sides, her heart pounding. Now that she was less than ten feet away it still looked like her painting. Could the mystery buyer possibly have decided – for reasons of his own – to exhibit it? Had another artist seen her work and decided to copy it? She was too confused to speculate further . . . the shock was too intense.

And then she saw the printed card pinned beneath it, bearing her name and a mark indicating that the painting was not for sale, and as realization flooded through her, so her eyes filled with tears of sheer joy.

At that moment Ross, coming to stand beside her with Olivia in his arms, decided that he had never loved Tessa more. The expression on her face was magical. She was beautiful and principled, proud and clever, talented and wilful, and she had given him a daughter who had awoken feelings in him which he had never even known existed.

Slipping her arm through his, Tessa whispered, 'I don't know what to say.'

He smiled, his gaze fixed upon the painting. 'Say yes.'

Still stunned, she shook her head. 'I can't believe this is happening. I can't believe that *you* submitted my painting to the Summer Exhibition . . . do you know how many paintings are sent up each year? And how many are rejected?'

'Yes.'

'But . . . whatever made you decide to do it?'

'Would you have done it?' he countered gently and she shook her head once more, absently stroking the inside of his wrist as she did so.

'Of course not. I wouldn't have dared.'

'That's why I did it.'

'And I thought you'd sold it.'

'Yes.'

Swallowing the lump in her throat, Tessa said in a choked voice, 'I still don't know what to say.'

'Yes,' he prompted with consummate patience, and she smiled.

'OK, yes. Now tell me what I've just agreed to do.'

'You're a clever girl,' he said triumphantly, tilting her face up towards his and kissing her pink mouth. 'I'm sure you can hazard a guess.'

'This time,' sighed Holly ecstatically, '*nothing* can go wrong. It's a *fait accompli*!'

'What is?' asked Tessa, who was feeding Olivia with one hand and attempting to open the post with the other. Incredibly, she was now receiving requests from all over the country for details of her work. Even more happily, Ross's painting was once more hanging in his office and as soon as the redecorations were completed at Hunter's Lodge it would be transferred there, to grace the huge sitting room and serve as a permanent and salutary reminder that she had once doubted his peerless integrity.

'Max is going to be best man,' Holly explained with exaggerated patience, 'and I'm going to be best girl. Need I say more?'

'I'm sure you will,' said Tessa, crumpling up a pile of envelopes and lobbing them in the direction of the waste-paper basket. It didn't seem quite the moment to mention that she had invited Adam Perry to the wedding reception.

Holly applied a celebratory second coat of lipstick with a flourish and blew a kiss at Olivia, who was opening sleepy dark eyes and flailing her tiny fists. 'Of course I'll say more,' she declared, checking her reflection in the mirror. She was due back on duty in ten minutes. 'In fact I'll make a prediction: your wedding night is going to be the night when I finally bundle that gorgeous male body into bed.'

There were so many preparations to be made that Tessa soon began to appreciate the wisdom of those who organized their lives in the traditional manner: wedding first, baby later. Ross was taking care of most of the arrangements but she was still stunned by the amount of work remaining and Olivia, gorgeous but time consuming, was thwarting her at every turn. Her painting, needless to say, had ground to a standstill. Bare canvases lay hidden beneath piles of Pampers and every time she managed to clear a small space in her overcrowded cottage some besotted grown-up – usually either Holly, Max or Adam – would turn up with yet another huge and impractical stuffed toy for Olivia.

She was, nevertheless, truly happy at last. Despite her longstanding doubts and misgivings she knew now that marrying Ross was what she most wanted to do.

And since she had cringed at the thought of a huge wedding and Ross had set his heart on one, they had reached a compromise: a small ceremony held at Bath's Register Office would be followed by a vast and lavish reception at The Grange.

It sounded simple, she thought helplessly as Olivia screamed for her feed and knocked a pile of invitation acceptances to the floor. Whoever would have thought that getting married could be so incredibly complicated?

* * *

Whoever would have imagined that being in love could be so complicated, thought Mattie as she sipped her tea and waited for the phone to ring, secure in the knowledge that it almost certainly would.

Having never imagined herself in the role of mistress she still found it hard to come to terms with the fact that she was one. With the right man, she had discovered with more than a twinge of guilt, it was appallingly easy.

In a seedy way, of course, it had been exciting. The thrill of secrecy was an added aphrodisiac and when they were together Mattie told herself – as Richard had instructed her to do – that since Antonia had herself been having affairs for years it didn't count. It wasn't as if he was being unfaithful to a faithful wife who waited at home for him with loving conversation and a carefully prepared meal.

But guilt and joy and new love and the knowledge that what she was doing was wrong . . . yet at the same time so blissfully right . . . was certainly a shock to the system. In the past fortnight she had lost ten pounds quite effortlessly. She was thinking of marketing the Sex-Plan diet. Lack of self-confidence, however, was the spoiler. Despite the fact that everyone was commenting on how much better she looked, and despite the fact that Richard had told her (last night, at the crucial point in their lovemaking) that he loved her, Mattie couldn't help wondering about the future. Did saying it *then* actually count? What was really going to come of this glorious affair?

For while she loved . . . adored . . . worshipped Richard, the terrifying thought that he was only using her still continued to haunt Mattie's day-dreams. A practical woman, she was only too uncomfortably aware that this could well be another Ross

Monahan-type affair . . . only more prolonged. Why ever, after all, should Richard want to leave a beautiful, streamlined, *young* wife for an older, plumper, un-chic woman with nothing more to offer than helpless devotion and stretchmarks?

Francine Lalonde had stretchmarks but they didn't deter Max. Holly, wearing a new and excruciatingly pink shade of lipstick which made him long to scrub her mouth with a tissue, had spent the entire morning practically leering at him. In retaliation, he went upstairs and placed a call to Madrid, where Francine was currently filming.

She was on set, of course, and unable to come to the phone.

When she finally managed to call him back three hours later he was disappointed to hear that returning to England in order to attend his brother's wedding was out of the question. She couldn't possibly get away.

And even more disappointingly – Francine being Francine – she insisted on telling him exactly why not. 'Darling, I am exhausted! This stinking director makes me work and work all day and half the night and then Armand makes love to me for the other half . . . I tell you, it is as much as I can do to take a bath without being seduced. Maybe when this terrible film is over I can come to see you but at the moment I am up to my eyelashes in hard work. Ahh!' He heard her gusty sigh and wondered viciously whether the unknown Armand – doubtless some mercenary gigolo – was with her even now. 'You have no idea, darling, how wearing it all is.'

Despising himself, he heard himself say, 'I've been pretty busy myself. The screenplay's almost finished.'

Francine let out an excited whoop. 'Max, you are magnificent!

And is it truly marvellous? Will it win me an Oscar, do you think?'

'You'll have to read it and decide for yourself,' he replied, attempting to sound offhand yet at the same time magnificent. Since the thought of his body wasn't enough to tempt her away from Armand, he was reduced to baiting her with the promise of an unseen – and as yet unfinished – script. 'Altman's very interested,' he added even more casually. Now he was further reduced to telling great big, totally shameless lies.

'Robert Altman!' exclaimed Francine, audibly impressed. 'He's a wonderful director . . . Max, I promise you that I will come to your dear little hotel and visit you very soon.'

It was just as well, thought Max when he finally replaced the receiver, that it *had* been a lie. If Robert Altman were to direct Francine in this film she would doubtless have even less time than ever to spare for its lowly writer.

Chapter 35

The day before the wedding promised to be a heavenly one. A light, gauzy mist had dispersed by eight o'clock and the sky, initially pale, darkened steadily to cobalt blue unmarred by a single cloud. Hotel guests took their breakfast on the terrace, basking in the warmth of the sun, admiring the perfect views and taking their time deciding which of Bath's celebrated sights they should see today . . . that was, if they could tear themselves away from the perfection already surrounding them.

Grace, serving breakfast to a party of Germans – two overweight businessmen from Dusseldorf and their equally fat, sunburnt wives – was surprised to see Antonia Seymour-Smith sitting alone at a nearby table. Always a regular visitor to the hotel in the past she had been conspicuous by her absence in the last six weeks and those who were aware of her longstanding relationship with Ross – which meant everyone who worked in the hotel – had presumed that Ross, cleaning up his act now that he was a father and husband-to-be, had terminated their affair and advised her to steer clear of The Grange.

As she unloaded the last of the dishes piled high with grilled bacon, mushrooms, tomatoes and scrambled eggs on to the Germans' table, Grace glanced across once more and hoped that Antonia hadn't come to try and stir up trouble. Her own tentative friendship with Tessa was enormously precious to her, she adored her little half-sister Olivia, and since Ross and Tessa had announced their marriage plans, Ross had been a changed person. Grace's day-dreams now revolved hopefully around the idea that one day she would finally be able to pluck up the courage to tell Tessa who she really was, and that she would be welcomed with joy and delight into the glamorous, loving and infinitely exciting Monahan family.

Recalling now the events of last Christmas, when Antonia had introduced herself to Tessa and had attempted to sabotage her relationship with Ross, Grace wondered whether she should find him now and warn him that Antonia was here. But even as the thought crossed her mind she heard the familiar roar of his car's engine and a couple of seconds later saw the gleaming white Mercedes snake off down the drive towards the main road.

At that moment Antonia raised her hand, gesturing for attention, and Grace realized that she would have to do the honours herself.

'Coffee please,' said Antonia, her face shielded behind huge dark glasses, her expression toneless. Grace wasn't the only one whose ears were attuned to the sound of that particular engine, and although Antonia hadn't deliberately come here this morning in the hope of seeing Ross, her stomach curled in disappointment as she realized that subconsciously that was exactly what she *had* wanted.

Never mind, she consoled herself, as the waitress before her fumbled in her skirt pocket for an order pad. Marriage wasn't the end of the world. As soon as the novelty wore off, Ross would come back to her.

'Just coffee,' she repeated with exaggerated patience as Grace stood, pencil poised, before her. What was this girl anyway, a half-wit?

'Gosh, sorry. We've all been so busy with the preparations for Ross's wedding,' said Grace cheerfully, 'that I don't know whether I'm coming or going. There's so much to do and everyone's so excited.'

'Mm,' said Antonia, glancing at her own wedding-ring. 'Well, weddings are exciting. They have to be, to make up for all that boredom later on.'

'Oh, Tessa and Ross won't be bored,' declared Grace stoutly, and Antonia hid a smile. Ross certainly wouldn't be bored if she had anything to do with it. 'They really are wonderfully suited,' continued Grace, seizing her chance. 'I've never seen Ross so happy and I just know that they're going to have a perfect marriage. He's changed,' she added meaningfully, her cheeks pink with her own daring, 'and now that he's finally fallen in love with someone he's going to make sure he keeps her for ever and—'

'Reading too many cheap romantic novels can seriously damage your health,' snapped Antonia, provoked beyond endurance and suppressing a wild urge to slap the girl's stupid little face. Rising abruptly from her seat she added, 'Cancel that coffee.'

'Good,' whispered Grace triumphantly as she watched Antonia leave, 'because we don't need your kind at this hotel.' And one day, *one day*, she would tell Ross of the part she had played in ensuring that his wedding-day proceeded without a hitch.

A notorious law unto themselves, journalists have always taken great pride in their ability to make an impact.

Sadie Labelle, being no exception, was particularly pleased with her article, published on the eve of Ross Monahan's wedding.

As a powerful Fleet Street journalist she was accustomed to respect from people far more important than Tessa Duvall and the girl's obvious disinterest, not to mention her flippancy, had needled her beyond belief.

But, as Ross had warned Tessa, nobody needled Sadie Labelle and got away with it and this time the woman famous for her lack of subtlety had really gone to town. 'I don't make a habit of interviewing non-celebrities,' began the opening paragraph, and Holly, who had crawled back into bed with a mug of tea, a mild hangover and the morning paper, experienced a crawling unease. 'But since this particular non-celebrity is Tessa Duvall, the soon-to-be wife of the wonderfully wicked Ross Monahan, I was persuaded to meet her.

'And a very educational meeting it was too. Why, I wondered, should an eminently eligible man like Ross want to marry an unknown, unsmiling artist whose talent for small-talk is limited and whose interest in meeting this humble journalist was on a par with her former financial standing . . . zilch?

'But Ms Duvall is a clever girl and the answer, of course, is that she caught him. And this is where I'd like to draw her tactics to the attention of single, successful men everywhere. During the course of our interview she told me a fib or two and I don't imagine they were the first of her young life. But I'd like to point out to Ms Duvall and those women who would seek to emulate her that single, successful men eventually see through such ploys. If Tessa truly believes that she has hooked her man for life then I beg her to think again . . .'

There was more of the same but Holly had already snatched up the phone and punched out the number of The Grange. Moments later, she reached Max.

'Oh Max, for heaven's sake don't let—'

'— Tessa see the paper,' he intercepted swiftly, knowing what Holly was like when she switched into gabble-mode. 'It's OK, she's already seen it. She laughed.'

Holly sank back against the pillows, deflated but still outraged. 'She really laughed? But it's so *nasty*! Is she going to sue?'

'No, of course not. You know Tessa, she's not going to let a little thing like that bother her. And she's never been one to care too much about what other people think of her, has she?' Max smiled as he spoke, recalling the time when she had tipped a bottle of rather good red wine down his trousers. Holly, however, was less convinced.

'Sometimes people pretend not to care,' she said, crumpling up the offending article and tossing it in the direction of her waste-paper bin. Since her aim, however, hadn't improved with age, it landed instead in the wide brim of the hat she would be wearing at tomorrow's wedding. 'But deep down they're still hurt.' The comment, she felt, was doubly apt; hopefully it would make Max think twice about their own relationship. It was about time he realized that she was more than an endless sheet of blotting paper for his insults.

'Sometimes that is the case,' agreed Max, who realized exactly what she was up to. 'On the other hand,' he added, because baiting Holly was something he could never resist, 'some people just aren't happy unless they *are* being hurt.'

The newspaper article had hurt Tessa, of course it had, but she had managed to persuade herself that it really didn't matter and she'd also done a pretty good job of concealing her true feelings.

She'd needed to as well, in order to calm down her furious future husband, who had called Sadie Labelle every ghastly name under the sun and threatened to sue her for every penny she'd ever earned. It had taken quite a time to reassure him and Tessa had been more than a little relieved when she'd finally managed to persuade him to drive into Bath and pick up a couple of extra cases of champagne.

'Don't let it bother you,' she'd told him as she kissed him goodbye.

'She's a fat bitch,' said Ross, putting his arms around her shoulders, 'but OK. Besides, I'm not going to let La Ugly spoil our wedding-day. Hmm,' he murmured, drawing Tessa closer and running his hands appreciatively down to her slender waist, 'I could think of much nicer things to do right now than trailing into town and buying champagne. How about a little practice run, just to make sure we'll know what to do tomorrow night . . .?'

'How about exercising a little self-control?' suggested Tessa with a reluctant smile. 'We have a million other things to do today . . . and it seems a shame to give in now, with only twenty-four hours to go.'

'If I'd known that you didn't approve of pre-marital sex,' Ross murmured, kissing her neck and breathing in the familiar, gorgeous scent of her skin, 'I would have married you six months ago.'

'I know you would,' she replied with a smirk. 'But in case you'd forgotten, Mr Monahan, I turned you down.'

Chapter 36

The cottage was almost completely empty now. Tessa stood in the centre of the sitting room with Olivia cradled in her arms amd gazed at the rough, whitewashed walls bereft of paintings. She smiled to herself as she realized that most houses looked much larger when they were empty but this one still seemed as tiny as ever.

But it had been *her* home. She had loved living here.

'And now we're going up in the world,' she told Olivia, who was far more interested in attempting to separate her toes from her fat little feet. 'Are you excited?'

Olivia let out a squeal of frustration. Her toes were very firmly screwed on indeed.

'Hmm, well don't let Ross hear you say that. When we move into that big new house he'll expect you to express your appreciation in the proper manner. And that doesn't mean throwing up all over those spectacular handwoven carpets he's so proud of.'

But her daughter, unimpressed, remained absorbed in the matter of her undetachable toes. Tessa, replacing her in the carrycot, glanced at her watch and decided that it was time to load the last remaining boxes of plants, books and paintings into the car. She really needed to be back at The Grange by twelve-thirty in order to thank the dressmaker who was delivering her own and Holly's finished outfits. The poor woman had worked so hard, altering her own dress three times as week by week she had shrunk back to her pre-Olivia shape and at the same time coping with Holly's histrionics when a bout of lovelorn bingeing had resulted in two extra inches around her hips.

Antonia realized that she was driving because she didn't know what else she could possibly do to pass the time. She felt as twitchy and uneasy as a reformed alcoholic on the verge of giving in. It was only eleven-thirty and she didn't know how she was going to get through the next hour, let alone the next two days. Because no matter how many times she reminded herself that Ross's marriage was nothing more than a temporary inconvenience, the words were somehow no longer ringing true.

She had begun to panic and that spiteful little waitress at The Grange – despite the fact that she'd probably been paid by Tessa to say what she had – had only made the uncertainty harder to bear. All Antonia knew now was that Ross was about to marry someone who was quite wrong for him ... he was making a hideous mistake ... and she simply couldn't bear to think of it, but since there wasn't anything else to occupy her mind she was unable to stop the terrible thoughts going round and round ...

Having managed to persuade herself that visiting the hotel earlier had been simply a pleasant way of starting the day, Antonia was forced to admit that turning into the narrow lane which led to Tessa's cottage was sheer compulsion, something she absolutely had to do.

But it was a harmless enough act, she reasoned, braking slightly as the amber roof of the cottage came into sight over the brow of the next hill. The place was empty now, and there would be no one to testify to the humiliating fact that Ross Monahan's discarded mistress was behaving like a lovelorn fourth former.

When she saw, however, that the cottage was not empty, Antonia's heart did a slow, looping somersault. Tessa *was* there, after all, her blonde hair glistening in the sunlight as she lifted and loaded the first of several boxes into the boot of her car.

Antonia realized in a flash that she was trapped. With the top down on her own car she was going to be instantly recognizable even if she shot past at eighty miles an hour. But the lane was so narrow that stopping and attempting to turn around would be a physical impossibility. And still she was stuck; even as these thoughts crossed her mind the distance between Tessa and herself was steadily shrinking. She was no longer in control of the situation. Whatever happened next was out of her hands. She would leave it up to instinct and fate.

'Hello,' said Tessa cautiously, when Antonia's car had slowed to a halt beside the front gate. It had been six months since they had last met, but she recognized her at once, as Antonia had known she would. Tessa had a memory for faces and Antonia, with her sleek, straight, dark blonde hair and expertly made-up deep blue eyes, hadn't changed at all.

'Hi,' said Antonia, switching off the ignition and taking in every detail of Tessa with equal efficiency. No make-up, pale pink cotton shirt tied at the waist above white Levis, oddly familiar pale pink leather pumps . . . 'Where did you get those shoes?'

Polite conversation was all very well, but Tessa still had a lot to do. Lifting a box of paintings and placing it carefully in the boot of the car – Ross's car – she said, 'Oxfam.'

'I thought so.' Antonia sounded pleased. 'They're mine.'

This time Tessa risked a smile. 'Well, they were.'

'But you're marrying Ross Monahan tomorrow,' said Antonia, lighting a cigarette and blowing a perfect smoke ring. 'Surely you don't need to buy second-hand shoes any more? Doesn't he look after you?'

Tessa glanced down at her feet. 'I'm still capable of buying my own shoes.'

Ross was mine too, thought Antonia, but before she could think of anything more to say the sound of a baby crying broke the silence. 'Is that Olivia?'

It could hardly have been anyone else but Tessa nodded anyway. 'I'd better go and see to her.'

'Would you mind,' said Antonia eagerly, 'if I came with you? I'd like to see her too.'

'Look, I'm sorry.' Tessa hesitated, hands on hips. 'But this is a weird situation. I really don't understand why you've come here.'

Antonia shrugged. 'I'm not sure myself. I suppose I was curious. But if you're at all worried that I might harm your baby . . . I'll go.'

Instantly ashamed of herself, Tessa said, 'I wasn't thinking that, I was just pointing out the fact that this is a bit strange. But if you'd like to see Olivia, then of course you can.'

Antonia smiled. 'Thanks.'

'Oh, she's adorable!' she exclaimed, her gaze softening as Olivia made a fretful grab for her necklace. 'You're so lucky . . . just look at those incredible eyes . . . I can't believe how like Ross she is!'

'But smaller,' said Tessa with a grin.

'You're so lucky,' repeated Antonia softly, moving across to the window and pushing her hands into her jacket pocket.

Turning back to face Tessa she said, 'Do you think you'll be happy with Ross?'

Here we go, thought Tessa, who had half-suspected that something like this would happen. Humouring the woman before her, she pretended to give the question serious consideration.

'Yes,' she replied finally. 'If I didn't think it was right I wouldn't be marrying him.'

'He's had a bit of a reputation in the past,' said Antonia, the knot of tension in her stomach tightening up once more. She hadn't meant to say it but somehow, now that she was here, she simply had to. Tessa *should* know what Ross was like, it wouldn't be fair not to tell her.

'What he's done in the past is his affair,' said Tessa, and immediately winced.

'Ah, you're assuming that he's changed,' Antonia pointed out, an edge of triumph in her voice. 'But how would you feel if I told you that he hadn't?'

'Maybe I'd think that you don't want me to marry him,' said Tessa, outwardly calm. Inwardly, however, she was beginning to feel both angry and afraid.

'If I thought you'd be happy I wouldn't be saying this,' Antonia told her, her expression sincere. 'And I'm not being a bitch, really I'm not. But I do think you deserve to know what Ross is like.'

Hating this and hating herself for even listening, Tessa murmured, 'Go on, then.' Whatever Antonia had to say would be the wishful thinking of a jealous woman. She needn't take any notice of it because it wouldn't be true.

'He came to my house a few weeks ago and told me that our affair had to stop – for a while,' said Antonia quickly. 'But he promised me that he would be back. I'm sorry, Tessa, but you see it isn't over between us at all. Ross and I have an understanding and—'

'I don't believe you,' said Tessa, shifting Olivia from one hip to the other and smoothing her dark head with trembling fingers. This was horrible. She *wasn't* going to believe it. Antonia was lying.

'Would you believe Max?' asked Antonia gently. 'Maybe you'd accept what I have to say if he confirmed it. Why don't you ask him where Ross was while you were in hospital giving birth to Olivia?'

Tessa froze. Perspiration trickled down her spine, yet she was cold and shivering. She didn't want to hear this.

'Max knows,' continued Antonia, who couldn't have stopped now if Ross had erupted into the room with a shotgun. 'Because I was in bed with Ross when he phoned him at the Ritz. We spent the night in Room One Eight Four and I picked up the phone when Max called the following morning. I truly *am* sorry, Tessa, but I couldn't bear to think of you marrying someone like Ross in the mistaken belief that he would be faithful to you, because he simply isn't that kind of man and I think you deserve better.'

'And I think,' said Tessa tonelessly, 'that it's time you left.'

There wasn't time to think. She didn't want to think. In an hour, Olivia would need to be fed and Ross would be wondering why they hadn't returned to the hotel. She was going to have to move fast, without thinking, and get away before the true horror of it all really hit her.

* * *

Obtaining the number from directory enquiries and punching out the number on the new mobile Ross had given her was easy. Telling the receptionist that her name was Mrs Monahan, and that she thought she may have lost a gold earring during her overnight stay in . . . Room One Eight Two . . . on the twenty fifth of June was easy.

The receptionist had apparently checked the reservation on a computer because within moments she was back on the line. 'It was in fact Room One Eight Four, Mrs Monahan, but I'm afraid we haven't found your earring.'

And hearing those words was the hardest, the very hardest thing she had ever had to do in her life.

Knowing that Holly would be up at The Grange by now, Tessa dialled her flat. The answerphone picked up on the fourth ring. This wasn't going to be easy either, but at least it would be an improvement on the last call. All pain was relative, she thought as she listened to Holly's ludicrously cheerful recorded message. Then, as the tone went, she took a deep, shivering breath and said, 'Holly, it's me. I'm not going to marry Ross. I'm sorry, but I'm leaving it up to you to tell him the wedding's off. Olivia and I are going away . . . to Scotland . . . but I promise I'll be in touch with you soon. Sorry . . .'

Chapter 37

'If this is some kind of joke,' said Ross slowly, 'then all I can tell you is that it's in fucking bad taste.'

Holly despised herself for her weakness but she knew she simply wasn't capable of getting through this without help. The half-pint glass clashed with her teeth as she took another gulp of wine and tears sprang to her eyes. He knew she wouldn't joke about something like this . . . he just couldn't believe that it was really happening. She still couldn't believe it herself, for heaven's sake. This sort of thing *didn't* really happen. Particularly to someone like Ross Monahan.

'It's true,' she said, taking another slug of wine. 'She left the message on my answering machine. She . . . told me to tell you the wedding was off. Oh Ross, why would she *do* this?'

At that moment Max burst into the office. 'Has Tessa shown up yet? I've checked the cottage but it's empty and—'

'She's gone,' said Ross evenly. Max took in Holly's distraught state at a glance. Mauve eyeshadow and black mascara were sliding down her cheeks and she was gulping like a child. Without even thinking, he pulled out a clean handkerchief and shoved it into her hands.

'Gone where?'

Ross shrugged, his dark eyes avoiding direct contact, his jaw tense. 'Scotland, evidently.' With a vague gesture towards the big, north-facing window he added, 'Funny how some people run away to Scotland to get married while others go there in order to avoid having to.'

'But *why*?' demanded Max furiously. 'What's happened?'

Ross, unable to speak for a moment, merely shrugged. Holly, who had been struggling to choke back her tears, burst into noisy, inelegant sobs.

'Nothing's happened!' she wailed. 'I saw her last night and she was fine! I just can't believe this is happening . . .'

'Doesn't she realize what she's *doing*?' Max began, then stopped himself. 'Oh shit, of course she does. Look, we've got a lot to do. If there's no way of contacting Tessa and getting this bloody mess sorted out, we need to face facts – the wedding has to be cancelled.'

The enormity of the task sent a shudder down Holly's spine. Even at this moment guests were arriving at the hotel. She knew that a party of Ross's friends were flying back from Marbella, breaking their holiday in order to attend the wedding of the year. And there were all those expensive gifts, the sumptuous food which the restaurant staff had worked so hard to prepare . . . van loads of flowers . . . the hideous gossip and excited speculation of staff and guests . . . however would Ross cope with the humiliation? And – oh God – what about the Press, due to descend in droves? They would hardly be able to believe their ghoulish luck; runaway brides and jilted husbands were far more enthralling than run-of-the-mill wedding ceremonies and tales of happy-ever-after.

It was a nightmare. And now her glass was empty. The nightmare deepened.

'I could do with a drink myself,' said Max, observing her stricken face. Then he glanced at his brother. 'Ross?'

'I don't want anything.' Ross moved towards his desk and picked up the phone. Within seconds he was through to the offices of one of London's leading press agencies.

'Steve? It's Ross. Look, I don't have time to fuck about so I'm relying on you to spread the word. I'm not getting married tomorrow. Yes, it's all off.' He listened for a moment, his knuckles tightening around the receiver. 'Sorry mate, but no comment. It's nobody's business but our own. Just make sure everyone knows, OK? And tell them that any member of the Press caught within half a mile of this hotel within the next week will have my guard dogs to answer to.'

'Sit down,' commanded Max, returning to the office with a bottle of Scotch and two glasses and practically pushing Holly down into the nearest chair.

'But I should be helping . . . ' she protested weakly, taking the fresh glass and downing a hefty gulp of the amber liquid.

'A lot of use you'd be,' he remarked, pouring his own drink. 'You look bloody awful. It's OK,' he added, turning his attention to Ross, 'I've let them know outside. Sylvie has instructions to tell anyone who's booked a room for tomorrow that they're welcome to stay free of charge if they want to. She's cancelling the flowers, the Register Office and the cars. All we have to do now is contact as many of your friends as possible and tell them it's off, and decide where you're going to go. You have to get away for a couple of weeks,' he explained, meeting Ross's blank expression. 'You can't stay here, for Christ's sake.'

'I work here,' replied Ross evenly. 'I live here. And I'm bloody well staying here. What am I supposed to do, fly off to Antigua for a solo honeymoon?'

* * *

'It's the shock,' said Holly, later that evening. It was ironic in the extreme that tonight of all nights she and Max actually should be having their most intimate conversation yet. She only hoped she'd be able to remember it all tomorrow morning, she thought woozily as he leaned forward and topped up her drink once more. 'I've never seen Ross like this before. He's like a robot.'

They were sitting in a dim corner of the bar, keeping as far away as possible from the rest of the guests. It wasn't necessary to be a lip-reader to guess their favourite topic of conversation tonight. Yet Ross stood among them, a glass of Perrier water in his hand, speaking and nodding and listening in turn as if nothing at all had happened. Only his eyes, fathomless and fractionally less bright than usual, gave him away; as Holly had pointed out, he was functioning on automatic pilot, silently daring anyone to either ridicule or pity him. Watching him, she could have wept all over again because he was being so brave, and it was all so unnecessary. He shouldn't be doing this, it could only be adding to his private agony. And they still had absolutely no idea why Tessa had run away . . .

Max, realizing that she was once more on the brink of tears, took Holly's hand. Her vulnerability had touched him today as no amount of wit and brashness and sparkling repartee ever had. Now, with her make-up long since gone – his silk handkerchief had borne the brunt of that onslaught – and with her red-gold hair free of bows, bright combs and lacquer, she looked younger, more approachable and more *real* than the Holly he had known and taken care to avoid for so long.

'Ross will live. Of course he's in shock, but he'll come through it. And you really didn't need to apologize to him earlier, you know,' he added with a brief smile. 'He doesn't hold you responsible.'

Holly, her gaze fixed on his hand clasping her own, was finding it difficult to concentrate. It was the first time Max had ever voluntarily touched her. It was typical, she thought, that after years of expensive manicures and literally hundreds of bottles of nail polish he should have held her hand on the one day when her nails were bare.

But the warmth of his touch, his gentle strength, the reassuring intimacy of the gesture, was nevertheless as exhilarating as she had always imagined. She wanted to kiss his tanned fingers and press them to her cheek . . . she wanted to press his whole body against her whole body . . .

'— can't stand the way people keep looking over at us,' Max was saying. Guiltily, Holly thrust her fantasies to the back of her mind and assumed an attentive expression. For a moment, two Max Monahans swam before her like formation dancers.

'Sorry?'

'Why does everyone think we know why Tessa disappeared?' he said, glaring across at a group of whispering middle-aged women and hauling an unsuspecting Holly to her feet. 'Come on, I feel like something in a zoo down here. Let's go.'

'Go where?' whispered Holly, clinging on to him for support as he veered between the tables. Gosh, she hadn't felt this dizzy when she'd been sitting down. But Max was being so wonderfully masterful that if he'd said Siberia she would have happily agreed.

'Upstairs,' he said casually, then glanced down at her. 'That is,' he added with a wry grin, 'if you think you can manage them.'

Max's rooms smelled unmistakably of Max. Holly would have

recognized the scent of that particular, unusual aftershave anywhere. Sinking down into the depths of the butter-soft beige leather sofa, she realized belatedly that she still hadn't let go of Max's hand. When he sat down beside her she heard her own heart racing. She only wished she could remember whether she'd put on a clean bra this morning.

'You smell nice,' she said dreamily, edging closer gradually so that he wouldn't notice she was doing it. 'Have I ever told you that? You always smell . . . wonderful.'

If she didn't stop sidling along the sofa she was going to end up on his lap, thought Max, but somehow the thought was no longer a terrifying one. Holly, devoted and uncomplaining, was simply someone he had never taken seriously before but right now he felt he deserved a little devotion. And since Francine was no doubt enjoying herself with Armand . . . or Giorgio . . . or Kurt . . . he didn't see much point in saving himself for the moment when she might actually deign to enjoy herself with him. Besides, if he closed his eyes he could almost imagine that Holly was Francine; their voluptuous figures weren't at all dissimilar.

Holly's eyes were already closed. All that alcohol on a completely empty stomach had knocked her for six and although she was vaguely aware that this was the happiest, most glorious moment of her life, the culmination of every fantasy she had ever . . . well, fantasized, she was nevertheless finding it extra-ordinarily difficult to remain sitting upright. Feeling Max's arm sliding across her shoulder she attempted to turn towards him but she was no longer quite sure where he was. Because her eyes were still shut of course, she scolded herself. This was silly, she had to open them in order to get her bearings . . . but darling

Max was murmuring her name from a great distance and now she felt as if she were in a tunnel, slipping helplessly away from him.

'Max,' she called weakly, holding out her arms and realizing that the room was spinning, gathering speed, and that at any moment she might topple right over on to the floor. 'Max, please . . . hang on to me . . . don't let go . . . Max, I do love you . . .'

Chapter 38

'You look like the little matchgirl,' observed Dominic, opening the front door and disguising his surprise with typical flippancy. 'Only wetter.'

Then without another word he took Olivia – asleep in her carrycot – and drew Tessa into the large, incredibly untidy living room. Within moments, her rain-soaked pale pink shirt was on the floor and he was pulling one of his own sweaters – black lambswool with cadmium-yellow paint staining one sleeve – over her damp head.

'Now sit,' he said, pointing to the rug in front of the gas fire and throwing her a towel. 'Dry your hair. What do you want, coffee or a drink?'

'C . . . coffee,' said Tessa, her teeth chattering uncontrollably. 'Please.'

'And Olivia? What would she like . . . Beaujolais Nouveau? Cognac?'

To his relief, Tessa managed a faint, barely-there smile. 'I'll take care of Olivia when she wakes up, thanks.'

Having planned on driving up to Bath for the wedding the following morning, Dominic hadn't bothered to buy any milk so he got out the cognac anyway and splashed some into Tessa's black coffee by way of recompense. Then he sat back and waited for her to drink it, and for her teeth to stop chattering, before he spoke again.

'I know I'm supposed to tell you that you don't have to talk about it if you don't want to,' he began, flipping the ring pull on his own can of lager and pausing for a second to take a swallow. 'But I'm not that polite. So tell me why you're here and not there.'

His matter-of-fact tone was exactly what she needed. At the first sign of sympathy Tessa knew she would break down in tears. Gratefully following his lead she said, 'The old, sordid story, I'm afraid. He's been seeing another woman and I was the last to know. Luckily, I found out before it was too late.'

Dominic thought for a moment. 'Antonia.'

She nodded.

'Christ, he must be mad.'

'Yes, well . . . the thing is, could you put up with a couple of flatmates for a while, just until I get something else organized?' She shrugged, dragging her fingers through the wet tangle of her hair. 'We don't have any references and one of us is incontinent and can be pretty noisy at times, but we'll try not to be a nuisance and we promise not to throw all-night parties more than twice a week.'

'Incontinent flatmates are my favourite kind,' he declared expansively. 'And you can stay as long as you like, so don't worry about looking for somewhere else. Now, why don't you give me the keys and I'll get your cases from the car.'

Tessa, who was still towelling her hair, sighed and said, 'How do you suppose I got so wet? The car belongs to Ross, for heaven's sake. I drove to the railway station in Bath and left it parked outside on double yellows . . . it's probably been towed away by now. And I haven't brought anything with me so until I can get out to the shops I'm afraid you're going to have to do without this rather expensive sweater.'

She had, however, had the presence of mind to remember the pink raffia knapsack stuffed with disposable nappies, clean clothes and other baby essentials.

When Olivia had been fed and changed and put down for the night in the spare room, Dominic and Tessa settled down before the fire once more with a bottle of Spanish red wine. She was still unnaturally calm about the traumatic events of the day and Dominic, realizing that the time had now come for the emotions to surface, said gently, 'Tell me exactly what happened, sweetheart. Come on, you need to get it out of your system.' Tessa, however, remained pale but composed. The wine was warming her and she was lucky enough to have a friend like Dominic; she was simply glad to be here in Cornwall, with him.

'It was my own fault really,' she said, her tone calm, her arms hugging her bent knees. 'I knew what Ross was like . . . *you* knew I knew what he was like! . . . but I was silly enough to think he'd changed, whereas what I should have done was stuck to my original decision and steered well clear of him.'

'The papers will be full of it when word gets out,' remarked Dominic. She was *too* calm. Now he found himself almost deliberately trying to provoke the inevitable outburst – anything was better than all this frozen acceptance. 'What will you say when they ask you for your side of it?'

'Nothing.' Tessa smiled. 'I'm staying here and Ross thinks I'm in Scotland. Look, are you hungry? Why don't I make us something to eat?'

'Oh, for heaven's sake, Tess,' he exploded, gesturing frustratedly at his shirt-front. 'Here's my shoulder! You're supposed to cry on it. It's the night before your wedding and you've done a runner . . . you should be weeping and wailing and instead you're offering to cook me a bloody meal!'

Leaning over, laughing now, she kissed his tanned cheek. 'I was gullible, I trusted someone and he let me down. Of course I'm sad, but how can I regret knowing Ross when if it weren't for him, Olivia wouldn't even exist? Having a daughter means far more to me than having a husband. And don't flatter yourself,' she added, rising to her feet and heading towards the kitchen, 'I wasn't going to *cook* you a meal anyway. What I had in mind was peanut-butter sandwiches . . .'

The change in the weather had been dramatic; after weeks of unrelenting sunshine and soaring temperatures, the storm had broken in spectacular fashion at around two o'clock that afternoon. The sound of unaccustomed rain hammering mercilessly against the windows had seemed quite strange, alien to the ears after such a prolonged dry spell. Dominic, finding himself suddenly and unexpectedly awake at four-thirty in the morning, lay in the darkness and sleepily assumed that it was this noise which had disturbed him.

But a moment later he heard the quieter rustle of paper and some sixth sense made him realize what was happening. Sliding noiselessly out of bed and dragging on the nearest pair of jeans to cover his nakedness, he made his way across the hallway and pushed open the door to the sitting room.

Tessa was kneeling on the floor, her blonde head tilted away from him, her slender shoulders heaving. Before her lay the discarded scarlet and white striped paper in which his wedding present – flamboyantly addressed to Mr and Mrs Monahan – had been wrapped.

Dominic, justifiably proud of the small, simply constructed sculpture he had worked on for almost three full days, wished now that he had bought them an electric kettle instead. The two entwined figures, male and female locked in a tender embrace and demonstrating with aching clarity the love and trust which bound them, lay in Tessa's lap and as he watched, ashamed by his thoughtlessness but at the same time relieved, a single tear splashed down on to the ivory glazed figures and Tessa's sobbing finally became audible.

Crouching down beside her, he pulled her gently into his arms. 'I'm sorry, I should have put it away.'

He had had plenty of experience in his time with the vagaries of female emotion; as he had expected, the gesture of comfort had a cathartic effect upon her tears. All he had to do now was hold her and wait patiently for her to finish. She would feel far better as soon as this first outpouring of grief was out of her system.

Chapter 39

It had been, decided Holly morbidly, the most hideous day of her entire life. As she crawled into bed at the ridiculously early hour of ten o'clock she shuddered afresh at the memory of the moment when she had woken up in Max's bed. The hangover alone had been pretty unbearable but mingled with the scent of *that* aftershave it had finished her off completely. Thank goodness Max hadn't been there to see her sitting up in bed retching helplessly into the nearest flower vase.

And then, when she had finally managed to locate her shoes and stagger from the bedroom to the sitting room, he had been there, showered and dressed and concentrating rigidly on the screen of the word processor at which he sat. Fumbling like an idiot for her handbag, which was squashed halfway down the back of the sofa, she had tried to smile at him and received a brief, less than reassuring, stare in return. The relaxed intimacy of the previous evening was clearly no longer on the agenda. She felt dreadful and probably looked it. Max, no doubt, was thanking his lucky stars right now that she *had* passed out before he could do anything he would certainly have regretted later. Cinderella had had her chance and she'd blown it. And if she didn't get out of here fast she was in very real danger of being sick again, all over his beautiful leather upholstery. Bitterly ashamed of herself – how, after all, could she ever have really imagined that she stood a chance with Max in clothes like these and no make-up?

– she gave up on the smile. Her teeth hurt too much anyway, along with the rest of her hideous body.

'I'll be off then,' she said, as Max typed a few words, swore beneath his breath and irritably deleted them.

'Mmm.'

'And . . . I'm sorry about last night.'

He was still concentrating on the screen. 'Mmm.'

The pig, he hadn't even had the decency to glance up at her. Not that she would have wanted him to, but still . . .

And the horrors of the morning hadn't finished showing their hand. Spending the night in Max's bed had been a long-cherished ambition but she wouldn't cherish this memory. Nor that of those endless ghastly seconds when she descended the main staircase and had to walk the length of reception in order to reach the front doors. Sylvie Nash, bursting with curiosity and disbelief and as tactless as ever, exclaimed, 'Holly, you look terrible! What on earth have you been up to?' Then, raising her voice instead of lowering it, she added archly, 'And who on earth were you *with*?'

By this time, of course, everyone had turned to look at her. Holly, bare-faced in every respect, said, 'Mel Gibson', and didn't stop walking until she reached the blissful sanctuary of her car.

Except that there had been no real sanctuary. By the time she realized that the filthy dark blue Rolls-Royce was actually following her, it was too late. Wearily, she drew up outside her flat and watched in her rear-view mirror as Adam Perry parked behind her.

'I'm tired, I'm not in the mood for jokes, I just want to go to bed,' she announced, and because it was only Adam she wasn't even ashamed of her derelict appearance.

For once, however, he wasn't smiling. To her astonishment he didn't even pick her up on her unintentional *double entendre*. Seizing her keys from her shaky grasp, he put one strong arm around her shoulders and led her up the steps to her front door. 'I know, sweetheart. You look done in. What a rotten time you've had.'

The warmth and sympathy in his voice was so unexpected that Holly found herself unable to speak. Almost before she knew what was happening she found herself lying on her unmade bed with a mug of creamy coffee in her hands and a plateful of hot, buttered crumpets on her lap.

'Thank you,' she said at last, glancing across to the window as the first spattering drops of rain began to fall outside. Like tears, she thought. 'I wonder where Tessa is now?'

'She's a sensible girl,' Adam reassured her. 'Wherever she is, she'll be in touch with you before long. You're her closest friend.'

'She must be feeling awful. And the worst part of it is, nobody has any idea why she should have done it. If I'm so close to her, why don't *I* know?'

'Shhh.' Breaking off a butter-soaked wedge of crumpet, he held it to her mouth. 'Come on, eat. And you mustn't feel guilty, because whatever has happened is between Tessa and Ross.' He paused, then said slowly, 'It did occur to me that it might have something to do with Antonia Seymour-Smith.'

Holly chewed and swallowed, thankful that the nausea had receded. The paracetamols which Adam had wordlessly handed to her along with her coffee also seemed to be working. Her headache was less severe; all she had to cope with now was her own shame. She had made the most appalling fool of herself and Max would probably never want to speak to her again.

'Ross wondered the same thing,' she admitted, dragging her thoughts back to the conversation currently in progress. 'He spoke to her on the phone yesterday but she didn't appear to know anything. Besides, Tessa isn't the kind of person who would be put off by wicked gossip; she knows perfectly well that Ross adores her and we *all* know that he hasn't done anything wrong. He ended his affair with Antonia ages ago and he hasn't even *looked* at another woman since he's been with Tessa.'

She pushed the plate away, unable to eat any more. Adam, finishing his own coffee, said, 'You still look absolutely wiped out. I'll leave now, and let you get some sleep. But look, you'll be feeling better by this evening – how about a quiet dinner somewhere? I could pick you up at around eight.'

He had been kind, but Holly wasn't about to fall into the gratitude-trap. Furthermore, she knew that she wouldn't want to go out. She had a great deal of thinking to do and she needed time alone to come to terms with her disastrous experience with Max. Wounded and humiliated, she craved solitude . . .

'It's nice of you to invite me, but I don't think so,' she replied. 'I want to be here in case Tessa tries to get in touch.'

'I could bring some food over . . .?'

'No, Adam.' Speaking more firmly, she shook her aching head. A lecherous male was the last thing she needed right now, even if he was revealing a new and unexpectedly compassionate side to his nature. 'I just want to be alone, really.'

'OK, sweetheart. Well, I'll be off then.' He tucked the duvet around her before moving towards the door. 'But if you change your mind, give me a ring. I'm in the book, OK?'

* * *

Despising herself for her weakness, Holly gave in at around seven o'clock that evening. Six hours of much-needed recuperative sleep had worked wonders and by the time she stepped out of a long, blissfully hot Badedas bath she found herself restored. Her ghastly hangover, as hangovers have a way of doing, had vanished without a trace and even the nightmare of last night seemed less threatening now. Maybe a quiet, companionable dinner with Adam wasn't such a terrible idea after all. And it would be nice to be able to talk to someone who knew Tessa, who shared her concern for her . . .

Adam's phone, when she eventually dialled the number, was engaged. While waiting for the line to become free, Holly rifled through her wardrobe, discarding a dozen or so outfits before finally settling on the daffodil-yellow silk dress which clashed so wonderfully with her hair, and which she knew Adam would like. He had been so kind to her this morning, he deserved that much at least.

Her nails took ages; this new nail varnish needed three separate coats before the required depth of colour and lustre could properly be achieved. In between the second and third coats she rang Adam again but the line was still busy.

By eight-fifteen she was ready, and not ashamed to admit to herself that despite the traumas of the past day and a half, she was looking pretty damn good. If only Max could see her *now*, maybe . . .

But she pushed that thought firmly from her mind and dialled Adam's number once more. Hooray, the phone was ringing at last.

She listened with mounting dismay and anger as the ringing continued, purring monotonously on and on in time with her own breathing. It was only twenty past eight and the bastard had gone out. She'd been stood up, abandoned, *forgotten*.

Holly kicked the coffee table, hard. So much for kindness and sympathy. Then she reached for her diary and turned to the list of numbers in the back. She was damned if she was going to stay in now; there had to be someone who would go out for a drink with her tonight . . .

'We're all meeting down at that new cocktail bar on Pulteney Bridge,' said Jennifer cheerfully. 'And Sophie Kendall's bringing along a team of drop-dead-gorgeous polo players she met up with at Lansdowne last week. Holly, you simply *must* come . . . apparently they have the most divine legs . . . and they're all absolutely loaded! Just think of the possibilities,' she concluded dreamily.

Holly, brightening at once, said, 'I'll be there.'

The Calypso, chic and streamlined and one of Bath's smartest places-to-go, was bulging at the seams. For a moment Holly hovered on the wet pavement outside, mentally gathering herself for the plunge into hectic sociability. Tonight she would do her best to forget Max and Adam, Ross and Tessa; she would smile and dazzle and enjoy herself . . . she *would* enjoy herself . . .

A fresh spattering of rain pushed her towards the door but even as she stepped across the threshold and the wall of heat and noise hit her, she felt a stab of uncharacteristic – almost telepathic – unease.

A moment later she realized why. For there, standing at the bar, was Adam. With his arm around the waist of Clarissa 'The Boob' Fox.

It hadn't been telepathy, of course, merely the familiar tone of his voice and the volume of his laughter. Ducking behind the nearest pink-marbled pillar, Holly pretended to search in her bag for her purse and waited for her heart to stop pounding.

But it was no good; she felt sick. And utterly betrayed. A glance around the pillar told her that her first impressions had been correct. Adam and Clarissa were alone together and his arm was now draped affectionately around her shoulder. While she, Holly, had been at home tarting herself up for Adam – even choosing an outfit she knew he'd like, for God's sake – he had forgotten about her and blithely gone out to meet another woman . . . a woman, furthermore, whose breasts weren't even her own. How she had the nerve to *flaunt* those silicone monstrosities, Holly couldn't imagine.

Although Adam appeared to be enjoying them, she observed sourly, resentment mingling with outrage as the extent of this fresh humiliation began to sink in. Who the hell did Adam Perry think he was, anyway? How *could* he treat her like this, letting her down and waltzing off instead with Clarissa Fox? And how *dare* he ruin her night just when she'd begun to think that maybe he wasn't so bad after all?'

Turning, taking care to remain unnoticed, Holly slid back towards the door.

Chapter 40

As dusk fell, sheets of grey rain swept across the valley and even the trees seemed to droop beneath the onslaught. Ross, watching from the isolation of the unlit sitting room, surveyed the dismal view and couldn't help thinking that if Tessa had been there – if the wedding had gone ahead after all – the weather would have remained fine.

Shit, this was no good. Running his hands through his hair he turned away from the window and reached for his drink. Yesterday it had been acutely necessary – for unformed reasons of his own – to remain sober but tonight was a different matter. He needed something to numb the pain, to take his mind off the fact that the unthinkable had happened. He had to get out of this room, this empty house where he and Tessa had planned to start their married lives together . . . or at least where *he* had planned that they should start their married lives together . . .

The darkness was becoming oppressive. Tipping his tumbler of Scotch into the nearest plant pot, he snatched up his car keys and headed for the door. He was damned if he was going to fall into the pathetic trap of drinking alone; jilted bridegroom or not, he still had some vestiges of pride.

He bumped into Sylvie Nash on the steps of the hotel, just as she was leaving at the end of her shift and just as Ross realized that The Grange was not where he wanted to be. Coming back here had been a mistake; bravado was one thing but sheer unadulterated torture was quite another.

And at that moment, for once in her life, Sylvie said exactly the right thing.

'Oh Ross, you shouldn't be here.' Her eyes glistened with sympathy as she touched his forearm. Droplets of rain, caught in her hair, reflected the light from the foyer behind her. Ross, a great deal wetter, said, 'Where should I be, then?' and watched her hesitate, stuck for a reply.

'I don't know,' she whispered finally, with a helpless glance at her watch. 'But you look awful and I'm sure the woman who checked into Room Fourteen this afternoon is a journalist – she's been asking an awful lot of questions. If you wanted to,' she added with a rush of bravery, 'you could always come back to my house for the evening. My Mum and Dad are in Benidorm this week and my boyfriend's working up in Liverpool so there wouldn't be anyone there to bother you . . .'

The expression on Ross's face was unreadable, but she'd started and now she had to finish. Her long nails dug into her palms as she concluded lamely, 'You wouldn't even have to talk if you didn't feel like it . . .'

'Good,' said Ross evenly, placing his hand on the small of her back and guiding her towards his car. 'Because I'm not in the mood for talking.'

The house in which Sylvie lived with her parents was small, semi-detached and modern. The extremely clean living room was very Laura Ashley, very flouncy, and every available surface was crowded with china animals, ornamental ashtrays and elaborately framed photographs of Sylvie.

Ross sat down on the pink and white upholstered sofa and

watched through the open doorway as Sylvie, in the kitchen, made a pot of tea and opened a packet of chocolate digestive biscuits. When she returned to sit in the chair facing him they drank their tea in silence, listening to the mournful howling of the wind as it gathered strength outside. After a while, Sylvie got up and put an old Carly Simon LP on to the turntable, then disappeared into the pine-panelled kitchen once more, coming back with a dusty bottle of Polish vodka and a single glass.

'Go on,' she said quietly, holding the glass towards him. 'You look as if you could do with it. I'm afraid there isn't anything else I can offer you apart from Ribena.'

Accepting the drink with a smile, Ross reflected that of all the women in the world only Sylvie Nash could come up with such an entirely innocent *double entendre* . . .

Two hours later, he realized that he had been mistaken; Sylvie wasn't innocent at all. Fairly drunk by this stage, he was nevertheless still capable of making the required moves. When she had said calmly, apparently out of the blue, 'We could go upstairs if you'd like to', he hadn't replied. Maybe this was another typically-Sylvie remark and what she really meant was that it was time to go to sleep because she had to get up early for work tomorrow morning.

But then it had been her turn to smile. Rising gracefully to her feet, she had moved towards him and held out one slender, pink-tipped hand.

'I'd like to, Ross. Really. And no one else would need to know, would they?'

For a fraction of a second, he had almost been tempted. It was his wedding night, after all, and what was a man supposed to do on his wedding night, if not screw himself stupid?

But Sylvie wasn't Tessa, and sleeping with her wasn't going to make him feel any better. Nothing on earth was going to make him feel better tonight.

'Thanks,' he said, dredging up a faint smile so that her feelings wouldn't be hurt, 'but no thanks. I think maybe I'll just go on up to bed. I could probably do with some sleep.'

Surprised to realize that she felt relieved rather than disappointed, Sylvie simply nodded, unperturbed.

'OK. I'll show you to your room.'

Grace, silent and watchful and utterly devastated by Tessa's disappearance, guessed at once where – and with whom – Ross had spent the previous night. She hadn't spent the last few weeks observing the dramatic change in her own mother without learning to recognize that 'I've-got-a-secret' look in the faces of others. And while Sylvie was behaving with perfect propriety this morning, her eyes decorously downcast whenever Ross emerged from his office, Grace wasn't fooled for a minute. And as far as she was concerned it proved beyond any doubt at all that Ross's amoral behaviour was the reason behind Tessa's decision to leave.

Having spent a delightful lunch hour in bed with Mattie, Richard relaxed against the stacked-up mound of pillows and watched with pleasure as she reached for her clothes. Over her head slipped the glossy, dark green camisole top he had bought for her just last week. On went the matching French knickers. Mattie, no longer shy, did a brief twirl and ran her hands appreciatively over the satiny material. 'They're beautiful. I've never had such gorgeous underwear before.' She smiled as she picked up her dress, yet another gift from Richard. 'But you really shouldn't be spending your money on me like this . . . you're spoiling me.'

'It's a replacement,' he reminded her, 'for the dress I ruined that night at The Grange. Besides,' he went on, reaching out for her and kissing first one breast and then the other before they disappeared from view, 'I love buying you things. And you are the least spoiled woman I've ever known.'

Fully dressed once more, Mattie made them both a pot of tea. She had to be back at work in fifteen minutes but until that time came she would savour every moment with Richard.

'How did Antonia react when she heard about that business up at the hotel?' she asked, stirring her tea and quite forgetting that she no longer took sugar.

Richard adjusted his spectacles and sat back in his chair. 'She hasn't said much, but I can't help feeling that she knows more than she's letting on. She's like a child when it comes to possessions – she doesn't give them up easily – and it wouldn't surprise me if I found out that she'd done something drastic in order to try and hang on to Ross.' Then he took Mattie's hand in his and smiled. 'But to tell you the truth, I'm not interested enough to want to find out. Antonia can do whatever she likes; as long as I have you I don't care.'

Mattie sighed. It had been on the tip of her tongue to tell him about Ross and herself but she still didn't know whether she should. It was, after all, Grace's secret as much as her own and while Richard was in turn a secret from Grace she didn't feel that she could. 'I do feel sorry for that girl though,' she said slowly. 'You know, Tessa. She's got that baby now, and all that responsibility . . . she must be going through a terrible time.'

Glancing at his watch, Richard pulled a face. 'Right now we

have our own terrible time to consider. It's five to and you have to be back at work by two. We'd better get going before you start feeling sorry for Ross.'

'I don't feel sorry for him,' she declared stoutly, getting to her feet and picking up her bag. 'Whatever has happened, he had it coming to him. He deserves to be unhappy.' Then she relaxed and hugged her lover. 'I'm sorry, I'm being a bitch. Give me one more kiss, darling, and then we really must go.'

'You could never be a bitch,' said Richard, only too happy to comply. 'You're wonderful.'

Chapter 41

Stepping carefully, taking care not to slip on loose rocks, Tessa made her way down the steep, barely discernible path which led on to the beach. Perryn Cove, cocooned on three sides by precariously angled cliffs, might be small but it was worth the effort. A crescent of dark gold sand lay exposed by the receding tide, lace-fringed waves slid hypnotically back and forth and beyond them the even more mesmerizing blueness of the sea blended at the horizon into a cloudless sky.

And by some miracle, Tessa found herself entirely alone.

St Ives had been Dominic's home for the past four years and he loved every overcrowded inch of the town, revelling in the élitism of being a resident rather than a tourist and enjoying to the full the hectic, dissolute life he had made for himself here. There were always fellow artists to drink with, to commiserate with when the work wasn't selling and to celebrate with when business was good. And the supply of beautiful girls was, needless to say, limitless.

But whereas Dominic thrived on the company of others, Tessa cherished solitude. The endless informal parties did nothing for her, despite the fact that she knew only too well that at least half of them were for her own benefit. Dominic was attempting to build her a new social life, introducing her to all his friends in an effort to help her forget the traumatic events of her too-recent past.

Sadly, but not surprisingly, she had so far been unable to oblige.

This morning, however, Dominic was looking after Olivia and Tessa had three uninterrupted hours in which to think. Reaching the foot of the cliffs at last, she took off her white espadrilles and wriggled her toes in the warm dry sand. The intention had been to walk and think and explore the intricate collection of rock pools but the heat had sapped her energy. Now that she was finally here it seemed more sensible to have a quick swim and then rest, simply soaking up the sun and enjoying the peacefulness of her surroundings.

But the blessed silence was shattered less than twenty minutes later with the arrival of what sounded like a school outing. Tessa, lying flat on her back, opened her eyes a fraction and saw a dozen children and several gaudily dressed adults burst upon the empty beach like fireworks, having taken advantage of the ebbing tide and made their way around the base of the cliffs.

Praying that they wouldn't stay, she closed her eyes once more and forced her mind back to more important matters. Despite Dominic's repeated assurances that she and Olivia were welcome to stay as long as she liked, she knew they couldn't. It wasn't solving anything. She needed somewhere of her own, a secure home for Olivia, somewhere like her own cottage on the outskirts of Bath . . .

She was awoken from a light sleep less than an hour later by the trickle of sand on her bare stomach. Shielding her eyes from the sun, she gazed up at Dominic – looking ludicrously paternal with Olivia strapped in her baby-sling to his chest – and said, 'What am I, a seven-stone weakling?'

'If that,' he remarked dryly. She had lost far too much weight in the last few weeks.

'What are you doing here, anyway?' she said, her brain still fuddled with sleep.

Dominic levered himself with care down on to the sand beside her. 'Olivia and I have been having a serious talk.'

'Really?'

'Scout's honour,' he protested.

Tessa raised her eyebrows. 'I'm amazed. I didn't think you were capable of having a serious talk.'

'Well, I threw in a few one-liners,' he said with a grin, 'but Olivia soon hauled me back on to the straight and narrow. Didn't you, sweetheart?'

Olivia blew lavish bubbles of agreement.

'I see.' Tessa looked thoughtful; Dominic hadn't made the arduous trek to Perryn Cove for nothing; he was here for a reason. 'And what exactly have you been talking about? If you think I'm going to let you paint my daughter in the nude, forget it.'

But he was being serious now. 'It's you, Tess. Hiding away down here isn't doing you any favours. It isn't your *style*, for heaven's sake. What are you planning to do . . . spend the rest of the summer hiding away on a beach and saying, "I want to be alone"?'

'I don't know,' she said, only semi-truthfully. 'I've just been asking myself the same question. I suppose I do want to go back to Bath – it's where my friends are, after all – but it might make things awkward. Ross isn't the kind of person who's used to being publicly humiliated, which is what I appear to have done, so he might not be too thrilled by the idea of my returning.'

'And he didn't do anything to deserve it?' Dominic demanded, exasperated to realize that she was, even now, considering Ross

Monahan's feelings before her own. 'Sweetheart, he *knows* why you left him. Sod him! You do whatever you want to do and if he starts making things difficult for you, just tell him to get stuffed. Bath is where you and Olivia live and you have as much right to be there as he does.'

The fact that his conscience was troubling him, troubled Max. Unaccustomed to feeling guilty, he was nevertheless less only too acutely aware of the fact that he had treated Holly not only badly, but very unfairly indeed.

Which was why, when he discovered – too late – that Caroline Mortimer would not, after all, be able to make it down from London for the following Friday's Mad Hatter's Ball, he decided to assuage his guilt and invite Holly to partner him instead.

'Read my tea leaves, oh please read my tea leaves,' Holly begged Rosa Polonowski as, in a frenzy of excitement, she cornered the little Polish woman in the hotel's kitchen. 'Oh God, my hands are shaking, which way am I supposed to swirl the cup? Shit, it's teabags! Rosa, we'll have to make some more . . . Marco, where's the normal tea? You can spare Rosa for just five minutes, can't you? She's going to reveal my destiny and that's got to be more important than cleaning a few saucepans!'

'Ah, I see you wiz a handsome tall man,' explained Rosa five minutes later, scrutinizing the contents of Holly's teacup and pursing her lips as she concentrated. 'You are wearing a red dress, very grand, very beautiful.'

Right, thought Holly determinedly. She'd rush into Bath as soon as she got off duty and buy one.

'And you are laughing and having such fun wiz your handsome man, it is a night to remember for the rest of your life.'

'Is he in love with me?' breathed Holly, her eyes shining as she searched Rosa's face for clues. If she knew that Max really did love her it would make everything so much easier . . . they could dispense with all those silly, time-wasting formalities . . .

But Rosa shook her dark head slowly from side to side, like a ponderous pendulum. 'Ah no, not loff. But there is great attraction, which may lead to loff. Zis is just the beginning, after all. And such great attraction is a very promising sign, my dear. Not to be sneezed at or tossed aside in moments of despair.'

'Rosa, you're incredible!' sighed Holly, her very toes curling in ecstasy at the prospect of Friday night. 'And don't worry, there aren't going to be any moments of despair. Now that I know what's what I'll be able to have the situation *completely* under control. Oh, however am I going to get through the rest of the week . . .?'

One really did need to spend an awful lot of time preparing for the best night of one's life, mused Holly happily four days later as, to the sensual strains of Dido she wallowed in her foaming, freesia-scented bath and lazily soaped her breasts.

She had even constructed a timetable; bath at four o'clock, all-over moisturiser at four-thirty, hair at five, nail polish at six, make-up at six-thirty, get dressed at seven-fifteen and finally primp for an hour or so until Max arrived at eight-thirty. And she would have to force herself to eat a sandwich or two, she reminded herself with a brief, rueful smile. She wasn't going to drink on an empty stomach and run the risk of passing out on Max a second time. Tonight was going to be absolutely *perfect*.

Chapter 42

The hotel was busy; the hugely popular Mad Hatter's Ball, held annually at Shilton Court just a few miles away, began at nine and many of those attending were making an early start in the bar at The Grange, getting stuck into the Bollinger before heading off for the all-night festivities and a great many more bottles of champagne.

'Could you tell me, my dear, where I can find Max Monahan?'

Sylvie Nash looked up and smiled at the woman in the olive-green turban and dark glasses who was leaning conspiratorially over the reception desk. Her husky, accented voice was vaguely familiar but the glasses effectively masked her face.

'He's upstairs,' she replied, eyeing the expensive outfit and recognizing a Donna Karan when she saw one. Sylvie's bible was *Vogue*. 'If you could give me your name I'll ring through and tell him you're here.'

The woman smiled, revealing wonderfully white teeth, and shook her head with a playful gesture. 'Ah, but that would spoil the surprise, I think. Just say that an old friend has arrived to see him. And when he comes down those stairs we shall watch the expression on his face, OK?'

Max's expression, when he finally appeared several minutes later, was indeed worth watching. Disbelief mingled with joy and Sylvie avidly drank in every detail as he pulled Francine Lalonde – for now that she had removed those dark glasses her identity had become obvious – into his arms.

'I can't believe it,' he murmured, breathing in the faint, exotic scent of her. 'Why didn't you tell me you were coming? How long can you stay? God, it's so wonderful to see you!'

'I missed you,' said Francine, smiling up at him and kissing him again. 'And I didn't tell you because I wanted it to be a big surprise. But the surprise might be too big, I think,' she went on, drawing back and pouting with mock concern as she eyed his dinner-jacket and dangling bow tie. 'It seems that you have other arrangements for this evening. Maybe you are going to abandon me for another woman, Max?'

'Are you joking?' he exclaimed, hugging her more tightly still. 'I wouldn't abandon you . . . I'm not going to let go of you for a single second . . . no, no, it was just a very casual arrangement. Give me two minutes on the phone and I'll sort everything out. Holly's a decent girl; she'll understand.'

'. . . so you do understand, don't you,' Max continued, blithely unaware of the havoc he was wreaking, of the complete and utter devastation he had caused.

'Of course,' said Holly, amazed that she was still capable of speech. Her entire body, including her brain, had gone quite numb; she couldn't understand what she had done to deserve this. And what the bloody hell did Max think *he* was doing? Rosa had foreseen them together at the ball, happy and laughing and greatly attracted towards each other . . .

'Look, I am sorry,' said Max, sounding anything but. 'And I know it's short notice but I'm sure you can dig up a friend somewhere. I'll send a cab round to you with the tickets and you can have a fabulous night without me.'

When the front door bell rang ten minutes later Holly, her eyes now as red as her dress and her breath coming in great gulps as she struggled to quell unstoppable tears, spent some time ignoring it.

But the taxi driver clearly wasn't going to go away until he had delivered his tickets and the bell continued to jangle gratingly on her already shredded nerves. Finally, slowly, Holly made her way downstairs, almost tripping over the long hem of her ruby-red taffeta dress as she went.

'Oh my poor girl, come here,' said Adam Perry, enveloping her in his massive rugby player's arms and letting her cry all over the front of his dinner jacket. 'I was passing through reception when I heard Max speaking to you on the phone. Sweetheart, it's about time you got him out of your system for good . . . he's not worth all this, really he isn't.'

Once she'd got over the shock of finding Adam on her doorstep, Holly began to panic. He always seemed to see her at her very worst and she couldn't bear the fact that he knew how much Max had hurt her.

'He's an absolute shit,' he went on, when they reached her sitting room. 'I know you don't have a great opinion of me but I'm not as bad as he is.'

'Yes, you are,' she countered between hiccups, her expression accusing. 'You stood me up the other week. I saw you down at the Calypso with Clarissa Fox. So there wasn't any need for you to come over here tonight and gloat,' she added bitterly, 'because I'm quite used to being chucked over for other women, really I am. Nobody else in the world has had more practice at it than me.'

'Here, dry your eyes and do your face,' said Adam calmly, handing her a box of tissues and propelling her towards the bathroom. 'I waited for you to phone and when you didn't I popped down to the Calypso for a quick drink on my own. I just happened to bump into Clarissa while I was there and you must know what she's like – once those man-seeking missiles she wears down the front of her dress home in on you, you're sunk.'

Holly dug her heels in at the bathroom door. 'I don't want to do my face. What's the point, anyway? I'm hardly planning on going to the ball on my own.'

'Don't be such a wimp,' he declared brusquely. 'I'm here, aren't I? And we don't need Max's charity, if that's what you're worried about – I do have a double ticket of my own. You're going to the ball with me, Holly, and you're going to enjoy it even if it damn well kills you.'

'There now,' he said many hours later as they came together for one last dance in the oak-panelled, petal-strewn ballroom. 'Tonight hasn't really been so bad, has it?'

Holly smiled. It was four-thirty in the morning and all around them sleeping couples were draped over furniture leaving only about three hundred guests to carry on dancing, singing and carousing until dawn broke, but she hadn't given in. She had continued to smile and socialize as if she hadn't a care in the world and no one, not even Adam, could have guessed how hard it had really been to maintain the charade.

Yet at the same time she was forced to acknowledge that it could have been worse. In a detached way she had also managed to enjoy herself. Adam had been a wonderful partner, his noisy friends – currently refuelling themselves with breakfast in the dining hall – were funny, spectacularly complimentary and entertaining, and several of Holly's own girl-friends had been equally appreciative of Adam.

'He's madly attractive,' Sophie Kendall had enthused while Adam was – thankfully – out of earshot. 'You lucky thing, darling! Is he just as gorgeous without his clothes on?'

But whereas other men had ears, Adam possessed sonar. From his position at the roulette table he had turned, grinning broadly, and declared, 'Even more gorgeous, I promise you. And if you don't believe me, meet me upstairs in five minutes.' With a wink in Holly's direction he had added, 'My muscle tone has to be seen to be believed, doesn't it, my darling?'

His cheerful badinage had certainly helped the evening along. Holly, secure in the circle of his arms, rested her cheek against his rocklike chest as the music slowed and told herself for the tenth time that it really *could* have been worse. It still astonished her that Sophie, Melissa and the others had actually found Adam so attractive but each to her own, after all. And she *was* glad that he had persuaded her to come here tonight instead of leaving her alone in her flat to mope.

But Rosa Polonowski, thought Holly sorrowfully, had a great deal to answer for. Because she would have been so much more glad, so very much more glad, if only Adam could have been Max.

Chapter 43

Word of Francine Lalonde's arrival at The Grange having spread like wildfire through the hotel, the other guests and a flock of reporters – who had descended from nowhere – were all dying to see her. Consequently Francine and Max spent the first three days of her week-long stay almost entirely closeted in his suite, which suited both of them perfectly.

Francine, recovering from the rigours of filming, ate and made love and spent a great deal of time asleep. Max, as besotted as ever with her beauty and capricious character, ate and made love and sat, ostensibly working on his latest novel but in reality watching her sleep. And since Francine took such great pleasure in all three forms of activity he couldn't imagine a nicer way of spending their time together.

But on Tuesday morning, as Max drew back the curtains and bright sunlight flooded the bedroom, Francine announced that her 'lazy-boning' was over and that today she wanted to explore Bath.

'And I must see this hotel,' she added, sliding out of bed and heading for the bathroom. 'To stay in bed for so long is too decadent. Now that I am restored I need to meet new people and have fun.'

'I thought we were having fun,' said Max. Her directness, at times, was alarming.

'Of course we were,' Francine consoled him, her sherry-brown eyes alight with amusement. 'But that kind of fun can get boring after a while. And we don't want to get bored, darling, do we?'

'Oh my!' declared Francine admiringly as they made their way out on to the sundrenched terrace. Ross, sitting alone at one of the tables with a pot of coffee and a pile of paperwork, rose to his feet as they approached. 'Max, your little brother is quite something. I tell you, it's a good job I met you first or maybe I could have been tempted—'

'Hi,' said Ross, shaking her hand and realizing at once that Francine had expected him to kiss it. 'It's nice to meet you at last – we were beginning to think Max was holding you hostage upstairs.'

'He was,' Francine confided, employing her huskiest tones, 'but now I have escaped. And I am thinking that maybe he hid me away so I wouldn't find out that his brother is more handsome than any film star. Ross, I know I shouldn't say such things but Max has told me what happened and I have to say that this girl of yours – Tessa, is it? – must be stark-staring crazy not to marry you. Absolutely loopy!'

'Sit down, darling,' said Max hurriedly, shooting her a warning look. Francine, arranging her skirt to maximum advantage as she settled herself into the chair, shrugged and laughed. 'Now he is cross with me because I don't keep my thoughts to myself like a good Englishwoman,' she told Ross. 'But since we both know that I am saying the truth, why on earth *should* I keep quiet?'

'Absolutely,' said Ross, with a wry smile. 'And I happen to agree with every word you say.'

'But are you still desperately in love with her, despite that cruel thing she did?' persisted Francine, her eyes round with concern. Max, unable to cope with such brutal frankness, left them to it. Maybe by the time he had ordered breakfast and made a couple of overdue phone calls they would have settled upon a more neutral topic of conversation.

'Yes,' said Ross simply, when Max had left.

'But it is so tragic! Look at you – you can have any woman in the world and here you are being sombre and desolated all because of one girl who is too crackers to know when she is on to a good thing.'

Such outrageous flattery was undoubtedly pleasant to hear, but Ross wasn't about to let it go to his head. All women, in his experience, were actresses and professional actresses were the worst of the lot. How could anyone ever believe a single word they said?

But Francine, it seemed, could read minds as well. 'I know, I know,' she declared impatiently, 'but I am telling the truth. Look, I have been in bed for too long and now I don't feel like sitting down. Why don't you show me that beautiful conservatory over there . . . do you have orchids in it? . . . oh please, Ross, come on! I have a great passion for orchids and by the time we get back our breakfast will be arrived. OK?'

The temperature and humidity inside the conservatory was tropical, but Francine didn't appear to be bothered by the heat. Exclaiming delightedly over the glorious effect of the stained-glass windows, she turned and took Ross's hand, drawing him away from his position at the door.

'My God, it's incredible – like standing inside a rainbow! And such flowers,' she sighed with an expansive gesture towards the lush foliage arching above their heads. 'This must be your favourite place to be.'

The conservatory reminded Ross too acutely of his first fateful meeting with Tessa to be able to afford him much pleasure nowadays and he tended to avoid it, but he wasn't about to tell Francine that.

'It's a popular feature of the hotel,' he said instead, his tone neutral. Francine, undoing a couple of extra buttons on her white camisole top, gave him an extremely knowing look.

'But not as popular as its manager, I think. Ross, I know I am a forward woman. When I think something I say it and it can alarm some people, but I want you to know that I find you very attractive indeed. Do you find me attractive also?'

Christ, she was coming on, thought Ross. This was all he needed.

'I should imagine,' he replied slowly, 'that every heterosexual male in Europe finds you attractive. You don't really need to ask questions like that, do you?'

'But it is so wonderful to hear,' pouted Francine, trailing the feathery fronds of a particularly fragile fern beneath her fingers. 'It's so nice for the ego, don't you think? And so encouraging to know that one's interest in a man is being returned.'

If the situation hadn't been so delicate it would have been funny. Trust Max, thought Ross wryly, to lose his head over a woman who was quite possibly an out-and-out nymphomaniac. But meanwhile Francine was still smiling that legendary smile of hers and moving slowly but deliberately towards him. The time had come, he judged, for some straight talking.

'Look,' he said bluntly, 'it wouldn't matter how attractive I thought you were. Max is my brother and I do have *some* scruples . . .'

'So?' countered Francine with an elegant shrug. 'I am not married to Max, am I? We have a working partnership, if you like – he has written a film script for me and when the film is made I shall star in it. We are of mutual advantage to each other, that is all. The fact that we also like to go to bed together is . . . how do you say? . . . by the by. It's fun, Ross, but it isn't a big love thing. Max knows that.'

'Maybe,' said Ross, who knew differently. 'But all the same, I really don't feel—'

'OK, OK,' Francine intercepted him, still smiling and quite unperturbed. 'But take it from me, I have an instinct for such things. We shall be lovers before the end of the week, Ross, I promise you.'

The hotel guests weren't the only ones eager to catch a glimpse of Francine Lalonde. Accustomed though they were to visiting celebrities, the staff were nevertheless equally curious to meet the famous actress with whom Max was so totally and uncharacteristically besotted.

Grace, having drawn the longest straw in the kitchen, took extra care not to spill so much as a single drop of coffee as she made her way carefully out on to the terrace, but to her disappointment Ross's table was unoccupied.

Assorted papers, however, still littered the table at which he had been sitting so she laid the tray carefully down next to them and, blinking in the bright sunlight, scanned the emerald lawns sloping down beyond the terrace. Still no sign of either Ross or their illustrious guest.

But moments later, as she turned back towards the hotel, she glimpsed a flash of white amid the tropical jungle colours of the conservatory. Ross and Francine must be inside, she realized. And since their breakfast should not be allowed to go cold she must let them know that it was waiting for them out here.

* * *

'. . . we shall be lovers before the end of the week, Ross, I promise you.'

Ducking hastily away from the white-framed doorway, Grace held her breath and listened to the honeyed, French-accented voice of Francine Lalonde. My God, was Ross so completely lacking in morals that not even his own brother's women were off-limits?

Her heart racing, she waited for his reply, but none came. Finally, risking a single peek through the glass she saw that watching out for eavesdroppers was the least of their worries; Francine Lalonde, stretching up and resting her fingertips lightly upon Ross's shoulders, lifted her face to his and kissed his mouth. And when Ross, moments later, drew back and said, 'Look, this is crazy, I can't—' she smiled and silenced him with another kiss.

'Ah, but we can,' Grace heard her murmur, her hand now caressing the back of his neck. 'As soon as Max is out of the way – don't worry, I'll think of a reason to get rid of him this afternoon – we will be able to do whatever we want. And I can think of so many wonderful things,' she added persuasively, 'that I want to do to you . . .'

As Grace slipped away unnoticed, Ross took hold of Francine's arms and pushed them firmly to the sides of her body.

'No,' he said, his dark eyes boring into hers, his tone deadly serious. 'It isn't going to happen. You're not on location now, and I'm no groupie. You're here as my brother's guest and you're damn well going to behave yourself. You might not be in love with him,' he continued, as she opened her mouth to protest, 'but you can at least have the good manners to remain faithful to him until the end of the week.'

Pouting was what Francine did best. 'I didn't realize you were so boring,' she remarked with only mild truculence. 'Ross, you are a big disappointment to me.'

'Sometimes,' he replied coldly, thinking of Antonia, 'I'm an even bigger disappointment to myself.'

Despising Ross with all her heart, Grace didn't step out of the way quite as smartly as she could have done when he came through the swing doors of the kitchen at lunchtime. He was a bastard, she thought, during the fraction of a second when she might have taken a recovering step sideways . . . and a shirtful of lobster salad was the least he deserved.

'Christ,' said Ross, staring down at the mess as garlicky salad dressing sank through to his skin and pieces of salad and succulent pink lobster scattered at his feet. Then, glancing up and catching the expression of terror and defiance in the girl's eyes – the young girl who had visited Tessa at the hospital following Olivia's birth – he held up his hands in a gesture of defeat and smiled.

'Sorry, my fault.'

The girl, bending to retrieve the silver dish which he had inadvertently knocked from her grasp, muttered something beneath her breath. Unable to believe that he had heard her correctly, Ross said, 'I beg your pardon?'

'I said I was in a bit of a tizz,' replied Grace. Her cheeks were flushed but she stood her ground, silently daring him to disbelieve her. 'Table nine were in a hurry for their meal.'

Ross surveyed her for a long moment, then turned away without speaking. He could have sworn she'd said, 'It always is.'

Chapter 44

Never having managed to keep a secret before in her life, Holly was doubly relieved when the train finally – and with agonizing slowness – slid into Bath station.

Within moments Tessa and Olivia had emerged from their carriage and Holly was hugging them both.

'I can't tell you how much I've missed you,' she said, holding Tessa at arm's length and studying her. 'It's seemed more like five years than five weeks. You look wonderful!'

Tessa, smiling, did look wonderful. Slender and very brown, and with her long blonde hair pulled back in a plait, her green eyes dominated her face. As usual, she looked unfairly elegant in nothing more exciting than a baggy white cotton vest and khaki shorts, tightly belted at the waist with a scarlet scarf. Tessa was the only person she knew, thought Holly, who could wear army surplus seconds and get away with it.

'And what's been going on here?' she demanded, laughing delightedly and scooping Olivia into her arms. 'Will you look at this baby's *eyes*, Tess! They're unbelievable.'

For the eyes in question, deep blue at birth, were now dark brown and uncannily like Ross's. 'I know,' said Tessa fondly, 'she doesn't look like me at all. Dominic says we just have to hope that she hasn't inherited Ross's character too.'

But a dusty station platform was no place to stand and

exchange news and Holly, still carrying Olivia, led the way back to her car.

'Come on, I've got lunch and a stupendous strawberry Pavlova back at the flat.'

Picking up Olivia's carrycot, as well as the haversack containing her own belongings, Tessa followed her. 'Have you really not told anyone else that I've come back?' she asked, sounding intrigued rather than concerned.

'Of course I haven't!' gasped Holly, clearly affronted. 'I promised not to, didn't I? What on earth do you take me for?'

Tessa grinned, unabashed. 'Someone who can't keep a secret to save her life. I'm impressed Holly, really.'

'And so you should be, darling,' Holly retorted. 'Because it hasn't been easy. Especially when I've had Ross asking me practically every day if I've heard from you.'

They ate lunch out in the garden, lingering over coffee afterwards and discussing Tessa's return home.

'Because it *is* my home,' she said, as if needing to justify her decision to her friend. 'And I know that Ross will find out sooner or later that I'm back but I just want the chance to get Olivia and myself settled first.'

'And what do you think he'll do when he does hear?' said Holly, refilling their cups and hoisting her skirt above her knees so that her legs would have every chance of catching the sun.

Tessa shrugged. 'I've no idea. But as far as he's concerned I've made a fool of him so he can't be pleased.'

'He asks about you,' Holly reminded her.

'Ah, but does he actually *say* anything about me?'

Holly pulled a face. 'Of course not. I lie through my teeth to him and he's absolutely convinced that I'm lying but he can't do a damn thing about it. Tess, he hates me!'

'Join the club,' said Tessa lightly. 'And now why don't we talk about something a bit more cheerful? Tell me how things are going between you and Max.'

When Tessa had phoned Fred Lennard, the farmer who owned her old cottage, he had been touchingly pleased to hear from her and even more delighted to renew her lease. Renting out tiny, one-bedroomed cottages hadn't been as easy as he had imagined – visiting tourists demanded luxuries like space and shower units, up-to-date plumbing and central heating – and reliable long-term tenants like Tessa were hard to find. Of course she could come back, he assured her; he'd leave the keys under the back-door mat and they would settle up financially whenever it suited her to do so.

But it certainly felt strange, thought Tessa, returning to those familiar surroundings and encountering such unfamiliar emptiness. Only the very barest essentials remained; all her belongings were in Ross's possession – if he hadn't burned the lot – and if Holly hadn't been able to lend her an eclectic assortment of crockery, cooking utensils and bedlinen she would really have been sunk.

Holly had been so wonderful that Tessa still felt awkward about not having told her the truth about her abrupt departure from Bath, although she reasoned with herself that it was as much for her friend's sake as for anyone else's. Holly wouldn't think twice about giving Antonia Seymour-Smith a piece of her mind. Tessa, not wanting her to run the risk of jeopardizing the only job she'd ever really enjoyed, had explained instead that

Sadie Labelle's newspaper article, on top of her own longstanding doubts, had sent her into a blind panic. She had bolted, pure and simple, and she was sorry she'd had to put Holly through the hideous ordeal of having to break the news to Ross.

'But what are you going to say to him when you see him?' said Holly, genuinely concerned but at the same time faintly suspicious. She knew Tessa too well to believe that Sadie Labelle's spiteful article could have been a real factor in her decision to call off the wedding.

'I don't know,' replied Tessa truthfully. 'I just hope he leaves me alone. I'm sorry I let everyone down but I have as much right to be here as anyone else, and I'm staying. I have Olivia, my home and my painting. And all I want now,' she concluded slowly, 'is to be able to get on with my own life. In peace.'

Living quietly, however, was no guarantee of anonymity. Emerging from the bath three days later, Tessa heard a car pull up outside the cottage and didn't need to look out of the window to know that her visitor was Ross.

Brilliant, she thought, considering her dilemma. Having washed her entire meagre wardrobe of clothes this morning – they were at this minute hanging out in the garden to dry – she was either going to have to climb back into the T-shirt and jeans over which Olivia had so ungenerously thrown up her breakfast or face Ross in a bath towel.

The smell of baby-sick was overwhelming. As the latch on the front door clicked open she tucked the pale green towel as tightly as possible around her body, briefly ran her fingers through her tangled wet hair and headed towards the stairs.

Watching her slow descent, Ross reflected upon the irony of

the fact that great sex was one of his favourite occupations, yet he had known Tessa now for almost a year and they had made love only twice. Events had conspired against him; such a situation was practically bizarre. But at the same time, he acknowledged as he admired her slender, tanned figure and experienced unbidden stirrings of lust, it was also incredibly erotic. He couldn't imagine ever *not* wanting Tessa . . . he had never known another woman like her . . .

'I suppose I should have knocked,' he said, the expression in his eyes unrepentant.

'I suppose you should,' replied Tessa evenly. Having long ago given up trying to work out a preparatory plan of action for this encounter, she was playing it purely by ear. Inside, however, she was jangling with nerves. Actually seeing Ross was quite different from just imagining him. With a vague gesture in the direction of the staircase she added, 'But since my lover left ten minutes ago it doesn't really matter. Would you like some coffee?'

'Your lover,' said Ross thoughtfully, following her to the kitchen but taking care to remain at a respectable distance. 'Hmm, that's something my detective didn't tell me about.'

Despite herself, Tessa smiled. Ross had always been able to make her smile. Well, she amended hastily, almost always.

'You hired a private detective? I wondered about that funny little chap in the kilt who kept dropping his bagpipes. Did he tell you about the time he followed me to Edinburgh and—'

'No,' said Ross calmly, forestalling her. 'He told me about the time he followed you to St Ives.'

The fact that he hadn't been joking after all seemed even funnier. Tessa realized that she wasn't even angry; knowing Ross as she did, she should have guessed that something like this might have happened. Knowing Ross as she did, she reminded herself as she spooned coffee into two mugs and added boiling water, nothing should surprise her at all.

They returned to the tiny, sparsely furnished sitting room and Ross made himself as comfortable as he could in a lumpy, dark green armchair which did not encourage relaxation. Tessa, perching easily in the window-seat, clasped her coffee mug in both hands and gazed steadily at him over the rim.

'So you had me followed,' she said at last, breaking the taut silence. 'Why?'

'That's a bloody silly question. I wanted to know what you were up to. I wanted to know,' continued Ross heavily, 'why you'd disappeared.'

Unable to resist it, Tessa said, 'And was he helpful, or did you finally manage to figure it out for yourself?'

'Well,' parried Ross, veering away from the real question, 'he assured me that you weren't sleeping with Dominic.'

'And how did he know that?'

'He asked you.'

Tessa's eyes glittered. Placing her half-empty mug on the window-seat beside her and folding her arms across her stomach she said, 'What?'

'He came to one of your parties,' replied Ross, beginning to enjoy himself now. 'His name's Henry.'

Dominic was forever throwing impromptu parties – it came as naturally to him as breathing – and Tessa had met dozens of new people during the course of those happy, informal gatherings where the food, if any, was basic but where there was always plenty to drink. She thought back to one particular Sunday afternoon party and pinpointed Henry in her mind. Small, round-faced and cheerful and looking nothing at all like a private detective, he had engaged her in an easy discussion of French Impressionism. From there the conversation had turned to her own work – Henry merrily confessed to being an enthusiastic amateur, a weekend dabbler in water-colours – and to her hopes for the future. And he had . . . of *course* he had . . . casually asked Tessa whether she and Dominic were 'a couple'.

Smiling in response to the question, so delicately phrased, she had shaken her head and said, 'No, no, it's nothing like that. We're simply friends.'

Gazing steadily back at Ross now, she said, 'Well, that was very clever, very neat. But then my own fidelity was never really the issue, was it? You know damn well why I left and I'm sorry for any inconvenience I caused but I don't regret it, one bit. Not getting married was the most sensible decision of my life.'

Sitting there in that ridiculous bath towel, her bare toes curling against the rough stone wall and her tangled hair curling damply past her shoulders, Ross thought that she looked more proud, more regal than any power-dressed princess. She had hurt him so much, caused him grief and humiliation . . . yet she possessed such integrity that it was impossible not to admire her.

He simply hadn't been able to stop loving her, not for a single minute.

And apart from anything else, he was the one who had been at fault.

'I'm sorry,' he said, wishing he could just rip the bath towel from her and make love to her here and now. He wasn't brilliant at verbal apologies, not being at all used to having to make them. His dark eyes searched her face for encouragement but Tessa wasn't giving an inch; her jaw was set, the line of her mouth uncompromisingly firm. He reassured himself with the thought that at least she wasn't hurling abuse at him.

'I didn't know at first why you'd disappeared,' he said, attempting to explain. 'When I tackled Antonia, she denied having had anything to do with it. It wasn't until the following week that she admitted what she'd done.'

With great difficulty, Tessa controlled the impulse to hurl something at him. In this depleted cottage, however, there was precious little to hurl.

'So as far as you're concerned,' she said icily, 'the fact that you spent the night with her isn't the issue – you're just sorry you were found out.'

He hated the way she argued. Shaking his head, he said helplessly, 'No . . . yes . . . well, both. Tess, I *know* what I did was wrong and I wish to God I *hadn't* done it, but I was so furious after we'd had that argument and you'd seemed so hell-bent on protecting Dominic and getting rid of me that when Antonia turned up in London I just . . . flipped.' He stared out of the window, at the rolling hills in the distance and at a single bird soaring effortlessly up into the cobalt-blue sky. 'If it makes any difference, I regretted it straight away, afterwards. I just prayed that you'd never find out. And I know now that I would never do such a thing again. Ever.'

Having known about it for several weeks wasn't making it any easier to listen to. Tessa felt sick. She didn't have the heart to challenge him further; Antonia had stated quite categorically that Ross intended their affair to continue but if she mentioned that now he would only deny it.

'How can I believe you?' she asked instead, her tone weary.

'How could you ever expect me to trust you again? Spending the rest of my life with a man I'm afraid to argue with – in case he leaps into bed with the nearest available woman – isn't my idea of fun.'

'I wouldn't—' began Ross, eager to reassure her, but she quelled him with a look.

'Don't say it. I wouldn't believe you anyway, so just don't say it. Look, I'm expecting Holly here any minute now, so perhaps you should leave.'

When Ross didn't make any move to do so, she slid down from the window-seat and went outside into the garden. Returning less than a minute later with a creased and still slightly damp black vest and a pale pink denim skirt, she found Ross descending the stairs with Olivia in his arms. All thought of their argument swept aside he said in a voice filled with wonder, 'She smiled! Tess, she really smiled at me.'

Tess, who hadn't forgotten the argument, said briefly: 'Wind.'

'It looked like a smile to me.' Ross ran a gentle finger along the curve of his daughter's cheek. Not having seen her for over five weeks he was stunned by the change in her appearance and by the rush of love he felt for her. Those eyes, dark brown now, were large and fringed with surprisingly long lashes and he didn't care what Tessa said – Olivia was smiling.

God, he had missed them both so much.

'I *can* come and see her?' he said, as Tessa moved forward to take her from him. Olivia's tiny fingers clutched at his grey and white striped shirt, her grip surprisingly strong.

Tessa, not trusting herself to speak, nodded.

'And you'll be needing your things,' he went on, for something to say. 'They're over at the house – I can bring them back tomorrow morning if you'd like.'

'Thanks.'

He wanted to kiss her, but knew that he mustn't.

'Is there anything else you need? Money?'

'I'm fine.'

'Right. I'd better go then.' Stepping back, he watched her smoothing Olivia's dark, silky hair, her head bent protectively towards her daughter as if to shield her from the rest of the world.

'Tess, I really am sorry.'

She glanced up at him, and at that moment he saw the hurt, the disappointment and the sorrow in her clear green eyes.

'Yes,' she replied slowly. 'So am I.'

Chapter 45

Having always enjoyed meeting new people, Holly nevertheless wondered why on earth, in a moment of either weakness or sheer madness – possibly both – she had agreed to meet Adam's parents. Now, as the dark blue Rolls purred up the motorway at a sedate eighty miles an hour and the North grew steadily closer, she was seriously regretting her decision.

'They won't think I'm your girl-friend, will they?' she asked anxiously, imagining the horrors of such a scenario. Adam, overtaking a clapped-out Mini and popping another Rolo into his mouth, grinned at her.

'I'll make sure they don't, angel. No need to panic.'

'But I still don't understand why you even invited me. Do you take every woman you've ever met to see them?'

He shook his head, still smiling. 'By no means. Hardly anyone, in fact, but I thought it would be helpful for you to meet them.'

It was no use, he was being deliberately, infuriatingly enigmatic and she wasn't going to get a single sensible word out of him. Unwrapping the last Rolo and deliberately not offering it to Adam, Holly ate it. This was the last time, she reflected moodily, the very last time that she was going to be stupid enough to allow Adam Perry to persuade her to do anything against her will.

* * *

Little Tollerton, nestling in a fold of the Yorkshire Moors, was pure James Herriot. The small but sprawling village with its grey, slate-roofed cottages, colourful front gardens and narrow, winding lanes was shielded on all sides by rolling, pinky-mauve moors dotted with farmhouses and sheep. With the sun blazing in a blue sky it was all too picturesque for words but in the winter, Adam had explained, the roads would disappear beneath several feet of snow and the village, cut off for weeks on end, became a small world of its own, entirely self-contained and relying for survival upon the sturdy, no-nonsense determination of its inhabitants.

'What are you, the local boy who made good?' said Holly, as the Rolls-Royce pulled up outside a row of terraced cottages and an old man walking past with his dog touched his cap in a signal of recognition.

'No,' replied Adam, refusing to rise to her bait, 'I'm just Bill and Netta's eldest son. As far as these people are concerned, running a profitable farm is their idea of really making good. And catching yourself a reliable wife, of course,' he added cheerfully. 'That's far more worthwhile than owning a few dozen gambling imporiums, as old Jethro Blacker always calls them.'

'But you've made so much money,' she persisted, still needling him. 'Millions! I thought people in your position bought their parents nice new houses. It's what footballers always seem to do.'

'Ah,' said Adam, helping her out of the car and doing up an extra button on her shirt so that no cleavage remained exposed, 'but I'm a Yorkshireman, pet. We don't waste our hard-earned money on fripperies. Besides, if I started splashing out like that, buying new houses for every Tom, Dick and Harry I'd ever known, I'd just end up back where I started, and where's the point in that?'

But they're your parents, Holly wanted to scream at him. At that moment, however, the front door opened and Bill and Netta Perry, together with their daughter Jeanette and an assortment of dogs, spilled out of the cottage.

'We didn't even know you were here until I happened to glance out of the window,' scolded Netta, reaching up and giving her son a hug. Then, turning to Holly and smiling, she said, 'When he had that Ferrari we could hear him coming for miles. This new car's much too quiet. Hello, my dear, you must be Holly. Adam's told us so much about you. Come along inside and I'll make us all a nice cup of tea.'

Holly was reminded of the afternoon at Tessa's cottage, when Ross had instructed everyone to make themselves as large and noisy as possible. Even as they made their way through the house Adam was introducing her to his father, his younger sister and the dogs. Netta, bustling ahead of them into the kitchen, was telling Adam that his car needed a good wash and that Susie Ackerton had given birth to twins the previous week. Jeanette reminded Holly that they had met before, at the wedding reception at The Grange, during which Adam had so publicly blackmailed her into going out to dinner with him. Bill Perry, gently but firmly removing the teapot from his wife's hands, said, 'Leave it, lass. Why don't we all go out into the garden and get acquainted over a proper drink? How about you, Holly? Now you look to me like a gin-and-tonic girl if ever I saw one. Or would you prefer a can of lager?'

Half an hour later, everyone was still talking non-stop. Holly, relaxing over her second drink – an astonishingly stiff gin – was

351

struck by the easy familiarity and good-humoured badinage flowing constantly from one member of the family to the next. Bill Perry, grey haired and dark eyed, was openly *flirting* with his pretty wife. Netta, whose own hair was of the same tawny shade as her son's, laughed and joked and gave every inch as good as she got. Their affection for each other was undisguised, their general air of happiness infectious.

'Thirty-five years, we've lived here,' Netta was explaining to Holly. 'And whoever would have thought it would last five minutes when we were first married? Why, almost every other day I was either packing my bags or throwing Bill's clothes out into the street. We argued so much that it's a wonder we ever managed to produce young Adam. We were terrible . . .!'

'Scarlett O'Hara, the rest of the village called her,' continued her husband fondly. 'We struck a few sparks, I must say. Still, it gave the neighbours summat to talk about. And then, after seven months of marriage, we simply ran out of arguments. Couldn't think of another blessed thing to fight about. It was a shock to the system, I can tell you. There we were, ground to a halt and having to come to terms with the fact that we'd been in love with each other all along, without even realizing it.'

'So we decided to make the best of a bad job and stay married,' supplied Netta cheerfully. 'And here we are, all these years later, *really* stuck with each other. After all, who else would have either of us now?'

'Hmm, I don't know,' said Adam with a wink in Holly's direction. 'Jethro Blacker's always had his eye on you. And then there's old Ted Marston up at Hillcrest Farm . . .'

'Away, son!' exclaimed Bill Perry, taking his wife's hand and squeezing it. 'Those two old scoundrels don't have more than seven teeth between them. They're nowhere near good enough for my beautiful wife.'

'Ted Marston's rumoured to keep his life savings under his mattress,' put in Jeanette, her tone persuasive. 'Apparently he's loaded.'

'And since when has money made the heart grow fonder?' demanded Bill, as Netta pretended to consider the possibility. 'Whoever could prefer a pile of dirty banknotes to a kiss and a cuddle from a man with a full set of teeth? And besides,' he added forcefully, 'this is the woman who turned down the offer of a fast car, a world cruise and a brand-new, five-bedroomed house up on Tollerton Heights. Money wouldn't turn her head if it fell from the sky like snow.'

Holly looked blank. Leaning across, Jeanette explained with a giggle, 'Poor old Adam was absolutely dying to spoil Mum and Dad in their old age, but they refused to move.'

'And why should we?' said Netta comfortably, gesturing towards the apple trees, the carefully tended banks of delphiniums, hollyhocks and honeysuckle bordering the immaculate lawn. 'We've spent over thirty years getting this garden how we like it! And as for fast cars, what on earth would we look like, two old geriatrics bombing around in something out of a James Bond film? We'd be laughed out of the village . . . Now Holly, how about another chicken sandwich, or do you think you could manage a slice of this walnut cake?'

As Holly bit into the moist, deliciously rich cake, Jeanette caught her attention once more. In a stage whisper, she said, 'So are you and Adam really serious about each other, or are you just after him for his body?'

Holly almost choked. Adam wore his most irrepressible grin.

Bill and Netta Perry tried not to look expectant, and failed miserably.

'Unfortunately, neither,' said Adam, as Holly, scarlet-cheeked and hating him for landing her in this most embarrassing of situations, glared accusingly at him. 'It's a sad story, trite but true. Mad as I am about this gorgeous girl, she is besotted with another man who in turn rejects *her* in favour of another woman. All that remains now in order to complete the daisy chain,' he concluded triumphantly, 'is for me to have an affair with the other woman, and then we can all be unhappy together.'

'How fascinating!' said Netta, her sparkling blue eyes alight with interest. She patted Holly's forearm in a gesture of encouragement. 'Now that I no longer have any of my own, I just adore hearing about other people's traumas. Tell us everything, my dear. Every detail. Maybe we can help you to sort it all out . . . '

'It was a complete and utter set-up,' stormed Holly, still seething three days later and oblivious to the fact that Tessa – in the precious and lamentably few free hours Olivia allowed her – was trying to work.

'Maybe he really was just trying to help?' suggested Tessa, narrowing her eyes and testing the perspective of the landscape she was roughing out on canvas.

'Help himself, you mean!' retorted Holly, throwing herself down on the sofa. 'That man is shameless. And if he thought that introducing me to his parents would make me change my mind about him he couldn't have been more wrong.'

'Why, what are they like?'

'Wonderful! Blissfully happy, still besotted with each other after thirty-five years . . . it almost made me cry, just seeing

354

them together. I didn't realize marriages like that really existed.'

Tessa didn't either. But she couldn't understand why the fact that they obviously did should be having such a profound effect upon Holly.

'But doesn't that cheer you up?' she asked, resuming her painting and determinedly averting her own mind from thoughts of Ross. 'You always wanted to get married and live happily ever after.'

'Of course I do,' wailed Holly, banging her fist against the side of the sofa in despair. 'But not with Adam bloody Perry. I want to marry Max!'

Ross, having mounted his own all-out attack on Tessa, was equally determined to win her back. The fact that she had returned to Bath of her own accord had been, he felt, a promising sign, but the going was by no means easy. The unspoken subject of his thoughtless, ridiculous, *careless* one-night stand with Antonia stood like a barrier between them; he had betrayed Tessa, dissolved her trust in him . . . and much as he wished it could, somehow, miraculously happen, there was no way in the world that he could go back and undo the deed.

But if there was anything else he could do – anything at all – he made very sure indeed that it was done. Despite the fact that he found the idea of Tessa and Olivia spending the following winter in the cottage utterly intolerable, he organized the installation of an efficient central-heating system so that at least they wouldn't freeze. Replacing the ancient stove with a state-of-the-art microwave was the next step, closely followed by an equally hi-tech fridge-freezer, decent carpets, and a telephone – an unbreakable one this time. Insisting that she needed reliable transport, he also returned the white Mercedes into her possession. And whenever she protested, which was every time he turned up with something else new and efficient and sensible, he was able to kill her arguments stone dead simply by employing that most irreproachable of alibis – Olivia.

'I'm not doing it for you, I'm doing it for our daughter,' mimicked Tessa, jumping in before he had a chance to say it for what seemed like the twentieth time in as many days. 'Ross, she's ten weeks old. She doesn't *watch* videos yet.'

But what Ross didn't realize was quite how hard Tessa was finding it, simply coping with the situation. Unfortunately, knowing that a man wasn't ideal husband material didn't automatically cancel out all that natural attraction which had so drawn her to him in the first place. Chemistry – or whatever it was, she thought despairingly during her weaker moments – was no respecter of common sense, as poor Holly knew only too well. Knowing what was sensible didn't make it any easier to remain constantly on her guard against the totally unfair onslaught to which Ross was submitting her.

But gradually, very gradually, as the summer lengthened and finally gave way to autumn, she found herself able to come to terms with the situation. It still wasn't easy, but Ross tried so hard, and he was so totally besotted with Olivia that attempting to reduce the frequency of his visits would have caused more difficulties and Tessa had become only too acutely aware now of the fact that since Olivia *had* a father, she should grow up knowing and loving him, irrespective of his faults.

And so, almost without noticing that it was happening, they had fallen back into that easy familiarity which had always bound them. The only difference now was that since she knew there to be absolutely no future in it, the relationship remained purely platonic. Tessa couldn't cope with the emotional turmoil which she knew would result if she were to weaken and go to bed with Ross, even once. After all, she reminded herself with sardonic humour, look what had happened the last time she'd risked it.

Chapter 46

'But you were supposed to be coming home tonight,' snapped Antonia, irritated beyond belief by Richard's casual tone. *She* was the one who was supposed to be casual, dammit, and the fact that they were supposed to be attending the opening night of a play at the Theatre Royal only served to increase her frustration. 'What the hell am I supposed to do now? I can't possibly go to this thing on my own.'

But Richard remained unconcerned. 'Take a friend.'

I haven't got any bloody friends, thought Antonia, gazing moodily at the gin and tonic in her hand. Other men's wives or girl-friends were always too wary of her and she, in turn, naturally preferred the company of males, but she had never nurtured platonic relationships of the kind which made inviting a man to the theatre acceptable. Sometimes she felt as if she existed within an impenetrable plastic bubble, knowing that people talked about her, but never actually hearing the defamatory remarks herself. But as long as she had had Ross – and Richard – it hadn't bothered her in the slightest.

'Hmm, I may just do that,' she said, her tone deliberately sly in order to make him think that if he was going to let her down like this he would regret it.

'Good,' replied Richard equably. 'I'm sure you'll enjoy yourself. Look, I'd better get back into the meeting now.'

'Say hello to Harvey for me,' said Antonia, smiling to herself.

Harvey Russell was a mega-successful entrepreneur and a notorious womanizer whose advances she had regularly rejected over the years. Maybe now, though, she could be persuaded to change her mind. If the man was wealthy enough the size of his paunch became magically less of a turn-off, she'd always found, although of course with Ross she'd been spoiled; that lean but muscular athlete's body was simply faultless.

'Harvey.' Richard paused. Then he said, 'Yes, of course I will. He's in great form, putting deals together like nobody's business. The Germans don't know what's hit them. My God, you should have seen the way he handled Franz—'

'Fine,' interrupted Antonia, adrenalin suddenly racing through her bloodstream. 'Right, you get back to your meeting. 'Bye.'

It had never occurred to her before, she thought as she replaced the receiver and sat back, nursing her drink in both hands. It would never have occurred to her in a million years and she still couldn't believe that it was actually true, but that momentary hesitation, followed by the hearty extraneous detail were dead giveaways, the stumbling blocks of inexperience so instantly recognizable to practised deceivers such as herself.

Richard wasn't with Harvey Russell. He might not even be in London. He, Richard, her husband, was having . . . an affair.

The shock of it made her feel breathless, as if all the air had been sucked out of her lungs. Reaching for the bottle of Gordon's, she poured an extra inch into her glass and drank it down in one go. How dare he? Who *was* she? Why the bloody hell was life so unfair? And why the bloody, *bloody* hell, she thought viciously, didn't Ross Monahan dump that stupid little tart who called herself an artist and come back to her?

* * *

Ross, having deftly fitted Olivia's chubby brown limbs into a scarlet Babygro – he had overcome his fear that the slightest pressure on her joints would result in those terrifying greenstick fractures he'd read about – hoisted her into the air, waiting for the precious reward of her smile. Olivia, uncritically adoring, didn't hesitate to oblige.

'You see?' he protested, turning to Tessa, who was putting the finishing touches to a summery, impressionistic water-colour, 'Olivia thinks we should go. Ah, what a magnificent smile! What a magnificent tooth you have, my darling! Quick, look at her tooth, Tess.'

'I've been looking at it for the last four days,' replied Tessa patiently, though his enthusiasm secretly suffused her with pleasure. 'Ever since it arrived. And since you've taken at least two rolls of film and used up four hours of videotape recording its existence, no doubt we shall be looking at that tooth for the next fifteen years at least.'

'Fifteen years?' he said, eyebrows raised. 'Why not fifty?'

'When Olivia is fifteen, if she has any spirit at all, she'll destroy the evidence before you get a chance to humiliate her in front of her boyfriends.'

But Ross was unperturbed. 'I'll keep copies in a bank vault. A first tooth should be preserved for posterity. And you're still avoiding the subject,' he continued, determined that she wasn't going to wriggle out of it. 'Theo Panayiotou is a perfectly nice guy, kind to children and animals and thoroughly respectable. The fact that he's a billionaire shouldn't put you off, either. You painted Nico's portrait, so why are you hesitating this time? It's a brilliant chance, Tess. You'd be crazy to pass it up.'

She was only too acutely aware of that fact, but she also knew that actually painting the portrait wasn't the issue.

The catch, the big catch, was that Theo Panayiotou would be staying in Edinburgh and the plan was that she and Ross should travel up together. He had an hotel to look over, he had explained, and Theo was interested in partnering him in the deal. In between business meetings, he would sit for her while she painted his portrait. It all sounded incredibly logical and innocent, on the surface. But could she really trust Ross? And worse, she thought as she pretended to concentrate hard on the water-colour before her, could she really trust herself?

'Your mother is stalling,' Ross gravely informed their daughter. 'I have this feeling she's running out of excuses.'

'I have letters here,' said Tessa, waving towards the shelf above the fireplace which served as her filing cabinet, 'from half a dozen people asking me to paint them.'

'And you can,' he reminded her with exaggerated patience, 'but Theo's only in the UK for a week. Besides, think how impressed those people will be, knowing that you've just completed *his* portrait . . .'

He was beating her down again; she recognized the signs only too well. She also knew that if she protested about the fact that Ross had set up this deal himself he would only trot out that infuriating old line of his about not doing it for her, but for Olivia.

'Right,' she said at last, putting down her brushes and turning to face him. To her dismay, she felt colour mounting in her cheeks. 'If you must know, I don't want to spend a week in an hotel with you. And that is why I'm not going to Edinburgh. OK?'

Ross grinned, his dark brown eyes alight with triumph. 'No problem at all,' he said, hoisting Olivia into a more comfortable position against his chest and reaching for her bottle. 'Forget the hotel, we'll rent a tent, instead.'

Mattie, having hurried out to the chemist in her lunch break, was lost in thought at the counter when someone behind her tugged suddenly and none too gently at her hair. Startled – and praying that it wasn't Grace – she spun round.

'Olivia, that's a terrible thing to do,' scolded the blonde-haired girl whose baby had reached out and committed the anti-social act. She gave Mattie an apologetic smile. 'I'm so sorry, she's fascinated by hair at the moment. I've only just begun to realize how embarrassing children can be.'

Mattie recognized her at once, of course, although the photographs in the newspapers hadn't captured the full vibrancy of her beauty. With those clear green eyes and that self-deprecating smile, Tessa Duvall was far more attractive, more *alluring*, than she had expected. And the baby, so dark and mischievous-looking, and so like her father, was equally beguiling. Waving her fist and kicking her legs, Olivia gurgled and lunged once more in Mattie's direction.

'Don't worry, you have years of embarrassment ahead of you,' said Mattie cheerfully. 'She's gorgeous.'

Tessa rolled her eyes in mock despair. 'She's supposed to be asleep.' Then, beginning to move away, she said, 'Come on sweetheart, we'd better leave before your charm wears off.'

But Mattie was both fascinated and intrigued by this unexpected encounter. 'Actually,' she said, as Tessa turned to leave, 'it's nice to have a chance to meet you. I believe you know my daughter, Grace.'

'Who works at The Grange?' Tessa looked surprised, then

smiled again. 'Of course I do, she's a lovely girl. She came to visit me at the hospital after Olivia was born, but I haven't seen her since . . . well, not for ages.' Having been about to say that she hadn't seen Grace since the day before the wedding, Tessa had faltered. But this was Grace's mother, and it was hardly a secret, after all. 'Ross and I had a few problems, as I'm sure you know, and I haven't been back to the hotel. But I'd love to see Grace again – she was so kind to me while I was there. I'm leaving for Scotland tomorrow but tell her that as soon as I get back I'll be in touch with her.'

Mattie, who hadn't even realized that Grace had become quite so friendly with this charming girl, was both surprised and relieved.

Following the revelation that Ross was her own natural father, Grace had stopped confiding in Mattie about any of the goings-on at the hotel. It had all been very worrying, and Mattie in turn, had even allowed the terrible thought that Grace might have had something to do with Tessa's abrupt departure, to cross her mind. Discovering now that her daughter had been innocent of such fateful meddling – of *course* she wouldn't have done such a terrible thing – she was doubly delighted.

'I will,' she said, nodding her head for emphasis. 'And I'm glad to see you both looking so well. Grace has told me so much about you that it's nice to actually meet you at last.'

'And you,' said Tessa, taking a precautionary step backwards as Olivia reached out once more, apparently intent this time upon grasping one of Mattie's earrings. 'But I'll leave you in peace now. Olivia and I are off to buy some really efficient nappies. Meanwhile, I just have to pray that the man who's serving at the nappy counter isn't wearing a toupee . . .'

* * *

Later that evening, Mattie surveyed the result of her visit to the chemist. Bizarrely – she couldn't imagine how – the small pink ring which had formed on the strip of white cardboard meant that history had indeed repeated itself. She was pregnant. She really *was* pregnant. Again.

Her thoughts drifted back to her chance meeting earlier in the day with Tessa. Thirteen years were all that separated them yet her own experiences of motherhood seemed lifetimes away; having suspected the truth for almost a fortnight now, she still couldn't envisage going through that terrible, wonderful ordeal all over again. She was forty years old, nearly forty-one, and a *spinster*, for heaven's sake.

At the same time, however, she knew that she couldn't imagine *not* doing it. Richard was the best thing ever to have happened to her, but he was married. She couldn't expect miracles – she knew from bitter experience not to expect even the smallest miracle. Yet somehow it didn't matter. Knowing that she had done it before only meant that she knew the obstacles could be overcome. And now that she was actually pregnant she also knew that another child would mean more to her, be *worth* more to her than anything else in the world. Richard too was the impossible dream but at least this way she would always have a part of a man whom she now knew she *really* loved . . .

Chapter 47

Theo Panayiotou was as charming as Ross had promised, as only the Greeks can be, but he was also terrifyingly direct. Cutting no corners and coming straight to the point may have helped to make him a billionaire, with worldwide interests in oil, shipping and hotels, but as far as Tessa was concerned his manner was downright scary.

'Tell me,' he protested during his first hour-long sitting with her. 'What is the point of "playing it safe", when any one of us could die tomorrow? I see in your eyes and in Ross's eyes that the two of you share some deep and incredible relationship, yet Ross tells me that you and he do not sleep together. I find this totally . . . strange.'

But since he was being so direct, Tessa felt she had no choice other than to compete with him.

'He isn't faithful,' she said, delineating the shadows of the rotund, smiling face and finding them lamentably few and far between. Billionaire or no billionaire, Theo needed to go on a diet. 'I didn't marry him because he slept with somebody else. I don't want to be married to a man I can't trust.'

'I know, I know, he told me.' Theo dismissed her reasons with a careless gesture which caused Tessa to grit her teeth; she had just been outlining the position of his pudgy hands. 'But men and women have their differences and this is precisely *it*! Sex is easy for men, but if it is without love it is unimportant. The problem with women, you see, is that they fail to understand this, but a roll in the sack simply doesn't *matter* . . .'

'Hay,' corrected Tessa automatically, hurrying to finish his hands before they took off again. 'And it matters to me.'

'But I see it, I *know*,' exclaimed Theo, gesturing wildly towards the ceiling, 'that if you were married he wouldn't even look at another woman. Not that I understand such behaviour,' he amended with a sorrowful shrug, 'but we are talking of an Englishman, after all . . .'

'Some tent,' said Tessa, later that night. Olivia, lying flat out in the centre of the four-poster bed, shifted and sighed in her sleep.

'It was all I could manage at such short notice,' said Ross, wishing with all his heart that it could be Tessa and himself occupying that bed. 'And there's no need to look at me like that, it has a roof, doesn't it?'

Eyeing the myriad folds of midnight-blue velvet, Tessa managed a small smile. If Ross could have known how hard it was for her to resist him when he was being this nice, she would have died.

'It has a roof,' she agreed equably. 'And your own bed, in your own room, has a similar roof. Try it, you may like it.'

'Tess.' He moved towards her and she took a prudent, reluctant step backwards. 'How often has Theo told you that men are men and women are different? This is killing me, you must know that.'

'And how much did you pay Theo to expound his ridiculous chauvinist theories?' she retaliated, keeping her tone light. 'He's Greek, Ross. He wouldn't recognize a monogamous relationship if he tripped over one in the street. We've only had one sitting and he's already sworn undying love over the phone to three different women while I've been there.'

'Theo loves women,' he replied with a careless shrug, although the expression in his eyes was now altogether more serious. Maintaining the distance between them – that *bloody* distance which Tessa insisted upon, and which kept them eternally, infuriatingly and so unnecessarily apart – he said, 'Whereas I only love one woman. And if she'd just give me a chance, *one chance*, I could prove it to her.'

'I expect you could,' replied Tessa coolly, willing away the frantic butterflies in her stomach and forcing herself to stand firm. 'I'm sure you're every bit as clever in that respect as Theo is. But we aren't talking about the number of women you love, Ross. We're talking about the number you're capable of remaining faithful to. And unfortunately,' she concluded with a brave, dismissive gesture which tore at her very heart, 'that number has never managed to dwindle to one.'

At that moment she knew how right she had been not to want to come here. Away from the cottage, she had lost the slight natural advantage of being on home territory and Ross was making the very most of her loss. That look in his eyes, the tone of his voice, his entire *manner* were all designed to distract her, to pull her even further off guard. Moving almost imperceptibly closer now, he said, 'But it would, if you'd only give me that chance. Tess, I'm not denying that what happened was absolutely my own fault but you sent me to hell and back when you disappeared the day before the wedding. The fact that I still want you – and *only* you – must tell you something about the way I feel. This is serious, Tess. This is once-in-a-lifetime stuff and I don't understand why you can't see it as clearly as I can.'

She was shaking now, desperately unnerved by his proximity and by the blatant honesty of his words. But she must not, *must not* give in.

'You're talking about sex,' she said accusingly and Ross – rising to the bait, thank heavens – backed off at once. Palms up, brown eyes registering injured innocence, he said, 'No, Tess. I'm not.'

'Good,' she replied in brisk tones, reaching for her dressing gown and heading for the bathroom. 'In that case, maybe you'd like to prove it. By leaving.'

She had particular cause to be grateful to Ross tonight, thought Mattie with a tiny smile. When he had altered the shift rota at short notice Grace had been less than amused – not having access to a video recorder meant that she would miss the penultimate episode of a television serial in which she had been particularly engrossed – but at least Mattie now had the house to herself for the evening.

And she certainly needed the privacy and security of her own home in which to tell Richard about the baby; sitting in a country pub, or in his car and relaying such news would be far too nerve-racking. Not knowing how he was going to react – he might lose his temper and make a scene or dump her in a dark country lane miles from anywhere – she couldn't take any chances.

Not that she honestly imagined he would do such a thing, but she was deliberately steeling herself for the very worst so that anything else would be a bonus. Whatever else happened, Mattie had sadly realized, he was going to be very, very shocked indeed.

Mattie was certainly shocked herself when, less than ten minutes later, Richard arrived. Pulling her towards him, he kissed her thoroughly in the hallway without even bothering to close the front door behind him.

Breathing in the beloved smell of him, a mixture of wool, aftershave and professionally laundered shirts, Mattie returned his embrace with equal fervour. Then, peering over his shoulder, she gasped, 'You've left the car outside! Oh Richard, can't you stay after all?'

His eyes bright with the enormity of his decision, he kicked the door shut and drew her into the sitting room. 'Darling Mattie, I have no intention of ever parking my car in an adjacent street again. I don't care who knows I'm here and I don't want you to care either.'

'But . . .' said Mattie, her heart pounding as he kissed her again. 'B . . .'

Minutes later, she smoothed her ruffled hair and attempted to get some sense out of him. Richard's normally anxious expression had been replaced by one of confidence. And he was showing every sign of being thoroughly, insatiably aroused. She wondered whether sex first, bombshell later would be like allowing the condemned man his hearty breakfast.

'But darling,' she protested once more, wondering whether he had in fact been drinking. 'What about Antonia?'

'I know, I know,' he said reassuringly, wishing he'd thought to bring along a bottle of champagne. 'This isn't a spur-of-the-moment decision, believe me. I've thought of scarcely anything else for the past week. But I *love* you, Mattie, more than I ever loved her. You've made me so happy in these last few months that the situation has simply become more and more ridiculous, and now I've decided to do something about it.' Taking her warm hands in his, he paused and swallowed hard. 'I'm going to leave Antonia. And if you want me . . . well, then I want to be with you. For the rest of my life.'

In the tradition of all those old black-and-white movies she'd watched and wept over for as long as she could remember, Mattie drew a deep, shuddering breath and promptly burst into tears.

'You'd better say something,' he prompted gently, when the sobs had finally subsided. 'It's somewhat unnerving, not knowing whether you're crying because you're happy or because the situation's just too awful to contemplate.'

Drying her eyes with a paper hanky, Mattie shook her head. 'Oh Richard, I don't know either. Of course, of *course* I want you. But you might not want me.'

'I do.' Kissing her nose and her wet eyelids, he had never loved her more. 'Haven't I just said that I do?'

'But that was before you knew,' wailed Mattie, hot tears rolling afresh down her cheeks, the oh-so-carefully prepared speech flying straight out of the window. 'Richard, I'm so sorry, I didn't mean it to happen. I'm p . . . p . . . pregnant.'

For perhaps the first time in his entire life, Richard's quick brain failed him. He could almost feel it failing him, slowing almost to a standstill as if he had been subjected to a stealthy syringeful of anaesthetic. Staring at Mattie, his face expression-less and his voice equally devoid of emotion, he said, 'You're what?'

'Pregnant,' whispered Mattie, terrified yet at the same time curiously elated. There, she'd told him. And although it would break her heart if he abandoned her now, at least the waiting was over and she could get on with the rest of her life. He couldn't force her to have an abortion, after all. Nobody, not even Richard, could prevent her from having this baby now that it was actually on its way.

All relationships are a matter of give and take. Nobody knew that better than Richard, who was perfectly well aware of the fact that if he hadn't been extraordinarily successful in his chosen career, and as a consequence become extremely wealthy, then Antonia would never even have considered marrying him.

But the knowledge hadn't bothered him because he had accepted it as the fact of life which it undoubtedly was; in return, he had acquired a young, beautiful, socially adept wife whom under other circumstances he could never have hoped to marry. And to be scrupulously fair to Antonia – not realizing at the time that chronic infidelity was her all-time favourite hobby – he *had* found certain aspects of her personality attractive. With her laid-back, devil-may-care attitude to life she had counteracted perfectly his own introspective and somewhat obsessive personality. Richard spent a great deal of time worrying about what others thought of him whereas Antonia couldn't care less. For the first year or two, he had been captivated by what he had thought was her charm but which he had slowly and painfully come to realize was, in fact, sheer selfishness. While he worked, Antonia merely spent her time and his money amusing herself. And the much-longed-for children he had been hoping for had never materialized, simply because his elegant, streamlined wife categorically refused to have any. Pregnancy, according to Antonia, was nature's way of ensuring a lifetime of undiluted misery and no way did she intend to fall into such a thoroughly revolting trap. Richard, realizing sadly that as long as contraceptive pills were being marketed he had absolutely no choice in the matter, had forced himself to understand and accept her decision. It was, after all, pretty much of a *fait accompli*.

But whereas his marriage to Antonia had never been restful, meeting Mattie had been like coming home. Her quintessential goodness warmed him like fine old cognac. Only with Mattie was he able to truly relax and be himself.

Now, hearing her astounding news, he knew beyond all shadow of a doubt that he had been right. Gathering the woman he loved into his arms, he said simply, 'Stop crying. I've never been so happy in my life.'

Chapter 48

Having failed spectacularly in her attempt to impose some form of schedule on Theo Panayiotou – meetings, people and planes waited for *him*, it transpired – Tessa soon realized that the promised sittings simply weren't going to materialize. Constantly on the move, Theo could seldom spare her longer than ten minutes at a time. She was also beginning to wonder whether his mobile phone hadn't been surgically grafted to his ear.

'I'm sorry,' he told her, shrugging and giving her his most charming smile, 'but this is the way I work. Business is business, Tessa. And I have to be back in Athens by the end of the week. If you really need this much time with me, I'm afraid you're going to have to travel around and catch me between meetings.'

It wasn't ideal by any means, but Tessa knew that he was right. He wasn't being deliberately difficult, he was just hopelessly pushed for time. 'What about Olivia?' she asked. 'I can't leave her behind.'

'Bring her,' replied Theo, with an expansive gesture. 'No problem; we have plenty of room. Besides,' he added with a wink, 'maybe she will want to follow her father into the hotel business. It will be good training for her, don't you think?'

Which was why, the following morning, Tessa found herself leaning against the balustrade of Drumlachan Castle while Theo, holding her small daughter with all the ease of a man who has fourteen nephews and nieces, courteously enquired, 'So would you care to tell me, Olivia, whether in your opinion this might be a suitable venture in which to invest? What are your views on this?'

Predictably, Olivia screwed up her face and bawled. Tessa was amused to note the rapidity with which her screaming daughter was returned to her. Theo, she decided, only really enjoyed the company of females who openly adored him in return.

At that moment Ross reappeared at the foot of the sweeping stone staircase. 'The river's bulging with salmon,' he told them cheerfully. 'And there are red deer grazing on the other side. These grounds are a tourist's dream.'

'But not the plumbing,' remarked Theo with a grimace. 'Ross, this place is going to need a huge amount doing to it. More importantly, the job needs to be supervised. We shall have to have someone *in situ*. Did you have anyone in mind for this?'

'I did, I do,' replied Ross, lighting a cigarette and narrowing his eyes against the spiralling smoke. 'Me.'

'What?' said Tessa, so taken aback that she spoke without thinking. Having spent the last hour and a half touring Drumlachan Castle with Theo and Ross, she knew only too well how much work would be entailed in bringing the place up to scratch. The surrounding scenery might be spectacular but the castle itself, having until recently been family-owned, had fallen into a state of incredible disrepair. 'But it's going to take months!'

Ross nodded. 'Eight or nine I would imagine. Maybe even a year if the weather holds us up.' Then he shrugged. 'But we need someone who knows what he's doing and Max can manage The Grange in my absence. As I see it, I'm the best man for the job.'

Tessa, saying nothing more, turned away. Ross's pronouncement had struck her like a hammer blow and she was shaken to realize quite how badly she didn't want it to happen. Having grown used to the fact that he was always around, she had never really considered the possibility that he might – of his own accord – remove himself from her life.

My God, thought Ross, glimpsing the expression on her face as she turned away and recognizing the proud straightening of her shoulders. She really minds. I'm actually getting to her. Miracles *do* happen . . .

'It's not as if I'd be emigrating,' he went on, with a barely discernible wink in Theo's direction. 'I could fly back to Bath every few weeks or so for a couple of days. After all, I wouldn't want Olivia to forget who I am.'

'Right,' murmured Tessa, no longer trusting herself to speak. She felt as if a part of her had been suddenly and savagely chopped off. It was the most awful sensation, yet in its own warped way it was teaching her a great deal. She was obviously far more deeply involved with Ross than she had been able to admit, even to herself.

'I'm sorry,' said Richard, pale but utterly determined. 'But I want a divorce.'

Ridiculously, Antonia's first thought was that only Richard would be polite enough, pedantic enough to apologize before he stuck the knife in. It was absolutely typical of him.

Her second thought was that he had to be joking.

'Darling,' she said with a tolerant smile, 'are you drunk?'

But Richard simply shook his head. 'Of course I'm not drunk. Look, we have to face facts, Antonia. This marriage hasn't worked out. I don't want to spend the rest of my life regretting the fact that I didn't have the nerve to admit it, or to do anything about it. I want a divorce.'

They were sitting at the dining table. Richard's lunch of poached salmon and broccoli remained untouched; while summoning up the courage to make his announcement, Antonia observed, he hadn't been able to eat any of it. She herself had almost finished hers. It was all terribly reminiscent of one of those exceedingly English stage plays, she decided. Noel Coward would have approved no end.

'But, darling,' she said politely, helping herself to another potato from the tureen and taking care not to drop melted butter on to the pristine tablecloth, 'I really don't understand why. I thought we had a perfectly satisfactory marriage. If you've been feeling like this, why on earth haven't you said anything about it before?'

The other woman, of course, was the reason behind this sudden rebellion. Not having ever had an affair before, Richard was getting carried away. He was testing her.

Beginning to relax, Antonia refilled her water glass and smiled at him. Now that she had overcome the initial surprise and recognized the situation for what it was, she knew she could handle it. Which was more than poor Richard seemed capable of, she thought with an emotion akin almost to pity; he was perspiring heavily and still as white as a sheet.

'I'm saying it now,' he said. 'And there's no need to look at me like that, Antonia, because I'm absolutely serious.'

She shook her blonde head, not bothering to hide her amusement and revelling in the fact that she was one up on him. 'No, Richard. You're just absolutely besotted with some other female and for once in your ordered life you have allowed yourself to be carried away. You see, I *know* all about your little affair,' she added, her tone gentle, 'and I understand. These things happen. The one mistake you mustn't allow yourself to make is to take it all too seriously. Have some fun by all means, darling, enjoy it while it lasts. But divorce is such a drastic – and expensive – pastime that I really wouldn't recommend it. It would only end in tears, I can assure you. And I do so hate,' she concluded with a flash of malice, 'to see a grown man cry.'

Richard, rising jerkily to his feet, realized that he couldn't stay in this house for another minute. Unable to compete with Antonia's sharp mind and cruel tongue – and caught even further off guard by the astonishing fact that she knew about Mattie – he had to leave.

'I'm going,' he said. 'I shall instruct my solicitor to commence divorce proceedings immediately. And don't worry, I wouldn't dream of dragging Ross into it; the divorce will be on the grounds of my adultery.'

At that moment, the grinding reality of the situation hit home and Antonia's stomach lurched. Richard was no Paul Newman, but she relied heavily on him for all the security she so desperately needed in her life. He was her uncomplaining, indulgent father-figure, forgiving of any wayward behaviour and providing her with the safety net she needed in order to enjoy life as it should be enjoyed. Without him she would be horribly, scarily alone.

'Richard, I'm sorry.' Following him upstairs, bitterly regretting her earlier flippancy, she tried to catch hold of his arm. When he flinched away, her alarm grew. He was serious. He really did mean to go through with it.

'Darling, I shouldn't have said those things,' she began, 'and I know I've been a bitch but I do love you. You can't just—'

'All true,' he replied shortly, opening wardrobe doors and flinging shirts, suits and sweaters on to the bed with quite uncharacteristic lack of concern for their well-being. 'And I can just leave. I am leaving. I *want* to leave.'

Within no time at all the clothes had been bundled into two suitcases and he was lugging them towards the stairs. Antonia, staring at the emptied wardrobe – for he hadn't even closed its doors behind him – realized that she didn't know what to do next. Mild amusement hadn't worked. Niceness had been a downright failure. Richard was leaving her – really leaving her – and she couldn't think of a single way of stopping him.

She was still sitting there on the edge of the bed when she heard the front door slam. The sound, detonating her anger, catapulted her to her feet. Crossing to the open bedroom window, she stood there and felt her anger spiral to exploding point.

Richard, hauling the heavy cases into the boot of the car, didn't look up.

'You bastard, you fucking stupid bastard,' screamed Antonia, clutching the windowledge for support. 'You'll regret this for the rest of your pathetic life! I'll make you sorry you were ever born!'

Continuing to ignore her, Richard slammed shut the boot of the car and adjusted his spectacles. He was perspiring so heavily that they had slipped down from the bridge of his nose. Taking slow, measured steps he made his way round to the driver's door.

'I'll get you,' shrieked his wife, from high above him. 'I'll burn this fucking house down . . . I'll take you for every penny you've got . . . you won't know what's hit you by the time I've finished!'

But still he didn't look up. Grabbing the nearest heavy object, a Caithness glass paperweight, Antonia hurled it with all her furious might, praying that it would smash the car's windscreen and that Richard would storm back into the house. He mustn't leave . . . he had to stay and fight . . . for *her* . . .

But the paperweight, glittering in the sunlight, merely landed on top of the car and bounced off, leaving a slight dent in the roof and a smattering of glass splinters on the bonnet. Richard, behaving as if it hadn't even happened, switched on the ignition and put the car into gear. Then, without even so much as a glance up in Antonia's direction, he set off down the drive.

He did not, however, get very far. The tension had affected him badly; his hands were clammy and the venom of Antonia's words still clung to him, haunting his conscience and at the same time causing him to shudder with relief. He felt hot and cold at the same time and his breath was coming in short, sharp gasps.

When the pressure on his chest grew more severe, stiffening the muscles in his shoulders, he realized that he was experiencing some kind of delayed shock reaction. His breathing was more laboured; he needed to pull off the road and rest for a couple of minutes, to calm down and compose himself before he saw Mattie. Although at the same time he couldn't wait to tell her that he had actually *done* it – that he had walked out on Antonia for good.

But he had to stop the car before he caused an accident. Spotting the lay-by up ahead on the brow of the hill, he forced his aching arms to perform the necessary manoeuvres, signalling, changing gear and hauling the steering-wheel to the left. God, it was hard work . . . but at least the car was now safely parked. All he had to do now was regain control over his breathing and ease the cramping sensation in his chest. If he could manage to adjust the position of the seat, if he could stretch out flat he knew he would feel better.

And then the cramping sensation intensified, became knife-like, and he realized that this wasn't stress at all. Something was seriously wrong. A bolt of pain shot down his left arm, his entire body was cold yet drenched with sweat and the Rachmaninov piano concerto playing on the car radio was distorting, ebbing and flowing beneath the buzzing in his own ears. Screwing up his face against the mounting onslaught of pain, Richard knew that he had to get out of the car, attract attention, call for help . . . but he no longer had the necessary strength. Antonia's vicious words mingled in his panicking brain with Rachmaninov, and although his eyes were closed he was clearly able to see Mattie, dear sweet Mattie in her pink dress, smiling at him and telling him that it didn't matter, it was only a cigarette burn, nothing to worry about at all . . .

Antonia, examining her face in the bathroom mirror, observed with pride and relief that the tears she had shed earlier had left no tell-tale marks. She hated to cry anyway, so it hadn't lasted more than a couple of minutes – just long enough to exorcise the frustration and anger. Richard didn't deserve more than that.

And now that she was feeling better, and since her eyes weren't in the least bit reddened or puffy, she was able to smile at her reflection and plan some suitable course of revenge. If she really wanted to hit Richard where it most hurt and cheer herself up at the same time, she decided with detached amusement, what better way of achieving it than by going beserk with the gold cards? How ever many ludicrously expensive dresses could she buy before hitting the limit on good old AmEx?

Chapter 49

Armed with the certain knowledge that Tessa, while still wary, was weakening, Ross redoubled his efforts to finally win her over. And now that he had also discovered the means with which to do it, he felt closer than ever to succeeding. For as far as Tessa was concerned, it seemed that a little jealousy – as long as no other women were involved – went a long, long way.

'So tell me, what do *you* think of Drumlachan Castle,' he said persuasively over dinner that evening in a secluded corner of the hotel dining room. 'Isn't it going to be incredible when it's finished?'

In the topaz candlelight his dark eyes seemed more mesmerizing than ever. It was dreadfully unfair, thought Tessa, that just when she most needed to be strong, to maintain that acceptable distance between them, Ross should be looking his absolute best, exuding health, charm, enthusiasm . . . and a great deal more than his fair share of sex appeal.

She was torn. Accustomed to speaking her mind, she knew that this was exactly what she mustn't do now. For those private thoughts were so wildly inappropriate that just thinking them stirred up a helpless, fluttering desire in the pit of her stomach. And Ross, most definitely, must not even suspect that such traitorous emotions existed.

Which was why she forced herself to smile and say instead, 'I don't know how you even begin to set about turning a mouldering old castle into a luxury hotel, but I'm sure it will be incredible by the time you've finished.'

She only half-listened to his detailed explanations. Having done it before with The Grange, he was clearly buoyed up by the challenge ahead of him. Ideas flowed, practical answers were supplied to seemingly insurmountable problems and as his enthusiasm gained momentum, Ross grew ever more expansive. All the time, even as he was roughing out plans on the back of their menu – the *maitre d'* was going to be thrilled about that – Tessa felt him slipping further and further away from her. And now that he was, she was no longer quite so sure that she wanted him to.

'. . . as I said before, it's going to take a while. If we get planning permission for the golf course as well, I'm going to have to allow for a year away from The Grange. But it'll be worth it.' Leaning back in his chair, he grinned at her. 'Don't you agree?'

'It doesn't seem altogether fair,' ventured Tessa cautiously, 'that you should need to abandon your own hotel in order to get this one set up, while Theo just leaves you to it.'

'Ah, well. That's one of the perks of being a billionaire. He's providing financial backing; I'm making the whole thing viable. You paint pictures and I turn old buildings into desirable places to stay. This is what I do best, Tessa. It's bloody hard work, but it's fun.'

She'd never seen him like this before, so engrossed in an idea that he'd even stopped flirting with her. More bluntly than she had planned, she said, 'It won't be fun in February, when there's six feet of snow on the ground and the electricity's been cut off for a fortnight.'

'Which is why,' he replied, unperturbed, 'we'll need our own generator. You see, that's what *makes* it so much fun. It's all about tactics, beating the odds, winning. Shall we order coffee now or would you prefer some to be sent up to your room?'

He hadn't even noticed that she'd taken special care to look nice tonight, she thought with a touch of uncharacteristic pique. She wasn't exactly proud of herself for having made such an effort, and the fact that he hadn't even noticed was doubly infuriating.

Slowly, slowly, thought Ross, employing every ounce of self-control he possessed and smiling at her in what he hoped was a brotherly fashion. She was wearing the black dress in which he had first seen her, just over a year ago now, and its elegant simplicity seemed to suit her more than ever, enhancing the startling emerald-greenness of her troubled eyes and the glossy golden-blonde hair which tumbled past her shoulders with such riotous abandon that he could scarcely bear not to reach out and touch it.

'I suppose I should make sure Olivia's all right,' she said, her tone determinedly neutral. Being packed off to bed at ten o'clock with a tray of coffee wasn't exactly what she was in the mood for, but if Ross wanted to be rid of her . . .

Before she had a chance to take him at his word, however, he caught her arm. 'There's really no need for you to go, is there?' he said beguilingly. 'Relax. The baby-sitter's booked until twelve and you know perfectly well that if there were any problems we'd be paged. Now, if you smile nicely I'll order us another bottle of wine.'

The excellent claret slipped down easily, warming her and weakening her resolve. When Ross had tipped the last of it into their glasses she finally asked the question which had been bothering her all evening. 'So, who will run this new hotel when it opens?'

Ross sipped his drink, then shrugged. 'I don't know. It might be me.'

'But why?'

'Why not?' he countered, a note of challenge in his voice. 'It's not as if I have any real ties in Bath. I don't have a wife to worry about, after all.'

She felt less warmed, less relaxed now. Keeping her voice low, so that diners at adjacent tables wouldn't overhear, she said, 'There is Olivia.'

'I'd see her whenever I returned to Bath. I told you that this afternoon,' he replied evenly. 'Tess, she's my own daughter. You *know* I wouldn't abandon her.'

But now that her defences were crumbling, she could no longer hold back. Inwardly horrified by the unmistakable trace of self-pity in her own voice, she said, 'But it's not the same.'

And Ross, exhaling slowly, smiled. 'Forgive me if I'm being presumptuous, Tessa, but does this mean that you might actually miss me if I weren't always around?'

She drained her glass and glared at him, hating him for making her say it but at the same time experiencing a rush of relief. It did, after all, need to be said.

'Dammit Ross, of course I'd miss you. Not that you deserve to be missed—'

'Sshh.' He reached for her hand, forestalling her. The smile, that wicked, mesmerizing smile which had got her into so much trouble in the past, broadened. 'Don't spoil it now. That first statement was perfect. You don't know how long I've waited to hear you say those words . . . or any kind words at all,' he added, leaning fractionally closer towards her. 'Do you realize, Tess, that you never say anything nice about me?'

She knew that she was in danger of sliding over the edge, of relinquishing her long-held principles and allowing herself to wallow deliciously in the sea of sheer, uncomplicated pleasure. But it had been so long, so very long since she had permitted herself such luxury . . . and it was so nice to be wanted, flirted with, desired . . .

'That's probably because you don't deserve to have anything nice said about you,' she retaliated, but gently. Her entire body was tingling with newly acknowledged emotions, her stomach muscles taut. 'But if you're fishing for compliments, OK. Ross, that's an extremely nice shirt you're wearing. It suits you.'

His dark eyes glittered with a mixture of amusement and desire. 'Why, thank you. It wasn't quite what I was hoping for, but it's a start. For someone so desperately out of practice, it isn't bad. Now concentrate, Tess, and see if you can manage another one. I'm particularly partial to compliments about my body . . .'

'Not fair,' she protested, dizzily aware of the warmth of his hand and the way he was stroking the inside of her wrist with his thumb. 'An eye for an eye, a compliment for a compliment.'

'In that case, you are the most beautiful, difficult, desirable, complicated, wonderful girl in the world,' he declared with an air of triumph. Then, lowering his voice, he added, 'And I love you.'

Tessa's heart lurched. She dropped her gaze and swallowed, hard. That *really* wasn't fair.

'Go on,' prompted Ross, infinitely gentle now. 'You can do it.'

'You have . . . very nice hands?' she said helplessly, realizing that she was well and truly lost. Humour was no longer appropriate; Ross wasn't going to let her wriggle out of this one. And the relief of knowing that, and of realizing that she no longer even wanted to resist him, was so indescribably wonderful that she didn't know whether to laugh or cry.

'Absolutely not good enough,' murmured Ross. He gave her hand an encouraging squeeze. 'Try again.'

'Mr Monahan,' said the *maitre d'* with a small, apologetic cough, 'there is a phone call for you, at the reception desk.'

Neither Ross nor Tessa had noticed his arrival; Tessa jumped and Ross looked up at him with barely disguised impatience. Then he relaxed and grinned, because it didn't really matter; Tessa was finally his again and nothing else mattered at all.

'I have to say that your timing is lousy,' he told the *maitre d'* with a friendly shrug to show him that it wasn't really his fault. 'Look, could they take the name and number of whoever it is? I'll phone them back later.'

'I'm afraid the caller insisted upon speaking to you,' replied the man, his tone apologetic but grave. 'Apparently it is a matter of extreme urgency.'

'Go and see who it is, Ross,' said Tessa, tumbling back to reality with a bump and wondering what the urgency might be. 'Maybe there's a problem at The Grange.'

'It's probably Theo,' he said, winking at her as he pushed back his chair. 'He's gone to the casino. Maybe he needs to borrow a couple of grand.'

When he returned almost ten minutes later, Tessa knew at once that something terrible had happened.

'What is it?' she said, suddenly dreadfully afraid.

Ross, pale and obviously shaken, sat down. 'It's Richard Seymour-Smith. He's dead. He died this afternoon.'

'Oh!' Meeting his troubled gaze, she exhaled slowly. Richard Seymour-Smith. Ross's accountant. Antonia's husband. Such a premature and unexpected death was undoubtedly tragic but having imagined the worst she was secretly relieved. At least it hadn't been Max or Holly. Nevertheless, the news appeared to have affected Ross badly and she took his hand. 'That's awful. Poor . . . Antonia.'

But Ross, paler than ever, shook his head. 'There's a problem, Tess. That was Max on the phone. And Antonia. Apparently she turned up at The Grange this evening in the most terrible state. She's practically deranged with grief . . . well, that's only natural, I suppose. But it seems that she insisted upon speaking to me and now she wants me to be there with her. She won't even speak to anyone else. It was so awful, listening to her . . . she can't stop crying and she's blaming herself and saying she can't go on living without Richard. Tess, she thinks I'm the only person who can help her.'

'I see,' said Tessa carefully. It was hard to believe that less than fifteen minutes ago everything had been perfect. 'She wants you to go to her. Right away?'

'I don't *want* to go,' exclaimed Ross. 'But I really don't see how I can refuse! Tess, you didn't hear her . . . she's distraught . . . she isn't strong like you . . . she's never had to cope on her own and now that this has happened she's gone completely to pieces.' He paused, then fixed her with a sober, unswerving gaze. 'Please don't make this any more difficult for me than it already is, Tess. Antonia's husband is dead and she needs me. I have to go.'

Chapter 50

Mattie, having slept extremely badly, finally gave up the struggle and got out of bed at six-thirty, telling herself over and over that there was no need to worry. If Richard hadn't phoned or visited her the previous day it was simply because he had been unable to and not because he had changed his mind about leaving his wife. Presumably Antonia had kicked up a fuss, pulled out all the stops, argued her case and wept ... despite herself, Mattie couldn't help feeling sorry for her. Being discarded wasn't the pleasantest of experiences, no matter what Antonia might have done to deserve it. But oh, it was hard not *knowing* what had happened. Glancing across at the phone and willing it to ring, she switched on the kettle and attempted to divert her mind with the prospect of tea and strawberry jam on toast, although strawberry jam was beginning to lose its appeal. The faintest twinge of nausea was making itself felt and she didn't know whether it was the onset of morning sickness or sheer nerves. What if Richard hadn't been able to go through with it after all? What if she was standing here waiting and worrying while at this very moment, following an idyllic reunion with Antonia, he was lying in bed, asleep in her arms? But he had seemed so utterly determined yesterday, and so overwhelmingly thrilled by the news that he was going to become a father ...

At that moment the morning paper was shovelled through the letter-box, flopping on to the tiled floor and making her jump.

Having made her tea, Mattie picked up the paper and settled down at the kitchen table to read it. Anything was better than dwelling on her own silly insecurities, after all, and there really was nothing like a little local news and gossip for diverting the mind.

Antonia was indeed in a dreadful state. Having refused point-blank to leave the hotel, Max had put her in one of the second-floor suites. Ross, who had flown down on the early morning shuttle and driven from Heathrow to Bath in pouring rain, reached The Grange at midday.

Antonia lay huddled beneath a mound of blankets in the centre of the bed, her normally immaculate dark-blonde hair tousled beyond recognition, her pinched face smeared with tears and the remains of yesterday's make-up. When she saw Ross she burst into a fresh storm of sobs and flung herself at him, her words at first incomprehensible, her fingers clutching desperately at his shirt.

Ross, who had been dreading the ordeal, had finally forced himself to imagine how he would feel if Tessa were dead. Now, all reserve and self-consciousness having melted away as he imagined the extent of his own grief in the face of such a terrible loss, he simply held Antonia and let her cry, hearing the dreadful, racking sobs and murmuring the reassurances she so desperately needed to hear.

'There now, sweetheart, cry as much as you want to . . . I'm here now . . .'

And eventually, finally, the flood of tears subsided and he was able to make her drink a little milk together with two of the mild tranquillizers her GP had left for her the previous night.

Gently wiping her face with a cool, damp flannel, he eased her into a sitting position in the enormous bed and held her trembling hands firmly between his own.

'Now, do you want to talk about it, or do you feel like sleeping for a while?'

'Of course I want to talk about it,' said Antonia weakly. 'I've been waiting for you to come home so that I can talk. Oh Ross, it's horrible, I keep expecting to wake up and realize that it's all been some ghastly nightmare.'

'Tell me what happened. Talk as much as you like, cry as much as you like, do *whatever* you want to do,' he said reassuringly. 'I'm here now and I'm not going to go away.'

'It was so awful.' Antonia reached for a tissue from the box beside the bed and wiped her reddened eyes. But that compulsion to talk was so overwhelmingly strong that she couldn't stop now. 'Richard and I had lunch together. He was in such good spirits and it was a beautiful day . . . he seemed fine, then. We made arrangements to go out to dinner together when he'd finished work. He . . . he told me to go out and buy myself something nice to wear – he was going to reserve a table at Zizi's – and I kissed him and told him that he was the most wonderful husband in the world . . . and then he got into his car and left for the office. I cleared away the dishes and messed around in the house for about an hour and then set off in my own car to go into town and buy myself a new dress. But when I reached the lay-by on Channon's Hill I saw . . . I saw Richard's car parked there, and there was a police car and an ambulance . . . oh God . . . and I pulled in just as they were putting his . . . him . . . into the back of the ambulance and when I asked the policeman what was wrong with him they told me that he was d . . . dead.' At this point she burst into tears once more, collapsing into his arms and burying her face in his shirt. And Ross, moved by the awful tragedy of the situation, feeling desperately sorry for her, held on to her and said again, because it was really all he could say, 'It's all right, I'm here now. I'll look after you, I'm here.'

God, he was tired. Last night having been a sleepless one – and not for the reasons he had been hoping it might be – all he longed for now was his bed. Being with Antonia was emotionally exhausting, but until she fell asleep he felt duty bound to stay with her; consequently he hadn't even been able to phone Tessa in order to reassure himself that she truly understood why he had had to return to The Grange.

A timid knock at the door reminded him that he had ordered coffee ten minutes earlier. Antonia's fingers tightened convulsively around his arm, preventing him from getting to his feet, and with an inward sigh he said, 'Come in.'

As Grace entered the room he observed with weary annoyance the expression on her pale, disapproving face and recalled that this was the girl who had tipped lobster salad over him. At the time he had apologized for causing the accident, but her remark afterwards had made him wonder if the action hadn't been deliberate.

Annoyance kindled to anger as she continued to stare at him with almost supercilious distaste.

'You can leave the coffee on the table,' he said brusquely. 'And if you want to carry on working here, I suggest you do something about your attitude. Guests at this hotel have a right to expect courtesy from our staff, at the very least.'

You bastard, thought Grace, an icy shudder of revulsion running through her as she surveyed the scene before her. Her father, his tie loosened at the neck and the top two buttons of his shirt undone, was actually sitting on the bed with his arm around Antonia Seymour-Smith. And he had the nerve to suggest that *she* needed to mend her ways.

'I am courteous,' she said, her unwavering gaze still fixed upon them as she planted the tray on the table. 'To guests at this hotel. And to anyone else,' she added with calculated insolence, 'who deserves courtesy.'

Ross had had enough. The situation was too ludicrous for words. 'That's it,' he said, no longer even bothering to conceal his anger. He did, after all, have more important things on his mind right now. 'You're fired.'

'Good,' said Grace. He was her father ... he wasn't going to get away with this ... he was her *father* ... 'Good,' she repeated fiercely, to show that she really meant it. 'I'm glad.'

One of the advantages of instant dismissal, she decided with almost manic cheerfulness, was that it left you with plenty of time to make a spur-of-the-moment trip to the hairdressers. Her appearance, such as it was, had never featured highly on her list of priorities but all of a sudden it seemed important, something she simply had to do. And although the price had been extortionate, she was pleased with the result, an ash blonde, ultra-short cut which made her look, according to the enthusiastic stylist, positively elfin.

The living-room curtains were drawn when she returned home at three o'clock. Puzzled, for she had expected Mattie to be at work, Grace let herself into the house and said cautiously, 'Mum, are you here?'

The living room, when she pushed open the door, was in almost total darkness. Mattie, wearing her old pink dressing gown, was curled up on the settee, a newspaper discarded on the floor beside her.

'Mum, are you ill?' she asked, automatically switching on the overhead light. At the sight of her mother's face, she flinched and grew afraid. 'What's happened?'

Slowly and with seemingly great effort, Mattie turned her head to look at her and the extent of her silent, helpless anguish sent a wave of real panic through Grace. Dropping to her knees at her mother's side, unable to imagine what could possibly have happened, she said desperately, 'Tell me. Tell me what it is!'

'Oh Grace,' said Mattie weakly. 'He's dead. I loved him, I loved him so very much ... and now he's gone. I just can't believe it's happened.'

So it was the lover, of whose existence Grace had been aware but whose identity had remained unknown to her. Reading between the lines – and working at The Grange had given her more than enough practice in this field – Grace had worked out for herself that secrecy had needed to be maintained because the man in question was married, and although she hadn't approved in principle she had appreciated the difference he had made to Mattie. Being in love had suited her wonderfully.

And now her mother, who had seemed so much younger recently, looked so old and grief-stricken that she could scarcely bear the unfairness of it all.

Overt displays of affection didn't come easily to Grace but now she put her arms around Mattie and hugged her. Mattie, dry-eyed and unable to cry, said, 'He was going to leave his wife and marry me.'

'Oh, Mum.'

Mattie nodded, almost to herself. 'He really was.'

'How did you find out about . . . what happened?'

'It . . . it was in the paper. Darling, you're kneeling on it . . . don't crease the page.'

Grace picked up the local newspaper and scanned the pages at which it had lain open. There it was, headlined: DEATH IN CAR. In silence, she read the accompanying half-column.

'Richard Seymour-Smith?' she said finally, unable to truly believe it. 'The man you've been seeing . . . it was *him*?'

Mattie couldn't speak. Covering her aching eyes – why, *why* couldn't she cry? – she nodded.

'And he was going to leave Antonia and marry you?'

'Yes.'

'You should have told me before,' said Grace, not knowing whether to laugh or cry. 'I'd have been so *pleased*.'

There was no point in keeping any of it from her now, decided Mattie wearily. She'd certainly have to know sooner or later, anyway.

'And I'm pregnant,' she said, reaching for Grace's hand, seeking its reassuring warmth. She had Grace and she had the baby. The only person she didn't have was Richard.

Chapter 51

Hunter's Lodge echoed with the emptiness which had, until very recently, seemed oppressive. Now, however, Ross welcomed it. Holly had tried her best to cheer him up during those brief periods away from Antonia, but the last three days had been an exhausting nightmare and since Tessa was still up in Edinburgh all he craved was solitude. And maybe a large Scotch . . .

When the knock came at the front door less than ten minutes later he swore quietly, wondering who on earth could be wanting to see him. Only Holly knew he was here.

But since not answering the door would be pointless – dusk had fallen, the sitting-room lights were on and his car stood outside on the drive – he rose to his feet and made his way through to the hall.

'Oh, great.'

'I have to talk to you. It's very important.'

He shook his head, pushing his fingers through his hair with a weary gesture. 'Look, contrary to what you may think, sacking members of my staff doesn't give me a great deal of pleasure. But if you've come here to ask for your job back, it's been a wasted trip. Do you seriously think you deserve it?'

Grace, her chin jutting in defiance, shook her head and at that moment he realized why she looked so different. Gone was the shoulder-length, mousey-brown hair; she had had it bleached and cut short and it didn't particularly suit her. She was also wearing rather too much make-up, inexpertly applied. What, he wondered despairingly, had he done to deserve this useless confrontation? Why the hell couldn't people leave him alone?

'I don't want my job back,' said Grace, determined not to be intimidated. 'I need to speak to you.'

'What about?'

'It *is* very important.'

Ross sighed. 'You'd better come in then.'

'Thank you.' She followed him into the sitting room, struck by the silence, struck by her own daring. At last, at long last she was actually *doing* something. And it felt great.

'Why don't you tell me why you're here,' said Ross abruptly, pouring himself another drink and deliberately not offering her one. Grace observed the slight and smiled to herself. She didn't want a drink anyway; she'd already had several.

'I want to tell you how stupid I think you've been,' she said brightly, digging her hands into the pockets of her jacket. 'You should be married to Tessa now, but you couldn't resist playing around with Antonia Seymour-Smith. And then you slept with that actress, Francine Lalonde. And now,' she said quickly, before he could stop her, 'you're *still* playing around with Antonia. Don't you ever stop to think about how stupid it all is?'

Ross couldn't believe he was hearing this. The girl was off her head. 'That's it,' he said sharply, moving towards her. 'You can leave now.'

Grace took a couple of steps backwards and smiled at him.

'How about me, then? Wouldn't you like to sleep with me?'

The expression in his eyes was chilling. 'For Christ's sake, do you think I'm completely desperate?'

'I think,' she retaliated bitterly, 'that you are an all-time selfish bastard who'd sleep with any woman as long as she had a pulse.'

This was ludicrous. What the hell was he supposed to do, call the police? 'Now look, this has gone far enough.' The girl obviously *was* deranged; he had to exercise a bit of diplomacy. 'I realize that losing your job has upset you but this is no way to—'

'No!' shouted Grace, her grey eyes blazing, her temper snapping like elastic. 'It's the way you treat women that upsets me. It's the way you treated my mother!'

Ross held up his hands in an attempt to persuade her to lower her voice. If he didn't calm her down somehow she was liable to do something really stupid. 'Grace,' he said in soothing tones, 'I've never even met your mother.'

'Oh yes you have.' Aware of the momentousness of what she was about to say, even more aware of the way her heart was pounding against her ribcage, Grace took a deep breath. 'Her name's Mattie Jameson.'

Ross looked blank. The name meant absolutely nothing whatsoever to him. Then, his expression conciliatory, he said, 'What happened? Did I turn her down for some job at the hotel?'

She might have known that he wouldn't remember. Biting her lip, she said evenly, 'No. You knew her a long time ago.'

'And?' he said, looking puzzled, but not particularly concerned.

To be so carelessly, completely forgotten by someone whom you knew so well was, Grace felt, the ultimate humiliation. How *dare* this man treat her mother – and herself – so shamefully?

'And,' she replied, her own voice echoing in her ears as her rage and long-suppressed frustration finally spilled over, 'you slept with her. Made her pregnant. And then dumped her.'

Wary now, his dark eyes registering genuine disbelief, he said, 'Look, this *is* wrong. You've made a mistake. I've never in my life had a girlfriend, pregnant or otherwise, called Mattie.'

'I didn't say she was a girlfriend,' Grace countered icily. 'I said that you'd slept with her. She didn't realize that it was only a one-night stand. She waited for you . . .'

Then, seeing the expression on his face, she shouted, 'You still don't understand, do you? She's my mother! And it was you, you who slept with her and got her pregnant and didn't even give her a second thought. So *think* about it – what does that make you? You're my father, Mr Monahan. *My father*.'

There was a brief, eerie silence during which she realized – quite superfluously – that it had grown dark outside. But she had said it, at long last he knew, and all she had to do now was wait for his reaction. One thing, though, was for sure; he could no longer ignore her.

She was prepared for any reaction except amusement. When Ross laughed, she felt as devastated as if he had taken a knife and cut out her heart.

The next moment, abruptly, he stopped smiling. 'Of course I am. We look so much alike. Now come on, this has gone far enough. You're leaving . . . and so am I. I'd offer you a lift,' he added derisively, 'but I'm going back to The Grange.'

'You bastard!' screamed Grace, realizing that he wasn't even going to take her seriously, and that if she didn't act quickly he would grab her and throw her out of the house.

Without even pausing to think, she darted sideways out into the hall, heading towards the staircase. Before Ross could stop her, she raced up the stairs. Reaching the top step, she glanced at the painting hanging on the wall before her – one of Tessa's, probably – then turned and gazed triumphantly down at him. 'I'm your daughter and you aren't going to get rid of me. You treated my mother like dirt, abandoning her . . . and now it's happened again . . . she's been abandoned all over again . . . and you can't go around *doing* these things! It's time you realized that. Oh shit, you're my father and you aren't even *pleased* . . .'

'You're completely mad,' said Ross, his tone flat, dismissive. 'And if you don't get down these stairs this minute—'

'You don't even recognize the truth when you hear it,' screamed Grace, beside herself with fury. 'But then how could you, when you never tell the truth yourself? You're a liar and a cheat and I'm going to make you sorry you ever *met* my mother!'

This was ludicrous, bizarre. Knowing that he should be humouring her, calming her down before he phoned for a doctor, Ross kept the thought that if he had ever met her mother then he was already sorry, to himself. But the girl, seemingly able to read his mind, let out a howl of anguish and ran along the landing in the direction of the bathroom. And realizing that she could be in real danger of harming herself, he went after her.

He caught up with Grace seconds later, grabbed her around the waist and half-dragged, half-carried her back towards the staircase.

'I hate you!' she yelled, hitting out, kicking him and wriggling like an eel. Ross, saying nothing, grimly withstood the flailing assault and manoeuvred himself into position at the top of the stairs.

But whereas he was only attempting to restrain Grace, she was fighting with every ounce of strength in her body. Kicking out wildly, she wrenched free and lunged at Ross, both arms outstretched, clawing fingers aiming for his face. The suddenness of the attack, the expression on her face, the ear-splitting, unearthly scream all caught him momentarily off guard and he took a steadying step backwards.

Except that the ground had disappeared. His foot searched for reassuring solidity but found only thin air. All sense of balance lost, he fell backwards. And then, with Grace's terrible screams still filling his ears, his back hit the unyielding, carved-oak edge of one of the stairs and pain radiated through his body like an explosion. The excruciating pain increased, terrifyingly, as he hit each consecutive step. And everything . . . his surroundings, that hideous noise . . . his mind . . . was dimming, fading into greyness . . .

Mercifully, by the time he reached the foot of the stairs he had lost consciousness.

I've killed him, thought Grace, staring down at the immobile body. Slowly, shakily, she descended the broad staircase and knelt at Ross's side. He was lying on his front but she knew without a shadow of a doubt that he was dead. His body, clad in white sweatshirt and faded denims, was so still. He didn't appear to be breathing at all. And when she leaned over him to look at his face in profile, the dark eyelashes didn't even flicker.

'Oh God,' she whispered, gazing down at her father and realizing that it had all gone horribly wrong. 'Oh God, I'm sorry. I didn't mean to kill you. All you had to do was believe me . . .'

Chapter 52

'If I'd known this was all I had to do to win you round, I'd have thrown myself down the nearest staircase months ago,' murmured Ross with a ghost of a smile.

Tessa, determined not to cry, stroked his warm, tanned forearm. 'What makes you think you've won me over?' she demanded lightly.

He glanced down at her hand. 'You were never this affectionate before.'

A lump formed in her throat and she swallowed, hard. 'Can you feel it?'

'No, but please don't stop. It looks wonderful.'

She didn't understand how he could be so brave, so philosophical, so goddam *cheerful*. When Holly had phoned her this morning and told her that Ross was in hospital she had flown down from Edinburgh immediately, unaware of the extent and potential seriousness of his injuries.

Now, having seen him and listened to the doctor's guarded prognosis, the enormity of what had happened . . . what might happen . . . was still only just sinking in. For although there had been no actual fracture, they had explained carefully, the cervical section of the delicate spinal cord had been so badly jarred that it had bruised and become swollen, effectively robbing Ross of the use of his arms and legs. In such a case of 'spinal shock' all they were able to do now was attempt to reduce the swelling with anti-inflammatory drugs. And wait. Only time would tell whether the damage was irreparable. And if the damage was irreparable, Ross would be paralysed from the neck down for the rest of his life.

'I still don't understand how it happened,' said Tessa slowly, continuing to stroke his arm. 'How on earth could you have fallen down those stairs? You aren't the falling-down type.'

Ross, unable to shrug, raised his eyebrows. 'Must have had an off-day. I suppose I just wasn't looking where I was going. One slip . . . and that was it. I'm just grateful that Holly turned up when she did, otherwise I suppose I could still be lying there now.'

Tessa shuddered at the thought. Evidently Antonia, screaming for Ross, had ordered Holly out to look for him, which was how he had been found. She supposed that in a convoluted way she should be grateful to Antonia, but she far preferred to save her gratitude for Holly, who had overcome her shock at seeing Ross in such an appalling state and had acted with commendable coolness and presence of mind.

Hit suddenly by a fresh wave of panic, unable to keep up the façade of cheerfulness for another second, Tessa felt her eyes fill with hot tears.

'Oh Ross, what's going to happen? I'm so afraid . . .'

'Sshh.' At the sight of her distress, his own guard nearly dropped. He longed so much to be able to take her in his arms, to hold and console her. But nothing worked. Nothing moved. And the doctors had already warned him that the paralysis could be permanent. 'Don't cry. I'm just glad you're here, that you came back.'

'Of course I came back! Did you really think I wouldn't?'

He grinned, doing his best to dispel her tears. 'I thought that maybe you might have stayed with Theo. It must have crossed your mind, too. He's rich, Tess. Very, very rich.'

'And very, very short,' she replied, wiping her eyes and managing to smile because it was so obviously what Ross wanted her to do.

He gave her a look of mock relief. 'So, no contest.'

'Well, I wouldn't say *no* contest . . .'

At that moment he grew serious, his dark brown eyes searching her face for reassurance.

'Tess, I want to ask you one thing. Could you make me a promise? A promise that you really won't break?'

She squeezed his hand, barely able to speak. 'Yes. Of . . . of course I will.'

'Great,' said Ross, breaking into his widest, wickedest smile. 'As soon as I'm out of this bed and in full working order again, you're going to seduce me. No holds barred. And it has to last at least twenty-four hours or I'll want my money back.'

'You blackmailer!' exclaimed Tessa, praying only that his optimism wouldn't be unfounded. 'I thought you were serious!'

'Never more so,' he replied with injured innocence. 'If that isn't an incentive to get better I don't know what is. But in the mean time, my mouth *is* in perfect working order. If you want to start getting into practice you could try giving me a kiss.'

Throughout each day Ross received far more visitors than he was officially entitled to. During the gaps between visitors he was subjected to the various attentions of nurses, physiotherapists, doctors, neurophysiology technicians and more physiotherapists. A lone psychiatrist, brought in to discuss with him the possibility of having to come to terms with permanent and devastating disability, lasted less than five minutes. Ross informed him that since he had no intention of remaining disabled, counselling was a ludicrous waste of both the psychiatrist's time and his own so would he please get the hell out of his room.

But alone each night in the clinical, white, single-bedded side ward, breathing in the antiseptic hospital smell and staring up at the pitted, polystyrene ceiling, he had plenty of time to think. And plenty of things to think about. The only thing he didn't need to think about was how he would begin to come to terms with permanent disability. Because although he loved Tessa and Olivia with all his heart . . . or maybe because of it . . . he knew he would rather die than spend the rest of his life in a wheelchair.

On the sixth day, Mattie came to visit him.

'Thanks for coming,' said Ross, studying her carefully, seeing a plump woman in her early forties wearing a dark blue dress, sensible shoes and rather nice perfume. Her eyes, wary yet at the same time proud, scrutinized him in return.

'You said on the phone that it was important,' she replied quietly. 'I assume it concerns Grace.'

'Yes. Well. She came to see me a week ago. She told me something which I didn't believe.'

'And?' said Mattie unhelpfully.

Ross sighed. This was proving even more difficult than he had imagined. 'And,' he said, meeting her cool, unblinking gaze, 'if you understand what I'm talking about, maybe you could tell me whether or not it's true.'

'If I understand what you're talking about,' she replied stiffly, 'then you must realize that it is. Grace is hardly likely to make up a story like that and try to persuade *me* that it's the truth, is she?'

There was a long silence whilst Ross digested – and at the same time couldn't help admiring – the simple logic of her statement. Finally, he said, 'So I am her father. God, this is a weird situation. I'm sorry, but I really can't remember you at all. Where did we . . . meet?'

'At a summer ball, in Bristol,' said Mattie with a brief gesture of dismissal. 'Look, it really isn't important. You were drunk and I was unhappy. I didn't blame you for what happened.'

'I am sorry, though,' repeated Ross. 'It can't have been easy for you. If you'd contacted me I would have . . . helped.'

I didn't want you to help me, thought Mattie, remembering the terrible humiliation she had felt at the time. I wanted you to love me as much as I thought I loved you.

Aloud, she said, 'It doesn't matter now. And it wasn't always easy, but I managed. *We* managed. Of course, all the upset could have been avoided if only Grace hadn't taken the job at your hotel. That *certainly* wasn't my idea.'

Ross frowned. 'If you felt that strongly about it, I don't understand why you told her who I was. Wouldn't it have been simpler just to—?'

'Of course it wouldn't!' Mattie burst out, then she saw the look of genuine incomprehension in his eyes and realized in a flash that he had never even been aware of the existence of Grace's teenage crush on him. Colour rushed to her cheeks and she sank down on to the chair behind her. 'I'm sorry,' she amended, flustered. 'No, maybe it would have been simpler not to tell her but at the time I just felt that I should.'

'Poor kid, no wonder she was so mixed up.' Ross thought for

a moment, then said, 'Where is she now? Has she managed to find herself another job yet?'

'I don't know. She disappeared last week.' Her expression strained, Mattie added, 'She left me a letter, saying that she was going down to the south coast to look for work and I haven't heard from her since.'

'When she does contact you,' said Ross carefully, 'will you tell her that you've been to see me, and that everything is . . . all right?'

Mattie, sensing the change of tone, gave him a sharp, intuitive look. 'When did you say Grace came to see you?'

Unable to help himself, Ross smiled. He *liked* this proud, brave, uncomplaining woman. She reminded him in a way of Tessa.

'It doesn't matter,' he said reassuringly. 'That's between Grace and myself. But do please tell her that I understand. And that I *am* sorry. I'm afraid I haven't treated her terribly well in the past, but now that we all know where we stand, maybe we can sort something out.'

Gazing at his immobile limbs, covered with a thin white sheet, Mattie pondered the vagaries of time. Having spent years remembering the perfection of that body, it had taken falling in love with Richard to make her realize how inessential physical perfection actually was.

Before tears had a chance to blur her eyes, she returned his smile. 'Of course. And I hope that you *will* be standing again, soon.'

'Don't worry,' said Ross, wondering whether the faint tingling sensation in his fingers was actually real, or a figment of his imagination. 'I will. I'm on a promise.'

Chapter 53

'Holly? It's Max.'

'Yes?' said Holly, with extreme caution. Her heart still somersaulted at the unexpected sound of his voice but she had, over the past couple of months, finally managed to bring some measure of control into play. Eternal optimism was painful, as she had learned to her cost. Now, at last, she was beginning to face up to the fact that the much longed-for love affair simply wasn't going to happen.

'Well,' said Max, sounding faintly put out by her lack of enthusiasm, 'I wondered if you'd like to have dinner with me tonight.'

'Fine,' she replied, picking up the remote control and flipping from channel to channel. Great, a Tom Cruise film was just starting.

'Right then. I'll . . . er . . . pick you up in an hour, shall I?'

'OK,' said Holly, and replaced the receiver. Then she stuck her bare feet up on the settee and settled down to watch the film.

Tom Cruise and Kelly McGillis were just about to give in to torrid, mutual temptation fifty-five minutes later, when the doorbell rang.

'For heaven's sake,' said Max, when she opened the front door. 'What's going on?'

Holly, her red-gold curls tumbling around her shoulders, was wearing old jeans, a falling-to-pieces Miami Dolphins sweatshirt and absolutely no make-up whatsoever.

'Well, Tom Cruise and Kelly McGillis have just gone back to her place and now they're—'

'I'm talking about *you*,' he interrupted. 'Are you ill? I've booked a table at Zizi's and you aren't even *ready*.'

'I didn't think you'd turn up,' said Holly simply, standing her ground, and beginning to enjoy herself. For the first time, the very first time in her life, she was redressing the balance. And it felt wonderful.

'But I said I would, didn't I?' demanded Max with a mixture of bewilderment and frustration. Then he remembered, and finally realized what this was all about. 'Ah, I'm with you now. You're paying me back for the night I stood you up.'

Far more than that, thought Holly, but didn't say it. Instead, she just nodded.

'And is revenge as sweet as they say it is?'

'Oh yes.'

Max smiled. 'Well, that's something, I suppose. Look, do you think I could come in, or was slamming the door in my face what you'd really set your heart on?'

While she watched the rest of the film, he cancelled the table at Zizi's, phoned for takeaway pizzas and made a quick trip out to the nearest off-licence. Holly, having manfully resisted the urge to slap on lipstick and mascara and screw an amber-tinted light bulb into her bedside lamp while he was out of the flat, forced herself instead to remain glued to the sofa. She had absolutely no idea why Max was here but this time, *this time*, she had no intention of allowing him to make a fool of her.

'How's Ross today?' she asked, when Max had returned with two bottles of Chianti Classico. The pizzas, huge and garlicky and spilling over the sides of the plates, were sheer heaven. Not even caring what Max might think, she undid the top button of her Levi's and reached across for another slice.

'Doing brilliantly. The physiotherapists are exhausted. Apparently he's recovering faster than any of the doctors believed possible. It's only been five weeks and already he's regained seventy-five per cent muscle strength.'

'Poor old Tessa,' said Holly with a smile. Ross had cheerfully related the story of the promised sexual marathon to all and sundry; it had become a standing joke among his regular visitors.

'Lucky Ross,' mused Max, and laughed at the outraged expression on her face. 'OK, OK, don't glare at me like that. It was a joke. And I couldn't seduce her even if I did want to – she's too much in love with my brother.'

'Remember how you used to hate her?' Holly said idly, as she sipped her wine.

'I didn't hate her, I just didn't trust her.'

'Hmm. Like I don't trust Antonia. Did she turn up at the hospital again today?'

It was a double-edged sword, dug slyly in just beneath the ribs. Faced with Tessa's almost constant presence at Ross's bedside, Antonia had begun to turn her less-than-subtle attentions towards Max. Since Richard's funeral she had returned to live at home, but, seemingly unable to tolerate her own company, still visited The Grange – and Max – on an almost daily basis. Everyone felt sorry for her of course, but public grief mingled with shamelessly flirtatious behaviour wasn't easy to cope with. Max, having taken over the running of the hotel in Ross's absence, had taken to closeting himself in the office whenever her car screeched up the gravelled driveway. Ross had been known to request physiotherapy in order to get her out of his room.

Tessa, trying to be philosophical about the situation, found Antonia's attitude difficult to deal with; as far as Antonia was concerned, she simply didn't exist.

'Hmm?' said Max, whose attention had been elsewhere. Quite suddenly, he found himself wondering why he *had* always treated Holly so offhandedly in the past. Chic and sophisticated she was not, but she undoubtedly had her good points and over the last few weeks, seeing the way in which she had worked so hard to maintain morale both at The Grange and at the hospital, he had come to realize that there was a lot more to Holly King than met the eye. Furthermore, as he had noticed before, the less she tried to alter her appearance with that bloody awful circus make-up she was so fond of, the better she looked.

'Antonia,' repeated Holly, realizing that she was in danger of losing her composure. Why did Max keep looking at her like that? It was unnerving. More than that – it was unfair.

'She was there,' he said dismissively. 'But I don't see why we should spoil our evening talking about the weeping widow. Look, I've been invited up to Goodwood the weekend after next. Crazy Daisy isn't racing but it should be a good day out . . . how would you like to come up with me?' Then, seeing the expression of sheer misery on Holly's face, he pulled a mock-miserable face in return. 'On the other hand, maybe you wouldn't like it at all.'

Holly, never one to beat about the bush, couldn't help herself. She had been doing so well, had thought that she was almost immune by now, and here was Max turning on the full force of his charm. She was confused. This was more than unfair . . . it was downright cruel.

'All of a sudden you're being *nice*,' she said bluntly. 'I don't know why you're doing it and it's making me nervous. Why *are* you being so nice to me now, when you never have before?'

Max's smile was rueful. 'I know, my track record in that department isn't great. But I do like you, Holly. I suppose I'm just wary of committing myself to someone who might demand more of me than I'm prepared to give.'

'Who said I wanted commitment?' demanded Holly, crossing her fingers beneath the table to counteract the awful lie.

'Nobody said it,' he replied with a shrug. 'It's just the way my mind works. I'm a suspicious bastard, I suppose.'

Her grey eyes sparking with righteous indignation, she said sharply, 'Well, you were wrong. I thought we could maybe have had fun, that was all.' The crossed fingers, hidden from sight, tightened. 'Settling down with one man isn't my style at all, I can assure you.'

When Max, still smiling, leaned forward and took her hand, turning the palm upwards and dropping a kiss into its centre, she knew that she was back on the slippery slope once more. She couldn't resist him. Maybe, she thought helplessly, this would get him out of her system. On the other hand, maybe she could change Max's suspicious mind, make him realize that settling down with the right woman wasn't such a terrible fate after all. . . .

'In that case, I'm sorry,' he said, leaning closer still. His mouth was now only inches from her own and the tone of his voice, together with the scent of *that* after-shave, was invading her senses like a drug.

Totally addicted, Holly surrendered herself to his kiss. When she finally drew back, giddy with pleasure, Max murmured,

'Since you aren't drunk this time, may I assume that you won't be falling asleep within the next hour or two?'

She shook her head, colouring slightly at the memory of that awful night.

'Good. And now that we understand each other . . . no promises, no ties . . . I want you to know that I would like, very much, to make love to you.'

A faint sound, a cross between a sob and a sigh, escaped Holly's lips. Drawing her into his arms, he said slowly, 'Was that a "yes" or a "no"?'

It was, she thought, like an entire lifetime of birthdays rolled into one. Running her fingers tentatively along the line of his collarbone, admiring the exquisite musculature of his shoulders beneath the blue and white striped shirt, she knew that this was what she had been waiting for, this was her fantasy come true.

'Yes,' she whispered, but by the time she finally managed to say it the slow, melting, magical seduction had already begun.

Chapter 54

'I still can't believe that you've done this much,' said Ross, standing back and studying the canvases, some of which were framed and hanging on the walls while others lay stacked in a corner of the small sitting room. Once again he was struck by her incredible range of style; moody, muted water-colours here, tropical, carnival-bright oils there, clever pen-and-ink sketches vying with classical, architectural studies of noted buildings which, in turn, competed earnestly for attention with those quirky, comical crowd scenes at which she excelled. 'These are seriously good, Tess. I mean it.'

'Thank you,' she said, hugging Olivia and struggling to keep a straight face.

Ross, leaning on the ebony walking-stick which seemed so at odds with his otherwise faultlessly healthy appearance, moved slowly towards one of the smaller paintings and studied it in detail for several seconds. Then, with that expression on his face which she had come to know so well, he turned back to face her and said, 'We really are going to have to get something organized now. You need your own exhibition.'

'Do I?' said Tessa, thankful that Holly wasn't here. She would have been rolling on the floor by now.

'Of course you do!' Encompassing all four walls with a sweeping, expansive gesture, he went on, 'You must have over a hundred paintings here. Look, let me talk to some people, get them interested, and then we can start looking at possible venues. I'll phone Marcus Devenish, he's—'

'Actually,' she said, interrupting him in mid-flow, 'there's an exhibition I'd really like to see in a fortnight's time, at the Devenish Gallery. Maybe we could both go along to that, and you could speak to him then.'

'Why wait? We could go today. God, you don't know how glad I am to be out of that hospital at last . . . I just want to get on and *do* things . . .'

Tessa had to turn towards the window this time in order to hide her smile. Outside, a gunmetal-grey October sky hung heavily over frost-encrusted hills. While Ross had been lying in the hospital a gaudy autumn had been usurped by the onset of winter, arriving unusually early this year. And while he had been out of action, she had been the one who had been getting on and doing things. Shifting Olivia's squirming body over to the other hip, she bent down and retrieved a leaflet from her bag. Deadpan, she handed it to him. 'This is the exhibition I want to see. It sounds interesting.'

'I hope it's not one of those bloody modern abstract things,' grumbled Ross, taking it from her. 'If you think I'm going to waste my time looking at a load of coloured squares—'

Then he halted abruptly. Tessa, still unable to look, braced herself.

'Is this real?' he said at last, and she turned to face him.

'Yes.'

'Who organized it?'

'I did.'

'An exhibition of work by Tessa Duvall,' he read aloud. Then he glared at her. 'Are you sure this isn't another of your jokes?'

'Oh, quite sure.'

'But you didn't even ask me to help you.'

'I thought,' she replied carefully, 'that it was about time I helped myself. It proved to me that I really was worthy of an exhibition. I suppose I needed to know,' she explained with a shrug, 'that I was being given one on my own merit and not simply because you'd called in a favour from a friend.'

He glanced once more at the clever, classily designed leaflet in his hand, then transferred his gaze to the clever, classy girl standing before him. At last, at *last*, he thought with a mixture of pride and relief, she was truly beginning to believe in her own talent.

'Does this mean you're going to become celebrated, rich and famous?'

'There is that chance,' she replied with a touch of amusement.

'In that case,' said Ross, countering with a wicked smile of his own, 'maybe we should be celebrating. In time-honoured fashion.'

'What a good idea,' Tessa replied cheerfully. 'Will you put the kettle on or shall I?'

'Not that kind of time-honoured fashion. Moving towards her, giving her the full benefit of his beguiling dark gaze, he slid his free arm around her waist and murmured, 'This kind of time-honoured fashion.'

It was a tempting proposition . . . too tempting . . . but someone had to exert a little self-control. She knew Ross well enough to realize that the kind of celebrating he had in mind wasn't going to fall under the heading of what the physio-therapists termed 'gentle exercise'.

Side-stepping neatly out of reach, she said, 'You aren't well enough yet.'

'Bet you I am.'

Tessa shook her head, refusing to rise to the challenge. 'Really, Ross,' she said, her soothing tones masking genuine regret. 'It wouldn't be fair.'

'Is *this* fair?' he demanded, eyebrows raised in good-natured despair. Feeling sorry for him, and also for herself, she patted his arm.

'You aren't back in full working order just yet,' she reminded him. Those had been the terms under which he had extracted her unsuspecting 'promise', after all. 'Give it another couple of weeks. Meanwhile, exercise a bit of patience.'

'I thought you were the one,' Ross countered ruefully, 'who was going to exercise the patient.'

'I'm just not cut out for this kind of thing,' cried Holly, slamming the car door and jamming her keys into the lock. 'I thought I could do it. I thought it would be terrific . . . but I feel worse than I did before and it's all so depressing that I don't even know any more why I carry on.'

'Last week you told me that everything *was* terrific,' Tessa pointed out reasonably.

'That was last week. This week he seems to have forgotten that I even exist. Right now,' concluded Holly, the epitome of gloom, 'I feel like an out-of-work hooker.'

A bowler-hatted passer-by, overhearing her declaration, gave her an interested sideways glance. Holly glared at him.

'You have to admit, though,' said Tessa, flinging the ends of her white scarf over her shoulders and digging her hands into her jacket pockets, 'that he hasn't actually been seeing you under false pretences. He did warn you what to expect.'

'Of course he did,' admitted Holly crossly. 'That's what makes it so much harder to bear. We're just good friends who see each other occasionally, enjoy each other's company and have great sex. No ties, no strings, no commitments.'

'And?'

'And those times are so great that they make all the other times – when I don't see him – that much *more* depressing. I'm just not a casual person, Tess. Pretending that this stupid kind of relationship is what I want is beginning seriously to get to me.'

'Then finish it,' said Tessa, safe in the knowledge that such a suggestion would produce an instantaneous protest. Holly would wail: 'But I can't, I can't possibly do that. I love him!'

The expected reaction, however, didn't materialize. With a miserable shrug, Holly replied in subdued tones, 'I know. I think that's what I'm going to have to do.'

As they rounded the corner, the Marcus Devenish Gallery came into view. Occupying a prime position on one of Bath's most elegant streets, its long windows glittered beneath their burgundy-and-white awnings. The paintings currently on show there were cleverly displayed, inviting closer inspection. By tomorrow afternoon, thought Tessa with a roller-coaster surge of pride, her own one-woman exhibition would have taken over the entire gallery. It was something of which she had always dreamt. And now at last the dream was about to come true.

'I'm a selfish old bag,' said Holly, watching the expression on her friend's face and giving her a quick hug. 'Look at you, on the brink of stardom. I'm so proud of you, Tess.'

'It might be a dismal failure,' said Tessa hastily. 'And anyway, artists don't become stars.'

'Then you'll be the first. How on earth are you planning to cart all your paintings down here, anyway? Seventeen journeys in the Merc?'

'Sylvie Nash's boyfriend has a van.' Tessa, taking her arm, drew her towards the gallery. 'He's picking them up from the cottage and bringing them down here tonight. I'll hang them tomorrow morning. Come on, I want to take a proper look around and decide where some of them are going to go.'

Mattie, having read in the local paper the announcement that Tessa's one-woman exhibition was being held at the Devenish Gallery, was hugely embarrassed when Tessa spotted her lingering outside on the pavement fifteen minutes later. Not knowing whether or not Ross had told her about Grace, she hadn't the least idea how to react. On the point of slipping away, however, she was prevented from doing so by Tessa, who shot out of the gallery and greeted her with enthusiasm.

'Hello, how nice to see you again! I meant to contact Grace to ask her if she'd like to come along to the opening tomorrow night, but I'm afraid there's been so much to do . . .'

Mattie relaxed a little. Clearly, she decided, Tessa didn't know.

'But now that you're here I can invite both of you,' she continued cheerfully. 'And please don't think that you'd be expected to buy something – all you have to do is eat and drink and look happy to be here. I'm going to be so nervous that I'll need lots of friendly faces around me for moral support. Please say you'll both come?'

Mattie hesitated. From the corner of her eye she could see Max and Ross getting out of Max's car just a few yards up the road. 'It's very kind of you to invite us,' she said hesitantly, 'but I don't really know whether—'

'Ross!' Tessa swung round as he came up behind her. And in that brief moment Mattie both saw and felt the inextricable bond of love which united them. Envying them that happiness and at the same time remembering that what she and Richard had shared had been every bit as wonderful, she instinctively pulled her coat more tightly around her. Ross, however, didn't miss a trick; his gaze flickered for a split second in the direction of her stomach. To Mattie's enormous relief, he said nothing.

'Ross, this is Mattie Jameson, Grace's mother. I've invited them to the opening tomorrow and she's wavering. Tell her that they *have* to come!'

'You *have* to come,' he recited, his tone reflecting amusement for Tessa's benefit. Then, meeting Mattie's troubled gaze, he added slowly, 'Although I understood that Grace had moved away. Is she back now?'

Mattie nodded. 'Two days ago.'

Seeing that Tessa's attention was temporarily diverted – a traffic warden was heading purposefully towards them and she and Max were hunting frantically for change for the unfed meter – he lowered his voice and said, 'In that case, why don't I come over this afternoon?'

Unable to reply, Mattie nodded once more.

'And hopefully you *will* both come along to the show. I mean that. No more excuses,' he added, as Tessa returned to his side.

'No more excuses,' agreed Mattie, smiling at Tessa and wondering how she would react when Ross – as he surely now must – broke the news to her that Grace was his daughter.

'That's great,' said Tessa. 'We'll see you both tomorrow, then. I can't wait to see Grace again.'

When Mattie had left, Ross attempted to steer Tessa in the direction of the car. 'Come on, let's go back to the cottage.'

She dug her heels in. 'Holly's still inside the gallery. I can't just leave her.'

'Yes you can,' put in Max, who was in a good mood. He hadn't realized that Holly was here. 'I'll take her out to lunch.'

Chapter 55

'So that's it,' concluded Ross, wondering what was really going on in Tessa's mind and searching her face for clues. 'Maybe I should have told you earlier but it isn't exactly a pretty story.'

When Tessa didn't reply he leaned forward and said urgently, 'Say something.'

She shook her head. The knowledge that Olivia had a half-sister . . . and that the half-sister was Grace . . . had hit her harder than she had imagined possible. It was such a strange idea. It also explained why Grace had taken such an interest in Olivia and why her attitude towards Ross had been so ambivalent. Most of all, Tessa realized how easy it was for this kind of thing to happen. Mattie's experience with Ross had been identical to that of her own and if it hadn't been for the merest chance – when Holly had unknowingly explained her predicament to Ross – he would have gone through life unaware of the fact that yet again he had become a father. How many men had been in the same situation? Hundreds of thousands? Millions? And for each of these men there was a woman, left holding the baby. She couldn't help wondering whether somewhere in the world Olivia and Grace might not have another sister or brother . . . it wasn't beyond the realms of possibility, after all.

'Tell me,' prompted Ross. 'Tell me what you're thinking.'

'It's complicated,' she said finally. 'But most of all, I suppose, I feel sorry for Mattie and Grace, for what they've had to go through.' Then she smiled. 'And now I realize how glad I am that it turned out differently for Olivia and me. It's much nicer having you here . . . and so much nicer for Olivia, knowing who her father is and not having to wait until she's eighteen before she finds out.' She paused, her expression thoughtful. 'What are you going to do about Grace, now?'

'I'm seeing her this afternoon.'

Tessa nodded, knowing that it wouldn't be easy for him but at the same time sensing that everything would be all right. 'Tell her,' she said slowly, 'that I'm looking forward to seeing her tomorrow night.'

'What's the matter?' said Max, frowning slightly as Holly pushed her plate to one side, virtually untouched. He had never known her to be so quiet. He hadn't even realized that she was physically capable of *being* quiet. Most alarming of all, however, was the loss of appetite. Of all the women he'd ever known, none had enjoyed their food as much as Holly.

'Nothing,' she said in such subdued tones that he wondered if she might be on the brink of tears.

Holly, however, was determined not to cry. It was sad, but it was her own decision and at least she knew she was doing the right thing. Like amputating the foot before the whole leg became gangrenous, she thought, willing herself to be strong. Finishing this quasi-relationship now would be painful, but not half as painful as waiting . . . becoming more deeply involved . . . loving Max and not being loved in return . . . It definitely needed to be done. It was just a shame, she thought with a quick glance around the bright, crowded restaurant, that there was nothing on earth she could do to make Max feel more for her than he did.

Watching her miserably tracing patterns in the peony-pink table-cloth with her fork, Max said, 'Look, you obviously aren't hungry. I don't have to be back at the hotel until six – why don't we go back to your place?'

And have casual, uninvolved, just-good-friends sex, she thought, momentary anger mingling with the automatic surge of longing. Well, why not? It had always been fantastic sex, after all. Maybe it would cheer her up, like pigging-out the night before the start of a particularly ruthless diet.

'OK,' she replied, laying aside her fork and mustering a small smile. Afterwards, she would tell him. 'That sounds like a nice idea.'

Max, glad to see the smile, took her hand briefly in his and squeezed it. He'd known she would come around, eventually. 'Nice?' he demanded, regarding her with mocking amusement. 'If nice is all I can muster I'll begin to think I'm losing my touch.'

This time she laughed, masking her own unhappiness and joining in. Failing to make the most of this – their last time together – would be the most shameful waste of an afternoon, after all.

'Sorry, my mistake,' she assured him lightly. 'I'm sure it will be . . . memorable.'

Mattie, sensing that a tactical withdrawal was called for, had shown Ross into the small living room and discreetly disappeared. Grace was sitting uneasily in one of the fireside chairs. Not having touched alcohol since the night of her last fateful encounter with Ross, she felt that if she could just get through this final ordeal without giving in, she would win the battle. Never had she wanted a drink more badly, and never had she been more determined not to have one.

'Well,' said Ross, seating himself in the chair opposite and propping his cane against the mantelpiece, 'I suppose I owe you an apology.'

And quite suddenly Grace was no longer afraid. He was here at last, and she didn't need to be afraid. The sense of relief was almost dizzying.

'I suppose I owe you one too,' she replied in a low voice. 'I thought you were dead. I was so scared that I just panicked and ran away. Then when I read in the papers that you were paralysed I was even more scared.'

'You weren't the only one,' said Ross with a brief smile.

'Well, I'm sorry. And I'm glad that you're OK now.'

'Yes.'

The silence that followed was broken only by the loud ticking of the carriage clock on the mantelpiece. Ross shifted in his chair and realized that he had to say what he felt.

'Look, I don't know what you were expecting today. This isn't exactly easy for me. Logically, I accept the fact that I am your father, but I don't *feel* like your father. If you'd like to come back to work at The Grange, that's fine by me, and maybe we can both get used to each other gradually. I'll help you . . . and Mattie . . . as much as I can, in any way that I can, but we still don't really *know* each other. If you were expecting me to come here today and give you some big fatherly embrace then I'm afraid . . .' he shrugged helplessly '. . . I'm just not cut out for that kind of thing. So if that's what you thought would happen then I'm sorry, but it wouldn't feel—'

'It's OK,' Grace cut in, relieved. 'I couldn't do all that stuff either. Too embarrassing for words.'

Ross grinned at her. 'Maybe we're more alike than either of

us realized. How about returning to work, then? Would you like to come back to The Grange?'

More visible relief. Now that she was relaxing he saw that she was looking better than she ever had before. The new hair cut, less aggressively short now, framed her face and flattered her delicate bone structure. With a little guidance, he thought, she could learn to make the best of herself. She might not resemble him physically, but she appeared to possess plenty of Monahan spirit. And Mattie had told him that she was bright; maybe with the right help she might be able to build a real career for herself at the hotel.

'I'd love to,' said Grace simply. 'Thank you.'

'Right, that's settled. And now,' he said, settling back in the chair and fixing her with his most direct gaze, 'I need you to answer a couple of questions for me. About your mother.'

Chapter 56

By the time the police managed to contact Marcus Devenish at seven-fifteen the following morning there was almost nothing left of his beloved gallery. Apparently triggered by a loose wire inside the fuse box, the Fire Officer explained, the flames had spread, setting off the smoke alarms, but doing their damage so rapidly that by the time the fire engines arrived on the scene the entire first floor was ablaze. Bringing the fire under control had taken three and a half hours and the building – or what remained of it – was now barely recognizable.

Heavily insured but shaken to the core nevertheless, Marcus Devenish thought back to the previous evening. Not wishing to be late for his dinner appointment with a New York buyer, he had handed the keys of the gallery over to Colin Rowland, the young man who, later on in the evening, would be returning with the consignment of paintings due to be exhibited the following day. With a shudder he recalled his hearty, joking reminder not to forget to lock up again afterwards because they didn't want a bus load of burglars making off with the contents of the gallery. 'I don't think young Tessa Duvall would be too thrilled,' he had added cheerfully, 'if she turned up tomorrow morning and found an empty gallery. Just stack all the paintings against the walls and make sure you reset the burglar alarm before you leave. OK?'

But resetting the burglar alarm hadn't helped. As Marcus Devenish stood, hunched inside his overcoat, in the middle of the road outside the smoking, blackened, windowless remains of his gallery, he wondered how on earth he was going to find the words needed in order to break the news to Tessa.

'Oh God,' she whispered, clinging to Ross as the full horror of the fire revealed itself. The initial frantic hope that maybe at least some of her work might have escaped intact was dashed now; the one hundred and twenty-six paintings – upon which she had pinned her hopes, her aspirations, her entire *future* – were gone. Destroyed. Reduced to wet ashes.

She was shivering so violently that all Ross could do was hold on to her. In the grey November half-light the scene of devastation was so total that there were no words with which to comfort her. It should have been such a happy day . . .

Tears rolled down Tessa's cheeks and she pushed them away with the back of her sleeve, breathing in the acrid smell of scorched wood which still hung in the air. 'I suppose I should be ashamed of myself,' she said eventually, the words catching in her throat as she fought for control. 'It's not a *real* disaster. No one's died. I just can't believe that all those paintings have . . . gone. I wanted so badly for the exhibition to be a success, so that you could feel proud of me, and now there's nothing left . . .'

Colin Rowland winced as the van swung around the corner, intensifying an already brutal hangover. Last night had been a hell of a night and when Sylvie found out that he'd met up with Barry Edgeson – 'that pond-life' she called him – she wasn't going to be pleased. But at least he'd remembered to set his alarm clock before he'd crashed into bed at around two-thirty. He had a vaguely uneasy feeling that he should have phoned

Ross Monahan at the hotel yesterday evening to let him know what had happened, but it was only eight-thirty now and with a bit of luck he'd reach the art gallery before anyone else arrived. If he could unload the van quickly enough he might even get away with it completely, and then no one need ever know what had happened.

'Bloody hell!'

Hangover forgotten, Colin braked hard and brought the van to an abrupt halt. Jumping down from the driver's seat he stared open-mouthed at the scene of devastation before him. Firemen, clambering through the now sodden debris, were winding up their hoses and a collection of shocked onlookers littered the pavement, surveying the remains of the most prestigious art gallery in Bath.

Then he saw Tessa, being comforted by Ross Monahan. And slowly, arising from the depths of his tired, dehydrated-by-alcohol brain, came the thought that maybe failing to make the delivery wasn't going to turn out to have been such a disaster after all.

Colin Rowland didn't smell that great – stale whisky fumes mingled unhappily with wafts of late-night vindaloo – but Tessa didn't care. Finally managing to make sense of his garbled explanations and realizing that her paintings had not, after all, been inside the gallery when it had burned to the ground, she kissed first Colin, then Ross, then Colin again. Finally, for good measure, she kissed one of the firemen who had been attempting to comfort her earlier.

'I still don't understand why you didn't deliver them,' said Ross, glad that he wasn't expected to kiss Colin in turn. But Colin, having in the space of less than five minutes cast himself in the role of conquering hero, was already telling his story to the team from a local radio station, who evidently weren't put off by the smell of curry.

'See, after we'd loaded the van up at Tessa's place, I started off back and realized that I was getting low on petrol,' he explained importantly, his rich local accent thickening with the excitement of it all. 'So I pulled in at the filling station, like, and who should I bump into but me old mate Barry Edgeson. Well, we hadn't seen each other for yonks – he's bin away in the Army, like – and there we both were, practically next door to the Golden Lion which was always one of our old stamping grounds, so we popped in for a quick one to celebrate. Next thing I knew, it was chucking-out time and I'd sunk a few so I thought I'd best leave the van in the pub car-park. Me and Barry went off for a chicken vindaloo – bloody 'ot it was an' all – and then got a taxi 'ome. First thing I knew about the fire was when I brought the van down 'ere just now . . . and all the paintings snug as bugs in the back of it. Blimey, if I hadn't kept 'em safe they'd have gone up in flames along with the rest of this place. Bloody lucky, I reckon, that me old mate Barry done 'is runner from the Army after all . . .'

'If my memory serves me correctly,' said Holly at five forty-five that evening, 'your mother once told me that there was nothing she hated more than parties full of strangers. And now here she is, just over a year later, hosting one of her very own. So what do you make of that?' she demanded, addressing Olivia and pulling a face to make her laugh. 'What has *happened* to your funny old mother in the last year? Would you have even recognized her then if you'd passed her in the street?'

They were sitting in the conservatory at the hotel, taking a brief, well-earned break. Following the seemingly miraculous reappearance of the paintings Ross had informed the attendant gaggle of press photographers and radio and TV crews that the exhibition would go ahead on schedule, and that it would be held at The Grange. And because the fire at the Devenish Gallery was such a newsworthy item, Tessa's show had become newsworthy too. The pre-publicity generated was far greater than it could ever have been if the gallery had remained intact.

They had never worked so hard before in their lives. The seven hours spent transforming the hotel ballroom into an impromptu gallery had been unbelievably hectic with everyone – florists, caterers, electricians, even the occasional journalist – joining in. The glittering chandelier, normally such a spectacular feature of the room, vied now with subtle but effective spotlighting, designed to enhance the pictures ranged around the walls. In the centre of the room stood a lavish buffet, laid out on a vast oval table and flanked at either end by cases of champagne. Three hundred glossy catalogues, lost in the fire, had been replaced by a stack of five hundred hastily constructed handsheets run off by Max on his word processor. It was almost six o'clock and incredibly, everything was ready for the opening.

'You wouldn't have recognized her, would you?' cooed Holly again, as Olivia made a grab for her earrings.

Tessa took a sip of white wine and grinned. 'She might; I'm wearing the same dress, after all.'

'And you won't be able to get away with that when you're a megastar! Don't worry, I can spend other people's money just as easily as my own – I'll come shopping with you, show you how it's done.' Tessa, envisaging herself in day-glo orange lycra and sequinned high heels, changed the subject.

'So, how did it go yesterday afternoon?' she demanded briskly. Since Holly hadn't so much as mentioned it, she had assumed that the crisis was over. 'Have you changed your mind about finishing with Max?'

But Holly's face fell. 'Thank goodness we've been so busy today,' she said with a rueful half-smile. 'At least I haven't had time to think about how rotten I feel. It was a nightmare, Tess, but I did it. I told him that I didn't want to see him any more.'

'My God!' Riveted, unable to believe that Holly had actually had the strength of will to go through with it, Tessa leaned closer. 'What did he say?'

'Well, he wasn't exactly prostrated with grief,' replied Holly, with a trace of bitterness. 'Surprised, of course. He obviously didn't expect someone like me to do that kind of thing to someone like him. But in the end he just shrugged and said that if that was what I wanted, then fine.'

'And?' prompted Tessa sympathetically.

'And so I got out of bed, put my clothes on and left the flat. When I got back an hour later he was gone. I suppose I thought that if I told him while we were in bed together it might make him try and change my mind,' she said, her eyes filling with tears. 'Heaven knows, it was what I wanted him to do, but it didn't happen. He's been terribly polite all day and I've been polite back, and it's all been horrible. I know I've done the sensible thing,' she concluded, picking at the plate of hors-d'oeuvres which Tessa had liberated from the buffet, 'but it doesn't make it any easier to deal with. I still can't believe that I've done it . . . and that I've done it to *myself.*'

Tessa, who knew only too well how that felt, said consolingly, 'But you know it was the *right* thing to do, and that'll make it easier. You'll get over him . . . meet someone else . . .'

'Oh yes.' With a disconsolate gesture Holly speared a morsel of monkfish with her fork. 'Plenty more of these in the sea. They can't all be bastards, after all.'

'Of course not. Some of them are really rather nice.' Tessa wondered whether Adam Perry would be turning up later. She'd sent him an invitation, but Holly had mentioned in passing last week that he was in Portugal.

'The trouble is,' replied Holly gloomily, 'they're not the ones I fall in love with.'

432

Chapter 57

By six-thirty it was obvious that the exhibition was going to be a raging success. The atmosphere in the ballroom, now filled to overflowing with guests, was electric, the impromptu change of venue only adding to the general air of excitement. It was, Tessa realized, promising to turn into a real party. And the giddy exhilaration of hearing her work being praised was further enhanced when she realized that they actually meant it; already, her paintings were being bought by customers – professional buyers and private collectors alike – who didn't even flinch at the sight of the prices which Ross and Marcus Devenish had insisted upon, and which she herself had felt to be so off-puttingly exorbitant.

'You're *worth* it,' Ross had explained for the tenth time earlier that afternoon, when she had panicked, afraid that every painting would remain unsold. 'Tess, you just need to have the courage of everyone else's convictions. Believe me, these are not outrageous prices; they're the price of your hard work and talent. Not to mention,' he had concluded with a lascivious wink, 'my commission.'

And to her enormous relief, her fears *had* been unfounded. All around the ballroom red 'sold' stickers were materializing on picture frames and every so often Holly would dash up to her in order to regale her with details of the more outrageous gossip and to smugly inform her who had bought what.

'Happy now?' demanded Ross, leaning on his black cane and surveying her with amused eyes. In his dark suit, and with his almost-black hair gleaming, he looked so heartstoppingly handsome that for a moment a lump came to her throat. The thought that he could have been crippled for life, imprisoned within an externally perfect but immobile body, seemed impossible to imagine now. He had been so lucky . . . they had been so lucky . . .

'Very happy,' she admitted, slipping an arm around his waist. 'Of course, it could be the champagne.'

'It could be the fact that those Bond Street dealers over there are describing you as a major new talent,' he murmured, having eavesdropped shamelessly on their conversation earlier. 'Come here, major new talent, and give me a kiss.'

As his warm mouth closed over hers, an explosion of flashbulbs captured the moment for posterity and tomorrow morning's papers. The Press, out in full force, recognized a great story when they saw one.

'It was a shame about Drumlachan,' Tessa whispered, her lips brushing his earlobe. The castle had been sold at auction the previous week to a London-based consortium.

Ross tilted his head, shooting her a sideways glance, but her face was the picture of innocence. 'Hmm. Well, never mind,' he replied enigmatically. 'There'll be other castles.'

Tessa, however, was unable to leave the matter there. 'Tell me,' she said with deliberate vagueness, 'would you really have stayed up in Scotland to supervise all that work?'

He couldn't help it. He burst out laughing. It must, he thought triumphantly, have been preying on her mind for weeks.

'Of course not, sweetheart. You hire other people to do jobs like that. I just said it to see how you'd react.'

Then, before she could say something undignified, he kissed her again, hard.

'We're being watched,' said Tessa, pulling away and attempting to restore normality to the proceedings. Pink-cheeked, she smoothed her hair. 'Where's Olivia?'

'The last time I saw her she was with Adam, and sporting a red sticker. I think she's been sold.'

So Adam was here. Tessa smiled to herself and hoped that fate would take a hand; Holly was out there giving a good impression of a single girl without a worry in the world, but she needed someone. And Adam was so *nice* . . .

At that moment a tanned arm snaked around her waist and a voice whispered seductively in her ear: 'So, how does it feel to be famous?'

She swung round, ignoring the expression on Ross's face, and kissed Dominic on both cheeks. 'I thought you weren't coming!'

'Would I miss this?' he demanded, his sweeping gesture encompassing the entire ballroom. 'Would I say "to hell with it, how am I supposed to travel up from the wilds of Cornwall to Bath when I don't even possess the money for the bus fare?" Besides,' he went on, stage-whispering into her ear, 'I just happen to have my latest future wife with me. She drove us up in her Lotus. And she's beautiful as well . . .'

Ross, who still didn't entirely trust Dominic, moved away. Dominic's grip tightened around her waist. 'Are you happy, sweetheart? Really happy?'

Aware that her hair was hanging precariously loosely from its combs, Tessa nodded and gave him another hug. 'I am,' she assured him. The occasional doubts which still haunted her . . . Antonia . . . her own ability to continue to hold Ross . . . his diabolical past history with other women . . . no longer mattered. 'I am,' she said again. 'So happy that I never believed it was possible. But it is. And I'm afraid I'm being horribly smug.'

Aware that Ross was still watching them from a distance – and thinking that he didn't really blame him – Dominic regarded her radiant face with affection.

'As long as you're sure, sweetie, and as long as you're absolutely sure that you aren't just doing it out of gratitude, then fine. Nobody deserves to be happy more than you do.'

Adam handed Olivia over to Holly and wished that he could take *her* in his arms. She was looking slightly tired – the strain showed in her eyes – but otherwise splendid in a taffeta dress of bubble-gum pink shot through with violet. An astute man, he had observed the careful distance she was maintaining between herself and Max, and his spirits had lifted immeasurably as a result.

But he was also acutely aware of the fact that he had to proceed with caution. His attempts to win her in the past – via the bulldozer approach – had been spectacularly unsuccessful. And right now she looked more in need of sympathy than a cartload of compliments.

'You look as if you could sleep for a week, pet,' he told her, steering her towards a chair and appropriating two glasses of champagne from the tray of a passing waitress. 'You've been working too hard.'

Holly, grateful for the chance to sit down and deftly removing her glass from Olivia's eager, grabbing fingers, gave him a wry smile.

'You're telling me that I look a fright, is that it?'

'Don't be silly. Have you noticed, by the way, that Tessa's portrait of you has been sold?'

He indicated with a nod the general direction in which the painting was situated, a quirky, colourful study of Holly, long red-gold ringlets tied up in an emerald scarf, sitting on the floor engrossed in the task of painting her toenails.

'Really? Who bought it?' For a moment, hope soared. Maybe it had been Max.

'I did.'

It wasn't exactly encouraging, he thought, seeing the flicker of disappointment in those wondrous grey eyes.

'Oh. Why?'

He shrugged and said simply. 'I like looking at you.'

Holly, unable to stop herself, searched the room for Max. There he was, laughing with Caroline Newman and obviously having a good time. It was cruelly apparent that the sense of loss she was feeling was quite one-sided. Max was wasting no time at all in finding himself a replacement.

And the thought of having to witness the procedure – and all subsequent procedures – was becoming increasingly unbearable.

Adam, finding her quiet distress equally hard to bear, could keep silent no longer. 'Sweetheart, he's treated you like dirt and he doesn't even deserve you. You should leave. You can't carry on seeing him day after day, torturing yourself for no reason.'

'Of course I can,' replied Holly automatically. Then her eyes grew bright with tears. 'I *like* working here.'

'You could like working somewhere else, away from Max Monahan,' he said bluntly. 'Every time you see him, it brings back the pain. If you're going to get him out of your system you need a complete break.'

During the last couple of miserable, sleepless nights she had told herself exactly the same thing. The cold-turkey treatment – brutal, indescribably painful but ultimately effective – was what she *should* aim for, but just ending the relationship with Max had required more bravery than she'd known she possessed and now she didn't have any left. She wasn't superhuman, after all. She was simply Holly, renowned for her bright clothes, big tits and lousy choice in men.

She kissed Olivia's dark head, unable to meet Adam's gaze. 'I know it's what I should do. I just can't actually bring myself to go through with it.'

'But you *could*,' he said urgently, his mind racing ahead even as he spoke. 'Look, I've just bought a restaurant in the Algarve. You could work there, run the bar. I *mean* it, Holly. It would be the perfect opportunity. You'd be in your element . . .'

It was such a ludicrous idea that she actually laughed aloud. 'I couldn't possibly run a bar in Portugal.'

'Why ever not?'

For a couple of seconds the old Holly resurfaced; she was herself again. Patting his arm and leaning across in order to whisper in his ear, she said slowly, 'Because, dumbo, I don't speak Portuguese.'

'Tell me if it's none of my business,' said Ross, 'but I couldn't help noticing yesterday that you'd put on a bit of weight since the last time I saw you. I asked Grace about it. She told me that you were pregnant.'

Mattie's answering smile was tinged with sadness. The last time she'd visited The Grange she had met Richard and walking up the floodlit drive this evening had brought the memories of that wonderful night surging back. She had never been able to bring herself to throw away the pink dress with the cigarette burn on the sleeve.

'I also asked her who the father was,' continued Ross, his tone gentle.

Her eyes searched his face. 'Did she tell you?'

'I'm her father. Of course she told me. Mattie, I'm not proud of the fact that I had an affair with Antonia. Richard was a good man. I can't imagine what it must have been like for you, hearing that he was dead . . . and now, through no fault of your own, you're having to cope with the same situation all over again.'

'Not quite the same situation,' she reminded him calmly, gazing over his shoulder at a charcoal portrait of Olivia. 'I know that Richard loved me. Sometimes it makes it harder to bear, but most of the time it's a comfort.'

'You would have been perfect together,' said Ross, realizing that it was true. She had dignity and warmth, and genuine compassion. She was as unlike Antonia as it was possible to be. 'Look, I wasn't around to help you when Grace was born, and I know I'm eighteen years too late, but I would be grateful if you'd allow me to help out this time around. Please don't say anything, but I've been in touch with my solicitors and arrangements have been made. You won't need to worry about your financial situation, OK?'

Mattie frowned. 'I don't want charity—'

'It's not charity,' said Ross rapidly. 'It's repayment of a debt, long overdue. Besides,' he added with a flicker of amusement, 'it can be expensive, raising a brilliant young accountant. By the time he's three he'll be screaming for fresh batteries in his calculator. For his fourth birthday he'll be demanding a desktop computer.'

'Yes,' said Mattie, smiling up at him. 'She just might.'

Taking advantage of the fact that Mattie and Ross were otherwise occupied, Grace ventured shyly up to Tessa.

'Hello.'

'Grace! I'm so glad you were able to come.' Reinforcing her words with a quick hug, Tessa then stepped back to have a look at her. With her artist's eye for fine detail, and with the added benefit of hindsight, she was able now to recognize the similarities between father and daughter which Ross had been unable to see. The colouring was entirely different, of course, but the firm set of the jaw and those sculptured cheekbones were the same. And although it wasn't a physical characteristic, their determination to get what they wanted in life was also undoubtedly a shared trait.

'It seems funny, being back here,' said Grace, casting around for something to say. 'I keep feeling as if I should be clearing away plates or something.'

'Just enjoy it. I am. And Grace,' continued Tessa, lowering her voice slightly, 'I want you to know how glad I am that everything's sorted out now between you and Ross. I was pretty stunned when he told me yesterday, but I'm beginning to get used to the idea now. How's it going between the two of you?'

'Not too badly, I suppose.' Grace shrugged, then grinned. 'Considering that I keep having to stop myself from calling him Mr Monahan.'

'It's not going to be easy,' said Tessa, attempting to reassure her, 'for either of you. He's only just got used to being Olivia's father. Now, all of a sudden, he's got a grown-up daughter to contend with as well. Give him time. Don't expect too much too soon, that's all.'

'I won't,' replied Grace simply. 'I know it isn't easy for him. But I'm just so glad that he knows.'

'So, how about a quote?' asked one of the female journalists with a suggestive smile. Max Monahan was even more spectacular in the flesh than he appeared on television whenever he went on to plug his latest book; those dark good looks combined with that deadpan arrogance were irresistible. 'What's really going on between you and Francine Lalonde? Have you been over to see her in Switzerland? Any plans for the future, hmmm?'

From the corner of his eye, Max glimpsed Holly, deep in conversation with Dominic, her bright hair surrounded by a halo of light from the doorway behind her. For a moment he imagined he could smell the scent of her perfume. He turned back to face the journalist. 'I've written a film script; she's reading it. I'm expecting her over here in a week or two . . . but for now, let's just say that we're good friends.'

'Bor-ing!' pouted the journalist, holding out her glass for a refill. 'Come on, Max, give me a break. You can be indiscreet with me. Is marriage on the cards?'

Max, who had been drinking since two o'clock – running off five hundred copies of Tessa's exhibition brochure on a word processor was thirsty work, after all – was aware that he was on the verge of being alarmingly indiscreet. But, he reasoned, did it really matter? He loved Francine and Francine loved him in return; she'd told him so when he'd phoned her just the other week.

With a faint smile he said, 'Well, I wouldn't rule it out . . .'

* * *

'How am I?' echoed Holly, not knowing whether to laugh or cry. 'How am I? I'm in love with Max, who treats me like something stuck to the bottom of his shoe. As far as he's concerned, I'm nothing more than a series of one-night stands without the hassle of having to remember a string of different names. I told him that I didn't want to see him any more and he had to pretend to be disappointed. I don't think I can cope with working for him any longer and I've been offered a job abroad but I don't think I could cope with that either because it means I won't see Max any more. Apart from all that,' she concluded wearily, 'I'm fine.'

He'd scarcely seen her since that night they'd spent together at her flat and on those few occasions when they'd met at Tessa's cottage afterwards the atmosphere between them had been strained to say the least, impotence being a first for both of them. Dominic recalled how his own humiliation, coupled with Holly's conviction that she must be about as physically attractive as a garden slug, had resulted in the unhappiest of nights. Their mutual failure – for she had insisted that the fault must lie with her – had remained their dark, shameful secret. At least he bloody well hoped it had; if she'd opened her mouth to a living soul he'd never speak to her again.

But now her own unhappiness had overcome that awkwardness between them and his heart went out to her.

'Well, he obviously liked your body,' he said with a crooked smile. 'Surely that must give you some comfort.'

'It makes it worse,' insisted Holly miserably. 'Sex was the only thing he *was* interested in, when he was with me. I felt like a blow-up doll. It was awful.'

'Then leave.'

'I don't want to leave.'

'In that case,' said Dominic with a trace of exasperation, 'stay.'

'How can I stay?' she wailed, spilling white wine down the sleeve of his denim shirt. 'He doesn't love me. That's even worse.'

Having been thoroughly jostled as she made her way across the hot, crowded room – Max was now talking to Sylvie and Colin, but Caroline Newman remained super-glued to his side – Holly pushed open the doors which led out on to the terrace and stepped outside. The cold night air fanned her hot cheeks. The floodlit lawns sloping away into inky darkness reminded her of the huge step into the unknown which she now knew she herself had to take.

Moments later, Tessa and Adam joined her. Adam, who had had the foresight to bring a bottle out with him, refilled their glasses.

'I shouldn't,' said Tessa. 'If I get drunk I might start telling Max what I think of him.'

'Shame on you!' mocked Adam. 'Just when he's finally forgiven you for adding him into that painting you did for Ross.'

'The Party', the only picture not for sale at the exhibition, was still attracting a gratifying amount of interest from dealers, critics and ordinary art lovers alike. If Ross had wanted to, he could have sold it twenty times over. Wary of stereotyping herself, Tessa was nevertheless coming to realize that this was the style people most preferred; paintings like 'The Party' were what they wanted above all else. However unwittingly this time, she thought with a rueful smile, Ross had sealed her future once more.

'It doesn't matter,' said Holly, carefully perching herself on the edge of a table. The ice-cold metal bit into the back of her thighs. 'Adam, is it warm in the Algarve at this time of year?'

In the darkness he was unable to see her face. Taking care not to overreact, he said simply, 'Yes.'

'And is Portuguese an easy-enough language to pick up?'

'It is.' He assumed it would be. He didn't care whether it was or not. If Holly was coming with him to Portugal nothing else mattered. But just to be on the safe side, he lied. 'Of course it is. The easiest language in the world.'

'Hmm.' Pausing, she took a calculated sip of her drink. 'In that case, maybe I'll be able to scrape by after all.'

'You're going to Vilamoura!' exclaimed Tessa, who was obviously *au fait* with the situation. Gosh, thought Holly, *au fait*. Maybe she should consider a job in France instead.

'If Adam's sure he doesn't mind,' she said, all of a sudden feeling unaccountably shy.

Mind? Adam, pondering her choice of word, shook his head and smiled into the darkness. Maybe at last, with Max out of the way, he might stand a chance of bringing her around to his way of thinking. He might stand a real chance with her.

'I think I may be able to bear it.'

Tessa gave Holly a hug. 'You're doing the right thing,' she assured her. 'But I'll miss you terribly. So, when are you going?'

Almost exhilarated now by the fact that she had made the fateful decision, Holly said, 'Tomorrow.' Then she paused and bit her lip. 'Well, tomorrow would be nice, but I suppose I'll have to work out my notice first.'

Grace, holding an exhausted Olivia, had appeared in the open doorway. The thought struck both her and Tessa simultaneously, but Grace would never have dared to voice it herself.

Tessa, however, recognized a neat solution when she saw one. 'We'll speak to Ross,' she said, removing her fractious daughter from Grace's arms and exchanging a brief, secret smile with her. 'I'm sure something can be arranged.'

Chapter 58

Antonia shivered as she stepped out of the taxi. On the way over to the hotel she had been taking a furtive swig of vodka just as the driver had swerved to avoid a rabbit and the icy liquid had spilled down the front of her white Alexander McQueen dress. Now the material clung wetly to her breasts, which didn't exactly look chic. Still, never mind; she could hang around outside for five minutes, use the time to compose herself. Mustn't get too drunk, though. She needed to ensure maximum impact and for that she had to keep her wits about her. Besides, she wanted to be able to remember every moment of it afterwards. Where was the fun in causing a truly memorable upset if all that remained the next morning was a foggy blur?

Her train of concentration was rudely interrupted less than a minute later. As she picked her way along the narrow, unlit path leading towards the back of the hotel, she tripped over an abandoned shoe.

Scooping it up and flinging it into the bushes, she hit Colin Rowland squarely between the shoulders.

'Christ! What's that?' he howled.

Sylvie giggled beneath him. Colin, still regarding himself as the hero of the hour, had insisted upon celebrating al fresco. The cold November air and mattress of dead leaves, however, left a lot to be desired in terms of comfort. As long as it wasn't Ross she didn't mind being interrupted at all.

'Disgusting,' pronounced Antonia, catching a glimpse of pale buttocks and crimson boxer-shorts as Colin scrambled to his feet and hauled up his trousers.

'My God, it's Antonia Seymour-Smith,' whispered Sylvie, in turn recognizing the white silk-clad figure and that clipped, derogatory tone. 'Tessa's going to love this.'

'I ain't crazy about it meself.' Colin, who regarded himself as Tessa's saviour, had heard enough about Antonia to know that he didn't like her. And since, unlike Sylvie, he didn't have a job to lose, he turned, unsimilingly, to face her.

'Look, nobody wants you 'ere, stirring up trouble. Why don't you just go 'ome?'

He was good looking enough in an unpolished way, Antonia supposed. Observing him carefully, giving him the old up-and-down, she shook her head. The original rough diamond. And that appalling accent . . . 'I'll do exactly what I want to do,' she replied with disdain, tossing her half-smoked cigarette at his feet. 'And it'll take a lot more than a brainless gorilla like you to stop me. Particularly a brainless gorilla who copulates without even bothering to remove his cowboy boots.'

Holly saw her first, carelessly helping herself to a glass of wine and spilling at least a third of it as she swung around to survey the scene.

Hell, she thought, irritation mingling with unease. Antonia wasn't meant to be here; Ross had supposedly spoken to her about it, explaining that it was Tessa's night. The last thing they needed was a clinging, over-emotional ex-lover causing friction and rotting up the evening.

Seconds later, Max spotted her too. Swearing beneath his

breath, he moved swiftly across the room to Antonia's side.

Party, party, thought Antonia, smiling at a middle-aged man in a hideous maroon-velvet dinner jacket. We're having a party, what fun.

'Antonia, what are you doing?' demanded Max in a low voice. His fingers closed around her upper arm and she looked pointedly down at them.

'Am I under arrest?' Her eyebrows arched in surprise. Pouting pink lips curved with sly amusement. 'My dear Max, you must know what a great lover I am' – there was a provocative pause, then she added delicately – 'of fine art.'

'You aren't supposed to be here, you know that.' She could be difficult; he knew he would have to tread with great care. 'You must realize how awkward the situation is.'

Antonia laughed and took another sip of her drink. 'Forgive me, but I was under the impression that this was a public exhibition. Don't I have as much right as anybody else to admire Tessa's work, and to maybe purchase a couple of her charming paintings if I so wish?'

She was glad she hadn't finished the rest of that vodka. Her diction was still crisp – God, even Julie Andrews would be envious – and her mind sharp enough to realize that if she could allay Max's suspicions from the outset, she would have cleared that first, all-important hurdle. A quick slanging match followed by unceremonious ejection from the hotel would mean an entirely wasted journey.

Still smiling up at Max, aware of curious eyes upon the pair of them, she watched him struggle with his conscience. She was the tragically bereaved young widow, after all. And nobody liked to upset a widow. It simply wasn't done.

'If it makes you any happier,' she whispered confidingly, 'I won't stay long. Let me just take a look at the paintings . . . make my choice . . . and then I'll go.'

It was such an eminently reasonable request that Max knew he couldn't argue with it. With a shrug, he let go of her arm. He'd done his bit, he told himself. If Ross didn't like it he'd have to do the dirty work himself.

'All right,' he said, taking a step backwards and for a fraction of a second meeting Holly's unsmiling gaze across the room. 'But don't take all night. And just be . . . nice. OK?'

Nice party, thought Antonia gleefully as he moved away. Nice people. *Nice* Tessa Duvall. It was enough to make a normal person throw up.

Aware more than ever now of the attention she was attracting from different corners of the room, she wandered obediently across to the nearest painting and studied with the appropriate degree of absorption a medium-sized portrait of Holly King – overweight and overdressed as usual – painting her toenails. What a waste of paint.

Concealing her own unease and determined not to allow Antonia's arrival to spoil her night, Tessa turned back to the young reporter who was covering the event for the local paper.

'I'm sorry. Where were we?'

'I was just saying,' said the girl earnestly, 'how lucky you are to have a boyfriend who was able to put his own hotel at your disposal. If it weren't for Ross Monahan, this exhibition wouldn't have been able to go ahead, would it?'

Arranging the exhibition with Marcus Devenish was something Tessa had been inordinately proud of doing, something she had achieved without the assistance of anyone else. Grateful as she was to Ross, it still rankled to know that her own solo effort had now been nullified. It was the fourth time in the space of less than three hours that the same challenging statement had been put to her.

'I'm sure the exhibition would still have been held,' she replied, taking care to conceal her irritation and speaking in even, measured tones. 'Not tonight, of course, but at some stage in the future—'

'Still,' interrupted the girl, 'having a rich boyfriend to help you out must be nice.'

'Oh yes.' Tessa, watching Antonia as she swayed back towards the drinks table for a refill, was unable on this occasion to keep the sarcasm out of her voice. 'It's the answer to a dream. If he hadn't had money I'd never have slept with him in the first place.'

Fucking hell, thought Ross, returning from taking an overseas call in his office and halting abruptly in the doorway as the crowds momentarily parted to reveal Antonia standing before one of the paintings at the far end of the room.

Grace materialized at his side, her expression equally un-amused. 'She turned up five minutes ago. Max spoke to her,' she said tightly. 'He says she's all right but I don't trust her. She's a troublemaker.'

Ross leaned on his stick, relieving the ache in his left leg. The sense of uncomfortable responsibility he felt towards Antonia returned. She was alone, conspicuously solitary, and although he had asked her not to come, the air of sadness underlying her cool façade wasn't easy to ignore.

'Maybe she'll leave soon,' he said, with a brief, reassuring smile in Grace's direction.

'Hmm,' said Grace, not returning his smile.

Although she tried hard not to look at her, Mattie found her gaze helplessly drawn in Antonia's direction time and time again. This was Richard's widow, she thought, studying the slim, elegant figure in shimmering white and wondering how Antonia would feel if she knew that standing less than six feet away from her was his mistress, pregnant with his child. Then she shivered, glad that Antonia didn't know. Such ice-cold beauty coupled with the sharpness of tongue for which Antonia was famous could undoubtedly destroy her at a stroke. And it didn't matter anyway, thought Mattie, because Richard had really loved her, not Antonia, and that was a secret really *worth* keeping . . .

They were all watching her, thought Antonia, swinging round and catching them off guard. It was actually rather amusing, picking them out: Max, Hugh Stone, Holly King . . . there was Ross, talking to that dreary little waitress, and Tessa Duvall, even Adam Perry . . . all watching her like prison-bloody-guards . . .

'And who the hell do you think you're staring at?' she demanded, her gaze fixing abruptly on the woman to her right.

Mattie, prickling with embarrassment and pretending not to have heard, hastily turned away.

'I said,' repeated Antonia with slow amusement, 'what are you staring at? Do I know you or something?'

'No . . . I'm sorry . . .' The woman was blushing furiously.

Antonia grinned, enjoying herself enormously. 'What are you, anyway?' she persisted. 'Fat or pregnant?'

Mattie dug her fingernails into the palms of her hands. Richard had loved *her* . . . nothing else mattered . . . Tears glistened in her eyes and her voice caught in her throat. 'Me?' she said, forcing herself to meet Antonia's glittering blue gaze. 'I'm pregnant.'

'What did she say to you?' Grace, fiercely protective of her mother, glared at Antonia's retreating back.

'Nothing.' Mattie shook her head, not wanting to cause any trouble. 'She . . . she asked me if I was pregnant, that's all.'

'You should have told her that it was Richard's baby.'

'Grace!'

'Well, maybe not,' conceded her daughter with a shrug. Then she smiled. 'But Richard paid for the silk knickers you're wearing, didn't he? It's a shame you couldn't at least have told her that.'

It was so unfair, thought Antonia, jealousy churning inside her as she watched Ross and Tessa together. If the calculating bitch hadn't managed to get herself knocked up it could all have been so different.

In the days following Richard's death, she recalled now, she had been devastated but at the same time happy, because Ross had come back to her. In its way, it had been almost perfect . . . just like old times . . . until he had had that stupid accident and Tessa had flown back and ruined it all, forcing her unceremoniously out of the picture. Now Ross was treating her, Antonia, like some kind of frail, elderly aunt; he was kind, solicitous . . . and distant. And she was damned if she was going to go along with this bloody stupid charade a moment longer. She loved him too much to allow it to happen. It was time he took notice of her, once more. Proper notice of her. Ignoring her like this, pretending that she barely even existed, simply wasn't *fair*.

It was achieved in less than five seconds flat. For Tessa, who saw it happen, it seemed more like five minutes, played out in agonizingly extended slow motion. One moment Antonia was standing quietly, clutching her drink and gazing up at 'The Party'. The next moment, without any warning whatsoever, she had bent to remove her left shoe and taken an uneven step forward. The stiletto heel shattered the glass and gouged a hole in the centre of the canvas. Someone screamed. The sound of the stiletto being dragged downwards, tearing through the canvas and scraping viciously against the backing board beneath it, seemed to echo around the entire room. There was a terrible, appalled silence, broken only by the sound of Antonia stepping back to survey the result of her work and crushing already fragmented glass beneath her feet.

Adam reached her first, his normally ruddy face white with fury. Not trusting himself to speak, he simply grabbed her and half-dragged, half-carried, her towards the exit.

This was it, thought Antonia triumphantly. This was exactly what she'd needed to do in order to make Ross realize that he couldn't just disown her when it was convenient for him to do so. The expression on Tessa's face was worth it all.

'Ross doesn't love you,' she said, loudly enough to ensure that absolutely everyone could hear. 'He loves me, he'll always love me—'

Adam's vast hand, salty and suffocating, clamped down over her mouth. She tried to bite it, but couldn't. Within moments they'd reached the doorway leading out on to the terrace. And Ross was right behind them, she realized with relief. It was all right, he was here, everything was going to be all right . . .

'I'll call the police,' said Adam grimly, but Ross shook his head.

'Christ, isn't it bad enough already? This is Tessa's exhibition; for her sake let's leave the police out of it, for now at least.' His fingers around her arm weren't exactly gentle but they were an improvement upon Adam Perry's ferocious, bearlike grip. Able to breathe once more, Antonia cast a sidelong smile up at him as he led her towards the conservatory.

'I knew you'd understand.'

Opening the door, pushing her through and locking it behind him, he shook his head. The expression in his dark eyes, an amalgam of anger and sheer disbelief, made her shudder.

'I don't understand,' he said slowly. 'I don't know what the fuck you think you're doing. You're crazy.'

'No, I'm not.' Trembling now, she collapsed into one of the cane chairs. Why didn't he understand? Why wasn't he reassuring her, putting his arms around her and telling her that everything would be all right? 'I'm not,' she insisted, her eyes filling with tears. 'I love you.'

At a complete loss, so angry that he thought he might hit her, Ross quickly turned away. 'Don't be so bloody stupid.'

'It's *not* stupid,' sobbed Antonia, wrenching open her bag and groping blindly for a handkerchief. 'And you love me. We were happy until *she* came along. She ruined everything. And then when Richard d . . . died you came back to me and we were h . . . happy again. You don't love her, you *can't* love her . . . it's not *fair*!'

It was all going horribly wrong. She couldn't even find a handkerchief. Still scrabbling in desperation at the bottom of her bag, her fingers closed around the small brown bottle of sleeping tablets which the doctor had prescribed for her following Richard's death.

'If that's what you think,' came Ross's derisive reply, 'then you really are mad. Jesus, you march in here and wreck Tessa's entire exhibition and expect me to *approve* of what you've done?'

He still had his back to her. Without even stopping to think, Antonia unscrewed the lid and tipped the contents of the bottle into her hand. There were maybe twenty pills in all, but they were shiny and lozenge-shaped, and ridiculously easy to swallow. Someone had left an untouched glass of wine on the table beside her, making swallowing them almost pleasurable. When she had shovelled them down, gagging slightly as their bitterness caught at the back of her throat, she smiled to herself. Now Ross would have to do something. He would have to show her, she thought with a surge of triumph, that he cared.

'Look,' she said, almost conversationally. When he turned, she held up the empty bottle. 'I've just taken these pills. The whole lot.'

'Good,' Ross replied, his tone bleak. 'Let's hope they bloody work.'

Chapter 59

'I'm sorry about this.' Shivering uncontrollably, Tessa hauled Adam's jacket around her shoulders, closing it around herself and Olivia. 'But I couldn't stay in there. Is that unreasonable? Hell, I don't care if it *is* unreasonable – I'm sick and bloody tired of being patient and understanding. That bloody woman does exactly what she likes and what does Ross do? Chases after her and leaves me on my own looking bloody stupid!'

Holly didn't know what to say. She'd never seen Tessa so angry. She was cold too, but Adam only had one jacket. At least they'd be warmer inside the car.

Adam unlocked the doors and helped Tessa and Olivia into the back seat. 'Where do you want to go? The cottage?'

'Anywhere,' said Tessa, through gritted teeth which wouldn't stop chattering. Then she covered her eyes with her hands and shook her head. 'I'm sorry, but could we just wait here for a few minutes? Maybe Ross has got rid of her . . . he might be looking for me . . . I can't just disappear without letting him know . . .'

'Of course,' said Adam firmly noting that Olivia thankfully had fallen asleep. 'Stop apologizing. We'll wait here as long as you like.'

'Tell me again,' instructed Ross, realizing that the situation was potentially very serious indeed. He could cope with the storms of tears – he'd grown almost immune to them in the past months – but this new, manic euphoria was chilling. Antonia was actually proud of what she'd done. And she had made it abundantly clear that if he didn't help her now, then no one else would.

'Mogadon tablets, about forty,' lied Antonia, her smile bright but her speech beginning to show distinct signs of slurring. 'Paracetamols, ooh . . . about thirty. Took those before I got here. And how much have I had to drink? Eight or nine glasses of wine, maybe a bit more. I could die, darling, right here in your beautiful conservatory. Then you'll be able to remember me every time you set foot in here . . .'

Ross recalled only too well the pretty sister of an old school friend of his. Dumped by her fiancé, she had taken fifteen paracetamol tablets and the teenage cry-for-help had backfired because unknown to her, it was a lethal dose. The effects of the drug were insidious; the following day she had been sitting up in her hospital bed holding her errant fiancé's hand and laughing at her own stupidity. Two days after that, liver failure had set in. Within a week she was dead.

And Antonia had taken twice that amount of paracetamol in addition to the entire bottle of sleeping tablets.

'I'm going to call an ambulance,' he said, moving towards the locked door.

'If you leave me,' Antonia replied sweetly, 'I'll smash this glasshouse to pieces and cut my wrists.'

Ross knew that he couldn't risk calling her bluff. Neither was he strong enough to overpower her. But if he waited for her to lapse into the inevitable coma, it might be too late.

'What,' he asked wearily, 'do you want?'

She smiled. 'You. I want you. I'll go to the hospital if you take me. But only you.'

'. . . he didn't even stop to *think* how I'd feel, with all those people staring and whispering. I just can't believe that I stood there like an absolute idiot, waiting for him to come back.' Tessa was rattling on, incapable of keeping quiet. All the frustrations of the past months, having welled up and been suppressed for so long, were now spilling out. And she didn't care. She was sick to death of Antonia Seymour-Smith and bewildered by Ross's humiliating betrayal. She had needed him and he had disappeared. She'd had enough.

'The Press will have fun,' she continued bitterly. 'I can't wait to see what they make of it all.'

'But sweetheart, Ross only—'

'Please Adam,' she snapped, intercepting his argument. 'Please don't make excuses for him. I want to go.'

She halted abruptly. Holly followed the direction of her gaze, her heart sinking as she recognized Ross and Antonia making their way slowly across the dimly lit car-park.

'Oh God,' said Tessa brokenly. 'And I really thought he'd be worried about *me*. And Olivia. What a joke.'

Adam's warm hand brushed her shoulder. 'Let me go and speak to him.'

'No! Look at them.' Through the tinted glass of the rear window, she watched Antonia stumble against Ross. His arm was around her waist and although his own limp was discernible he was clearly supporting her, murmuring encouragement as they made their way towards his own car, parked less than twenty yards from Adam's Rolls-Royce. 'She's ruined the entire evening,' Tessa whispered incredulously. 'She's ruined one of the most important nights of my entire life and he's comforting her instead of me.'

'Oh Tess, you can't just stay here all on your own,' wailed Holly, following her into the darkened cottage. As Tessa flicked on the light switch, the phone began to ring. Despite everything, she felt a surge of hope.

'Hello?'

'Is that Tessa Duvall? This is Andy Llewellyn of the *Evening Post*. Do you have any comment to make about—'

She slammed down the phone, then disconnected it.

'Holly's right,' said Adam brusquely. 'What do you want to do?'

Pale but dry-eyed, Tessa tightened her hold on Olivia, her only remaining comfort. As long as she had Olivia, nothing else mattered. Feeling almost sorry for Adam and Holly, now caught up in this whole miserable mess and clearly worried about her, she managed a faint smile.

'Well, my passport's upstairs.'

Adam, stepping forward, took the sleeping Olivia from her grasp. 'In that case,' he replied with characteristic bluntness, 'get packing.'

'It was a joke,' Tessa protested weakly.

'Bullshit,' he said. 'This isn't a joking matter. You're coming to Vilamoura with us.'

'No comment,' hissed Ross, having limped downstairs at ten o'clock the following morning to find himself being confronted by a disgustingly eager Andy Llewellyn.

'Can you tell me where Tessa Duvall is, then?' demanded the reporter, determined to get his scoop. 'Her cottage is empty and—'

'Shit.' On less than two hours' sleep, Ross didn't have the patience to cope with bright-eyed journalists and their inane comments. He *knew* that Tessa wasn't at home. Nor was she at Holly's flat. Having left Antonia at the hospital, he had driven – strictly against doctor's orders – all around Bath in search of her. She was nowhere to be found. 'No fucking comment,' he repeated bitterly, since Andy Llewellyn continued to hover. 'I mean it. Just get lost.'

'Coffee,' said Grace, when the journalist had grudgingly departed. For some inexplicable reason she was standing behind the reception desk dressed in a dark blue jacket and matching skirt. Taking the proffered mug, he glared at her.

'What are you doing?'

'Holly's left.' Grace, who had been mentally bracing herself for the last two hours, spoke calmly. Somebody had to, after all. 'You need a receptionist. Sylvie's been teaching me what to do.'

Sylvie couldn't teach a puppy to pee, thought Ross, but since Grace appeared to have made up her mind he couldn't be bothered to argue. He had more important things to think about. Tessa and Olivia had disappeared. Holly had disappeared. It stood to reason that they were together.

'Where has Holly gone?' he said, forcing himself to sound merely interested. Grace eyed him with evident disapproval. 'I don't know,' she replied truthfully, 'but I do know that she's with Tessa, if that's what you're trying to find out.'

'Of course it's what I'm trying to find out,' snapped Ross. 'She's disappeared. Again. I want to bloody well *find* her.'

'You're the one who disappeared last night,' Grace reminded him pointedly. 'She was upset. And I don't blame her.'

The memory of Antonia lying unconscious in the hospital's casualty department having her stomach pumped out and intravenous drips inserted into her arms flashed through his mind. It could be touch and go for a while, the doctor had warned him. She might still die.

'I don't blame her either,' he said tonelessly, imagining how Tessa must have felt when he hadn't returned. 'But I didn't have much choice at the time. When I see her I'll be able to explain.'

For the very first time in her life Grace found herself feeling sorry for her father. His dark eyes were underlined with shadows; he looked terrible. 'I don't know when you'll see her,' she said, more gently now. 'When Holly phoned me last night she was calling from Heathrow.'

Max, finally putting in an appearance downstairs at midday, stared at Grace and said, 'What are you doing here? Where's Holly?'

'Holly doesn't work here any more,' replied Grace, on this occasion enjoying herself. Having treated poor Holly abominably for months, sympathy was the last thing he deserved. 'She's gone away.'

'What? She can't have!' Max, incredulous, glanced along the reception desk as if half-expecting to find Holly hiding behind the filing cabinet. 'Where's she gone?'

'I don't know.' Grace wished she had a camera. The expression on his face was superb. 'Abroad.'

'But she can't *do* that.'

'Yes she can,' she replied evenly. 'She already has.'

Chapter 60

Tessa, glad of the clean, salty breeze coming in off the sea, twisted her hair up in a scarf in order to keep it out of the way. Beside her on the scarlet rug, Olivia sucked her fingers and happily kicked her heels. Seeing her, visitors to Adam's beachside restaurant automatically assumed her to be the daughter of Juliette, the black-haired, dark-eyed waitress. With her golden, all-over tan, Olivia looked more Portuguese than the Portuguese and clearly revelled in the heady, temperate climate of the Algarve.

At least someone was happy, thought Tessa, as she pulled out her sketch-pad and a box of pencils and attempted to drum up a bit of enthusiasm. But enthusiasm had been in pretty short supply for the past five weeks. Coming to terms with her own unhappiness had been difficult enough, but maintaining a façade of cheerfulness had been sheer torture.

Maintain it though, was what she felt obliged to do. Adam and Holly, touchingly concerned for her well-being, had been so kind, and she herself had felt so deeply ashamed of herself that concealing her true feelings had seemed the only way of repaying their kindness. She had trained herself not to cry – at least, never when anyone else was in earshot – and to smile as if she meant it whenever a smile was required.

But the feelings which she refused to allow anyone else to see, or to even guess existed, churned endlessly within her like a nestful of snakes. She was never unaware of them; they were always there, from the moment she woke up each morning to the time she eventually succumbed to another night of fitful sleep. The marvellous Portuguese food failed to tempt her and she had lost weight. Holly was openly envious whereas Tessa could only gaze down at her concave stomach and berate herself for her lack of control. Never one to indulge in self-pity, she found herself quite helplessly consumed by it.

And the awful sensation wasn't showing any sign of going away, or even lessening. Each day was as depressing, as dishearteningly hard to bear as the one before. Time didn't appear to be healing the wound at all.

Chewing the end of her pencil, Tessa gazed at the cluster of fishing boats hauled up above the shoreline, their nets spread like spiders' webs over the bleached sand. It was such a tranquil scene, she didn't understand why she couldn't absorb some of that effortless tranquillity, why she couldn't simply count her remaining blessings and get on with the rest of her life.

But thoughts of Ross continued to haunt her. Every time she reminded herself that he was undependable, her mind betrayed her, dragging up shared moments of laughter, closeness and simple, gut-wrenching love. Whenever she told herself that *he* had betrayed her, memories of his bravery, tolerance and many extravagant gestures flashed to the fore.

It was a no-win situation, depressing in the extreme. And having to pretend that everything was fine – that she was, as always, in control of her emotions – was the most dreadfully depressing part of all.

* * *

Adam wanted Tessa to be happy almost as much as he wished that Holly would fall in love with him. Sadly, he wasn't at all convinced that either wish was likely to be fulfilled. Holly was a huge hit with the customers in the restaurant and she was working with touching diligence to expand her Portuguese vocabulary, but the necessary magic – that indefinable chemistry – had so far failed to materialize. She never even so much as mentioned Max, but he sensed nevertheless that Max was there, in her mind. The only good news, he thought dryly, was that he wasn't the only man in Vilamoura who didn't possess that elusive chemistry. Locals and visitors alike, charmed by her wonderfully voluptuous body and russet curls, did everything in their power to charm her in return and were smilingly rejected every time. She was impervious to their outrageous flattery. These handsome, dark-skinned, dark-eyed men interested her not at all, which was a relief in one way, thought Adam, except that he would have been a great deal happier if only he could rid himself of the lingering suspicion that this cheerful, hard-working, morally impeccable member of staff was a mere two-dimensional clone of the real Holly King.

It was mid-afternoon, the quiet period between lunch and dinner, and the restaurant was virtually empty. Holly, sitting behind the bar, had her head bent over a book. When Adam approached, she leapt a mile and the book, sliding off her knees, dropped noisily to the floor.

'I thought you'd read that one already,' he said, knowing perfectly well that she had. Max Monahan's fast-moving, tightly plotted thrillers occupied the entire top shelf of her bookcase at home and she had freely admitted months ago to having read and reread every one of them.

'Not for years,' lied Holly, embarrassed. Those precious books *were* Max; they made her feel closer to him. Leaping to her feet and shoving the paperback hurriedly beneath the counter, she picked up a soft white cloth and began polishing glasses as if her life depended on it. Flushing beneath her tan, she said, 'Where's Tessa?'

'Out on the beach.' Adam pulled a stool across, helped himself to a San Miguel and sat down. 'Look, I'm still worried about her. Do you really think she's happy here?'

It was a conversation they'd had before, not helped by the fact that Tessa herself invariably insisted that she was. Holly, busy maintaining her own façade, found it hard to gauge the state of Tessa's emotions. Sometimes she wondered whether they weren't battling on like two characters in a particularly dreadful play, struggling to please the hard-working producer – Adam, of course – because it really wasn't his fault that they were working with a truly God-awful script.

'She seems OK.' Holly shrugged. 'We've always told each other everything. If she was really miserable, I'd know about it.' Then she paused, not wholly convinced by her own reasoning. 'At least, I'm sure she's as happy here as she would be at home. And she certainly doesn't seem to want to go back . . .'

'Do you?'

He had seen the book, caught her out like a father discovering his young son with a copy of *Playboy*. Still polishing and stacking glasses with automatic agility, she returned his sober gaze.

'Yes. But only because I'm a pathetic wimp.'

'Will you go?'

She shrugged again, and turned away. 'No, because it wouldn't do any good. There's no happy ending either way, but at least by coming out here I'm doing something different.'

There could be a happy ending, thought Adam helplessly, as he finished his beer. *He* could make the ending a happy one. If only Holly could get Max out of her system and realize how very, very much he cared for her himself.

By the time Max paused for a rest it had grown dark outside and only the green glow from the screen of his word processor illuminated the room.

Sitting back in his chair and fishing his half-smoked cigarette from the overflowing ashtray, he surveyed the words on the screen before him with enormous pleasure. Everything else might be up the creek at the moment, but at least his writing was going well, this latest novel unfolding with miraculous ease practically of its own accord. The original meticulous synopsis having fallen by the wayside, Max was now learning to trust his instincts; he didn't have a clue what would happen next, but he knew that whatever it was, it was going to be bloody good.

Which was just as well, he thought ruefully. This book was the only decent thing to have come out of the past few weeks. Although it was only the beginning of December, the Christmas celebrations had already begun and night after night, riotous office parties were being held at The Grange. Ross, not in the sunniest of moods, had taken to closeting himself in his office with piles of paperwork, to the intense disappointment of the female guests and the relief of his long-suffering staff. If Ross could have banned Christmas he would have done so. As it was, he simply refused to join in. Tessa, thought Max with a mixture of sympathy and exasperation, had a lot to answer for. Wherever she and that bitch Holly might be.

The other irritations in his life at the moment were Francine and Grace. Francine was an irritation because he had been unable to get in touch with her for almost two months now. Grace, on the other hand, was ever-bloody-present. And while Ross had apparently got used to the idea that she was his daughter – their friendship, though still tentative, was gradually strengthening – Max was quite unable to come to terms with the fact that this quiet, watchful, self-possessed teenager was his niece.

Thank God for Caroline Mortimer, he thought, flicking a switch and watching as the printer began to churn out pristine sheets of completed manuscript. His agent was coming down from London to see him tomorrow and he would be even more than usually pleased to see her. He couldn't wait to show her what he'd written. And with neither Francine nor Holly currently around, he was also looking forward to taking her to bed.

When the phone rang at seven-thirty the following morning, dragging him into semi-consciousness, he grunted with sleepy annoyance. When he heard Francine's voice, however, he became fully alert in an instant.

'Max! You sound like someone who is half-dead. Are you OK?'

He hauled himself up on one elbow. Suddenly all was right with the world. Francine might have lousy timing but the fact that she'd contacted him was all that mattered.

'I'm fine. Where are you?' He wondered whether she could possibly be back in England, then realized that even if she wasn't, he had to see her anyway. And now that the book was so far along he could easily afford to take off for a couple of weeks.

'Barbados, darling! Such a beautiful island, and so hot . . . I think I am in paradise! And you should *see* the view from this window . . .'

Barbados. It was an enticing thought, even without the added attraction of Francine's voluptuous presence. God, he was halfway to an erection already, just thinking about it.

Glancing out of his own window at the decidedly unenticing grey sky and mist-shrouded hills he smiled and said, 'I can think of far nicer things to do on a tropical island than sitting and admiring the view. If I was there, you wouldn't have time to—'

'Oh Max,' breathed Francine with that famously sensual sigh. 'You're so wicked! And you're right, it would have been so nice if you could have been, but . . .'

'I *can* be there,' he cut in, his tone triumphant. 'Francine, give me the address. I'll catch the first flight out.'

'Darling Max!' This time the sigh was a sorrowful one. 'You don't understand. You simply can't come.'

His erection subsided, as if in silent agreement. For a moment he was unable to speak.

'You see, I had to speak with you, to explain that I won't be doing your film,' continued Francine. Her husky accent intensified, as it always seemed to do when she was about to tell him something she knew he wouldn't like.

His fingers, gripping the receiver, turned white. 'Why not?'

'Well, the other week I fell in love with this beautiful man – you must have heard of him, his name is Pietro Giannini – and tomorrow morning we are getting married. I am so happy, Max! He is everything I ever wanted . . . I would die for him . . . but he has read your film script and he doesn't think that such a role would be good for me.' There was a pause, then Francine continued gaily, 'So, of course, I have to do as he says, like a good wife-to-be, and tell you that the deal is off.'

Max couldn't believe this was happening. Pietro Giannini wasn't beautiful; he was disgustingly rich – reputedly a billion-aire – and sixty-five if he was a day. He was also – naturally – one of the most powerful film producers in the world.

'I see,' he said finally, wondering why he didn't put down the phone. He'd heard all he needed to hear, after all.

'I knew you would understand,' purred Francine. 'We always did understand each other, didn't we, Max? And I know your film will be a success, even without me in it. You'll find someone else to play my part.'

'I'm sure I will.'

'Oh, and Max! I have the funniest thing to tell you.' Oblivious to his lack of enthusiasm, her voice chattered on. 'My press agent sent me a newspaper clipping the other week stating that you and I were going to be married! Isn't it hysterical, darling? Where do these crazy journalists get their ideas, I ask you! Can you imagine anyone seriously believing a story as silly as that . . .?'

Fed up with work, and with the sounds of drunken frivolity emanating from the ballroom where a local insurance company were holding their Christmas bash, Ross pushed the mound of files into his desk drawer and reached for his jacket.

'Tell Hugh to keep an eye on that lot,' he said to Grace, nodding in the direction of the party. 'I'm going out for a couple of hours.'

'Right. Don't forget that you have a meeting scheduled for two-thirty, with the man from Comsel.'

Ross had forgotten.

'Jack Dreyfuss,' added Grace helpfully. 'He wants to organize a sales conference for two hundred, in mid-January.'

'Right.' He smiled briefly. The silver lining to Holly's precipitate departure had been Grace, without whom the hotel might well have ceased to function. She knew everything, often even before it knew itself, and he was inordinately grateful for her discreet efficiency. 'Thanks.'

As he made his way towards the doors, she called after him, 'Could you let Mum know that I won't be home until eight o'clock this evening?'

Astounded, Ross turned to face her. 'How on earth did you know that I'd be seeing your mother?'

Grace coloured and shrugged. 'Sorry. I just did. You looked as if you needed to.'

It was bizarre, he thought, as he pulled up outside the house fifteen minutes later, that Mattie should be the person with whom he felt most at ease now. Having somehow got into the habit of visiting her once or twice a week purely to make sure that she was all right, her company had become gradually more and more necessary; these days it seemed to be his only lifeline.

Only with Mattie could he really relax, only she truly understood his own private torture. Their conversations – hers about Richard, his about Tessa – were intensely private and strangely, if temporarily, cathartic. Nobody understood better than she did how he was feeling, because she herself felt exactly the same way. It was masochistic, he supposed, but also comforting. Not to mention ironic . . .

Chapter 61

'Well?' demanded Max, not exactly in carnival mood. Even Caroline Mortimer's presence – and her reputation as the most beddable literary agent in London – had failed to lighten his spirits this afternoon. He was in the mood to argue, and by the stern light of battle in her eyes it appeared that she was as well.

'Max, it's good,' replied Caroline evenly. Then she adjusted the shoulder pads of her conker-brown suede jacket, a sure sign of trouble. 'But it's no good, if you understand what I'm saying.'

They hadn't been to bed yet, he reminded himself. She was probably just frustrated. A hurried lunch, followed by an hour of the speed reading for which she was equally renowned, wasn't exactly conducive to good humour. Or maybe, he thought darkly, it was some kind of joke. Dammit, he *knew* that this latest novel was great.

'What are you talking about?' he asked crossly, gesturing towards the discarded manuscript piled neatly before her. 'It's brilliant. I've never written anything so easily before in my life. It practically wrote itself . . .'

Caroline sat back in her swivel chair and lit a cigarette, her shrewd grey eyes fixing upon Max with semi-amusement.

'Look, the brutal truth is my job. It's what pays me my paltry ten per cent, for heaven's sake! Max, as a novel it's fine, but it simply isn't *your* kind of novel. It won't work. Your readers expect action, sex, thrills, violence and more sex. What you're giving them here is a goddam love story.'

'What?' Max, unable for the second time that day to believe that this was actually happening to him, stood and glared at her. 'What the hell are you talking about?'

He swiped the cigarette from her fingers. Caroline calmly pulled another from the open packet and lit it.

'Trust me,' she said, blowing a perfect smoke ring. 'I'm good and you know it, so you *can* trust me. We could publish this novel, of course, but it isn't what your readers expect from Max Monahan, so if you take my advice you'll bring it out under another name. It *is* good, Max, it's wonderful. If I weren't an agent it would bring tears to my eyes. But it's still a love story, and what interests me most at this point in time is who *is* this woman you're so crazy about? Come on Max, I'm intrigued. Tell me all about her. You *know* you can trust me.'

She didn't understand at all. It was the final fucking betrayal. Max, unaccustomed to criticism from anyone, least of all Caroline, continued to glare.

'I'm not crazy about anyone,' he snapped, but Caroline merely shrugged and smiled with the irritating demeanour of one who knows best.

'You're wrong!' reiterated Max, stubbing out his half-smoked cigarette and forcing from his mind the faint, niggling notion that she might be right. It was a bloody good story, that was all, and the fact that it contained a little more love interest than usual meant absolutely nothing whatsoever.

'I'm never wrong,' replied Caroline, smoothing her sleeked-back hair with her left hand and glancing at her watch. 'Max, think about it. Maybe it's time you settled down. It isn't such a terrible idea, so stop fighting it. Look, I have a train to catch in just over an hour. Are we going to spend that hour in bed or not?'

'Absolutely not,' snarled Max, irritated beyond belief by her attitude. She wasn't the only one who could be uncooperative when she set out to be.

'My God, and he's faithful too,' said Caroline with a faintly mocking smile. Rising to her feet, she straightened her immaculate skirt and tapped the manuscript with an expertly manicured, glossy beige fingernail. 'Believe it or not, I'm pleased to hear it, Max. Men like you aren't built for bachelorhood.'

'You're out of your mind.'

'Read it again, sweetie.' Picking up her bag, she slung it cheerfully over her shoulder. 'When you've calmed down. If you possess half the brain cells I think you do, you should be able to figure it out for yourself.'

Max swore beneath his breath. This was all too much. He couldn't handle it.

'And stop thinking that it's something to be ashamed of,' concluded Caroline, pausing with her hand on the door. 'It's quite natural. And if it's any consolation, I rather envy her. Whoever she is, she's a very lucky girl.'

With the phone off the hook and the bottle of good wine – which Caroline Mortimer hadn't stayed to share – to keep him company, it took Max four and a half hours to reread the five hundred pages of completed manuscript. By the time he had finished, the bottle was empty, he had run out of cigarettes and his back ached.

Even worse, however, he was forced to admit to himself that Caroline had been right.

Bloody hell, he thought, glaring at the untidily strewn pages spilling over the bed. He didn't understand how something like this could happen . . . he genuinely hadn't realized what he was doing . . . he couldn't *comprehend* how such a character could have wormed her way into *his* novel and taken it over so completely. Particularly when that character, in every quirk and detail, was so undeniably Holly King.

Granted, he no longer actively disliked her. The reality of Holly was a vast improvement over the impression she had first made upon him; her gregarious nature and over-the-top style of dress no longer actively offended him and she was undoubtedly good company, both in bed and out. In the beginning, when she had tried so hard to impress him, he had instinctively drawn back, appalled by such blatant puppy-dog devotion. But once she'd calmed down and treated him normally she had improved – in his eyes – beyond all recognition. She had been fun to be with. During their times together they had got along famously. And best of all, they had understood each other. Max could certainly understand how a man – if he *was* the marrying kind – might fall in love and want to marry Holly.

But now he had to come to terms with the idea that he had unwittingly become more involved with her than he'd either anticipated or consciously realized.

Whoever would have thought it, he mused, running his index finger idly around the rim of his empty wine glass. Life was indeed strange, although if Caroline thought he was going to let his heart rule his head, she didn't know him as well as she imagined she did. He supposed he should be grateful, at least, for the fact that he absolutely *was not* the marrying kind . . .

* * *

It was probably just as well, thought Ross, that Grace wasn't on duty. Even Sylvie, diplomatic to the last, had sounded decidedly frosty when she'd buzzed through to his office in order to announce that he had a visitor.

Moments later the door had opened and Antonia appeared before him, her expression wary, her features taut with pride.

He hadn't seen her for over six weeks. The overdose of Mogadon had been real enough, but she had lied about the paracetamol tablets; the gastric wash-out had done the trick and within a week she had been discharged from the hospital. According to the psychiatrist who had attended her, she was suffering from a reactive depression. She had to give herself time in which to come to terms with her grief and learn to put the past behind her. Impulsive, anti-social behaviour wasn't the answer . . .

'You have to put the past behind you,' Ross had reminded her when she had relayed the conversation back to him. Residual guilt mingled with anger and relief. Antonia hadn't destroyed her own life, but she had certainly succeeded in wrecking his. 'As far as I'm concerned, I never want to see you again.'

And now here she was, enveloped in an olive-green trench-coat, cream leather boots and a cashmere scarf, looking scared but determined. If she even tried to give him any trouble he swore he'd pick her up and toss her through the nearest window. If anybody was justified in displaying impulsive, anti-social behaviour, he was.

'I know you didn't want to see me again,' said Antonia, 'but I thought you might like to know that I'm off to the States this afternoon.'

'Really.'

'Florida. Miami. My aunt's invited me to stay with her . . . indefinitely.'

Thanks to Antonia, Ross hadn't seen Tessa or Olivia for seven weeks. He didn't know when, or if, he would ever see them again. He was glad Antonia was leaving, but if she thought he was going to fling his arms around her and kiss her goodbye she could bloody well think again.

'Good.'

'I thought you'd be pleased,' said Antonia with a crooked half-smile. She paused, then added with a rush, 'I decided that it would be the best thing to do. I'm not exactly flavour of the month around here – I know that – and over there I can start a new life, without having people pointing and whispering about me behind my back. Besides,' she concluded with a touch of defiance, 'I think Miami Beach will suit me. And I've always found American men attractive. Who knows, by this time next year, I could be married again.'

God help him, thought Ross, but wisely refrained from speaking the words aloud. Instead, in neutral tones, he said, 'So you've sold your house?'

'All going through.' She nodded. 'My solicitor's handling it.'

'Good.' He was beginning to run out of patience. Why didn't she just leave? Glancing up and seeing her flip open her handbag, he thought for a mad moment that she was going to pull out a gun and shoot him.

'I'm leaving now,' said Antonia hurriedly. With shaking fingers she dropped a small, folded piece of paper on to the desk between them. 'I know you hate me and I know I deserve it, but I'm not a complete bitch and I've always paid my debts. You may not believe this, but I am sorry I wrecked that painting. Give this to Tessa . . .'

Her voice trailed away. Ross stared back at her, saying nothing.

When she had left, he picked up the folded cheque, made out to cash for three thousand pounds. Since the painting had been his, he felt entitled to claim the compensation. And since Tessa – if she were here – would undoubtedly have refused it, and the money had been Richard's anyway, he felt it only fitting that it should go to Mattie and her unborn child.

For the first time that day, as he pocketed the cheque, he smiled.

Chapter 62

Sadie Labelle, in uncharacteristic holiday mood, sat back in her chair and smiled at the waiter. 'That was a wonderful meal. We'll have our coffee and brandy outside, I think, and take advantage of the rest of the sun.'

'Certainly, madam,' replied Jose, thinking as he did so that this woman looked capable of taking advantage of anything and anyone she chose. The meal and the wine had softened her, but she was undoubtedly used to getting her own way and he had no intention of wrecking his chance of a hefty tip by telling her that the spacious verandah was currently occupied by a half-naked artist and a teething baby. If that was where she wished to sit, he wouldn't stop her.

But when Sadie led the way through to the back of the restaurant and stepped out on to the sun-baked verandah, with its sweetly scented profusion of flowering plants and elegant white seats, she found only a solitary baby in semi-push-up position, peering solemnly up at them over the side of its cot.

'Well hel-lo!' cried Sadie, chucking her bag on to a nearby table and dropping to her knees. 'Look at you, aren't you adorable! Will you just look at those *eyes* . . .?'

'If your friends could see you now . . .' remarked her companion dryly, settling into a chair and lighting a cigarette.

'Well, they can't,' retaliated Sadie with a touch of defiance. 'Besides, I'm on holiday and I can do whatever I like. Can't I?'

she continued, addressing the infant once more and reverting to baby-speak. 'I can do whaddever I like because even if you were old enough to talk you wouldn't be doing it in English, so I'm perfectly safe.'

When the little mouth drew down at the corners into a bulldog grimace and the first whimpers threatened to erupt, Sadie laughed and scooped the child up into her arms. 'Oh no, no, no,' she cooed, kissing the dark, silken head. 'Oh no, you mustn't cry, come on now, there's a good boy, mustn't—'

'Actually, it's a girl.'

Tessa, returning with Olivia's bottle, had been standing in the doorway for almost a minute attempting to persuade herself that the unlikeliest sight of the twentieth century was not, after all, a mirage.

Now her mouth twitched because she had wondered whether Sadie Labelle would recognize her and from the expression on her face there was no doubt whatsoever that she had.

'There goes your street cred,' observed her companion, blowing a series of perfect smoke rings.

'Yes, well,' said Sadie defensively. 'She was starting to cry.'

Stepping forward, enjoying the woman's discomfiture, Tessa handed her the formula. 'Here, give her this, she's hungry.'

'So,' said Sadie, when they were at last settled – in an oddly amicable manner – around the table. 'This is where you've been hiding.'

'I'm not hiding.' Tessa's voice was calm but the pain was evident in her eyes. 'I just needed to get away.'

'Fancy you two knowing each other,' put in Sadie's companion. 'I'm sorry, but I'm afraid I don't recognize you. Are you famous?'

Tessa smiled and shook her head. 'I don't know you, either. My name's Tessa Duvall and this is my daughter, Olivia.'

Her outstretched hand was shaken, very firmly indeed. 'How d'you do, my dear. I'm Barbara Labelle and this ill-mannered creature is *my* daughter, Sadie.'

Somehow, Tessa had never imagined that Sadie Labelle would have a mother.

'And how did you two meet?' persisted Barbara, downing her brandy with relish and tilting her wide-brimmed straw hat away from her face.

'I interviewed her,' said Sadie flatly, and her mother laughed aloud.

'Ha! In that case, say no more.' Turning to scrutinize Tessa she said bluntly, 'Did she make you cry?'

'No. As a matter of fact, she was a pretty shrewd judge of character. Not of my character,' Tessa added, then glanced across at Sadie. 'You were wrong there. But of course you were absolutely right about Ross.'

Upon hearing that the Monahan-Duvall wedding had been called off at the shortest possible notice, Sadie had experienced a rare spasm of guilt. She hadn't meant to provoke quite such a dramatic reaction. Sometimes her own power alarmed her.

As if reading her mind, Tessa added flatly. 'It wasn't your article. I'm not that gullible.'

'Oh. Good.' Sadie was feeling distinctly uncomfortable; this kind of encounter wasn't what she was used to. And the presence of her mother – who positively revelled in such potentially awkward situations – wasn't helping matters at all.

'Why?' intercepted Barbara. Shrewd, gunmetal-grey eyes assessed the slender, bikini-clad girl sitting next to her. 'What happened? I assume we're talking about a man, here?'

'Mother . . .' Sadie shot her a warning look.

Barbara shrugged. 'Darling, I'm interested!'

'It's OK,' said Tessa, in her turn highly amused by the exchange, and by the infamous Sadie Labelle's obvious loss of composure. That she *had* a mother was a revelation in itself. That she was so clearly ruled by her was sheer bliss. 'I was involved with Olivia's father,' she continued, turning back to address the formidable Barbara. 'And I had a lucky escape. I found out just in time that he wasn't . . . right for me.'

'I heard what happened at the exhibition,' put in Sadie. A trained observer, she was able to see behind the calm front. Tessa wasn't fooling her for a moment and now that she was meeting her under such different circumstances the old animosity – possibly still coupled with residual guilt – was melting away. 'Antonia Seymour-Smith took an overdose and Ross had to get her to the hospital.'

'I know, I've read the papers,' said Tessa slowly. 'But the fact remains that he abandoned me when I most needed him, and I didn't see why I should put up with it any more. Antonia was always *there*, crawling out of the woodwork whenever things seemed to be going well between us and managing to ruin it every time . . .'

Sadie gazed down at Olivia, cradled in her arms. Having frantically gulped down the contents of her bottle, she was now lying in a contented, post-prandial stupor, dark lashes batting lazily against the sunlight, rosebud mouth pouting with pleasure, tiny hands like starfish curling and uncurling beneath her chin.

'Ross must be missing her,' she said, addressing Tessa but smiling at the drowsy baby on her lap.

Tessa, her eyes promptly filling with tears, shook her head. 'I expect he is, but I can't go back. If I'm going to make a proper life for myself . . . for both of us . . . I need time to get over him. And my friends here have been so kind . . .'

'Friendship is one thing,' said Barbara Labelle, who had a past most biographers would die for. Even her clever, sharp-witted daughter didn't know everything. She finished her black coffee and stubbed out her second cigarette with a peculiarly conclusive gesture. 'But it's not what makes the world go round, sweetheart. Believe me.'

'I'm not going back,' repeated Tessa, her expression desolate. 'I loved Ross, but it hurt too much. It's better this way, really it is. I don't want to be miserable for the rest of my life.'

'You're stubborn,' said Barbara Labelle, patting her hand. 'I like that in a girl. No doubt,' she added dryly, 'it's what attracted your young man to you as well.'

Chapter 63

'I'd like to speak to Ross Monahan,' said Sadie, a week later. It was the day before Christmas Eve and she had given the matter a great deal of thought. In the end, however, she'd managed to convince herself that she was right. And even if she wasn't right . . . well, it was something she simply had to do anyway.

'I'm afraid he isn't here at the moment,' Grace replied, juggling the phone as she reached for a note-pad and pen. 'I could take your number and ask him to call you back, if you wish. Or I could put you through to Max Monahan if it's a business matter. I expect he'd be able to help you.'

It wasn't the first time she'd subtly discouraged such calls. Since Tessa's disappearance the number of women phoning to invite Ross to this dinner and that party had gradually escalated, and although it wasn't Clarissa Fox this time – she being the most persistent of the pack – Grace suspected that the person on the other end of the telephone was just another in that long line of pushy, eager women in whom he wasn't even remotely interested anyway.

Damn, thought Sadie, who had wanted to break the news to Ross herself. But she was due in less than an hour at the first of three notoriously riotous Christmas parties. It was now or never – or at least until Boxing Day morning. Maybe speaking to Max instead wouldn't be such a bad move anyway, she decided, drumming her fingers rapidly against the arm of her chair. He could tell her if she was way off-beam. There was always the possibility, after all, that for reasons unbeknown to her Ross might not even want to know Tessa's whereabouts.

'Fine,' she said briskly. 'Put me through to Max.'

'Please,' muttered Grace beneath her breath.

When she knocked and entered his office fifteen minutes later, she found Max leaning back in his chair with his feet up on the desk, looking distinctly thoughtful.

'I'm sorry to disturb you,' said Grace, placing a sheaf of order forms in front of him, 'but Ross isn't here. If you could just countersign these I'll be able to send them out this afternoon.'

Transferring his brooding gaze to her, he said brusquely, 'Where's Ross?'

'He left half an hour ago.' She looked uneasy. 'He's gone to see a friend.'

'Your mother, you mean.' With an irritated sigh, he reached for a pen and scrawled his signature on the first form. 'What's going on, are they having an affair or something?'

'Of course not,' said Grace hotly. 'You know they're not! Ross loves Tessa and Mum knows what he's going through, that's all.'

'Hmm.'

Leaning forward, concerned that the pen he was wielding with such force could be about to rip right through the entire sheaf of order forms, Grace merely glanced at the writing on a scrap of paper at his elbow. The next moment she'd whisked it off the desk.

'I don't believe it! Is this where Tessa's staying? Do you mean to tell me that you've known all along where she is and you haven't told Ross . . .?'

She was white with fury. Max's first instinct was to snatch the paper back from her. Then he realized that it was too late. She knew he had it. And she *was* Ross's daughter, after all. At least the dilemma would no longer be his alone.

'Of course I haven't known all along,' he said wearily, indicating with a nod of his head that Grace should sit down. 'That call you put through to me just now was from Sadie Labelle, of all people. Apparently she ran into Tessa last week while she was on holiday. For some reason, she appears to have had a change of heart over Tessa. She gave me the address.'

'But that's fantastic!' cried Grace, her fingers itching to pick up the phone on the desk before her. 'Look, why don't you call him now? I'll give you Mum's number.'

'Grace, calm down. I've given the matter a lot of thought.'

'Oh yes?' She fixed him with a challenging stare and in that moment, for the first time, Max caught the slight but unmistakable resemblance to Ross. It was just how he used to look as a teenager, whenever someone had told him that something was impossible. He had invariably gone on to prove them wrong.

'Yes,' he replied firmly. 'Look, tomorrow is Christmas Eve. The hotel's never been busier . . . we're all going to be working flat out until after the New Year . . . there is absolutely no way that Ross can just take off now, to go and sort out his differences with Tessa.'

'But—'

'I'm being logical about this,' he continued in stern tones. 'Don't interrupt. I'm perfectly well aware of the fact that he misses her, but it's been almost two months now and at least he's grown used to missing her. If he phoned her – tonight, or tomorrow – and they had a screaming row, it would only make

Christmas that much harder to bear for both of them. So what I'm saying,' he concluded, 'is that we should keep this to ourselves for now. Preserve the status quo, if you like. And as soon as Christmas and the New Year are over, we'll give Ross this address. Then, he can do whatever he likes.'

The look Grace gave him was one of incomprehension mingled with pity.

'Max,' she said at last, sounding strangely like a disappointed school mistress, 'you've written a lot of books, so I know you must be intelligent. But for an intelligent man, that has to be the stupidest idea you've ever had.'

'The most stupid idea.' He glared back at her. Correcting her grammar seemed to be the only avenue of retaliation.

'Exactly,' said Grace with a note of triumph.

Realizing that he was beaten – the bitch; he'd fallen for that one – Max sat back in his chair and laughed.

Grace responded with a tentative smile.

'So, what do *you* think we should do?' he said finally, a kernel of grudging admiration beginning to unfold for the pale, determined young girl sitting before him. Maybe Grace – his niece – wasn't so bad after all.

'I'll tell you,' she replied with perfect composure. 'It's simple.'

It wasn't going to be the happiest Christmas on record, thought Holly with uncharacteristic understatement, but at least she and Tessa would be together.

And the fact that the Algarve was so very unChristmassy was something else to be grateful for. Sun, sand and Ambre Solaire were enough to trick the most traditional English brain and even Adam hadn't been able to conjure up a Christmas tree. Which was just as well, she decided gloomily as she shrugged on an old, faded denim shirt and pushed the tails haphazardly into the waistband of even older, barely respectable Levi's. If they could get away with pretending that it simply wasn't happening – that tomorrow, December the twenty-fifth, was just another ordinary day – maybe it wouldn't be totally unbearable after all.

Chapter 64

Adam and Tessa, together with Jose, Luisa and Ana, were gathered around the bar when Holly joined them downstairs ten minutes later. With the lunchtime session over, the restaurant was now closed until Boxing Day and everyone was either celebrating or giving an almost entirely convincing imitation of it. Adam was breaking open the third bottle of champagne and Ana had brought a vast bowl of seafood paella out from the kitchen. Olivia, happily ensconced on Luisa's ample lap, was rolling olives like polished marbles along the bar and screaming with delight each time Adam lobbed them back at her. The next moment, as one of the olives landed in Luisa's splendid cleavage, Holly glimpsed the secret smile passing between Luisa and Adam and realized with a jolt that the chemistry which had never existed between Adam and herself was showing definite signs of life at the other end of the bar.

It should have cheered her up – the fact that she had been unable to force herself to return Adam's feelings had troubled her conscience for weeks – but the jolt wasn't a particularly pleasant one. It made her feel even more alone than ever. With a consciously defiant gesture she picked up a glass, downed her drink in one go and immediately reached for a refill. In thirty-two hours Christmas would be over. If she was lucky, and if she drank enough, she might manage to sleep through twelve of them.

Minutes later she received another, quite different kind of jolt. For, unnoticed by the rest of the party, a tall dark figure had appeared in the open doorway. His face, silhouetted against the golden afternoon sun, wasn't visible. But Holly, with her mouth full of paella, knew without a shadow of a doubt who it was. Her entire body prickled with recognition, her stomach disappeared and swallowing the paella became a physical impossibility. All she could do in order to gain Tessa's attention was to point weakly in the general direction of the door with her fork and say, 'Phmghh . . .'

Holly had known instantly who it was because every detail of the man in the doorway was indelibly imprinted in her mind, but Tessa, wild hope surging and mingling with a momentary trick of the light, looked across at the outline of a tall, dark-haired man standing with one hand thrust casually into his trouser pocket and saw Ross. Her heart thundering like an express train, she was already half out of her seat before she realized she was wrong.

Max, moving towards them, didn't even glance in Holly's direction. After nodding briefly at Adam he turned to Tessa, the expression in his dark brown eyes quite unreadable. Then he paused, because although he had been planning what to say for the last twenty-four hours, now that he was here he didn't know how to start.

Tessa, however, filled the gap. Furious with herself for thinking that he could have been Ross, and forcing the sense of crushing disappointment angrily aside, she resorted to flippancy.

'What's this, the gunfight at the OK Corral? If you're going to shoot, Max, maybe we should do it outside.'

'Thanks,' said Max to Adam, who had silently handed him a

drink. Since he still hadn't even looked at Holly, whose face was as white as the marble-topped bar, Adam refilled her glass as well for good measure. She looked as if she needed it.

'Don't be flippant,' Max continued, drawing a deep breath and silently daring Tessa to interrupt him now. 'I know why you left but you should have given Ross a chance to explain. He didn't have any other choice that night – if he hadn't stayed with Antonia she might have died. And now he's impossible to live with because he loves and misses you so much that he doesn't know what to do with himself. He's not interested in anyone else, Tess. He wants you. And I've flown over here because I want you . . . to really think about what *you* want. And to come back home, today.'

This time the silence lengthened. All eyes were on Tessa. A single tear rolled unnoticed down Holly's cheek, because she hadn't known that Max was even capable of making such a poignant speech. God, she loved *him* so much . . . why had he never been able to say something like that to her . . .?

But Tessa had been hurt before and she proceeded with caution. Fixing Max with her most penetrating emerald-green gaze, she said, 'What I *don't* want is to be one third of some bizarre love-triangle. I don't want to make any more of a fool of myself than I already have. And I certainly don't want to spend the rest of my life wondering what Antonia Seymour-Smith is going to say . . . or do . . . or destroy . . . next. Max, you probably don't even realize what it's been like. Ever since Ross and I first met, she's been there to—'

'She's gone to Florida,' Max cut in. 'She knows there's nothing left for her in Bath. She won't be back.'

Tessa pushed her hair away from her face. 'And if Ross is

missing me so much,' she continued, with a note of accusation in her voice, 'why hasn't he flown out here himself? Why has he sent you on this mercy mission? Or is he just too busy with his bloody hotel?'

She was running out of arguments, thought Max. Tessa might look outwardly calm but he was able to see the way her tanned legs were pressed against the leg of the bar stool, so tightly that the surrounding skin had turned white. Every muscle was taut. And he'd bet the proceeds of his next book that beneath that baggy black T-shirt her heart was pounding like a jack-hammer.

'Ross doesn't know you're here,' he said evenly. 'He doesn't even know that *I'm* here. It was Grace's idea, actually.' He paused, a glimmer of a smile playing on his lips. 'We just couldn't think what else to get him for Christmas.'

Now there were tears glistening in Tessa's eyes. She knew she would go. She'd tried to be strong but it hadn't worked. Sometimes life just wasn't that simple. Loving Ross Monahan was something out of her control; no matter how hard she had tried, she'd never been able to stop loving him for even a moment.

'So I'm the cheap, last-minute Christmas present?' she said, tilting her head to one side and failing to hide her own smile.

'Hardly bloody cheap!' With mock exasperation, Max glanced at his watch. 'Have you any idea, Tessa Duvall, how much it costs to charter a plane and keep it sitting on the tarmac at Faro Airport while you sit here arguing about money and letting all these ludicrously expensive minutes tick by? For God's sake, woman, we have a schedule to keep! Now, will you get off that stool and start packing or do I have to do that for you as well?'

* * *

While Tessa was upstairs throwing belongings into an assortment of bags, Ana and Jose moved into the kitchen and began washing up the last of the plates and glasses. Adam had disappeared outside with Luisa and Olivia, leaving Holly alone in the restaurant with Max. She felt like the last, dilapidated sponge left on the cake stall at the end of the church fête, which was a huge boost to her morale.

Desperately on edge, unable to bear the awkwardness of the silence which had abruptly descended around them, she cleared her throat . . . tried and failed to think of something to say . . . and cleared her throat again.

'What's the matter, have you got a cold?' asked Max.

That was a great help, too.

She hung her head. 'No.'

'Hmmm.' Pulling up a stool, he sat down and lit a cigarette. For almost the first time, it seemed, his dark eyes flickered in her direction.

Holly wished fervently that she'd put on some make-up earlier, or even just a squish of perfume. She felt naked and undesirable and so miserable that she wanted to curl up and die.

'So.' Max tried again. He didn't know whether she was being deliberately unhelpful, but she certainly wasn't making it any easier for him to say what he knew he had to say. 'Well, how are you anyway? Enjoying life on the Algarve?'

'Yes,' mumbled Holly unhappily.

'Right. Good.' He crushed his cigarette into the ashtray and reached for another. 'Nice climate . . . is the restaurant doing well?'

This was awful. Max couldn't even *speak* to her any more. He was reduced to making stilted small talk as if she were a stranger.

She nodded. 'Yes, very well.'

'And how about you and Adam?' he persisted, his tone deceptively calm. 'Is that going "very well" too?'

Holly's head jerked up. 'We aren't together,' she said, not knowing whether to be relieved or angry that Max should have thought they were. Relief won; at least he didn't know that he had been her sole reason for leaving The Grange. Desperate enough to grasp at the flimsiest of straws, she realized that at least she hadn't humiliated herself totally. It was a small consolation, but better than none.

'You aren't together,' he echoed thoughtfully, pausing to draw on his cigarette. A lazy plume of smoke spiralled towards the ceiling. 'In that case, why *did* you come out here?'

'I . . . I just wanted to.' She felt the heat rise in her cheeks and knew she was going pink. 'Like you said, it's a nice climate . . . there's the sea . . . sunbathing . . . lying on the beach . . .' She faltered, unable to go on. Max was too clever and he knew her too well. Holly bowed her head once more, floored by the knowledge that she had, as she had feared, humiliated herself. Totally.

The time had come, Max decided, for the second of the two speeches he had come here to deliver. Spontaneous declarations not being his forte, he had needed to plan the words with great care, going over them again and again in his mind – this time without Grace's assistance – until he was sure they were right. It wasn't as if he was declaring his undying love and asking Holly to marry him, after all. He didn't want her to turn round in six months' time and sue him for breach of promise.

'Right,' he said brusquely, stubbing out the second cigarette and realizing that his hand wasn't entirely steady. 'Well, this isn't easy for me to say, but now that Tessa's coming back to Bath I don't know how you feel about staying on here. If you *do* want to stay, then fine, that's perfectly all right. But I just thought that maybe you might be thinking of coming back as well . . . you see, after you left, something happened to make me realize that my feelings for you weren't quite as . . . although of course you know how I feel about long-term relationships . . . I'm not talking about marriage here, because you know my views on that, too . . . but, on the other hand, just being with someone that you know and like . . . well, more than like, really, although that doesn't mean you automatically need to be married to them . . . but being *with* someone like that isn't such an awful fate as I suppose I'd always imagined, so I thought that maybe if you *were* thinking of coming back, we could . . . well, you know . . . just try it.'

Perspiration trickled down the back of his neck. He couldn't even recall lighting the third cigarette, now burning merrily away between his fingers. Once, years ago, he'd been called upon to speak without any prior warning whatsoever to a symposium of seven hundred people in the publishing trade. Compared with this, it had been a walk in the park.

But now it was done; at last he had said – clearly and concisely – what he had come here to say. The rest was up to Holly, his unnervingly silent audience of one.

She blinked. Finally she spoke.

'What?'

'Goddammit, Holly! Weren't you even *listening*?'

She gave him a puzzled look. 'Of course I was listening. It didn't make any sense, that's all. Maybe if you try again, more slowly this time . . .'

His heart sank. She really wasn't joking.

Max pushed his damp, dark hair away from his forehead with a gesture borne of deep despair. This was like Russian roulette with only two shots to go.

'Look, I'm not asking you to marry me, I'm just saying I'd like to give it another go. A proper go. Holly, I think I love you.'

More silence.

'Well?' he demanded. His white shirt was sticking to his back and there was only one cigarette left in the packet. 'Say something, for God's sake.'

Swaying on her stool, Holly clung on to the edge of the bar. 'I'm not absolutely sure,' she murmured, 'but I think I'm going to faint.'

'You aren't supposed to be crying,' Adam observed mildly. Through Holly's bedroom window he could see Max outside, loading Olivia and Tessa's belongings into the waiting taxi.

Holly, who had been frantically stuffing her own things into an assortment of suitcases, had stopped and stared at Adam when he'd appeared in her doorway, and promptly burst into noisy sobs.

'This is what you've always wanted,' he reminded her. 'You should be happy.'

'I am h . . . h . . . happy,' Holly gulped. 'This is the happiest d . . . day of my life . . . oh Adam, you've been so kind to me, and I've treated you so badly . . . you must hate me . . .'

As she stood helplessly in the centre of the little room with her arms full of clothes, Adam moved towards her.

'You daft creature,' he said with genuine affection, 'of course

I don't hate you. And you haven't treated me badly, either. You just weren't able to fall in love with me.'

'I did try,' sniffed Holly, wiping her eyes with a crumpled white silk shirt. 'I wish I could have done. Everyone kept telling me how wonderful you were, but . . .'

'These things are born, not made,' supplied Adam. Then, with a grin, he added, 'Although it certainly took Max long enough to realize how *he* felt.'

'You *are* wonderful.' The tears were gathering speed once more. Tossing the silk shirt aside, Holly said, 'Maybe it's just as well it didn't work out between us. You're far too nice for me.'

And then she was in his arms, sobbing great heaving sobs against his chest and wailing, 'We'll still be friends, won't we? We won't lose touch . . . I want us *always* to be friends.'

'We always *have* been friends.' Adam kissed the top of her head, then prised her away from him so that he could look at her. Having realized some time ago that Holly's feelings for him would never match his own, he had come to terms with that fact with customary good humour and stoicism. 'Whatever you do, sweetheart, don't waste time worrying about me. If it's not too much of a blow to your ego, I'm not intending to spend the rest of my life in an emotional decline.'

'You'll meet somebody, I know you will,' said Holly fervently. 'And you'll be the most marvellous husband in the world.'

'Of course I will,' agreed Adam with customary modesty. Smiling down at her, he added, 'And if I should ever need to produce a reference to underline that fact, you'll be the one I come running to, I promise.'

'I shall give you *glowing* references,' Holly declared expansively.

'Great.' He gave her one last kiss on her wet cheek. Over her shoulder, he could see Max and Tessa outside waiting beside the taxi. 'Er . . . could you write it in Portuguese?'

Holly gasped, then laughed aloud. 'You sneaky animal! Luisa?'

Assuming an expression of injured innocence, Adam said, 'Well, however did you think we'd been spending our nights for the past week or so? Playing bi-lingual Scrabble?'

Chapter 65

'This place is a bloody madhouse,' said Ross irritably, as the master of the local hunt led a noisy, disreputable conga-line through reception, demolishing Christmas trees in its wake. 'And where the bloody hell is Max? I thought you told me he'd gone out to pick up some presents.'

It was nine-thirty. Grace, who had been rushed off her feet all day, put down the phone and swiftly retrieved her tumbler of orange juice from his grasp. 'He'll be back soon. And please don't drink my drink – it could be hours before I get another one.'

Having tasted it, Ross grimaced. 'Ugh, no vodka. I thought I was the one who was supposed to be lacking in Christmas spirit.'

'Oh, cheer up,' said Grace, with a sympathetic smile. The call just now had been from Max, ringing on his mobile to tell her that they'd just come off the M4 and that they would be home within ten minutes. 'It's a great party. And it's Christmas Eve, Ross. You ought to try and enjoy yourself. Couldn't you at least pretend to be having fun?'

'Ho, ho, ho,' he said sardonically, bracing himself to re-enter the ballroom. 'Thanks a lot, you're a great help.'

'That's all right,' said Grace, risking another surreptitious glance at her watch. 'This is what daughters are for.'

'I'm nervous,' said Tessa as they pulled up at the top of the gravelled driveway. 'Really nervous. My God, what if this is all a horrible mistake?'

498

'Well, in that case,' drawled Max, 'I suppose I'd have to turn round and throw you straight back on to that plane.'

'Don't make fun of me!' Tessa wailed. 'This is scary. Look, there are hundreds of cars here – that means there's another party. And you know perfectly well that every time I come to a party at this hotel something hideous happens.'

'No, it doesn't,' chanted Holly. 'What about the first time? That wasn't hideous.'

'You mean when I woke up the following morning to find myself alone in Ross's bed? He left me fifty pounds and a note telling me to see myself out, but he couldn't address the note to me because he didn't even know my name.' She had twisted the facts slightly, but in doing so had at least managed to prove her point. She almost laughed at the expression on Holly's face. 'You see?' she concluded with wistful reproach. 'I told you it was hideous.'

'I do not believe this!' shrieked Holly. 'You didn't tell me about that.'

Tessa shrugged. 'Would *you*?' Then, from her position in the back seat, she glimpsed the quick exchange of glances between Holly and Max.

'I suppose not,' said Holly with a grin, thinking back – as they both were – to the night when she had passed out in Max's bed. In an undertone she whispered, 'You didn't leave me fifty pounds.'

'Sweetheart, you didn't do anything to deserve it,' he replied, winking at her as he unfastened his seat belt. 'You don't get something for nothing from a Monahan, you know. When it comes to doing deals we're ruthless ba—'

'Will you shut up and help us out of this damn car?' demanded

Tessa, still nerve-racked but, at the same time, suddenly bursting with impatience. Now that they were actually here she just wanted to get on with it. If Ross was going to tell her that he didn't want her back – and despite what Max had said, she still regarded it as a possibility – the sooner it was said, the better.

'Hmmm,' said Max, his expert gaze sweeping her slender body as he opened the rear door for her.

Tessa, holding Olivia, gave him a suspicious look in return. 'Hmmm what?'

'Hmmm fifty pounds,' said Max, grinning down at her. 'That's a lot of money for a cab. All I can say is that it must have been an interesting evening.'

Ross was standing at the far end of the ballroom when he caught sight of Max. At bloody last, he thought. At least now the group of Max's friends who had been pestering him for the last two hours would leave him alone.

Then he saw Holly and he froze with his drink halfway to his mouth, the numbing, mindless lethargy which had gripped him for the past few weeks abruptly swept away. What was she doing here . . .? How and why had she come here . . .? And did it mean that Tessa was also back in Bath?

Hope surged as he scanned the crowd around Holly and Max but there was no sign of Tessa. Without turning around – determined not to take his eyes off them for a second – he put his drink down on the table behind him. For a split second it teetered on the edge of the table before another hand, diving to the rescue, brushed against his and caught the falling glass in mid-flight.

'Thanks,' murmured Ross absently, his thoughts elsewhere. Then, as the owner of the hand moved from behind him, something registered on the very periphery of his vision. A fleeting glimpse of long, golden-blonde hair . . . a slender brown arm reaching up with a gesture of aching familiarity to push the hair back from her face . . .

'That's OK,' said Tessa, striving desperately to sound casual. 'It would have been a shame to waste it.'

Ross couldn't believe that she was really there. Unable to speak, he simply stared at her.

'After all,' Tessa continued, wondering whether her knees were capable of keeping her upright. She was burbling again, but she couldn't help it. 'You rather look as if you need a drink. It isn't just orange juice, is it? On Christmas Eve? I wouldn't have—'

'Tess, shut up.'

She nodded with relief. 'OK.'

The only thing that mattered now, thought Ross, was finding out *why* she was back. Before he made a complete idiot of himself. His dark eyes, carefully registering no emotion whatsoever, surveyed her slender, tanned figure. She was wearing a wildly impractical clinging white T-shirt dress that was little more than an elongated vest and a necklace of tiny, iridescent white shells. Her legs were bare and very brown. He glanced down at the simple, low-heeled gold sandals on her feet, then back up again. Impractical the outfit might be, but it was undeniably Tessa's style. She looked absolutely stunning.

'Where's Olivia?'

'Being spoiled to death by Grace,' replied Tessa, standing her ground and realizing that she was quite unable to tell whether he was pleased or angry to see her.

'So, where exactly have you been?'

'Portugal. The Algarve.'

'With Holly.'

'With Holly,' she agreed, holding her breath.

'And why are you here, now?'

It was like a decidedly unpleasant interview with the headmaster. She was beginning to think that Max had been very, very wrong. But since she *was* here now, she had to go through with it. At least she would know where she stood . . .

'I missed you,' she said simply, her brilliant green eyes meeting his. 'I tried not to, but it didn't work. And I suppose I came back' – she gestured vaguely, searching for the words but unable to find them – 'because I couldn't *not* come back. Damn, this is difficult . . . I just missed you and had to see you again. I shouldn't have run away. Running away doesn't solve anything . . . Oh, for heaven's sake, Ross . . . why don't *you* say something? You know I hate it when you look at me like that and don't say a word. It's not fair.'

'You aren't really giving me much of a chance,' he replied, sensing the interest of the crowds surrounding them. Several people, having recognized Tessa, were eavesdropping shamelessly. 'Look, why don't we move somewhere a little more—'

'No!' declared Tessa, alarmed. 'You might shout at me.'

She looked so genuinely scared that he was no longer able to maintain a straight face. 'In that case, what do you want me to do?'

'Tell me what you want. Do you want me to go . . . or not?' She shifted uneasily from one foot to the other. 'I'm sorry, but I have to know. Preferably this year.'

'OK.' He paused, as if considering the question. 'I want *you*. You must know that. Haven't I always wanted you, ever since we first met?'

She felt almost sick with relief. It was going to be all right after all.

'So now what do you want me to do?' persisted Ross, when she didn't reply. 'Prove it?'

Slowly, and with a hint of a smile, Tessa nodded.

'Right here, in public?'

He glimpsed momentary apprehension, but she'd committed herself now. She nodded once more.

'Maybe we *should* go somewhere more private.'

'No.'

'You're absolutely sure you won't be embarrassed?'

'Absolutely.'

'OK.' As he took a step towards her, his hands moved to the zip at the front of his trousers. 'Here goes . . .'

With a muffled shriek, Tessa stopped him. 'I'm embarrassed,' she whispered, trying not to laugh. And suddenly – somehow – she found herself in his arms and it seemed as if everyone in the ballroom was watching them. The general noise level of the rest of the party had definitely dropped. Several hundred pairs of party-lungs appeared to be holding their collective breath.

'I told you we should have gone somewhere more private,' Ross murmured, sounding pleased with himself.

She nodded, her head resting against the warm, reassuring solidity of his chest. 'Never kid a kidder,' she whispered back. 'You'd think I would have learned that lesson by now. Ross, everyone's still staring at us, and I'm even more embarrassed now than ever. Why don't we go to your office?'

'You might shout at me,' he mimicked gently. 'No, I'm happy just where I am, and I don't care who's watching. The more the merrier as far as I'm concerned . . .'

Tessa opened her mouth to protest but that was as far as she got. Tilting her face up to meet his, Ross kissed her with tantalizing slowness and all the old magic . . . that irresistible magic . . . came flooding back. She clung to him, no longer even caring that they were the focus of attention, and that the entire party had now ground to an enthralled standstill. Ross was all that mattered . . . being back with him was all she needed to be truly happy . . . and happiness had eluded her for so long that she could scarcely believe it was finally happening.

'Excuse me.' Max, breaking the spell, called out across the room. 'But do you two know each other?'

Ross's mouth, against Tessa's, curved into a smile. 'Not nearly well enough,' he murmured. Then, with his hands resting on Tessa's shoulders, he pulled away. Beguiling dark brown eyes studied her gravely for several seconds before he spoke. Tessa, trembling uncontrollably, longing for him to kiss her again, wondered what on earth he was going to do next.

'I love you,' said Ross, and although his voice was low it carried easily to those around them. 'I want to marry you. And I never, *ever* want you to leave me again.'

Tessa's eyes were bright with tears. Ross hadn't been blameless by any means, but she knew just how much she had hurt him – had publicly humiliated him – when she'd stood him up, practically at the altar. That he could still love her was amazing enough, when one took into consideration his pride, not to mention the fact that he was one of the most eligible men around. That he should still want to marry her was nothing short of miraculous.

Meanwhile, however, four hundred party guests stood mesmerized, awaiting her reply.

'Speak up, we can't hear you,' yelled Holly. For the first time Ross realized that Max had his arm around her waist. If he had been less preoccupied with more pressing matters he would have been astounded.

'Yes, speak up,' he told Tessa in an undertone. 'This is gripping stuff. Better than *EastEnders*.'

Tessa knew now why he had done it this way. The confidence was a front. Beneath the calm, famously flippant exterior lay a man who was genuinely unsure of himself and she loved him for it. Under circumstances such as these, how could she possibly refuse him?

Thankfully, no matter what the circumstances, she wouldn't have dreamed of doing so.

'Of course I love you,' she said at last, and was greeted by a chorus of 'Aaahs' from all corners of the ballroom. 'And if you're sure you still want to marry me, then I will marry you. And I *promise* never to run away again.'

Their audience went wild. The sound of cheering and applause reverberated around the room. For good measure – and because he couldn't think of anything he'd rather do – Ross enveloped Tessa in a hug and kissed her once more which only earned him another tumultuous roar of approval.

'Thank God for that,' he whispered against her cheek. 'You really had me going there for a moment.'

'In that case,' replied Tessa, 'maybe we should get to your office fast, before it becomes too obvious.'

'You should have ideas like that more often. I'm just glad I'm wearing a jacket long enough to cover my embarrassment.'

'I've got news for you,' said Tessa, kissing his neck. 'You forgot to do it up.'

As they made their way through the crowd, Ross whispered, 'Just think how much trouble you'd have saved, if only you'd agreed to marry me the first time I asked you.'

'And lose out on all the fun?' said Tessa, pretending outrage. 'This is seriously romantic. I wouldn't have missed this for the world!'

'Speaking of not missing this for the world.' Ross coughed and glanced meaningfully in the direction of Max and Holly. 'What *is* going on over there? I thought I was hallucinating before, but there's no doubt about it now. My older brother is definitely kissing your best friend.'

'Ask Rosa Polonowski,' said Tessa, wondering if she'd ever been happier in her life and realizing that she definitely had not. There, ahead of them in the open doorway stood Grace with Olivia in her arms. 'Oh Ross, I hate crying in public.' She fished in his jacket pocket for a handkerchief. 'But I think I'm going to have to.'

'Don't cry,' he said firmly. 'Listen, I've got some good news. I took your painting to an art restorer in London and he managed to fix it. "The Party" is as good as new.'

'Really?' sniffed Tessa, smiling through her tears. 'I painted another one. It's called "Party-Two".'

Wiping her eyes and keeping his other arm tightly around her waist, Ross grinned and said, 'I'm just glad that tonight's party is a private one. No Press, thank God. At least this is something we can keep out of the papers.'

'Can't have everything your own way,' cried Andy Llewellyn triumphantly, as Ross and Tessa reached the doorway at last and Ross scooped Olivia up into his arms. 'Smile for the camera. *And* again. Thank you . . .!'